Tangled HEARTS

TANGLED IN TIME BOOK 3

CAROLINE CORVIN

First published in 2023 by Grenwyvern Publishing

Auckland, New Zealand

Content Warning

The Arms of An Angel

Dallblane Castle, Scotland - August 2019

"THIS WOMAN'S A FRIGGING artist," Finn muttered under his breath. Concert footage from the final night of the festival rolled across his laptop screen.

"You don't say." Euan's languid response, thick with disinterest, drifted from the couch. His eyes remained fixed on the massive television that dominated one wall of the lounge. The canned laughter accompanying an old episode of *Only Fools And Horses* spilled from equally enormous speakers.

A miasma of cigarette smoke blanketed the room. *Fucking Euan.* Although they all hated it, Euan's two-packet a day habit and his entitled attitude made everyone smokers in this household.

Annoyed by the spiralling smoke almost as much as his brother's lack of attention to an event so vitally important to their family, Finn grabbed the remote. Ignoring Euan's indignant, "Hey, I was watching that," he killed BritBox and set about casting his desktop to the television.

"*This* is what's going to save us," he said, stabbing a finger towards the screen, now overtaken by life-size images of the last hours of Rock The Castle 2019. "This year was just the start. Charlie Christensen's documentary is what will cement our festival in people's minds. This is what will get them clamouring for tickets, coming back year after year. This is what will make them say 'Fuck Glaston-bury, we're going to Dallblane'. This is what will get them to choose us over Slane."

God, if that happened, it would be more than they could ever have hoped for. They'd drawn fifty thousand people here a month ago to Dallblane. Impressive for a new event, but he and his business partner, Eric, had their sights set on more. When the big name music promoter had unexpectedly come to Finn nine months earlier, in the depths of the Scottish winter, with a belief they could, even in a limited time frame, pull off something special that summer, the sheer intensity of the man's enthusiasm had captured his imagi-nation. Eric's total conviction that they would succeed had proven prophetic. They had.

Their target was to match Slane: seventy thousand people. The venue could easily hold it; they could create the infrastructure to support it. They'd never aim to replicate Glastonbury; no way could they accommodate two hundred thousand. But they could position themselves as a serious alternative. Just the thought of it sent a renewed wave of the excitement that had gripped him since Eric Walters arrived unannounced on that bitter December morning. The moment he had heaved his untidy bulging frame onto one of the leather couches in the study and started talking, Finn had felt something he hadn't felt for a long time: hope. Even before Dad died, he'd been in a slump. Caught in a strange half-world between leaving university and the rest of his life, whatever that was supposed to look like, the last few years had passed him by in a blur. Now, once again, he felt fully alive. Now he could see the future and it was good. Better than good. It would be fucking amazing.

"Charlie's got hours of footage, her own and some she's pulled in from others," he said to Euan, who, recovering from the unexpected interruption to his tv viewing, now attempted to muster a look of bored indifference and failed. No one could ignore the images on that screen. "This is just a taster she's thrown together for us to get the idea. And she's got literally thousands of stills, too."

"Fuuuck," Euan said, peering at the television. "Holy shit! How is it I've never realised it till this moment that Phoenix Alferez is sex on legs?" The object of his sudden attention strutted across the screen, clad in the briefest of denim cut-offs, screaming out the words of her hit single.

"Well, if you'd stuck around instead of swanning off to the south of France, I'd have taken you backstage to meet her. She's even better up close. A set of deep brown come-hither eyes." He noted with pleasure Euan's scowl of annoyance, realising what he'd missed.

Getting in a small jibe still wasn't enough to make Finn let go of how pissed off he was at his brother, even now. Euan had buggered off and left them to do it without him. Although rather useless at anything practical, with his financial knowledge, they could certainly have put him to work. But unfortunately, Euan had quite an aversion to the 'w' word. He didn't yet understand that being the Earl of Dallblane was no guarantee he could enter the ranks of the idle rich. In his case, far from it. The estate teetered on the brink of ruin and the nineteenth century castle was literally about to become one if they didn't find some cash to shore up its crumbling walls and dodgy roof. The festival had been the first milestone on that journey, but this documentary would put them out in the fast lane.

While Euan remained mesmerised by the sleek, writhing body of the stunning Ms Alferez, Finn's eyes were drawn to the crowd beneath her. And to one particular woman. She perched bare-legged atop a guy's shoulders, laughing in exhilaration, her head tipped back and her face luminous in the pure joy of the moment. The camera angle made it seem as if the powerful stage lights that caught her blonde curls in a blaze of gold had deliberately spotlighted her. As the camera panned around, it revealed elaborate tattoos on the slender arms clutching the shoulders of the man beneath her. Without thinking why, he suddenly needed to see more of her. He grabbed the remote and paused the video for a moment.

Euan didn't object. His eyes focused intently on the still shot of Phoenix crouched low in the middle of the screen, only the barest sliver of fabric covering her crotch. "Fuck," he said under his breath. "That should be illegal."

Finn ignored him, unable to drag his attention away from the girl in the crowd lit up like an angel, her hair a shimmering halo, perched on the shoulders of a man—a man that looked exactly like him. He flicked the rewind and ran those thirty seconds again.

Euan let out a low whistle of appreciation, having no objection to watching Phoenix dance once more, assuming his brother had it on repeat for his enjoyment. Meanwhile, Finn scrutinised the man on the screen. In the midst of a sea of people, the bobbing bodies largely obscured him. His t-shirt back was plain white, and for sure he owned a few of those—like a couple of million other guys.

"One more time," he said, letting the film flip backwards at speed.

Euan grinned. "I think you're enjoying this as much as I am, you dirty dog. Maybe that backstage visit meant a little more than you're letting on, huh?"

Finn narrowed his eyes, squinting at the screen so hard it hurt. It was the hair that cemented the resemblance between him and the guy in the crowd—the unfashionably long dark hair his mates ribbed him about. He hated all this manscaping that seemed to be essential these days. That made him a rare breed—but not a unicorn. It seemed there was another man amongst those fifty thousand people with a similar dislike of barbers, because he knew this couldn't be him.

He had been in the crowd at some stage each one of the five nights of the festival. However, he remained absolutely positive during this set on this particular night he wasn't. He remembered exactly where he was: backstage with Eric attempting to pacify Mick Harrison, who was acting like a diva and demanding they produce some coke or he wasn't going on. Reduced to scrounging around for some shady scumbag to procure drugs for an arsehole rock star who had them over a barrel was the only experience that had tarnished an otherwise dream week. And for that reason, it was particularly memorable.

That's how he'd met Phoenix. Not really met her; encountered her for one brief moment. She'd slipped past them, heading back to her dressing room, and it wasn't come hither, but sympathy he'd seen in her eyes. He'd decided there and then, despite the skimpy outfits and provocative gyrations that seemed to spill out unbidden at the same time as her spectacular voice, she might indeed be the sweet thing her PR people made her out to be. Much too sweet to let people like his brother near.

So, it was an illusion. He had a secret twin, a doppelgänger. Lucky bastard, he thought, looking at the tattooed angel perched on the guy's shoulders. He wished it was him.

Part One

HERE

1

Commute

Mt Eden, Auckland, New Zealand - November 2013

PARKING AT 59 MOUNTVIEW Road resembled hot-bedding on an oil rig. As Layla reversed out of the driveway of the old villa, Will's car shot in front of hers to take the newly vacant spot.

The sprawling house was perfect for the five of them, except that like most of inner-city Auckland, the properties reflected a time where cars were few, and multiple-vehicle houses almost non-existent.

She raised a wave as he sprang out of the car, still as athletic as the lanky teenager he'd been when they first met. Although he'd grown into that gangly body; in fact, grown into it in ways that were incredibly distracting. But she wouldn't let herself go there. She knew where that might lead.

Somehow, an unspoken agreement had sprung up between them; heading down that path wasn't wise. It wasn't an agreement she'd wanted to make, but she'd sensed that was how he wanted them to be: just friends. No, not just friends, the best of friends.

It didn't stop those feelings that surfaced, sometimes when she least expected it.

The little shiver of attraction when he appeared shirtless in the kitchen, a pair of sweatpants hanging low on his hips and mussed up bed hair that begged a girl to run her hands through it. The tiny tremor of happiness that ran through her when he came in from the surf, the joyous touch of the waves still imprinted on his mood. The soothing safety of his arm around her shoulder those times when he knew by instinct alone that she needed his comfort.

That was the one real downside of this current living arrangement: she witnessed all these tiny but exquisite moments. They caught her with her guard down, triggering emotions she'd tried not to feel. Once again, she must bury deep the feelings that she'd battled against and failed. Once again, she must pretend that she loved him only as a friend, in the same way she loved other members of this crazy group they called 'the tight five'.

Who could have predicted when she'd arrived in Auckland six months earlier to take up her dream job that they'd all be together again? Who would have known that this role in a busy city ED, precisely the thing she needed to expand her experience and embellish her CV, would coincide with a spare room in a house with her four high school mates?

Here they were once again, in the same city, in the same house, a fond echo of their Dunedin university days, when unable to bear separation for long, they'd all gravitated south, reuniting in a dingy student flat in notorious Castle Street. And now fate had brought them together again.

As she slipped onto the motorway on-ramp, boxed in behind a crawling tourist coach, her mind tossed forward memories of the morning they'd met, the first day of the school year when she'd stepped onto a similar bus and her world had changed forever.

She'd never expected to find friends like them, ever, let alone as the new kid from the derelict part of Papakura on a posh bus on the way to a posh school. They'd welcomed her with open arms and never let her go. Even when separated by distance, she'd always felt their warm embrace reaching out across the miles, a separation that no longer existed.

For the third time, Layla jabbed her code into the machine at the barrier arm, her mind too unsettled to retrieve four simple digits she'd used every day of her working life for the past six months. The arm finally jerked up, allowing her into the hospital staff car park. Caught in a patch of stop-start traffic on the Southern Motorway that final twenty minutes of her commute, her mind had kept returning to one image. The niggle of worry triggered by that image had grown. There was something about Will's face as he'd lifted his hand towards her earlier; something not right with him.

She'd merely seen a friendly wave, but now she was second-guessing that. He'd looked kind of tense. Perhaps a tough surgery today? Or had the thing they all knew came calling from time to time devastated his day? Losing patients was tough. No amount of sympathetic noises from their other friends could get you through those events. Only another doctor, who'd experienced that helplessness at bringing all your knowledge to the battle, and yet still lose it, could even begin to understand.

As she made her way into the locker room, guilt nipped at her. There would have been time to stop for a moment, check he was OK. Wrap him in a quick hug that might be enough to get him through if indeed he'd lost someone. She cursed herself for not taking the time.

This damn job. While she loved the ED, sometimes she wondered if she'd let it become too important, overshadowing the people and things who were most important in life. Maybe the time had come to investigate the option of the GP programme. She shut the clunky locker door with a metallic clatter, unsure if her huff of frustration was more aimed at the ageing mechanism or herself for her neglect of the people who mattered more to her than any job. She headed for the triage area, bracing herself for the onslaught of Friday night incoming.

"So, does it feel to you like we were standing here a mere five minutes ago?"

Layla turned to meet the friendly smile of Stephen Turner, a young resident. Did she look like that when she started? That mix of exhaustion and exhilaration stamped on her face as the punishing reality of her dream job descended on her? Probably. The system didn't change, expecting the least experienced doctors to make good calls on the back of double shifts. It made no sense, but still the system prevailed.

"Tell me you *are* going home soon," she said. "It's Friday night. Party night."

"Party?" he said, through a brittle laugh. "What's that? I've never heard that word before."

She tossed him a rueful smile, not wanting to reveal that even in her third year out of med school, 'party' wasn't a word she knew too well either.

"Ok," she said, "well let's get *this* party started. Who've we got crashing our ward tonight?" She picked up the first clipboard, ready to start the handover briefing. "So let's start with this one. Tell me about Mr Bruce Nickel."

2

Night Shift

Rutherford Hospital, Auckland, New Zealand - November
2013

"Dear, I don't mean to be a nuisance, but I wonder if I could see the doctor, please?" Polite words uttered in a whisper thin voice. Papery lips struggled to push out the sound. A trickle of blood half-dried on a wrinkled brow. A hand dappled with age, placed over Layla's, asking for help. She leaned over the elderly patient, offering a reassuring smile.

"Barbara, my name's Layla, and *I'm* the doctor who'll be taking care of you for now. And this is Hector, your nurse." Layla nodded towards the young man who had followed her through the gap in the curtained cubicle. He unfurled the blood pressure sleeve, and with a smile, arranged it snugly around the sagging skin of Barbara's upper arm. Although the Filipino nurse was new, Layla already noted his quiet competence and kind manner. Good nursing looked the same irrespective of gender or country of origin.

"He's going to check your blood pressure, and then he'll clean up that nasty gash on your head." The angry slash of scarlet still bled a little, but she'd get Hector to finish dressing it before they took Barbara down to the monitoring unit. She'd had a lucky escape as far as they could tell. However, Layla hoped they'd discover why Mrs Barbara Heskith, aged seventy-eight, had woken to find herself sprawled on her bathroom floor. At her age there were many possibilities: heart attack, a small stroke, low blood sugar, or simply accidentally tripping on the sheepskin slippers that still clung to her gnarled feet. The bony legs protruding from them revealed a network of varicose veins. At least she'd been capable of pushing the alarm pendant around her neck, summoning an ambulance. It might have been much worse otherwise, a night on the cold hard tiles, waiting and hoping for someone to check on her come morning.

"Oh, doctor, it's so good to see you." Barbara turned grateful eyes on Hector as he strapped the velcro band tighter, and inflated it with strong rhythmic pumps. "Thank you for coming, doctor. I'm a little embarrassed, to be honest, falling over like that and causing such a fuss."

Layla was used to this. They didn't tell you in med school: some people didn't have the look of a doctor and never would—despite all those years of grind while studying, the massive student debt, the gruelling hours as a junior doctor, if you didn't look the part, patients would inevitably sit there eyeing you with distrust while demanding a more stereotypical alternative.

She didn't mind so much with the elderly ones like Barbara. Their generation, although having grown up with the concept of women doctors, still snapped back to gender expectations. Especially when stressed and in pain. An addled brain took the easy route. But she certainly objected when confronted with rude arseholes like the one awaiting her in the next curtained cubicle. He'd already delighted in goading her, but she hadn't let it get to her. She wouldn't give him the satisfaction.

Patients like Barbara were a welcome respite from the usual Friday night clientele in the Emergency Department of Rutherford Hospital. Polite, grateful, sober. Three rare qualities amongst the human debris that streamed into the ward from pubs, nightclubs and the city streets. It was now officially Saturday morning. Eight hours into her shift, Layla feared it would be another eight before she'd escape home. Then, while others enjoyed the first day of the weekend, she'd barricade herself against the daylight and steal what sleep she could. By six tonight, she'd be back, ready to do it all over again. The need to maintain a calm professional demeanour, no matter who the patient in front of her, made the long shifts more exhausting. Leaving Hector to finish with Barbara, she paused for a moment, steeling herself for the next encounter.

Layla sighed, took a deep breath and pulled back the curtain with a decisive flourish, revealing the charge nurse she'd call in to help. The staunch Helena still battled with the most unpleasant patient of the shift so far. Colin's pudgy face wore the same sneer as the last time she'd seen him. Helena was attempting to take a blood sample, the writhing man making the task twice as difficult.

"Ouch. Go easy. You're so bloody rough. An old girl like you should've had enough practice to do the job with a bit more care."

Grey-haired Helena kept her face neutral and her eyes fixed on the task, but Layla could tell the woman seethed inside. They'd made an unspoken decision to divert Stacey, the pretty junior staff nurse, to another patient, rather than subject her to the scrutiny of this thoroughly revolting man. His piggy eyes swivelled towards the sound, alighting on Layla's face with a glower.

"Oh, so the little lady doc's back, is she? Still couldn't find a proper one? What's the bloody world coming to?"

He emitted a grunt as Helena extracted the needle with more finesse than he deserved. She sealed the vial of deepest red liquid, likely to be as much alcohol as blood.

Layla inhaled slowly and put on her best bedside face. That someone in a pub had punched Colin in the head, breaking his cheekbone and blackening one eye, was no surprise. It disappointed her his opponent hadn't hit him harder, rendering him unconscious. He'd certainly be much easier to deal with.

"Colin, one of our staff will be here soon to take you over to radiology. We need to get a better look at that nasty break. And then one of our orthopaedic doctors will be in to see you to discuss what the x-ray shows. In the meantime, I'll leave you in Helena's capable hands."

She turned and left poor Helena to administer some pain medication. Although she couldn't help a smug smile when she thought of the look on Colin's face when feisty Cynthia Chen, who resembled a bristling angry bird, arrived from orthopaedics. What a shame she wouldn't be there to watch.

Cynthia would also pay her next patient a visit. Bruce, a mountain of a man, dwarfed the hospital bed. He'd failed to take a bend on his motorbike, ending up in a ditch and now sporting one of the ugliest compound fractures she'd ever seen. But he remained in good spirits, partly aided by the contents of the drip hooked up to his heavily tattooed arm.

He cast admiring glances as he glimpsed Layla's own tattoos peeking out under the sleeves of her scrubs when she leaned forward to adjust the machine monitoring Bruce's steady heartbeat. Not the usual reaction. The hint of navy ink on the arms of a young professional woman shocked many of her patients. It would horrify them if she were to strip off her top, revealing the full extent of her body art. Spiralling flowers and intertwined Celtic knotwork adorned her upper arms and shoulders and sprawled across her back. Mostly, she forgot about her tattoos. They'd been part of her so long she felt like she'd been born with them.

"Nice ink." Bruce nodded in approval.

"Thanks. Yours too." She grinned back at him. "So, Bruce, the doctor who I came here with before, when they admitted you—Stephen?" Bruce nodded in acknowledgment, remembering despite the terrible pain he'd been in. "He's gone off now, so I'm taking over. My name's Layla."

"Layla."

He turned her name over in a low voice that rumbled up from deep inside his broad hairy chest. He sported a wild beard that almost reached his navel. She imagined Bruce, six-foot tall and almost as wide, would be an intimidating sight in his full bikie regalia. But propped up here in a hospital bed, with his eyes twinkling in amusement, he resembled an enormous amiable bear.

"So I take it your daddy's a Clapton fan?"

"Right on the mark there, Bruce," she said while tapping in the latest readings from the heart monitor. Bruce's thatch of chest hair had bald patches where the nurse had shaved areas to stick on the sensors. She smiled, thinking how odd they would look peeking out of the traditional biker's open leather vest. Although given the injury, it might be some time before he'd be in his club uniform again.

"And if you'd been a boy, would it have been Eric?" he asked.

"Yeah," she laughed. "Jimmy was already taken. I've an older brother."

"Hendrix or Page?"

"Page. Although when my two younger brothers came along, Dad would have named a second one Jimi with an 'i' to cover all bases, but mum wasn't having it."

"So," he said, "let me guess. The next two..." He paused, eyes cast upwards while he mulled over the names of other legendary guitarists. "Keith?"

"No. Although Dad likes the Stones. And admires Keith's ability to function despite drugs and alcohol, but his guitar playing not so much." Yes, her dad and Keith Richards had quite a lot in common. He could probably count on one hand the number of sober days he'd had in the last twenty years.

"OK, let's see." Bruce looked thoughtful. Meanwhile, Layla checked the packing around the break. Seeing all appeared in order, she drew the sheet back, taking care not to jar the damaged leg.

"Pete? As in Townshend?" Bruce knew his British music.

"Yes. Well done. That's my youngest brother. Dad's a massive fan of The Who. Drives the neighbours mad with their music pumping out of his pride and joy, the biggest set of speakers you've ever seen."

Her dad never seemed to have money for anything but booze and cigarettes, unless it came to his music. Bruce's deep baritone laughter echoed off the grey vinyl-covered walls. The conversation was at least keeping her patient's mind off his injury. Best he didn't think too much about the impending surgery and the lengthy recovery time ahead of him.

"Think you can guess the other one?" she asked.

Bruce narrowed his eyes as he returned to scrolling through a list of rock guitarists in his head.

"Nah, I give up," he said after a moment. "So many axe-men to choose from. We'll be here all night playing that guessing game. Hard to pick my own favourites, let alone someone else's. Just tell me."

"Jeff, middle name Beck."

"Ah, nice. And not too way-out."

"Yeah. We're all thankful that he didn't name one Slash or The Edge."

"I presume your mother would have vetoed those?"

"Too right." Layla grinned back at him. Her mother always had the final say in the family. Not only when naming children. She made a couple of quick final notes on the laptop, murmured instructions to the nurse at her side, and turned back to Bruce.

"OK, Bruce. Things are looking fine there. As well as we might expect. You've made a right mess of yourself, haven't you?"

"Yeah, bloody embarrassing to be honest, doc. Totalled my bike too."

"Well, all is going to plan. You're scheduled for surgery later this morning. Someone from orthopaedics will come in soon, and the nurses here will keep you as comfortable as possible."

According to his notes, poor Bruce's last meal involved making a sizable dent in an all-you-can-eat buffet spread, washed down with a few pints. Now, he faced a lengthy wait before they could give him anaesthesia. But he seemed a tough character, putting a brave face on his predicament. She probably wouldn't see much more of him. Soon, they'd whisk him off to prep for surgery. But she'd appreciated the banter. It provided a pleasant interlude.

Ahead of her, an orderly wheeled a bed towards the next empty cubicle. Groans of pain announced another patient's arrival. She waved over a nurse and began again.

Although she'd been having some doubts lately, there was a lot to love about this work. It suited her. Emergency medicine might be challenging but never dull. A new patient presented a problem to be solved. On meeting each one, Layla's quick mind leapt into top gear, weighing up options, ordering the response, prioritising the actions. More than good under pressure, she thrived on it.

She brought other less practical assets to the job, too. Her bombshell blonde hair, full lips, and wide eyes caused difficulties with flirtatious male patients and inspired doubt in her capabilities with others. But the advantages of her appearance sometimes outweighed the drawbacks.

"The face of an angel and the hands to match," she'd heard a woman say. Her son, sitting beside her, had flashed Layla a grateful smile.

"Thought I'd died and gone to heaven when that lady doctor appeared," one elderly man had said, holding his wife's hand, elated that, through the work of her team, he'd beaten the heart attack that had threatened to send him to heaven for real. God, just as well they hadn't got close enough to her ID card to read her surname. Layla Angell. That would have really freaked them out.

By the time she knocked off around 9:30 am, Layla had lost count of the number of patients she'd seen. Most merged into a blur of names, faces, and injuries. A few unpleasant ones like Colin or the friendly, appreciative types like Bruce, stuck in her mind. But even those would trickle away into a vague past as she slept, clearing her mind for the next onslaught. Saturday nights were even busier, usually compounded by weekend sports injuries and waves of people who thought they'd be OK leaving their problems till their GP opened on Monday, then realised it couldn't wait.

She trudged to the staff car park. This is what it meant to be dead on your feet. Not really safe to drive, but since taking this job, she'd shunned the other option: two buses and one train between the hospital and the leafy central city suburb she now called home.

Her V8 Holden stood out amongst the practical Japanese hatchbacks. With a massive student loan, she should have bought a car like those, but after all the years of study, she'd allowed herself this one indulgence. Although the eye-watering amount of fuel it sucked sometimes caused her to consider swapping it for something sensible but boring. But then she'd slip into the moulded leather seat, turn the key, and the throaty thump of its heart, like a lullaby to her ears, would cause her to forget all thoughts of trading it in. Her brothers would also never forgive her if she did. They were part of the reason a young female doctor drove a testosterone-laden Aussie tank.

She found the flat empty. No surprises there. The other four inhabitants of the house were most likely off doing their own thing on a sunny Saturday morning. They retained a friendship still as strong as in their high school days when they had first earned the nickname 'the tight five', although now the demands of jobs and increasingly complex lives pulled them in different directions. But just like the players in a forward rugby pack, from which they'd earned that name, they remained bound together. In these people, Layla had found a second family, one that she could count on with more certainty than her own when things got tough.

Charlie was photographing a wedding today. It wasn't her usual scene. Typical of Charlie, with a warm heart buried inside that cool exterior, it was a favour for a friend. Her photography tended towards gritty realism rather than staged fairy floss. And her idea of a happily ever after didn't involve a guy and a girl saying "I do" under a fake floral archway. But she was too nice to say no.

And so she'd spend the morning recording all the primping and preening: hair, makeup, a nervous bride, laughing bridesmaids, the mother of the bride fussing. Far removed from the behind-the-scenes work that took Charlie backstage at rock concerts or into sweaty changing rooms after a big game. She'd earned quite a name for herself. The tangible proof of her talent, an award for photojournalism, hung on the wall in her room upstairs. Today's work wouldn't win her any awards, only grateful thanks.

Tristan would be down at the park watching the cricket. His sister's twins, a boy and a girl, phoned Uncle Tristan most weeks, begging him to come see their match. Tristan, although not a fan of early weekend rising, obliged regularly. He'd make a great dad one day. When he finally moved on from the spectacularly unsuitable string of women, he had a habit of finding in bars.

Leo was away for the weekend. By now he'd be pounding the Queenstown river trails, chasing a personal best time in his nineteenth marathon.

And Will, although not such a fitness fanatic as Leo, still never missed a day at the gym unless out surfing. The pair of them made her feel a little ashamed of her own slovenly attitude to physical fitness. She imagined he'd be down there lifting weights and working the rowing machine, or tumbling in the punishing Piha surf, mastering the waves chasing that one perfect ride. Hopefully, whatever he was doing, it had carried away the burdens of the previous day she'd seen in his face.

It seemed wrong to turn her back on this beautiful spring, almost summer day, even though she should be in bed. So, back at the house, she made herself a cup of tea and some buttered toast and headed for the bay window in the dining room, book in hand. Escape into a fictional world was a recently rediscovered pleasure after years of nothing but textbooks and research papers. It wouldn't hurt to take twenty minutes for herself. Otherwise, it would be sleep, shower, and off to work again, with no reprieve. At least this was her last night shift and then three blissful days off.

She had barely made herself comfy on the sun-drenched window seat when a muffled choking sound suggested that she wasn't alone in the house after all. It came from across the broad hallway, behind the closed lounge door. The distinctive sound of snoring. Male snoring. In fact, it sounded like the sort of snoring men did when sleeping off the aftereffects of a hard night on the booze. God knows she'd heard that sound enough growing up to recognise its harsh vibrations reverberating through the house.

She hoped Tristan had a good excuse lined up for missing the kids' cricket. Tiptoeing over to the door, she opened it stealthily so as not to wake the sleeping beauty.

The stale smell of alcohol wafted through the small gap, followed by the distinctive stench of vomit. God, she'd better go in and check he was OK. Although snoring was a good sign; it meant he was still breathing. The heavy drapes totally blocked the sunlight, and she had to feel her way around the solid furniture to where she could faintly make out a lumpy form on the couch.

She leaned over him, wrinkling her nose in disgust. She had to deal with enough of this at work, without it following her home. Bloody Tristan. It really was about time he grew up. He was a respectable lawyer, not a twenty-year-old student any more.

But it wasn't Tristan. Grey eyes stared back at her, wide in sudden shock at waking to find her gingerly pulling back the vomit-caked throw rug.

"Will?"

Sensible Will. Dependable Will.

Hardly-ever-drinks-because-he's-training-as-a-surgeon Will.

Just-rolled-over-and-threw-up-again Will.

3

Coming Clean

Mt Eden, Auckland, New Zealand - November 2013

"Layla?" He forced out her name, a rough crackle between dry lips from deep in his strangled throat.

"Will?" She flicked on a table lamp. It might be morning, but in this room the heavy drapes, designed to keep the warmth of an open fire in, also blocked out every shred of light. Definitely Will; his eyes squinted shut against the glare, his mouth set in a grim line.

"It's OK. I'm OK. Go away. I'm fine." The words slurred.

"You're not bloody fine. You're still pissed for a start. And you reek." Even though you learned to tolerate unpleasant smells in her line of work, it didn't mean she was oblivious to them. And it would be hard to miss the musty stale alcohol wafting off him, the acrid smell of vomit that lingered in the air and the surprising hint of cigarette smoke on Will's breath. "How the hell did you get yourself in this state?—No, don't answer that. Might be best I don't know."

'Why' would be the better question, but she feared that answer more. Thoughts of what had provoked this disaster caused her to once again silently berate herself for not acting yesterday. Her gut instincts had been correct—something was up—but to send Will on an all-night bender, it had to be bigger than anything she'd imagined.

He opened his eyes a sliver in response, and she saw shame written there. Waves of it rippled across his face. She understood his discomfort. Will never let himself get totally smashed like this. But somehow he had. She regretted her words. Who was she to judge? Somehow she'd become 'Miss holier-than-thou'. It was not as if she didn't enjoy a good session at the pub with her friends. Or a lively party. True, she was always cautious, the niggling thought that if she wasn't, she'd become her father: a drunk.

But her life, like Will's, simply had no time or space in it for that sort of fun anymore. Not while they were on this career-focussed treadmill they'd chosen. Not unless they were prepared to throw it all away, and they'd come too far to do that. Not this close to reaching the prize. There'd be plenty of time for fun after that.

"Here, sit up. Let's see if I can get you up. I think you need a shower and bed. Sleep it off."

At five-two compared to his six-foot, standing alongside him, she barely reached his shoulder. But he was lean. And she'd had plenty of practice at escorting drunks. She would have been barely ten years old when she'd first supported her father, weaving his way down the hallway to collapse in a heap on the bed, while her mother gave him a bollocking for yet another missed dinner.

"It's OK, Layla. You don't have to do this." He protested weakly, his face flushed as a surge of shame pushed its way through the fog.

"But I am doing this." Of course she would. She would do anything for Will. It went without saying—he was her ride or die, and she was his. She put on her best bossy doctor's voice. "Sit up." Tucking one arm around his shoulder, she managed to lever him into a sitting position. He stared down at the front of his shirt. It too had smears of puke, a putrid mustard coloured slash already dry and crusted.

"I'm sorry Layla. Really sorry." His eyes were glassy, but she read embarrassment in them. They'd never hidden things from each other. He knew her secrets, and she knew his. They'd never been afraid to bare their feelings, with the one glaring exception on her part—her impossible love for him. But today she sensed a reluctance to tell the full story lurking behind his discomfort.

"It's really not a problem," she said, softening her voice, and allowing her genuine concern for him to slip through. "Not as if this is a regular occurrence." In fact, she couldn't recall the last time she'd seen him even the slightest bit tipsy, let alone still pissed in the morning like this. "I thought it was Tristan. This is more his style."

"No, he's not home. Gone to the cricket, I think. He put me to bed here. He's a good mate." He smiled fondly as he recalled Tristan's part in this.

She fumed at that. A good mate wouldn't have let Will get in this state. A good mate would have at least seen him to his room. And a really good mate wouldn't have left him here unattended. Tristan might not be a doctor who fully understood the risks of aspirating vomit, but surely he had enough experience with booze himself to know that a very drunk friend might need someone to keep an eye on him.

"Do you think you can stand?" He looked a little less wobbly now she had him upright. It was a short walk down the passage to the bathroom.

"Yeah, think I can."

She wedged her arm under his and braced herself. "OK, on the count of three... one... two... three."

Will strained to take his weight on unsteady legs. Although swaying a little like a poplar tree in a breeze, he didn't need her to fully support him. Just as well, as she was questioning the wisdom of trying to do this on her own. But now upright and heading for the door, she let this sudden burst of forward momentum carry them the short distance to the bathroom. Once inside, she shut the door with a firm click. He leaned against the shower glass, head flung back, mouth open, breathing heavily as if the brief exertion had sapped all his strength.

"Right, let's get these off you," she said with the briskness that hadn't always come naturally, but she'd learned over the years. She began to unbutton his stained shirt, shuddering a little at the crumbly substance embedded in the buttonholes that now coated her fingertips. He let her peel the shirt off him, and she flung it into a far corner. She'd deal with that later. Her hands moved to unbutton his jeans. They too had some questionable stains, but these looked more like spilled beer. As she reached for the zipper, his hand sprung to life, jerking up to clasp hers.

"What?" she said. "Come on, these are filthy. We need to get rid of them and get you in the shower."

"Layla," he said, looking at her with a bashful smile. "Are you sure *you* should do this?" The words still rolled around in a drunken whirl before sliding from his mouth.

"Well, you don't seem to be capable of doing it yourself."

"Yeah, but..."

"But what?" Then she understood. "Oh bloody hell, Will. It's not as if I haven't seen it all before."

"Yeah, but you haven't seen mine before." It struck her as funny, that even though not at all with it, he could still summon enough energy to protest her seeing him naked. She swallowed hard. She'd come damn close to seeing all of it that morning back in the Castle Street flat when they were both just nineteen. Had wanted to see all of it. Still did, if she was honest. She pushed those thoughts aside and tried to push Will firmly back into the friend zone. That's how he wanted it and that's how it must stay. A mate helping another mate.

"And you think I'm going to be so dazzled by its uniqueness that I'll throw you on the ground and have my way with you? Come on Will, with that amount of alcohol on board, I doubt it's going to look the least bit impressive. Pretend I'm your mother."

That wasn't really the best analogy. Will's mother, the formidable Virginia Leroux, wasn't in any way the motherly type. How ironic that both of them should grow up in such different homes, but still experience the absence of their mothers from a young age: his, lost to her career as a medical researcher, leaving a series of nannies to raise her children; hers, captured by long hours juggling multiple low-paying jobs, while Layla and her brothers learned to fend for themselves.

"OK, OK." He raised his arms in surrender.

She looked around for a way to help him preserve his modesty. Seeing a large towel on the rack, she whisked it off in one hand. With the other, in one swift movement, she swept both his jeans and the boxers underneath to lie in a heap around his ankles. Keeping her eyes carefully trained on his face, she wrapped the towel around his waist, offering him back a little dignity in this most undignified situation, and secured it with a deft twist.

"Now, lean on me while you step out of those." He did as she directed, one arm heavy on her shoulder, half-slumped over her, while obediently lifting first one foot, then the next, in slow, awkward movements. Propping him on the side of the bath, where he sat eyes closed, she turned the shower on full blast. The water would not only wash away the stench, but hopefully revive him enough so he could make it upstairs to his bedroom.

"Oops. You've still got your socks on. Give me your foot."

One by one she took off the socks, trying hard *not* to think of what might have caused the soles to be damp. She waved one hand under the stream of water. Judging it to be sufficiently warm, she encouraged him to swing his legs around the side of the bath and rise to stand under it.

"You OK to stand there on your own?"

He nodded, letting the towel fall as he inched under the cascade of water, and she turned away. She'd have preferred to keep her eyes on him, so she could take action if it looked like he was about to topple over. But number one: he wasn't her patient, and it did seem a bit weird to be scrutinising your male best friend in the shower, even if it was for a good reason. And number two: even in this state, he might catch a glimpse of something in her eyes that she couldn't afford to let him see.

She sat on the floor, back against the wall, eyes carefully averted, and her fickle mind, now she'd fed it a brief thought of that time back in Castle Street, determined to deliver the memory in all its excruciating detail.

Layla remembered she and Will abandoning a study session, just for that one night exchanging work on an assignment for what every other Dunedin student seemed to spend Saturday nights doing: drinking. Caught up in the heat and excitement of a wild student party, they'd consumed way too much alcohol, stumbling home down the road in an unaccustomed haze of inebriation.

She remembered tripping over a dining room chair, and Will attempting to steady her. She remembered sprawling in the hallway as her legs buckled beneath her, and his unsteady hand stretching down to help her up. And then nothing. Till waking up to the sight of unfamiliar curtains, the folds of an unfamiliar bed, and a familiar body pressed up against hers. With relief, she realised she still had on a t-shirt and her underwear was intact. But there was no doubt that the man spooning her—and oh damn, if it didn't feel so good—was naked. A heavy arm curled around her waist, and she lay drinking in the comfortable warmth of him. One of his long legs angled between hers, and a little tingle radiated from that point of contact, working its way upward, taking up residence in the low centre of her body, morphing into an almost painful ache. He nuzzled against her neck, the light stubble teasing her skin, each exhale of breath a provocative caress. She wasn't sure how they'd got here, but she was OK with this. Very OK in fact. She let out a small sigh and relaxed into the bed, the mattress far more comfortable than her own, and enjoyed the added bonus of an attractive man wrapped around her.

As if he sensed her wakefulness, Will startled from sleep beside her. "Oh, shit, Layla," he said. He leapt away from her as if she'd burned him. He sat bolt upright, clutching the sheet to his chest. His grey eyes were wide, his mouth an 'O' of surprise. "Oh my god Layla, I'm so sorry," he gasped.

She hesitated for a moment, crushed by the realisation of what that look and those words conveyed: he didn't want this, didn't want *her* like this. Instinctively she sprang into action, her natural need to put things right taking over the agonising disappointment. He needed reassurance. She gave it to him.

"Hey, it's OK," she said, "see—" she swept the sheet back on her side to reveal her clothed body, "—*I* kept my clothes on." Maybe a bit of their usual banter could smooth over the awkwardness of the moment. Seeing his jeans discarded on the floor, she reached for them and tossed them his way. "Come on, Leroux, put some bloody pants on." *That's the way, keep it light.*

"Oh, God Layla, I hope—I mean—did I, did we?" She swivelled her head towards him, keeping her eyes firmly fixed on his face, every ounce of focus brought to bear on controlling her expression. He coloured a little under her gaze. "Shit," he said. "I'm really sorry for anything—for anything I did and I shouldn't have." The words came out in a clumsy stutter, far removed from Will's usual casual ease.

"I think it's fairly safe to say nothing happened, Will." *Reassure him, keep it light.* That was the best way out of this.

She knew that something *had* happened, but not what he feared. The world had upended itself. She turned away now, shielding her face from his scrutiny, fearing this new knowledge might be written there in all its terrifying truth. Inside, Layla knew she could never look at William Leroux in the same way again—her friend, her study buddy, her supporter who believed in her more than she did herself, never doubting she could do this doctor thing. Because, despite the residual fog of the alcohol and the niggling hangover that promised to launch a full-on attack on her tender head and nauseous stomach, there was clarity. She had feelings for Will; perhaps she'd had them for a long time. Wonderful, dizzying, but altogether frightening feelings—because it was obvious they weren't mutual.

"God, that feels good," he murmured. "Can you pass me something to wash myself with?" he called over the gushing stream of water.

"Stick out your hand," she said, and grabbed the nearest bottle, pumping a large puddle of thick, golden liquid onto his palm. She could hear him lathering it on his body and it brought an unhelpful longing to help him out with the task; slide her hands over that chest, follow the lines of his back. A fresh soapy smell wafted her way, carried on the billowing steam. The thought of inhaling that scent on his skin swamped her senses.

"Shampoo?" His hopeful voice pulled her out of her traitorous brain. He definitely sounded a little better. She repeated the process with a bottle of shampoo, squeezing a good measure into his hand while still keeping her back to him. The tap twisted off with a squeak, and the water stopped. "Do you think you could find me another towel?"

She pulled a fresh one from the cupboard. "Here," she offered, and an invisible hand reached over her shoulder and took it from her. "When you've finished drying yourself, wrap it around you and I'll help you out."

He definitely sounded much livelier, but it might be too soon to expect him to balance on one leg while climbing out of the deep, old-fashioned bath. Once he had both feet safely on the ground, they made their way upstairs. He took slow, halting steps, moving on his own now, but with her lingering alongside in case he should have need of her. His hands grasped the balustrade as he hauled himself up.

The huge question of why still hung between them. But seeing him so vulnerable, she didn't have it in her heart to probe. There was time enough to talk tomorrow, when he was fully sober and she wasn't so bone weary.

"Time for some sleep," she said, guiding him in the direction of his bed, where she pulled back the pristine covers. Smoothing the sheet down with her hand was like a whispered invitation. Even with Will in this state, she'd happily slide under it, wrap herself in a protective arc around him, and fall into a blissful sleep.

"Time for you to get some sleep too," he said. He might have read her need for sleep correctly, but she knew the mask she'd perfected to hide those other thoughts remained firmly in place. "I'm so sorry, Layla." His red-rimmed eyes were full of remorse. "You should have been in bed hours ago. What time do you start tonight?"

"Six," she said.

"Oh, shit, I'm really sorry." The bedside clock showed 11:00 am.

"It's OK. You know me. Five hours and I'm good to go again."

"Not when you've got at least twelve ahead of you."

"Nah, I'll be fine. Last night shift, three days off, and I'm back on days after that."

"Thank you, Layla," he said. "I owe you. Thanks for looking after me."

"More than bloody Tristan did," she said with a frown.

"William? Layla?" A voice echoed up from below. Right on cue.

"On my way," she called. "On my way to give him a piece of my mind," she muttered under her breath.

"Go easy on him, Layla. I did this to myself, you know," said Will, registering her angry tone. "He didn't pour it down my throat. I did. And he did at least get me home." Will's voice was the steadiest she'd heard so far. The shower had worked miracles. "Go easy on him," he repeated.

"Mmm," she said. "Maybe." She closed the door with a resounding click and made her way to the kitchen to pounce on Tristan.

4

Again

Mt Eden, Auckland, New Zealand - November 2013

"WHAT THE HELL WERE you thinking?" Tristan raised his hands in defence, as she burst through the kitchen door. "You know I love you like a brother Tristan, but sometimes I'd like to slap you."

"Yes, I know, *I know*. I shouldn't have gone off and left him." He knew all right. He knew what she was upset about before she'd even said it. "I'm sorry Layla. I thought he was OK. We'd been home an hour. I made him a coffee, settled him on the couch first." So they'd been up *all* night. Well, so had she, and she felt decidedly cranky as a result. "And you know what Sophie's like. I thought it easier to pop down to the park for an hour, rather than have her blast me for letting the kids down."

Tristan found his close knit family both a blessing and a curse. Since arriving back in Auckland, his sister expected him to take a full role as loving uncle, including regular attendance at Saturday sport. That meant football games in the winter. Spring brought no reprieve with weekly cricket matches underway. Tristan looked forward to the summer holiday break as much as the kids did. Six weeks of Saturday sleeping in. Yes, he was right: where her offspring were concerned, Sophie accepted no excuses for anything less than model uncle behaviour.

"Yeah, I get that, I suppose," she said begrudgingly. "What I most want to know is how he ended up totally off his face, anyway?"

"I can't take any responsibility for that. He was already well on the way when I got home. It was late—about eight. I went for a few drinks at the Viaduct after work. Anyway, I found him already half a bottle of whisky down when I got here."

He nodded at the near empty bottle and two glasses on the dining table. She hadn't noticed those.

"Shit. Whisky? Will? He never drinks more than a beer." No wonder he was annihilated.

"Yeah, I had a couple with him. Figured having some company might slow him down a bit. Which it sort of did. But then he insisted he was meeting Casey at The Glasshouse at nine, and I should call a cab for us both."

Casey was William's latest sort-of-girlfriend, as much as he ever had girlfriends. She and Will were alike in that respect, two sides of the same coin. He was the guy they took home and let into their bed, but never stayed the night and didn't bother to call. She was the girl who was happy to hook up for a bit of fun, but never expected them to call. Somehow this school teacher he'd met at the gym a couple of months ago had proved either more resilient than most, or a slow learner. The reward for Casey's persistence was semi-regular dates in between his crazy work schedule. Layla had even met her once, and reluctantly admitted that she was OK. But the William that Casey had been dating wasn't the William who'd shown up last night.

"And how did that go?"

"As expected. Badly. He should have phoned her and begged off. But no. Instead, we arrived there an hour late. And when she called him out on it, he was so surly and argumentative that after about half an hour she left with her friends. I have a feeling that relationship might be down the toilet. Unless she's the extremely forgiving type."

"That's a shame," Layla said, letting the familiar lie roll off her tongue and feeling guilty about her lack of truth, as well as the small thrill of possibility that Will being single always triggered in her. "I liked her." That bit wasn't so much a lie—Casey *was* nice enough, if a little bland for her taste. "I thought she was good for him. After all, you know how work-obsessed he's become. It's not healthy." That was the truth.

"As *you* should know," said Tristan, tossing her a pointed look.

"Touchè." That's why, out of all the 'tight five', she remained closest to Will. The others thought they were mad. Only he understood what it took to build a successful career in medicine. And only she understood what an aberration this behaviour was. Will was chasing his dream—to be a surgeon. And everything he did, or didn't do, focused on that goal. Including living the ascetic life they'd both chosen for now, making sure nothing derailed them from the path to the prize. "Talking of work, I'm due back there in five hours. I absolutely must get some sleep."

"And what's that if not work-obsessed?" he said, not afraid to make the accusation. It was her turn to raise her arms in a shrug of defeat. "Yes, well, get yourself to bed," he said. "I promise to creep around the house and not wake you. And don't worry about Will. I'll check on him."

"Thanks Tristan. I'm sorry for being so bitchy. But I'm buggered and, to be honest, seeing him in that state really threw me." The whole sorry saga still left her off balance. Fleeting feelings of dread rippled across her, as if her subconscious mind could sense something bad hovering narrowly out of reach in the shadows, waiting for an opportunity to pounce. She tried to brush them off, putting it down to her dragging tiredness.

"Yeah, I'm pretty tired myself. We should have gone straight home after the standoff with Casey. But he insisted on making a night of it. Must have been to five different bars. I tell you, for some unknown reason, he was a man on a mission to obliterate himself last night. And he needed someone as his wingman, or it would have been way worse. I'm sure it's only a one-off. Maybe he simply needed a bit of a blow-out and then he'll be back to normal."

"I hope so." She definitely didn't want to arrive home to find him in that state again. It frightened her. Just as he rode the waves out at the wild west coast beaches with respect for their power, but without fear, so Will approached life. And when tough times in her own life had loomed large, threatening to sweep her away, Will had always been the one who helped her ride out the storms. In a few short hours, her whole world had flipped, forcing her to be his safe place in the midst of some unknown danger.

"And I'll clean up too." Tristan offered an olive branch. "The lounge is a disaster area."

She also didn't want to arrive home to another mess like that. It would take days to get that nasty vomit smell out of the house. She could still catch a whiff of it here in the kitchen.

"Thanks Tristan. Bathroom's not looking too good either."

She headed for sleep, keeping her weary footsteps quiet as she edged past William's door. Five hours and it would all start again.

"Charlie?" she said, reaching for the curtain.

It couldn't be. The voice answering the nurse's questions in the next cubicle sounded exactly like hers. But it couldn't be. Layla blamed it on weariness from the lack of sleep coupled with the constant stream of incoming. Even now, close to midnight, it showed no sign of abating. No, Charlie would have arrived home after a full day trailing around the wedding, put her feet up, watched trash on tv, had a glass of wine, and turned in early. No, it couldn't be her.

It was. Charlotte Christensen sat on one of the hard vinyl chairs, seats that appeared deliberately designed to deter visitors from lingering. Her deathly pale face tensed at the sight of Layla, her eyes grave. The white-blonde Nordic hair usually tamed in a shiny pony-tail hung in tattered strands. A vivid streak of blood slashed across her white shirt.

"Not mine," she said, noticing Layla's eyes focus on the stain. "His." She jerked her head towards the bed.

Will lay head thrown back against the pillow, eyes closed, mouth a thin grimace of pain. A small trickle of blood oozed from a cut above his left eye. Just large enough to need stitching. Purple bruising already blossomed around one side of his jaw. His face appeared a little slack on that side, too. Possibly broken.

"Jesus," she swore under her breath, her professional filter slipping at the sight of him. She ignored the raised eyebrows and sideways glance of the nurse at her elbow and leaned across to survey the damage at closer range.

He looked even worse than he had that morning, if that was possible. His skin had a definite greenish tinge, and he breathed in shallow huffs. At this distance, she decided the jaw wasn't broken, but it would be painful all the same. And the reek of stale alcohol overlaid the distinctive metallic tang of blood. She turned back to Charlie.

"What happened? I can smell the booze. But his face?"

"He's been in a fight." The look on Charlie's face told her she wasn't joking.

"*A fight?*"

"Yes. A fight."

"Who the hell would pick a fight with William?" Will's natural amiability fit him for the role of peacemaker, not assailant.

"Normally, no one. But in the mood he was in tonight, well, he was asking for trouble. And it was him who picked the fight. That's what the bouncer told me." Layla couldn't help it. Her mouth fell open in disbelief and no words came. "Yep. He walked down to Maguire's about nine. The doorman didn't like the look of him. Said he was too pissed. Wouldn't let him in. So Will hit him."

"And the doorman hit him back?" Charlie didn't answer, but her thin smile confirmed it. Layla had seen the size of those big Polynesian lads working the door at Maguire's, every single one of them built like a brick shithouse. That guy had restrained himself. With such a mismatch, it could have been a lot worse. But all were genial giants, employed not solely for their intimidating physical presence but an ability to good-humouredly deal with the punters—nothing except totally obnoxious behaviour on Will's part would have provoked this. "So how come you're the one picking up the pieces?" Maguire's wasn't the sort of bar Charlie frequented.

"Yeah, lucky fucking me," she said, her mouth as sulky as her words. "Exactly how I love to spend my Saturday night. So much for my hot night in with Milla." Charlie threw a furious look in Will's direction. The relationship between Charlie and Milla seemed a bit off and on lately and this would not flick the switch firmly in the 'on' direction. Charlie sighed deeply. "One of the girls I know on the sports desk at Channel Four called me. She was in the queue to get into the bar. Saw it happen. She remembered Will from that night I scored us those tickets for the box at Eden Park." Layla remembered too. Back in the winter. They'd had a blast watching the rugby game and hanging out with the media crew. One girl had taken quite a fancy to Will. If it was this one, she'd have changed her mind after tonight. "He's lucky they didn't call the police. But perhaps because the bouncer hit him back, they decided it might cause more trouble. I found him slumped in the bookshop doorway two doors down. Threw him in a cab and came here."

"Steph, I'm going to need a suture kit, please." Layla dispatched the nurse while she took a closer look at her patient. As she leaned over, his eyes flickered a little. She reached to take his hand and saw him wince at her touch. Glancing down, she realised why. His hands, his beautiful slender surgeon's hands, were bloody and bruised. She lifted one gingerly, noting that although certainly battered, the fingers didn't appear misshapen. Maybe he'd get away with it. She hoped the damage was superficial. He couldn't lose the tools of his trade over one stupid lapse. It would be so incredibly unfair if one night of completely out of character behaviour cost him his dream.

His eyelids fluttered and snapped open, now focusing on Layla, as if seeing her for the first time. He let out a groan.

"Charlie. Why the hell did you have to bring me here?" His voice came out in a tortured whisper.

Charlie rose to her feet. Her eyes flashed, their placid blue transformed into a glacial glare. "I'll tell you why, William Leroux." She spat out the words. "Because the other option was City, and you wouldn't want to be lying in a bed there looking like that, would you? While they record the sordid details of how it happened for all to see?"

He let out a small grunt of acknowledgment, accepting Charlie's reprimand in the same way they all accepted her tough love. Charlie loved hard, and she loved fierce. Looking suitably chastened, he opened his mouth to speak again, and said nothing. Either he'd thought better of it, or it hurt.

And it *had* been an astute call on Charlie's part, choosing the more distant but less problematic hospital. Layla knew the last thing Will needed right now was to see one of his work colleagues peering down at him, judging him. At least by coming to her hospital here, down in South Auckland, he might survive this indiscretion without it blotting his spotless reputation.

She and Charlie had forgiven him plenty over the years. And he'd returned the favour. After all, none of them were perfect. Their friendship had seen each of them through tough times in the past, and no doubt would again. They'd forgive him this. But even so, Layla pasted a suitable look of exasperation on her face, and leaned over him.

"Again? What the hell is up with you, William?" He wouldn't expect anything less than her giving him a blast. She and Charlie were alike in that respect. But behind her words, a flaring worry threatened to swamp her. She narrowed her eyes, hoping to mask her concern with a show of displeasure. A lump rose in her throat.

To see him hurting like this brought all kinds of confusing emotions swirling upwards. But she mustn't let them surface. This was time to be her 'tough love' self.

"Sorry Layla," he said, the words slurred from the sagging curl of his lips. The pleading expression hovering in his eyes disturbed her nearly as much as the reason he lay here in her ED. For now, she'd do what she could to mend the obvious physical damage. Fixing it was a straightforward procedure even a first-year doctor would consider routine.

As for the underlying cause of Will's sudden self-destructive bent, he was hiding it. That was to be expected, raised in a family that didn't show their feelings or talk about them. Whether love or hate, anger or despair, the Lerouxs considered public displays of emotion to be beneath them. And you didn't air your problems. No, a Leroux presented a brave face to the world. Although she knew Will fought against what they'd made him, it was a battle he couldn't always win. Some things were so ingrained that under pressure, you fell back into them, a lesson she herself knew.

And she doubted she was ready for him to reveal his reasons. This dramatic change in him brought back the sickening fear that even when he chose to open up to his friends, this problem lay beyond what any of them could solve.

"Don't worry," she said, fighting to keep control, to not let guilt at being so hard on him overtake her. "After all, it's me who will be apologising in a minute. Since I'm about to hurt you." Steph raised her eyebrows at this callous comment as she handed over the syringe filled with local anaesthetic. "It's OK," Layla said. "I know him. Unfortunately." Turning towards him, hand poised over the wound, she paused for a moment, before launching back into her bossy friend act. "Just because I'm not having words with you about this now, don't think I'm not going to."

There it flashed again, that look in his eyes: bleak, beseeching, but wary. As if needing something from her, but also fearing it. She couldn't battle it any longer, couldn't pretend to be mad at him, when all she wanted to do was wrap him up tight and tell him that whatever it was, it would be OK.

"Will, what's all this about?" she said, her voice almost a whisper as she leaned in close to begin the work of mending the ugly gash. "Whatever it is, you know you don't need to do this on your own. We're all here for you. Like always." She said we, but she meant me. *I'm here for you, my love, one hundred percent. All you need is here with me.*

She'd made the job her priority for a very long time. But in that minute, she vowed to make him her priority. It was her turn to step up and become the safe harbour, the steady comfort, the loving supporter. Whatever storm he faced, she'd be there beside him and they would face it together, head-on.

"I'll tell you," he said, softly under his breath. "Not now, but I will. I'll tell *you*."

Layla swore she saw tears well in William's eyes. And knew the sting of her needle plunging into the open wound wasn't the cause.

5

Risk

Mt Eden, Auckland, New Zealand - November 2013

WILL'S JAW HURT LIKE hell and while he'd have preferred a big breakfast fry up to soothe his unsteady stomach, his current inability to chew ruled that out. A protein shake seemed the best of the liquid options. But the last thing Layla needed was the nasal whine of the blender to wake her, so he was attempting to quietly disperse lumps of green powder with a fork and having little success. Each puff as one disintegrated filled the air with the faint seaweed smell of spirulina. When he heard the front door open with a quiet click, and then a soft thud as it closed considerately, he didn't need to turn away from his task to know who had entered the house.

Charlie had gone out and wouldn't be back for hours. She'd accepted his offer of reparation: a hundred bucks to take Milla out for brunch and hopefully encourage her out of her bad mood. Of course, that mood was solely attributable to Charlie bailing on her the previous night, attending to him after his antics down at Maguire's. It seemed rather depressing to think they would probably ban him for life from their favourite neighbourhood pub. Although it was minor compared to the rest of his problems; he needed to let that one go.

Tristan was over at his sister's place doing lunch with his family. The guy was such a contradiction. Who'd know that hidden behind the exterior of this loud, brash and sometimes obnoxious extrovert, lurked a closet family man? One day, some girl would find her way behind that bravado, coax him away from his laddish ways, gaining a pretty decent husband as a reward for her efforts. One day, but maybe not yet.

So Will absolutely knew it was neither of them. But he would also have known Leo had arrived home simply by the careful way he'd opened and closed the front door. Of the five of them, only Leo possessed an awareness of others so keen that after two days away, he'd think of Layla sleeping upstairs after a night shift.

"Hey, man," Will said, feeling his grin involuntarily slide into an unintended lopsided smirk. "How did you go?"

Leo hesitated for a moment, scanning Will's face, with its distorted jawline, mottled purple skin and Layla's precise handiwork above his brow. When he'd studied himself in the mirror this morning, Will had once again wondered why the woman thought she'd never make a surgeon; he'd be proud of a row of sutures that tidy.

"Cracked three-forty," Leo said, with his modest smile, always so bloody understated. What Will would give to even complete a marathon, let alone go sub-four hours?

"Congratulations mate, that's bloody fantastic."

"Yeah, it's always good to set a new PB. I knew I had it in me this weekend, but I'd never have thought I'd do three-thirty-eight."

"So, you're home early. Thought you might have hung around Queenstown for the day. Celebrate the milestone."

"Yeah, well, I did a bit of that last night. And I wanted to get home and sort myself for next week. I'm off to Wellington in the morning."

"The land claim?" Will asked.

"Yeah," Leo said, a slow smile spreading across his face. "We're so close I can almost touch it," he said. "I'm thinking they're about to hand over at least two hundred million."

Even through his damaged mouth, Will forced out a low whistle of admiration. No one would ever guess that mild-mannered Leo's soft baby face masked a kick-arse negotiator. At the moment, he put that skill to use in the Land Court, hammering out one of the biggest ever settlements between a Māori tribe and the Crown. In his characteristic selfless way, he made use of his top flight legal mind for the greater good rather than emulate Tristan chasing big dollars in the corporate world. Will wouldn't want to be a government lawyer sitting across the table from Leo. He'd lull his unsuspecting victims with those softly spoken words and pleasant demeanour and then leap in for the kill, leaving them reeling that they hadn't seen it coming.

"You look like shit, by the way," Leo said, pulling up a stool at the counter. "Take a thrashing from those west coast waves? I hear the surf's been pretty fierce out at Piha."

He may as well get it over with. Leo would hear it from the others soon enough, anyway. "Nah, drank too much and had a slight altercation down at Maguire's."

"Shit, for real? Never thought it was the sort of place that would attract a rough crowd. You OK? Apart from the obvious..."

"Well, unfortunately, the rough crowd was me." As expected, Leo sat in stunned silence. "Yeah, well, at least you're not giving me shit about it," Will pressed on. "Charlie's all pissy with me, and fair enough too, I suppose—she missed her date night with Milla to pull me out of there. And then, Layla..." He pointed to the cut on his brow.

Leo looked at him, the raised brows and a quizzical expression conveying his expectation of more information. When it didn't come, he leaned forward on the counter, hands steepled in front of him. "I don't know what the problem is," he said, "and hey, I'm not even going to ask. But sounds like you need to sort yourself out, mate. Though I don't think you need me to tell you that."

"No, you're right. Got to get my shit together. In fact, I think I might go upstairs and give myself some time to think over a few things right now."

Just a few things, like the fact there was a time-bomb ticking in his head and what that meant for his future. If it went off suddenly, then he wouldn't have the luxury of worry. But more than likely it would just sit there, expanding at leisure, the tumour stretching slow tendrils, choosing at will what it might touch next. Perhaps it would nudge at his vision, forcing a degree of deterioration that the wonders of corrective lenses or advanced technology couldn't overcome. Or he'd lose fine motor control, robbing him of the precision in his hands that he took such pride in. Would it eventually take more? The ability to run, to walk, to ride the waves, or even to speak? It could. And in a cruel irony, he knew that surgical intervention to stop it could also take some of that from him too.

But the self-indulgent outrage out of the last two days had to end. Venting his anger on the world may have given some small relief, but he'd only ended up hurting himself and others. He had to throw off this stupid shit and start taking some considered action.

"OK," said Leo. "And you know, if you ever need to talk..."

"Yeah, thanks Leo, appreciate it mate." And he really did appreciate it. Friends like Leo, who went way back with you, were precious.

"Well, yeah," Leo said, "happy to help. But nah, I was going to say—you should talk to Layla." And then, in true Leo style, after dropping that enigmatic bombshell, he casually turned his back on Will, walked to the fridge and rummaged inside, humming to himself.

Bloody Leo, he saw everything. Perceptive little bastard was practically psychic. He was right. They'd been friends long enough to know. To know what Will knew. Even these last two days, caught up in this self-destructive spiral, amid his crazy spinning out as he grappled with the new reality of his precarious existence, there had been that nagging voice in his head, nudging him towards the one person who had a hope of saving him from himself.

But he needed more than rescue from Layla.

Perhaps the single good thing to emerge from this nightmare weekend was a surprising clarity. When he'd woken up this morning, his mind churning, struggling with the reality of the total arse he'd made of himself, and confronting the possible death sentence hanging over his head, one thing had pushed its way through. His future might be uncertain, but one thing about it he understood with absolute certainty: the person he wanted to share his life with, whatever remained of it, was her.

However, therein lay the other huge uncertainty. When he laid it all bare for her, what would she say? What would she do? He thought he knew Layla better than anyone else, almost as well as he knew himself. He would trust her with his life. But trusting her with the admission that he loved her—that was taking a leap into the unknown. But he had no option but to risk it all. When she woke, he needed to be ready to tell her everything. Calm, sober and ready.

6

Sorry

Mt Eden, Auckland, New Zealand - November 2013

THE PATIENT AFTERNOON SUN eventually found its way around the almost impenetrable barrier of the blackout curtains. It stabbed through a tiny slit near the edge of one, illuminating a strip of the imitation Turkish rug with an otherworldly glow. The clock showed 5:30 p.m. If she got up now, she could enjoy daylight for another two hours, enough to make her feel she hadn't spent her entire weekend in darkness. With three days off to look forward to, followed by a week of day shifts, there was plenty of time to catch up on sleep. But the bed was so comfortable. Layla peeled back the sheet and lay there a little longer, enjoying the kiss of cool air from the fan that lazily whirled in the corner.

This hazy, blissful drowsiness dissipated as her brain kicked into action. The events of last night came tumbling back to her in all their disturbing, bright-coloured reality. And the image etched so sharply in her mind was that of Will's eyes; a bleakness in them that sent chills across her bare skin. She gripped the sheet in tense bunches, pulling it back up over her knees, hugging them tight as if by retreating into herself she might ward off this creeping icy dread.

Muffled movements hinted at the presence of others in the rooms below, accompanied by the quiet hum of a radio kept to a considerate low volume. Then came footsteps as someone made their way along the upstairs hallway, the light tread respectful of a sleeping flatmate. Despite the careful placement of those feet, the odd creak escaped as hundred-year-old floorboards protested the weight. Whoever it was came to a halt outside her door and she waited for a knock that never came. A sudden swishing noise, and then they headed back along the hallway. She leaned forward, intrigued. In the gloom, she could make out the shape of a large envelope that someone had slid across the polished wood under her door. How strange.

Layla flung off the sheet and tiptoed across the room. As she bent to pick it up, she recognised its size and shape; a cover for x-rays or scans, to protect the film from damage. Definitely odd. But at least she had the answer to her first question. Only one person would have slipped that under the door. It confirmed her suspicion when she saw the single phrase, written across the top in a precise hand she knew so well: *This is the reason, not an excuse.*

She swallowed down the rising unease triggered by reading those few words. Thinking about what lay in this envelope filled her with trepidation. The reason for that behaviour last night had to be something big, something so unexpected, just as Will drunk and brawling in bars was unexpected.

When she read the name at the top of the first film: LEROUX, William Montgomery, bile rose in her throat, the fear of what it would reveal clenching her stomach. She fanned through the collection of images, recognising them as the output of an MRI scan. Spreading them out on the white bedspread, better to see each individual image, she saw they represented multiple cross sections of William's formidable brain. And as she peered at them more closely, she also knew why he was spinning out of control. The unmistakable shadow that marred one section of otherwise healthy brain tissue wasn't definitive proof of a tumour. If it was her patient, she'd be asking for further tests. But she suspected William had already predicted the results of such tests. Or perhaps he'd even had them. It was all perfectly clear to her now.

She placed the films carefully back inside the envelope, as if removing them from her sight could somehow wish them away. But it couldn't. Pulling her knees back up under her chin, she squeezed them close, trying to still her racing heart.

It was pointless. Working through the facts fed her growing panic. *Fuck*. This was bad. Far worse than anything she could have imagined. If this was what he suspected, the surgery to eliminate the tumour—presuming it was indeed operable—would save his life but potentially end his career.

Will, on the specialist neurosurgery pathway, desperate to emulate his father's renowned achievements, knew better than anyone what the odds were of such surgery not having any lasting negative impact: pretty much zero. He knew he'd no longer have the steadiness in his hands; some loss of fine motor control was an almost inevitable side effect. Even if it was slight, those talented hands could no longer do their delicate job. And that intense focus that he could bring to bear on any task and sustain for the hours necessary to complete a surgery—that too could—no, most probably would, suffer. That was the best-case scenario. And the worst? He might lose his life. She would lose him.

That harrowing thought spurred her into action: didn't stop to throw on a robe over the singlet and panties she'd slept in; didn't hesitate to politely knock on his door. But as she stepped through that door, even the sight of him was enough to shatter her heart into tiny pieces. He stood in the bay window with his back to her, silhouetted against the afternoon light. He seemed smaller than his six-foot frame, as if he'd somehow shrunk in on himself, shoulders dropped, head hung low in thought. It frightened her to see him like this.

Will the confident one, who'd front up to anything with a brave face. "Come on Angell," he'd said, when she'd faltered in the face of failing Professor Bergman's group assignment. "We're not going to let old Hamburger beat us." She'd picked herself up and made the old bugger begrudgingly give her an A+ for her term paper. And the times she'd almost drowned, pulled under by the weight of her family, their careless disdain for her attempts to become the person she was now, a person who was the things they were not. He'd taught her how to swim against the tide of her upbringing. He was the one constant, the one who'd always promised a reassuring certainty of a positive outcome. But there he stood, a man defeated.

He turned and stretched out his bandaged hands towards her, arms wide, and she stepped into them, drawn to him like a powerful magnet. As their eyes met, she saw all the wild emotion that swirled inside her reflected in his, the blue-grey turbulent like a stormy sea: fear, uncertainty—and unexpectedly, as they flickered across her bare shoulders, did she even see her own flash of desire mirrored there?

It was that last possibility that confused her. She'd always thought that it was she who carried that small smoulder of hope. Her that had pushed it down deep, assuming that he wanted no more from her than this friendship. But no, as she folded against him, as he took her in close, she felt him harden against her.

The thrill at this small sign of his want coursed through her; the graze of his chest against her erect nipples tingled with electricity. When she trailed her hand down the fabric of his t-shirt, the light brush of her fingertips triggered a little shiver. Perhaps it wasn't only she who had denied this possibility between them in the past. And now as she sensed this unspoken admission of a secret truth pass between them, their bodies betraying what their minds had tried to suppress, a melancholy ache in her bones overshadowed it, a reminder that a cruel present might deny them a future to fully explore it.

This devastating thought overwhelmed her. No sound came, but her body shook, the sobs wracking her in uncontrollable waves. He leaned his chin on her head; pressed a kiss on her hair.

"It's OK, it's OK, it's OK." He whispered it like a mantra, as if it might hold them in a moment in time where it *was* OK. Where it was simply two people drawn together in a small safe place, holding back the world.

She shouldn't be the one crying. She should be the strong one. He shouldn't be the one comforting. But sadness possessed her; a response to the callous unfairness and crushing regret. She'd known this man half her life, and only now, when she might lose him, she admitted the truth.

She lifted her head to him, not caring that he should see her like this. This was the person who had always truly seen her, known all the facets of herself she'd guarded from the world: the scared little girl she hid with composure; the woman who doubted herself despite projecting competence; the playful child that lay underneath her serious exterior. She trusted him with all of them without hesitation, but with one momentous omission—she'd never let him see how she loved him.

"Layla," he said, his voice soft, her name like a prayer on his lips. He lifted one finger, smoothing away a tear. Dipping his head low, those lips brushed against her cheek, ever so gently tracing the trail of tears. She closed her eyes and leaned into him as he moved her hair aside, exploring the little space between shoulder and neck. Her breath caught in her throat as he murmured her name against her skin. "Layla." The way he said her name would forever be imprinted on her. "Oh, god Layla." It came out as a sob.

She opened her eyes to meet his gaze, and what she saw there broke something inside of her, the mixture of sorrow, and want, and fear. And then his lips dropped to meet hers, the first faint kiss a messy fusion of tenderness and sadness. He sighed into her mouth and she felt an echoing sigh rising within in her, relief they'd finally made it to this point. The soft press of his lips became less patient, more confident, insistent even as their tongues met in a mint-flavoured dance.

They drew apart a moment, coming up for air. "How bloody stupid am I?" he whispered against her ear. "To get this close to leaving without you ever knowing?"

She felt her face crumple. The thought that Will, the one constant in her life, might not make it out the other side of this enveloped her in another tidal wave of fear. The tears fell again, and he crushed her to him, letting her collapse against his reassuring embrace.

"Tell me," she said, when she could finally speak, soothed by the gentle strokes of his hands on her back, and the warm comforting pressure of his body against hers. He released her carefully, led her over to his bed and they huddled amongst the mountain of pillows.

The room's simple, almost casual elegance reflected the good taste cultivated in a home with money; in contrast to her space with mismatched secondhand furniture and a hotchpotch of cheap and cheerful K-Mart decor items. But although it had been years since she'd spent time in a bedroom inhabited by Will, not since those days of pulling joint all-nighter study sessions in the Castle Street flat, she was comfortable here. It felt like him, calm and peaceful; smelled like him, his fresh aftershave hanging lightly in the air, reminiscent of the sea he so loved. She sat under the shelter of his arm, cradling one of his damaged hands in her lap.

"It was sheer luck they found it," he said, the words so matter-of-fact. How could discovering you had a brain tumour be lucky? "If I hadn't had that skiing accident in October, I doubt it would have come to light in time to do something about it."

Will's older brother, Carson, owned a place in Wanaka, the expected lavish holiday home of a successful merchant banker. The family frequently used it for skiing weekends. Even Virginia and Hilton sometimes joined their golden-haired children on the slopes at Treble Cone. Most of the time Will was so ordinary she forgot the rich kid he'd been. But anything that pulled him back into the web of his family was sure to smack of money. Like skiing. All the rich people were skiers.

"Of course. They would have checked for concussion," she said, knowing the drill of the ED at Lakes District Hospital in Queenstown would mirror that of her own workplace.

"Yeah," he said. "I mean, I was sure I'd broken my leg. That's all I thought about in the ambulance, not about how I'd smacked my head on the ground when I went down. After all," he said with a wry smile, "that Bollé helmet cost me a fortune. I'd have been pissed if it hadn't done the job. But yeah, they insisted on a CT scan to be safe. And they didn't like what they saw, recommended the MRI. So, the outcome of one skiing escapade: my leg's not broken, but I discover my brain could be fucked." He delivered the words dispassionately, his eyes fixed on the wall in front of him, as if talking about someone else. But then he leaned in against her, his voice dropping to almost a whisper against her hair. "And of course, the things that need to happen, if I'm going to beat it—well, the career is pretty much fucked too."

This was the heart of it. This was who Will was, who he was always going to be: a talented surgeon, an admired professional, a magician who saved lives with the skill in those hands, the lauded son of a lauded father. She understood it, probably more than anyone else did. She'd stood beside him on this journey, and now so close to completely fulfilling that potential, he had a choice: lose it all, or lose his life. But damned if she would stand by and see the latter. The person she needed most in the world now needed her too, to be the strong voice that told him every day that he was enough, just as himself.

"Can you imagine what Dad and Mum are going to think of that?" His voice cracked at the harsh reality of his parents' warped view of the world. Her heart broke for him, understanding as he did there was a list of conditions, always front and centre in his family, defining what he must be to deserve his place in it, to be worthy of the Leroux name, to be loved—for him to meet those conditions would now be impossible.

She felt a stab of fierce determination, a blinding need to convince him that there was a life beyond his career. She could offer him the chance to build a life with someone whose love was unconditional, for much as she respected his talent and skill as a doctor which far outstripped hers, she'd take Will if he was just an ordinary guy doing an ordinary job.

And then there was that pang of regret. God, they'd wasted years. But perhaps not totally wasted; their friendship was a strong base on which to build a future together. She knew things about Will, intimate things he'd shared with her: his hopes, his fears, his aspirations and his doubts. And he knew hers too. Except for that one small hope she'd hardly allowed herself to consider: that she might someday mean more to him. But today, in those minutes clasped tight in his arms, he'd broken down the wall she'd built around her secret love. It was a secret no more. She felt no fear that light now shone on it, simply relief that she didn't have to keep it hidden any longer.

She leaned in towards him, tracing the clenched jaw, brushing the golden stubble with her hand, training it down the tense muscles in his neck. As he dropped his head towards her, she couldn't help it. Her lips grazed his: gentle, tentative, soothing. His lips stumbled across her mouth at first, as if discovering it by accident. And then determined not to let this serendipitous find escape him, he became more insistent, seeking her out with a desperate hunger as if he meant to devour her.

So many times, she'd wondered what it would be like to kiss Will. Wondered, as she'd watched him laughing, what it would be like to capture the very joy of him in her mouth. Wondered as she'd seen him kiss another girl with eyes tender and welcoming, what it would be like to have him invite her in with that same tenderness. In those moments, she'd pushed it aside. Told herself it would be wrong to act on those feelings. The risk of losing this friendship was too great. It had sustained them both through some tough years. But now, faced with the possibility of really losing him, risk be damned.

She couldn't believe they'd spent all this time warily circling each other, frightened to make their relationship anything more. All this time they could have been doing this, wasted on others. Other men's hands had caressed her body, and now as Will's hands traced those same pathways, his fingertips burned, erasing those other prints on her skin, replacing them with his own mark, forever imprinted on her, indelible.

"My god you're so damn beautiful," he murmured, his mouth dragging down her throat, his hands upon her becoming more insistent. Surely when he rested his mouth right there against her neck, he could feel the heat of her pulse, a hot steady throb.

She felt his grin spread across her skin as he dipped his head lower resting lips against her collarbone. "Clavicle," he breathed, and a giggle bubbled up between them. The playfulness of their old game provided a momentary reprieve from the intense sensations sweeping across her body, rolling in waves under his bold hands as they traced the lines of her stomach, her hips. Finding the gap under her singlet, one made its way upward, clutching at her breast with strong demanding fingers, his thumb and forefinger trapping her nipple with electrifying strokes, his talented fingertips lending themselves to this work with a precise skill. She whimpered at the touch, a burning heat ignited down low between her legs.

"Take it off," he said, his voice low, his jaw rough against her neck, his mouth hungry to seek out every inch of her. She pulled away to stand with eyes locked on his, drinking in the hunger with which he scanned her exposed body as she peeled off the top, discarding it on the floor. "All of it," he said. She slowly rolled down her panties, the heat of his unwavering gaze upon her. He stretched out a hand, drew her back to nestle between his thighs, her head rested against his chest. One arm wrapped from behind cupping her breasts, the other strayed downwards, tracing a path that made her shudder in anticipation. In a haze of pleasure, she let him explore, his nimble fingers seeking and finding, stroking and pressing, until the whimpers became gasps. But moments away from the inevitable climax, she clutched her hand to his, stilling his touch just a breath away.

"No," she whispered. "Not yet." She didn't want this to be a selfish act. After all this time, she could be patient, determined for this to be the moment when they truly connected, together in this. Turning to kneel between his legs, her hands bunched the t-shirt, and he cooperated, tossing it to land beside the bed.

She trailed one hand through the soft springy hairs of his chest, her fingers following the neat line where they disappeared into the band of his sweatpants, going to the place her eyes had discreetly been before, now available to her touch. With her free hand, she tugged at the cord. "I think these need to go."

She shuffled back, creating space for him to shimmy off the pants, his boxers too, all joining the pile of discarded clothing on the floor. Freed from their confines, his erection reared up between them and she moved to lie across him, trapping its hard length against her stomach. He groaned as she moved herself against him, and he angled one leg between hers, pressing it against the heat between her legs and she too groaned with the renewed sensation. She floated in the intimacy as their bodies relaxed into each other. When for a moment he stopped, in one deft movement rolling her onto the bed, the world stopped too and she gasped at the loss of sensation, wanting the weight of his lean body against hers so much that it hurt. And when he responded, blanketing her, she revelled in how neatly they fit together, him tall, her small, like two pieces of a puzzle locked together, perfectly matched.

"Layla." The word came as a low growl in her ear. How many times had he said her name over the years? Hundreds? Thousands? But never like this. Never in a way that unleashed this tornado of feelings inside her, as he dipped his head, and his lips took possession of hers. She responded to his probing tongue with her own, wanting to fall into him, fade into him, become one single blistering sensation.

As her hands traced the perfect even ripple of his spine, he let out a moan, his hips thrusting into hers, hers involuntarily rising to meet him, her own low hum of desire springing from somewhere deep in her throat.

"Layla," he said, breaking away with a short gasp, "are we really doing this? Are you sure this is what you want?" His eyes were dark with need, a need she couldn't deny, just as she couldn't deny her own.

"I'm absolutely sure," she said.

"OK," he said, his breath still ragged. He sat up, bringing his hands to his temples for a moment before reaching for a drawer in the bedside cabinet. "Please let there be a condom in here."

He rummaged around while she welcomed the momentary reprieve to catch her breath. And in this moment, another need overtook her: the need to tell him the truth. This wasn't merely a sudden impulse on her part. This wasn't a gesture of pity.

His usually deft hands fumbled with the foil packet and struggled to unroll its contents as if he'd never done it before. But he'd never done this with her before. And it was important to her that, before they took this next step, he knew this wasn't simply some reaction to the emotions swirling around his illness, some primal response to the threat of his loss. She stretched out a hand to help him with the task and then lay back on her side. He pressed his body, still taut with desire, against the length of her.

"Will, I want you now, but it's nothing new," she said into his shoulder. "I can't remember when it started, but it seems like forever. All I know is I've tried not to think about this, tried not to imagine how it would be for us to be together. Now we're here, I'm not going to deny it. I've always wanted you," she whispered into the warm skin.

"I want you too, Layla," he said, quietly moving against her, stirring those thrilling pulses low down in her centre. "I've never wanted anyone as much as I want you right now."

And with her permission, they plunged back into the maelstrom. His kisses fell upon her, fierce and demanding, his body igniting hers with a rush of flame. Layla lost herself in this new language between them, a language of heat and pressure, rising and falling, the arch of her body in response to the thrusting of his hips, and finally an explosive scream of tension and release.

After that, there was no need for ordinary words. For there could be no words to describe the complexity of sensations and emotions that echoed in her brain. Layla just accepted that it was real, and it was amazing, and let herself doze against his broad shoulder, allowing her glow of happiness to push back the dark things that awaited them beyond this moment.

She awoke to see him looking down at her. His thumb traced her mouth, encouraging her lips to part in a lazy smile. There was an odd look in his eyes, and she felt a jolt of sadness that no matter what had happened between them, the gift of her love wasn't enough to protect him from what lay ahead. She stretched a hand up, to caress the tense set of his lips as he swallowed, as if gathering his thoughts.

"I'm sorry," he said in a gentle voice.

They were not the words she expected to hear. Two little words. How could two words take her heart from soaring with happiness and plunge it into freefall? But here it was—he was sorry. A mistake. A blunder in the midst of an emotionally charged moment. An action already a regret. She lay in stunned silence, tried to swallow down the feelings that bubbled up inside her but they choked in her throat. A shudder ran through her, settling in her gut as a stabbing physical pain.

"Layla?" he said, a question in the cadence of her name, seeking an answer for the sudden tension that gripped her.

He'd sensed the way her soft compliant body had hardened to cold steel. And hearing his question, she grew angry. How could he fail to see that apologising for what had happened between them had taken her hope and shredded it into tiny pieces? She sat bolt upright in the bed, flinging off his arm that rested on her stomach, tossing back the tangled knot of sheet from where it bunched around her legs.

"Sorry?" she said. "You're *sorry*?" Despite the tremor inside, her voice came out low, smooth, threatening. The words tumbled out in a bitter stream. "Well, thanks for nothing, Will. At least you could have waited a little longer to tell me you regret this. Could have given me some time to enjoy the lie."

"What?" he said, an expression of incredulity sweeping across his face. "No. No, Layla, that's not what I meant at all."

She wanted to believe the lack of guile in those eyes, but her emotions were all over the place and the dangerous vortex of fury that whirled amongst them snatched her up. She lunged to her feet, eyes scanning for what little clothing she'd arrived in. They landed on Will's t-shirt and she pounced on it, dragging it roughly over her head. She yanked it down brusquely, checking it at least covered her butt, and took one step towards the door. But he was already in front of her, blocking her way, and his arms sprung up, his hands grasping her wrists, determined to prevent her flight.

"Layla, stop," he pleaded. "I'm not sure what you thought I was saying, but it—"

Part of her wanted to let him finish, to believe in the man she knew who would never hurt her. Surely he wouldn't have treated her this way? But she also knew there was a side of him that did exactly this: fucked women and then slunk out in the middle of the night before moving on to the next one. She hadn't judged him for it because it was what she did too, all fun and no attachment. But she would never do that with him. He was her exception, but a rising nausea accompanied the distressing possibility that she wasn't his.

And the Will who stood before her was a different man to the one he'd been two days ago. This was a man who drank himself senseless, who brawled on the street, who had nothing left to lose. And perhaps *that* Will was a man who could have sex with his best friend, take her want for him and use it before casting her aside when he had no more need of it. Perhaps that Will saw this whole thing as a mistake, an error of judgement not to be repeated.

She hated that man. She wrenched her wrists free of his grasp and balled her hands into white-knuckled fists. She glared up at him and his eyes met hers, hurt and wary. Unable to bear that look, she leapt to her feet.

"Fuck you William Leroux," she spat at him in one last defiant gesture and then launched herself through the doorway, in the hallway colliding with a startled Leo who had arrived home oblivious to the events of the weekend and was unfortunately headed to his room at that precise moment. Brushing Leo and his look of concern aside, she escaped into her room and plunged into the refuge of her bed.

7

Truth

Mt Eden, Auckland, New Zealand - November 2013

HE DIDN'T CALL OUT to her and wait for her to invite him in, didn't bang on the door and demand entry—it wouldn't surprise him if she'd barricaded it, seeing the state in which she'd left his room. He needed a moment to summon sufficient courage to barge in there and sort this out. But if he had any chance of retrieving Layla from the crushing despair triggered by his words, he needed to think, and fast.

The weekend had been an unmitigated disaster. In fact, he'd been on a highway to hell before it even started, with that Friday afternoon specialist appointment. And while he couldn't blame himself for the outcome of that, he'd been completely at fault for every single catastrophic event since.

The only difference with this latest one was he had no idea why it had happened. Except to realise Layla had imbued those two words "I'm sorry" with a completely different meaning to what he'd intended. He was such an idiot. Perhaps it was evidence that, like his father, he was best at dealing with people who were unconscious, lacking the subtlety to understand the nuances of a gesture, or a word. True, he hadn't had too many proper relationships. But he'd always thought he'd handled those few adroitly, and hadn't left too much carnage in his wake when, as they all did, they'd ended. But here, with Layla, the best friend he had in the world, the person who he knew best and who knew him better than any other human being, somehow he'd totally fucked up. And there was no other option he could live with but to fix this.

His memory of the last hour had a surreal quality, like a beautiful interlude, where he'd briefly felt protected from the torrent of shitty things raining down on him. There was no going back to that time before, and he didn't want to. But he was uncertain of her. He thought in Layla's eyes he'd read the feelings he had towards her reflected back at him. Now he hesitated because going through that door meant either confirming that, or facing he'd been very wrong and that brief moment of perfect connection between them would never come again.

He couldn't keep loitering here in the hallway, fixated on Layla's bedroom door, wearing only his jeans; his t-shirt lay on the other side, with her in it. He desperately needed to find the guts to confront her.

Rustling from Leo's room down the hallway gave him the last tiny push of motivation he needed. God, he couldn't face Leo seeing how badly he'd messed this up. Talk to her. That was Leo's advice. Well, he'd taken it, but it had gone way beyond talking. Maybe Leo guessed that. Maybe in his usual subtle way Leo had been letting him know he saw it all. Those feelings for Layla he'd thought smoothly hidden under the casual banter, the time spent together under the guise of supporting one another on their shared career path.

The diagnosis had stripped away all the barriers he'd put up between them, breaking down all the subtle ways he kept himself at arm's length, never getting too close. The protective shield that allowed him to avoid feeling too deeply was also gone. The things he feared coming to the surface were now laid bare. And in that raw state, he'd had no defence against her, no choice but to let her sweep him into a whirlpool of emotions. He'd plunged in with her willingly, let himself succumb to a need for her that had lain under layers of 'shouldn't' and 'couldn't'. He turned the doorknob slowly and slipped into her room.

Layla sprawled on her bed like some graceful feminine interpretation of Vitruvian man. With wide green eyes fixed to the ceiling, only a brief flicker gave a slight indication she'd registered his presence. That seemed a good sign, her stillness a dramatic contrast to the raging wildcat she'd been minutes ago. But he knew Layla, and he knew that calm exterior still harboured a sea of roiling emotions that mirrored his own; a tempest they must navigate, or end up nothing but a wreck on the shore.

He sat on the bed beside her and placed his hand over hers. He wanted to tell her again that he was sorry, but explain that he regretted not *what* had happened, but *how* it had happened. He needed her to know that today, even before she'd appeared in his room, his uncertain future had delivered moments of blinding clarity—no, certainty, about what he must do in whatever time he had. He might not get to live long, but he would live big. And he wanted to live big with her.

Guilt still nagged at him. He'd loved this woman since he'd first set eyes on her, a wild-haired teenager making her way down the bus towards him, and yet he'd done nothing about it. He'd waited until she was vulnerable to take action on his feelings, and he felt like a coward for it.

She didn't shake off his hand; her acceptance of his touch was another good sign. And then her small palm turned slowly, her lithe fingers coming to nest under his. She was ready to listen to him. He struggled with the words, not only what he wanted to say, but even coaxing his taut throat to produce sound was a challenge. His hand reflexively tensed around hers, clutching it like a lifeline, a way back to her.

He decided to simply say it how he felt it, no embellishment, only the truth, laying it there in front of her. He couldn't bear this silence, almost as terrible as her anger, for even a second longer.

"Layla, you need to know that you're more precious to me than anyone or anything in this world." The bed shifted ever so slightly, absorbing the tension of her body as she let out an audible breath and relaxed into it. "I think deep down I always hoped that one day, when the time was right, we'd be together." Green eyes swivelled to meet his, tinged with redness—all his fault. He lifted a hand to trace the still damp path of her tears, hoping she wouldn't brush him away. His stomach clenched with shame that he'd hurt her, needed her to understand that was the last thing he'd ever want. "But I've taken that for granted. Wasted so much time. Waited till today, when your feelings were all over the place to do anything about it. It wasn't fair of me to do that to you." She squeezed his hand a little tighter. "I love you Layla. I think I always have. And back there, in my room, I just wanted to tell you I'm sorry that I never told you that, never showed you that before today. And I needed to know—despite me neglecting you so badly—whether today means the same to you as it does to me, that you could love me back in that way." He paused, as the thought she might not choked the words right there in his mouth. He swallowed, knowing they must be said. He must give her the out, if that's what she needed. "Or if you don't, if this was simply part of the overwhelm in knowing of my situation, and you want to put it behind us, go back to how it's always been, I'll try to live with it. But I'll never be sorry to have loved you. And I'll never regret that just for an hour I felt like I was yours and you were mine."

He dragged a bandaged knuckle across his eyes in a rough attempt to wipe away the tears that welled up at the thought. And an unwelcome image of his father flashed in his mind, the hard expression of a man watching a small boy cry over the death of the family dog, telling him he needed to toughen up.

His hand moved to pinch at the frown that gripped his face, his lids crushed together as he attempted to compose himself. He already harboured the awful thought she had come to him today, allowing him to make love to her out of pity for the situation he faced. He didn't want her like that, giving herself to him as a balm to ease the pain of his diagnosis. Oh, it had done that, but it would never be enough of Layla for him.

She moved quickly, and he jumped, a reflex reaction after her wrestling herself away from him with such violence only a short time ago. One moment she lay there on the bed, her silence and stillness absorbing his words; the next she was in his lap, arms clasping his head to her chest, fingers twined in his hair, the dampness of her own tears falling there. Her legs wrapped around his waist, and he traced the smooth skin of her thighs. She breathed her answer softly into his neck, the faint touch of it as soothing as her words. "The only regret I have is that we took so long to get here."

He crumpled back onto the bed, taking her small weight upon him. She sat there and gazed down at him, as if she was the triumphant victor in a wrestling match, pinning him down, forcing her opponent to yield. And he was. He would yield to her now, in this moment, and tomorrow, and all the days ahead. He would give over everything to her, and it still wouldn't be enough.

As if sensing this decision, she took control. Before, she had been pliant and willing, letting him make love to her; him choosing the direction of his hands; him deciding the focus of his mouth flicking at will from her hard buttoned nipples, to her warm languorous mouth, to the sweet secret folds between her legs; him determining the moment to plunge into the pulsing depths of her, setting the rhythm, reading the signs, teasing it out until she pleaded for him not to stop. He'd taken her as he wished, and she'd come with him on the journey. This time she was in the driver's seat and he felt a thrill of excitement at letting her take charge.

She whisked his t-shirt off over her head in one swoop. Her golden tousled curls emerged, still damp with the sweat of their earlier lovemaking, settling in tight spirals to frame that sweet face.

He eased one hand from underneath hers, feeling drawn to the art that adorned her body, tracing up the delicate vines that trailed her wrist, to rest on a cluster of petals in the crease of her elbow. He recalled the slender unembellished arm of the teenage Layla, the skin as yet untouched by many summers, taunting him with its luminescence. And then coming home after his gap year, to discover this intricate indigo foliage in full bloom across her limbs. His fingers continued to climb, reaching the curve of her shoulder, coming to rest on a spiralling knot. He followed its inky lines, the symbol drawing him in like a hypnotic mandala, bringing him a peaceful calm in the moment.

Lulled by his touch, she smiled down at him languidly and he felt himself stiffen beneath her. She felt it too, and it spurred her back into action. Her sparkling eyes had a look of determination as she leaned back and roughly unbuckled his jeans, and he raised his hips a little so she might tug them down. His cock sprang to life, meeting her small hand, and she grabbed it firmly with a wicked grin. She teased the tip delicately at first with one pointed forefinger and then leaned over to offer a flick of her little pink tongue. He groaned with pleasure. God, she was torturing him already; and then she stopped, tormenting him even more.

Leaning forward, her tongue now flickered at his neck, in that delicate space behind his ear. She paused there a moment, and whispered a single word in a tantalising, breathy voice.

"Tragus." A quiver of delight rippled through him, as she picked up his earlier reincarnation of their childish game, now playing out between them in a new, thrilling and very adult way.

She drew back, sitting astride him, gazing down with a teasing curve to her lips, a look of power in her eyes.

"I know you want me to just climb aboard, don't you?" she said, with a subtle rocking motion, the slight friction of her bare thighs against him. The obvious sensual pleasure of her centre meeting his was written on her face, whipping his senses into overdrive.

"Oh, yeah," he gasped, "of course I do." God, what he'd give to feel that tight wetness, those rippling muscles pulsating around him again.

She leaned in close once more, her tongue lapping at his chest, then whispered through a smile that he couldn't see but knew was there, "Well, as punishment for your crimes, I think I'm going to make you beg." And as her hand settled back to work, with gentle teasing strokes, he knew he would.

"Why do you think we took so long to work this out?" she asked, a rueful smile playing on her lips. She lay across him, so tiny that he marvelled he hadn't crushed her in the midst of their wild lovemaking. She gazed down at him with cheeks still flushed and dewy with sweat. The question was casual, but her eyes bored into him. There was no room for anything but honesty here. So he gave it to her, even though he was about to reveal the stupid misguided reasons he'd put the possibility of their relationship into a box and locked it down tight.

"God knows how many times I considered taking a step in that direction," he said. "But each time I thought about it, I pulled back. Truthfully—I thought you deserved better."

"And the other girls? I mean, you haven't exactly been a monk. Were you good enough for them, but not good enough for me?"

His face flushed, as with a pang he thought of the parade of girls he'd worked his way through in the time he'd known Layla. With most, the sex had been good, and they'd had fun together, kept it light and breezy. But things had never developed beyond that, presumably because they'd read his lack of interest in doing so. And honestly, he'd never felt any loss when they'd moved on or he'd moved on from then. None of them had been important enough to regret their absence. But he'd allowed them a little of that side of himself. And the most important woman of all—he'd offered her nothing. He sighed, furious at all the stupid decisions his past self had made.

"I suppose so." He struggled to explain it. "I mean—you know—I found a few people along the way to have a bit of fun with, but that's all it was. I'd never have started something like that with you—you're more than just a bit of fun. As I said, you deserve better than to be a pleasant diversion. And you know how I've been—obsessed with study and work—that was all I had to offer anyone."

She studied him carefully. He could sense the analytical mind that served her so well in the ED, always nailing the heart of the problem and calculating the appropriate next step, was at this moment weighing her next words.

"You know, I think I would have taken anything you had to give."

Those words gutted him. This exceptional woman thought so little of herself that she'd have settled for even a crumb of his affection. He was also curious that although she'd felt that way, besotted with him enough to accept any part of him no matter how small, she'd still kept it to herself. He reached a hand up, tracing the smooth curve of her cheek, wondering how he'd never seen that in her, and then suddenly felt glad he hadn't. Glad he hadn't started something superficial with her. Because if he had, they might not have this.

"Layla, I'm kicking myself for the idiot I've been, not seeing that the best thing was right here in front of me. But maybe it was meant to be now. This is meant to be our time. I think I always hoped that when this whole craziness of establishing a career came to an end, you might still be there. But I didn't expect you to wait around for that time. Layla, you deserve a guy who'd make you his number one. Someone who you could come home to after a long day, who'd rub your feet, and pour you a glass of wine, who'd take care of you. And I wasn't that guy."

She smiled down at him. "But you've always taken care of me."

"Not like that. Not how you deserve to be cared for. I couldn't see what I had to give you, beyond what we already had. In pursuit of this career, I've been single-minded and selfish. You know, it's been like that since the day we met. How could I expect you to wait around while I chased the dream?"

"I thought we were chasing the dream together, you and me."

"We were chasing the same dream, heading in the same direction. But that's not the same as being together. I think if you're really going to be together with someone, loving the other person has to be more important than any dream. You forget, I've lived my entire life seeing the opposite. You've seen my parents: they respect each other, admire each other, and they've supported each other to get where they are. But it's not love."

"Will, I've said it to you before: you are *not* your parents. I don't know why you have this crazy idea that because you've made some of the same decisions about your life as they did, that you're condemned to repeat all of them." Her face staring down at him was fierce. "And *they* might not be capable of love, or of being loved—but you are."

"I think part of me knows that," he said, "but shaking off that belief—it's hard. Up till now, I've taken the easy option; stuck to the plan. But that option isn't there anymore. On Friday, after the specialist appointment, although he didn't say it in as many words, I knew my career as a surgeon was over. Who I am, what I believed I'd be, is gone. And so I've rampaged around the place for two days, avoiding the need to face it. But last night, when I saw you there, trying to be angry with me, but seeing how much you cared, and Charlie by the bedside trying to look pissed off but really she was worried, it jolted me back into reality. I realised I can't run away from it. I have no choice but to face it. I have to let go of what was, and think about what will be. I don't have much control over how long I'll live—I'm going to have to hand that over to other doctors. But I do have control of how I live. And I want to live whatever time I have with you. If that's what you choose."

"You see, that's such an easy thing for me," she said. "Given the chance, I'd always choose you."

"So why didn't you ever let me know that?"

She'd never given him any sign. Or perhaps she had, and he'd been too stupid to see it. Again, he wondered if he was as emotionally inept as his father. He forced that thought aside with the same swift rejection as he always applied to any comparisons with Hilton.

"Because I thought you deserved better, too. Would want better. I mean, you know—" She dipped her head shyly, avoiding his eyes "—well, you've known me long enough to understand. You know my family, my background. I'm rough around the edges. And this—," she said, trailing her fingers down her tattooed arms, "well I don't look like the sort of girl a surgeon would have on his arm at all the posh conference dinners, or fundraising galas. I thought you wanted something different. I mean, none of the girls you went out with were like me."

Was she determined to shatter him totally? That she should think him so shallow.

"Layla—" He had to make her understand. "—there *is* no one like you. And if you're at all rough, well, you're a diamond in the rough. I was never in any doubt of the beauty inside of you. Or outside too," he said, trailing a casual finger down her pert nose, to meet the delicate lips that parted just a little in response, triggering another wave of that wanting. She dropped her head, shying away from the compliment. He stored that away with all he'd learned today. And that knowledge made William Leroux vow that he'd do all in his power to make this woman see how amazing she was. He wanted her to see what he saw; he wanted the whole world to see what he saw: a rare and precious woman named Layla Angell.

"Don't sit there!" Tristan's warning came a moment too late as they launched themselves onto the couch in a tumble of laughter. "Oh, OK," he said. "Ignore the damp spots then. Still not dry after cleaning someone's spew off it."

He gave Will a pointed look. The rather unpleasant tang of pine disinfectant wafted up from the cushioned surface.

"Sorry mate," Will said, through a laugh. "I think the score is still decidedly in my favour on that one though. God knows I've dragged you home in a state way more often."

"Absolutely," Layla said, backing him up. "Shit, Tristan. The number of times the rest of us have cleaned up after your excesses, it would take years for you to pay us back."

Tristan, looking chastened, flipped the tv channel over to the sports news. The remote had barely hit the coffee table when Charlie burst into the room, seized it with a flourish and killed the tv. She stood facing Will and Layla, arms folded across her chest, her face a frown of fierce determination aimed directly at them.

Tristan began to splutter in protest and thought better of it. Leo visibly cowered in the adjoining armchair and pretended to study his phone. He knew better than to draw the attention of a fired-up Charlie.

Will looked at Charlie and then at Layla. She met his eyes and even though they both knew laughing at Charlie when she was like this was very, very unwise, neither could help it. As expected, that caused her icy eyes to narrow even further, triggering a barrage of words.

"Right, you two, I've had enough for one weekend. Drunken spewing." Her eyes flared in Will's direction. "Drunken *brawling*."

She focused on him with even greater intensity and he felt a little surge of discomfort at the truth.

"Not to mention the symphony of sounds from upstairs that we've all been trying to ignore for the last two hours." Her eyes swivelled to Layla at this point and Will could see a flame of colour bloom on Layla's face. "And then you appear all giggly and making cow-eyes at each other."

She fixed them with a stare, but Will was certain he sensed a small flicker of approval in her eyes at this point.

"No one leaves until I get an answer." He absolutely believed that statement. None of them had the skills to sidestep Charlie. She paused and took a breath, then pushing them apart, wedged herself on the couch between them. "What the fuck is going on?"

8

A Terrible Idea

Mt Eden, Auckland, New Zealand - November 2013

"It's still a fucking terrible idea."

Charlie's head rested on her shoulder, her low voice in Layla's ear barely audible over the sound of Pearl Jam reverberating from a speaker. Layla was wedged next to her on the narrow mustard plaid couch that served as outdoor furniture. No one looking at this tacky piece of 70s kitsch, a relic from their past, would realise five well-paid professionals lived in this house. It still held the faint reek of long ago spilled beer. But Charlie had insisted on bringing it with her, too hideous to put in the house itself but holding too much sentimental attachment to send to the refuse centre.

"Probably." Layla agreed, pretending ignorance of the true meaning of Charlie's question. "At least we've got two doctors in the house," she said, attempting to deflect.

Her eyes remained fixed on the top of the wooden stairs that passed for a fire escape. Somehow it met council regulations, but the abrupt angle rendered it only suitable for a true an emergency—or a spot of stair surfing.

Tristan stood poised on the small platform, an ironing board tucked under one arm, and a shot of tequila in the other. Despite being the ringleader of this evening's stair surfing session, he'd insisted on alcohol to provide artificial courage for the wild ride ahead.

Will hovered at his shoulder. His blonde hair was backlit like a halo, illuminated by the light from Leo's bedroom, the access point for this insane event. The grin of sheer joy on his face gave him the appearance of some maniacal angel about to drop from the heavens. Leo leaned out the open sash window. He'd wisely decided to see if his mates survived before committing to his turn.

All three of them bore equal responsibility for the crazy idea. Tristan laid claim to inventing the sport. He'd first suggested it back in their student days, on a southern winter night when it was too cold to even venture a few hundred metres to the 'Gardies', their favourite student watering hole.

And the idea resurfacing tonight was entirely Will's doing. He'd been reminiscing about the old days in their Dunedin flat, talking about the good times; how few their worries had been. Even with the pressure cooker environment of med school, student life was a carefree existence compared to the challenges of adulting. It was a time that seeded all sorts of creative and sometimes daring pastimes.

But they could lay the final blame on Leo. Normally the most sensible, it was he who'd mused about what it might be like to ride the stairs outside his window. "Couldn't really do it inside," he'd said. They'd all agreed this villa was far too nice to risk holes in the walls from bodies plummeting down the internal staircase, borne on the back of the ironing board. They hadn't realised by agreeing with him his thoughts might turn to a dangerous alternative. "But I think there might be another option." They should have known from the uncharacteristic wicked gleam in his eye that something unprecedented was about to happen.

"Actually, we might be one doctor down soon," Layla said, "given Will's not backing down from the dare." Stupid as it was, she hadn't tried to talk him out of it, or tell him what he already knew: those four neat stitches she'd put in his brow might not survive him barrelling down a two-storey drop. What the heck, she could always do makeshift surgery on the dining room table. With his face flushed with exhilaration, his eyes alight with their old spark, and Will so alive in this crazy moment, able to put the looming problem aside for this one night—no, she wasn't about to spoil his fun.

"No, that's not what I meant," Charlie said, blowing out an exasperated breath, "—although—" she paused, startling at the crazed expression on Tristan's face as he lined up the board on the top step, "that *is* a really bad idea. No, I think you know what I'm talking about—you and Will." She sat upright, turning to Layla, her lips pursed, pale brows knotted in a frown.

Layla met her eyes with a steady gaze, prepared to defend it, even though deep inside a little voice still echoed Charlie's side. "Look," she said, "Contrary to what you might believe, we did a lot of talking up there today. We have no illusions about what this is, what might happen. But whatever the outcome, we will be fine."

"Layla, I'm not going to sit here and simply agree with you. Not when I see two of my best friends starting something that could lead to disaster. You know we all love him. All of us are heartbroken at the news. It's just the rest of us aren't leaping into bed with him to show it. Well, of course, that's not likely anyway given—" she stumbled over the words. "You bloody well know what I mean."

"Yes, I know what you mean." Even in the gloom, Charlie registered Layla's sharp look, but rather than warning her off, it seemed to encourage her to go on.

"OK, so you've worked out you have feelings for each other. Fine. But Layla, this is not the time to be acting on them. Wouldn't it make sense to park them for a bit? Let Will get through this. And then if you still feel the same, well..."

"And what if Will doesn't get through this, Charlie?" She hated putting it into words, as if speaking of it might conjure the spectre of Will's demise. "I get to spend the rest of my life wondering what if—what we might have had if we had grabbed this time? No, that's not an option."

"OK." Charlie's voice dropped back to a more conciliatory tone. "But say he does get through this—and you find out this was just some flash of passion fuelled by the shitty stuff that he's going through right now? What happens if after that the relationship goes wrong? You might end up with nothing. Think about how it might destroy the friendship you already have."

"Do you think I haven't thought of that? That he hasn't?"

"I'm worried that with things so emotionally charged at present, maybe your judgement isn't the best—yours or his."

"Charlie, it's precisely because of it, we're sure. There's a kind of clarity that comes from knowing you could lose it all."

With a resigned sigh, Charlie flopped back, her head on Layla's shoulder, heavy with the weight of unhappiness.

"Sounds like I've got as much chance of stopping you as I have that," she said, as Tristan took a theatrical bow, lay on the ironing board and let Will launch him into a terrifying downward plunge. He arrived at their feet in a tangled heap, sprawled on his back, still clutching the ironing board to his chest like some strange flailing beetle, unable to right itself.

They all screamed with laughter as he flung it off and staggered to his feet, seemingly unscathed.

"Will, I defy you to top that, mate," he roared in a defiant challenge.

"Didn't look too pretty from where I'm standing," Will called back. "What do the judges think?"

Layla and Charlie held up their fingers to indicate their scores: Charlie a five, and Layla a more charitable six. Tristan gave them a sulky middle finger and stalked off back inside to deliver the ironing board to the next competitor.

"OK." Charlie turned back to her, placing her two hands on Layla's shoulders. Her gaze was tender, her blue eyes calm and reassuring, like a summer sea. "If you two are all in, then I guess we're right behind you. Whatever it takes to get you two a 'happily ever after', we're all in."

"Thank you, Charlie," Layla said, placing a hand over one of Charlie's, giving it a grateful squeeze. With the other, she smudged away a rogue tear.

"No point trying to hold back the tide. Just a damn shame—I owe Tristan fifty bucks. I'm hoping he doesn't remember. I knew I was wrong within five minutes of accepting that bet."

"What? What the hell are you talking about, Charlie?" Layla wondered if she'd secretly tossed back some tequila, too.

"Don't be mad at me." A most un-Charlie like bashful expression crept across her face, and she sighed. "Back when you first started at St Aidan's—like the very first day—he sidled up to me and said 'Bet you fifty bucks Will hooks up with her' and stupidly I accepted the bet. I don't know what's worse—losing money to Tristan, or having to admit that for one brief moment he was a better judge of people than me."

"Oh my god, that's fucking hilarious," Layla snorted. "Tristan?"

"Yeah, well, like I said, I knew almost immediately that I would lose that bet. Although you did give me a bit of hope there by taking so damn long about it."

After the competition was over, all three stupid males surprisingly intact and no broken bones, Charlie gathered them in around her. She stood on the couch, balanced precariously on the lumpy cushions, looking down on them like a queen about to make a pronouncement from the throne. She held the empty champagne bottle in one hand and her full glass in the other and surveyed them with an appraising eye. Yes, they all had their own glasses raised and at the ready. Layla smiled up at her. It was so like Charlie to have a secret champagne stash for special occasions. And she had decreed this was one.

"To Will, who's going to kick cancer in the butt. Fuck off cancer!"

"Fuck off cancer!" They yelled it to the sky, valiant warriors preparing for battle.

Then, in the softest voice Layla had ever heard from her, "To Will and Layla. Love conquers all."

"Love conquers all." Layla drank in the warmth of them, Will wrapped behind her, his chin resting on her shoulder, his words a breath on her neck, while the people who loved them most in the world, formed a messy scrum around them, and gave them quiet affirmation. "Love conquers all."

It seemed the most natural thing in the world to slip in between the expensive cotton sheets, lay her head on the softest of pillows and simply breathe in the smell of him. She buried her nose in his hair, dropping a light kiss on the small patch of exposed skin tucked behind his ear. She trailed a hand down his side, coming to rest on his hip.

He gave a faint hiss. "Ahh," he said, "bit tender there. Might be a bruise by morning."

"If that's the only bruise you've got after that ride, then you got off lightly," she admonished.

"Just that and a bruised ego. The one real surfer and I take the award for the biggest wipeout."

"Might be a hint you should stick to watersports," she said. "Or not stair surf on the back of a hangover."

"I think both stair surfing and hangovers might be out of the picture for a while. Other priorities."

"So, what is your next move?" she said, feeling sick at facing the reality of his situation once more.

It disconcerted her to observe the uncertainty forced upon him. Confusion was not a feeling he was comfortable with, nor was a future suddenly hazy. From the time he was a small child, he'd had a clear line of sight. In Will's mind, he was born to be a surgeon.

"I had three weeks leave owing—bonus of being a workaholic—and on Friday I told them I need to take it," he said. "Thomas was a bit pissed off. Leading up to Christmas, they want to get through the surgery lists before they all go on holiday. But that's their problem. I've put them first, now I'm going to put me first. Get onto beating this thing."

"And what are your thoughts on that?"

She propped herself up on one elbow, wanting to see his face, see the truth of what he might tell her, even if it wasn't an easy one to hear.

Professionally, she was out of her depth here. This area of medicine hardly ever collided with her ED work. They patched people up and handed them on. Nothing like this.

But Will was standing in the shoes of his patients.

It was an immense advantage, knowing the options. The disadvantage was, of course, he knew the odds attached to those options. There was no one to act as intermediary, softening the blow of the facts—like the frightening morbidity statistics for brain cancers.

"Despite having the worst hangover of my life, and hands so fucking painful I could hardly work the keyboard, I did a solid few hours work this afternoon. Found some great stuff, really exciting stuff."

His eyes were alight with the buzz of knowledge. Sharing his endless passion for medicine and knowing the exhilaration of discoveries and innovations that brought hope to previously hopeless situations, she recognised the signs.

"You didn't talk to your father? After all—" Hilton Leroux, although a failure at parenting, was a highly successful surgeon, in fact one of the country's preeminent neurosurgeons.

"Layla, honey, you are a clever woman, but that is a fucking terrible idea."

"You don't think—"

"I know that if it was anyone else, say one of my patients, I'd possibly consider asking his opinion. But with this, I can't go there. There are too many emotions tied up in our relationship. I can't trust myself to look at his advice objectively. Hell, I might do the exact opposite simply to spite him, even if it is the best option. No, I've already decided. Whatever path I take, I plan to tell Mum and Dad when it's a fait accompli."

"Fair enough," she said.

She understood his complicated family situation enough to trust his judgement on this was sound.

"Anyway," he went on, the light of excitement returning to his eyes, "there's a guy in Baltimore—Brandon De Luca. He's based in a private research centre, some people who spun off from Johns Hopkins. There're a couple of philanthropists putting big money behind them. The stuff they're doing is cutting edge. Less radical surgical interventions followed by stem cell therapies. The results are impressive."

This was a brilliant alternative. Less invasive surgery meant an improved likelihood of him coming through it with less collateral damage.

That little bird of hope sitting curled tightly in her chest, tentatively unfurled its wings.

"Have you asked? Will they take you?" She could feel the small optimistic flutter grow stronger as it prepared to take flight.

"I emailed him. No reply yet. God knows I've checked enough times. But it's the early hours of Sunday morning over there, so chances are he won't have seen it. And who knows how often these guys check their email over a weekend?"

"He will," she said, her words confident. He must. "So, stem cell treatment?" Even though she was tired, her curiosity demanded satisfaction.

"Yeah," he laughed. "Take some fat cells out of my arse and then send them back in to fight on my behalf."

She was currently lying pressed up close around that sexy curved arse, and she lifted her hand from where it rested across his stomach to trace the shape, a smooth muscular butt, that looked exceptionally hot in a pair of jeans but felt even better naked.

"Just as long as they don't spoil it." Her giggle vibrated against his ear. "I like this arse exactly as it is."

His side of the bed was empty, but still warm, the shape of his body imprinted on the mussed up sheets. She could hear the gentle tap of fingers on a keyboard, and she sat up to see him at his desk, the light from the laptop screen illuminating his serious features. He leaned in to peer at it and then scrabbled to find his glasses.

God, she'd always found a man in glasses a bit of a turn-on, but this man in glasses, well, he turned the dial right up on full power. Laser surgery might have been an obvious choice, but he'd been adamant he wouldn't take the tiny risk that it might fail and jeopardise his surgical career. That he'd abandoned the glasses for contacts as soon as it was an option in his teens was probably just as well. Seeing Will standing all studiously sexy next to one of those other women who had come before her would have been too much to bear.

"Any news?" she called across to him.

"Yeah, there is," he said. "De Luca's replied."

She sprang out of bed and positioned herself at his shoulder, arms clasped around him, willing it to be good news. She scanned the screen, as he was, and decided from the friendly opening to his response that she liked the sound of this Brandon De Luca already.

Will's body was tense, coiled tight in anticipation, and at first, when she felt him slump under her arms, she thought it was with relief. But as her eyes caught up to the second to last paragraph, and she read those words: *'Not accepting any overseas patients at this time'* she knew that what she felt was his crushing disappointment, the same feeling that now brought all her hopes crashing to the ground.

"You have to ask him again." She couldn't let him accept no for an answer. There had to be a way to convince this De Luca person. Her mind raced in ten different directions at once, but one idea pushed its way forward. "Did you tell him the patient was you?"

"No," he said, "I thought I'd keep it professional, not personal."

"But you should tell him! Think of the opportunity for them. To have a surgeon in the trial. Just think of the insights you would bring. Will, you *have* to go back to him." She saw a tiny flicker of realisation cross his face. It wasn't an angle he'd considered, and it was a good one.

"OK," he said slowly, his chin propped in his hand, his eyes thoughtful. "At the risk of looking like I'm begging, I will. I've got nothing to lose except my pride. And right now, what good is that to me, anyway?"

"Here, let me help," she said, pulling across another chair. "We are going to offer Dr de Luca an opportunity he can't refuse."

9

Battle Lines

Whitford, Auckland, New Zealand – December 2013

LAYLA TIPPED HER HEAD back, eyes closed, letting the exhilarating rush of the wind play across her face. That same wind that tantalised her skin had already wreaked havoc with her blonde curls, twisting them into knots. But she didn't let that trouble her. Where they were headed, even a perfectly preened face and hair wouldn't score her any points. She'd endured the stony-faced scrutiny of Will's parents only a few times, but it was enough to know they had certainly never approved of their son's friendship with her. God, old Hilton would probably have an apoplexy if he even suspected things between them had moved beyond the friend zone. Despite the undeniable anxiety, that was later. For now, the combination of warm wind, a dusting of sunshine and the soothing thrum of the engine elicited a contented smile.

"Weather good on Planet Layla today?" Will called from behind the wheel of the Porsche convertible. It was the one concession he'd made to his upbringing: an expensive car. And she couldn't hold that against him. OK, the Carrera S wasn't the sort of car she could afford or would buy even if she could. Sporting a far more distinguished pedigree and the marque's typical extravagant sloping body, it was a totally different beast to her beloved Holden. But the refined beat of 400 horsepower that thrummed behind their heads, brought the same smile of pleasure to her face as it did to his.

"Just thinking how much I love this car," she said. "OK, it's not a Holden but…"

"Pity about that—" he said with a smirk. "—your aversion to all things not-V8. You'd look good behind the wheel. In fact, you know what? I think it's time we tested how much you're really wedded to that Aussie gas-guzzler. How about you drive the rest of the way?"

"No, it's your car," she protested, "and goodness knows you hardly ever get to enjoy it." It was true. In the traffic-clogged city streets, this lithe vehicle rarely got the chance to stretch her long legs.

"No, I insist," he said, already pulling over to make the driver change. "I'm going to convert you to a Porsche fan if it's the last thing…"

He stopped there, seeing the pang of anguish pass across her face as her mind raced ahead, finishing the sentence: *If it's the last thing I do.* How long would he have before reaching that point? Months? Years? Or a lifetime together—she had to believe that fate, aided by innovative medical knowledge would gift that to them.

"You're really determined to piss off your parents, aren't you?" she cut in. "Not going to be pleased to see me, let alone me driving your car."

"Let them be pissed off," he said. The swap made, he buckled her into the leather cocoon of the driver's seat that still held the shape and warmth of his body. "You know Layla, I'm up for this today. Not just telling them about the cancer, the treatment; I'm going to tell them about us, too."

"Oh, God." She gulped the air in panic, felt her knuckles tense as she clutched the steering wheel. "Are you sure?" Telling Hilton and Virginia Leroux that she and Will were together was akin to unleashing the four horsemen of the apocalypse.

"Absolutely," he said. "That's if you're OK with it? I mean, it's not going to be pretty, but I can handle it if you can."

What could she say to that? Not pretty was an understatement. Things were going to get ugly. Words would be said. Hurtful words. But maybe also words that showed he really did love her, defending his choice to be with her against the two people in the world who would be most upset by it.

"I can handle it. I can handle anything if it's with you beside me." It was true. She'd always seen herself as strong, but looking back, she wouldn't be the person she was if it wasn't for this person who'd been by her side. In those eyes, she saw how much her words meant to him. He'd always tried to help her, protect her, even as her friend. He loved knowing that she saw that in him.

"Ditto," he said. "Ouch!" he yelped, recoiling at the swift punch she'd laid on his arm. This thing between them was too new for her to have lost the matey reflexes of their years of friendship. "What the fuck?"

"Ditto!" she squealed at him, outraged. "You said 'ditto'! You know that's not an acceptable answer. Ever." How many times had she made him watch *Ghost* with her over the years? Surely enough to know how that word 'ditto' was such a cop out. Looked like she'd have to remind him. "You know, in *Ghost,* when Molly tells Sam she loves him, and he says 'ditto'. And she *hates* that. You *have* to say it."

"All right," he said, a slow smile spreading across his face. "I love you Layla Angell." He'd forgiven her the punch for providing this simple opportunity to say the words. It seemed he needed to do it a dozen times a day. Not that she needed to hear it to know. He bent over and kissed her. "And like in the movie, if I don't make it, I'll come back and haunt you."

Her stomach lurched. It surrounded them. No matter where they were, what they talked about, somehow the very real threat of his fragile life pressed its way forward. And just like Will to handle it this way. Joking about it when it wasn't a joke. She swung the car onto the road, tugging on her sunglasses so he couldn't see her welling eyes, and pressed her foot to the floor, trying to lose herself in the thrill of the frightening acceleration.

The Porsche ate up the sweeping back country roads like a ravenous panther. Black and sleek, it bowed to her bidding, but not without that slight push back, always letting Layla know that if it chose to, it would take charge.

As often as she dared, she shot glances at Will. And every time his eyes were upon her. The grin on his face broadened as she came to tight bends, wrestled with his baby and won the argument. She was a capable driver. She'd had a lot of years of practice. Jimmy had taught her when she was twelve in the back paddock at her uncle's farm. It had come in handy when, as a teenager, the publican summoned her to collect her legless father from the local when his money had run out and they'd tired of his company.

"See," Will said, "this car was made for you. I knew my two favourite girls would become besties."

She'd adored this man since he was still a gangly boy. So uncomplicated, so loving, so unfailingly happy. Even now, a month on from a frightening diagnosis. Even now, on the way to his intimidating parents, about to give them two bits of news they were certain to hate. If you could take sunshine and distil it into human form, it would be William Leroux. And she could never soak up enough of those rays.

"I think it's safe to say she and I are now BFFs," she said through a laugh. "Just don't tell *my* girl in case she gets jealous. She's already annoyed this sassy bitch has stolen the garage."

She nosed the car in behind Carson's hulking four wheel drive. She was pleased to see it there. On the few occasions she'd met Carson, she'd found him to be far more likeable than either of his parents. Although you'd be hard-pushed to pick him and Will out of a crowd as brothers on looks alone. Carson sported the trademark dirty-blonde Leroux hair, but cut in a neat conservative style to match the uniform of suits he wore to work, a distinct contrast to Will's unruly locks. It was as if Carson still adhered to St Aidan's 'hair must not touch the collar' rule, whereas on leaving school, Will had been quick to abandon that for a relaxed surfer vibe. Carson sported his father's powerful frame, Will the lean, angular build of his mother. But the moment you saw the brothers together, the easy banter flowing and the relaxed style, it became obvious. Having Carson present might make all of this a lot easier.

As the Porsche's growling motor faded to a low hum, the thwack of racquet on ball drifted across to them. Leaving the car, she followed Will over to where his father and brother battled on the tennis court. Hilton cut a dapper figure for a man of his age. In traditional tennis whites, his strong, confident returns kept his much younger son fully occupied. They arrived courtside in time to see Hilton deliver one last killer lob, the ball landing narrowly inside the line and a smidgen beyond Carson's desperate dive.

"The weekly ritual," Will said with a wry smile as his father walked over and put a consoling hand on Carson's shoulder. The younger man's resigned look said it all. "The day our father suspects either of us might beat him will be the day he gives up tennis. Until then, poor old Carson turns up every Sunday. The story is that it's so they get to see the grandchildren. But we all know it's so Hilton can assuage his fear of getting old by demolishing him at tennis."

She'd always thought it odd this way he referred to his parents by their first names, and had done so forever. So impersonal, as if keeping them at arm's length, as Virginia and Hilton seemed to have done to their children in return.

"So how come you don't normally come out here? Don't want to get your arse whipped by him every week?" she said. She'd never realised Sunday lunch was a family expectation that he'd been avoiding.

"Let's call it my one consistent act of rebellion," he said. "My mother has tried to shame me, bully me and, as much as Virginia ever does, beg. But no, I don't feel the need to be out here all the time. After all, that's who they most want to see." He nodded towards two little girls who had appeared on the side of the tennis court. They raced over and wrapped themselves around Carson's legs. Meanwhile, Hilton came across and tousled his hand on each curly head, a look of affection transforming his otherwise severe face. "So no, I don't feel bad leaving Carson and Kirsten to do the heavy-lifting when it comes to family."

Carson, the eldest, the golden boy. Somehow, he could never do wrong. If he didn't share Will's sunny personality and gracious manner, you might hate him for the way his parents always put him on a pedestal. Despite daring to sidestep the family's medical lineage for a career in commerce, it seemed he would always be the favoured child. While Will, dedicated to becoming a great surgeon like his father, seemed destined to always be second best in their eyes.

As they sat by the pool waiting for lunch to be ready, the conversation was polite, most of it revolving around what the girls had been up to. Who knew that three-year-olds had such a whirl of activities and a social life that would be the envy of most adults? But as they moved inside, the chatter of dance classes, swimming lessons and play dates subsided.

Hilton's shaggy head swivelled towards Layla. All her confidence evaporated under his withering stare. She met his type all the time in the hospital: arrogant older men who saw themselves, as surgeons, at the top of the food chain; they treated doctors like her who'd chosen other paths as some lower life form. But there, in the workplace, they held no fear for her. While she respected their experience, she didn't let it intimidate her. But here, the worry of his reaction to the as yet unknown fact that she and Will were together, sapped all the brave thoughts she'd tried to hold on to.

"So, I hear you're still slumming it in the ED with all the great unwashed."

No wonder Hilton had chosen a surgical path. He didn't have the empathy or generosity of spirit to deal with patients outside the veil of anaesthesia. She noted he didn't address her by name. As if by naming her it recognised her existence, and omitting it bolstered his power.

"For now," she said. "I've been offered a place in the GP programme next year. And I think I'll take it."

The huff of disapproval as he angled his large frame into the chair at the head of the table said it all. Virginia, sitting at the opposite end, mirrored his disdain, conveying it soundlessly with those appraising blue-grey eyes. It was a mystery how eyes so identical in colour to the ones she loved could possess such a different quality in the person who'd given birth to him. In Will's face, they were soft and friendly, in Virginia's stern and confronting.

"I think Layla's going to make an excellent GP," Will said, easing into a chair beside her. "She's such an astute judge of people. I saw it when we were on the wards together. The patients like her, trust her." He smiled at her reassuringly, and her heart skipped with love at the way he bolstered her in their presence. Not that it would have any effect on them, but she loved him all the more for knowing that and still trying. "And I fully intend to support her in that. She's certainly going to have better work stories than me to share over a glass of wine at night." He flashed her another one of those smiles and then tossed a final damning remark in his father's direction. "And of course, after all, you two are proof that you don't have to be carbon copies of each other for a relationship to work."

The silence was oppressive. He'd dropped it in there almost casually, but he might have stood up on the table and announced it. Layla's face burned. All flavour seeped out of the piece of sweet potato in her mouth.

Virginia's intense glare focused on the way Will's hand lay over hers, offering protection. Hilton scrambled to erase the momentary look of shock that he'd allowed to spill onto his face, and with a harrumph of displeasure set about furiously stabbing the slices of roast lamb as if attacking it with a pitchfork. Carson and Kirsten studied their plates in embarrassed silence. They were too diplomatic to pursue this line of conversation. Carson shot a surreptitious glance at the two of them. Obviously, there was more than one thing Will hadn't shared with his brother at their early morning surfing meet-ups.

The two little girls continued to aim spoonfuls of pasta at their mouths, oblivious to the tension between the adults at the table.

"Mummy, look," said Tahlia, attempting to use a tube of pasta like a straw to suck up the sauce. The adult eyes all swivelled towards the small girl, and her twin, Tabitha, who now tried to emulate this feat, much to the horror of her mother. The awkward moment passed. Layla knew that wouldn't be the end of it, but it gave her space to breathe.

At the end of lunch, Hilton rose from his seat and this seemed to be the cue for the women to clear the table. A cue that Layla missed as she stood, but was saved, catching Kirsten's almost imperceptible nod to join in the task.

"Dad, there's something I need to have a chat about." Will's voice had the slightest tremor, like the faint quiver of a plucked guitar string as the sound ebbed away. "And you too, Mum."

He wandered over to retrieve the large envelope he'd left on a sideboard. Virginia's eyes lit upon it and an expression of curious interest slid across her face. The pair most likely suspected he was about to discuss some case with the two of them. He was, but their enthusiasm would no doubt be dented when they found out the case was his own.

"Layla needs to be in on this, too." Now Virginia's eyes narrowed as confusion set in.

Carson, realising this conversation wasn't intended for the entire family, took the platter Layla held, and nudged her towards the lounge. Will stood at the door, ushering his parents through and then, guiding her in with a reassuring hand on her back, closed it firmly behind them.

Hilton sat in a huge leather wingback chair that made him appear larger than life—the king on his throne; Virginia took her place by his side in a smaller brocaded version, her erect posture conveying a queenly aura. Layla and Will took the low, wide leather couch opposite. The furniture arrangement appeared deliberate, designed to cast them in the role of supplicants.

Will dealt the films smoothly onto the broad coffee table between them.

Hilton raised each one to the light in turn, squinting at them thoughtfully. "Hmmm, yes, I see," he said, before casually casting them back onto the table and turning to Will. "So? I know what my assessment is, but I'd be curious to hear yours. See if they've taught you well."

"OK," Will said. "Glioma, more specifically, pilocytic astrocytoma. So not as worrying in type, and as there's been no noticeable change in the shape and size since it was first detected in early October, it suggests it's not one of the more aggressive mutations. But the location is tricky. Overall—good prognosis if they can get it all but I'd not be making any promises to the patient about that. If they can't, then the long-term prognosis is uncertain."

Hilton nodded in agreement, unable to suppress a small smile of pride in his son's knowledge.

"And that's why," Will pushed on, "I'm flying to Baltimore in a week's time."

Virginia and Hilton exchanged puzzled frowns.

"Look again," Will said, handing one film to his father. But it was Virginia, still with the evidence in her hand, who saw it first, and her mask of composure crumpled. Behind that exterior, Layla saw the rawness of a mother's pain for her child. Even Hilton's severe expression melted, as his eyes finally lit on the name.

"No," he said. "No." His voice became more emphatic. "Look, obviously the best person in the country to handle this would be me, and that's totally out of the question. But Baltimore? Why the hell would you be considering that? I'll talk to Bernard. I'd never tell him to his face, but the man's gifted. I've seen him handle surgeries far more complex than this."

"No," Will echoed back at him. "No, you won't contact Bernard. And I *am* going to Baltimore. Flights are booked for next Monday. I didn't come here to ask you to arrange anything. I thought you should know, as my parents."

"But why? Give me a good reason you would fly halfway round the world. When the solution is right here."

"Because we're not planning to take the usual path."

"We?" Hilton spat the question at him. "We? Is that you and her? You're taking advice from an inexperienced dime-a-dozen ED doctor just because she's your current lay?"

Layla felt Will grow in stature beside her. His voice when it came was low and threatening, a shade of menace in it that she had no idea he was capable of.

"The first thing you need to understand is this: you will never, *never* speak about my future wife in that way again. Not in my presence or behind my back."

Hilton, to her surprise, sat in stunned silence. He would never have predicted his son would stand up to him in this way. Neither would she. In the past, Will had always taken the approach of passive resistance against his parents. Now Hilton was forcing Will to choose. He chose her.

And those words: *future wife*. They'd talked around the idea of marriage, but only as some abstract possibility to come back to once they'd faced down this brain tumour. Certainly they'd never put it into such concrete terms. But it triggered such a burst of hope and happiness inside her that she could withstand the shock of Hilton's appalling words.

"And the second thing is," Will said, now risen to his feet and towering over them. "I am perfectly capable of making decisions about my life, my health, and my future without any input from either of you. For your information: the 'we' in this picture are Brandon De Luca and I." She heard Victoria's quick intake of breath at the name. "Yes, mother," he nodded, "the one and the same. Brandon has some spectacularly innovative trials underway. And I'm joining one. Both as researcher and subject."

He scooped up the films in one hand and with the other tugged her to her feet, leaving Hilton and Virginia still reeling.

As they made their way through the dining room, the flicker of raised eyebrows was the only sign that Carson, still finishing the last of clearing away lunch, had overhead the raised voices next door.

"Hey mate," he said, gripping Will in a brotherly handshake. "You keen to catch some waves one morning? It's been too long. I checked the tides—looking good for Piha this week—Tuesday, maybe? I'll pick you up." She could see in the way Carson searched his brother's face that he had questions that might be asked on that drive out to the west coast beach.

"For sure," Will said. "I'm on leave. Any day's OK with me." Another ripple of curiosity crossed Carson's face—Will would never walk out on work for no reason.

"Right, I'll check the weather and flick you a text," Carson said as they escaped the house.

At the end of the driveway, Will floored it and the car leapt from standing start to open road speed in seconds. The impressive acceleration pinned her back against the seat, and she enjoyed the secure feeling of the leather-lined cockpit and his capable handling of the vehicle along the sweeping rural roads.

"So..." she said, when they finally came to a halt at the first set of traffic lights inside the city limits. "Future wife?" The words had replayed themselves over and over in her head on the drive. She glanced across at him and he broke into a dopey grin.

"Of course you're my future wife," he said, looking a little sheepish. "I know, I know, we should have discussed it before announcing it to them like a done deal. But I couldn't help it. It was either tell them now or they find out after the fact—because I've got no intention of seeing them again for a very long time."

"It's OK," she said. "It was worth it just to see the look on their faces."

The light turned green, and the car surged forward again. Forwards was the only direction for them from here. No looking back and no regrets. She would be his future wife. He would have a future.

10

From The Heart

Papakura, Auckland, New Zealand – December 2013

"Look baby, it's snowing."

He sat on the sill of a heavy framed wooden window. His bedroom looked out on a white wilderness, fringed with brooding conifers. He might have been a figure in a snow globe. And there it was behind him, feathery flakes tumbling from a grey Maryland sky. Beautiful for sure, but not as beautiful as the sight of him, his colour a little better each day now, his arm extended holding the phone a little steadier, his voice showing no lingering trace of a tremor like in those first few days.

From this angle it was even hard to spot the mess they'd made of his hair on one side. She'd mourned the loss of it, and longed for the day when she could once more run her hands through it, all golden and salt-crusted bearing the tang of the sea. But she mustn't let any of these little sorrows tarnish the phone call. There was no room for any hint of doubt on her part. She would hold it together, for him, for now, knowing that in the quiet hours of the night, with the cold space in the bed emphasising their separation, those doubts would come back to taunt her.

"Baby?" she teased, forcing a smile. "Will Leroux, you've been there two weeks and they've got you talking like an American."

"Sorry," he said with a grin. "Two days with Brandon's family, hearing him call his wife that a dozen times a day—I guess it just crept in."

"It's OK," she said. "I think I kinda like it. And wow, that snow sure is pretty. And you get to enjoy it inside where it's warm—not like the old flat in Dunedin. God, I hated snow days there. It was so cold even the inside of the fridge felt warm. His place looks amazing."

"Yeah, this house is beautiful. Sort of rustic charm, but certainly not the backcountry cabin I expected when he invited me to join his family in the mountains."

"It was so sweet of him to ask you. I would have hated seeing you stuck in some hotel room over Christmas. It's bad enough that you're so far away."

"He's a good guy. I came here as a patient, but it's safe to say we'll part as friends."

It was painful to see the way his face lit up whenever he spoke of Brandon de Luca. Anyone would have admiration for the man who'd saved your life. But for Will, it was so much bigger—he wanted to *be* Brandon de Luca. And once, that would have been entirely possible. With ten years between them, over time, Will's career trajectory might easily have mirrored the American's. But in saving Will's life, Brandon had also robbed him of that opportunity. She just wasn't sure Will had accepted that yet.

"That's great Will." She kept her tone upbeat.

"So, *baby*, tell me then," he said, his smile broad, "how's your Christmas Day going?"

"Take a look for yourself," she said, swivelling the iPhone he'd bought her, a twin to his own. She panned across her parents' back-yard, zooming in on Jimmy first. Stationed at the barbecue, clad in his uniform black t-shirt and jeans, he wielded a set of tongs in one hand and clasped a beer in the other.

"Jimmy's our chef today. Hey, Jimmy," she called across to him, "say hi to Will."

"Hey, Will. Good to see ya. Cheers, mate." He raised the bottle in a toast. "And merry fucking Christmas," he added, before returning to the serious task of turning the steaks. He wasn't about to take his eye off the task for long—not when his reputation as the best barbecue cook in the Angell family was at stake.

"Jeff and Pete are being lazy arses sleeping off their Christmas Eve celebrations." She focused in on her two younger brothers, slumped in a pair of rickety deck chairs, sunglasses on, each clutching a 'hair of the dog' beer. "God knows their heads might not hurt so much if Dad would turn down the music, but there's no chance of that. Oi, you two," she called. "Be polite and say hello."

"Hey there, Will man. Merry Christmas." Jeff waved at the camera with a cheerful smile that belied the massive headache he'd been moaning about since surfacing an hour earlier. If it wasn't for her mother stalking into his room, stripping back the blankets and declaring—"It's bloody Christmas. I'm not having you lying in bed all day"—he'd probably still be asleep.

"Yeah, have a drink for us," Pete added, his words still slurring from the residual alcohol circulating in his system. "Not that we need another to add to the tally—it was a *big* night last night."

"Sorry, can't do that for you," Will replied with a rueful grin. "Alcohol ban I'm afraid. Doctor's orders."

"Oh man, sucks to be you," said Pete. "Well, take care, mate. We expect you back here with a six-pack under your arm as soon as you can, OK?"

"It's a deal," Will agreed through a laugh.

Her brothers loved Will. But of course, like her, they'd known him since he was at high school, just Layla's surfer friend who wore faded jeans, torn t-shirts and drove a battered old van with his board strapped on top. And, unlike her, they'd never seen him in his native environment, amongst the well-heeled landed gentry of rural Auckland. The disdain they normally reserved for those sorts of people had never spilled over towards Will. He was the exception to their rules.

"And here's the big man himself."

Her father wasn't, in fact, a big man physically. None of the Angell family were known for their stature, but Terry Angell brought a big attitude, like a cocky bantam rooster bristling with confidence. She turned to the ranch slider where she could see him twiddling with knobs on an amp, as he adjusted the levels of the rock music blasting out of two giant speakers set up on the concrete patio.

"Dad," she called. "It's Will."

"Hey Will, how's it going?" her father's rough voice, the product of a lifetime of smoking, rasped above the sounds of Bruce Springsteen.

"Great, Terry, just great. Bit nippy here, not like you lot soaking up the sunshine."

"Yeah," her father said, taking a deep draft of his cigarette, "can't beat good old En-Zed. Bet you can't wait to get home. Get away from all those loud-mouthed Yanks."

"Yeah, well, I do want to get home, but they've been treating me pretty well," Will replied with a smile. He was so tolerant of her father with his blinkered opinions and cranky ways. "So, Terry, is that Bruce Springsteen I hear? Your Christmas music?"

Her father's face lit up with a broad smile, showing his yellow nicotine-stained teeth either side of a yawning gap—he'd had two knocked out years ago in a fight at the pub. Nothing made him happier than talking music, and Will used it to his advantage, finding common ground with this stroppy little man. Despite the huge divide between her family experience and his own upbringing, across the years he'd won over the lot of them.

"Oh, look, here's Mum," Terry said.

Layla's mother appeared in the background, clutching Nana's crystal salad bowl on its annual outing. She knew without looking what it would contain—her mother's one and only salad combination of finely diced iceberg lettuce, wedges of tomato and slices of hard-boiled egg topped with a swirl of homemade mayonnaise. No fancy foreign food or strange combinations at the Angell household, just traditional old-fashioned Kiwi fare. Her mother hesitated for a moment, confused as to why Layla should thrust the phone at her. Then, seeing Will's face on the screen, she carefully placed the bowl on a plastic folding table, wiped her hands on her jeans and took the phone.

"How are you, love?" she asked. "Doing OK?"

"Yeah, Sharon, I'm good," he said. "Improving every day."

"So, when are they going to let you come home? My girl here—she doesn't let on—but she's bloody miserable. Putting on a brave face aren't you love," she said, with a nod at Layla, "but us mums know when their kids aren't happy."

"About a month, they say, Sharon."

"Oh well," she said, shooting Layla an enigmatic smile, "in that case, I better give this phone back to her so the two of you can talk some more. Take care, love."

Layla took the phone and flopped into one of the enormous black vinyl recliner chairs that dominated her parents' lounge. Here at least the sounds of "Born In The USA" wouldn't drown out her words. She cranked up the footrest and lazed back, enjoying the chance to rest her weary feet. When she'd offered to do the Christmas Eve shift, she hadn't realised how hectic it would be.

"What are you smiling at?" Will asked.

"Thinking about how funny Dad is. He obviously doesn't lump Bruce Springsteen in with 'those Yanks' he's so suspicious of."

"He sure is a character your dad. But I like him. You always know where you stand with him. He tells it like it is. Not like mine—the king of hidden agendas."

"Well, Dad likes you too," she said, stifling a yawn.

"Hey, I hope you're not getting too comfortable there."

"Why not?" she said. "Think I deserve it after the shift from hell."

"Ah—it's just that I need you to do something for me. You need to go up to your bedroom."

"My bedroom? Here?"

"Yeah, your old bedroom."

"OK," she said, intrigued by the odd request, and the strange crooked smile that tugged at his mouth. "Although I'm not sure what the hell anyone would want to go in there for."

As the only girl in the family, she'd merited her own room in the cramped ex-State house, but it was certainly basic, with the same decor that was already tired when they'd moved there in 1995. She padded down the hallway, the familiar threadbare hall runner rough against her bare feet. Her Mum was so proud of this modest house, purchased on the back of her relentless drive, working all the hours she could to provide the home for her children that their father never would.

Layla sat on the familiar bed, with the same lumpy mattress and still sporting the blanket of bright crocheted squares her grand-mother had given her for her tenth birthday. A moody Kurt Cobain stared down at her from an old poster.

"Now," Will said, "open the top drawer of the bedside cabinet."

She followed his instructions, encouraged by the look of inter-est—no, of anticipation—on his face. The drawer caught a little, the tired wood warped with age, but she managed to wrestle it open. To her surprise, even after all this time, there were still a few of her things inside. She picked up a well-read copy of *Creme* magazine with its tagline 'a girl's best friend' and smiled at the memory of her angsty teen self finding refuge in its pages. Underneath, the scratched Foo Fighters CD brought a frown to her face even years after her brother's carelessness had rendered it useless.

"Wow, I thought Mum would have thrown out all this stuff," she said, sorting through the jumble. It was strange seeing these treasures, reminders of the kid she'd been.

"Can you see it?" he said. "Perhaps it's underneath."

"See what?" she asked, lifting a battered notebook, but didn't wait for the answer. She saw it. There, nestled in the midst of these remnants of her teenage years, was an indigo leather box. She recognised the etched silver logo, a wide W-shaped constellation, the stars intertwined with the initials 'NF'. She adored Nik Francovic jewellery. Such a talented young man.

To think that in between all of it—flights to the US, all the pre-op procedures, a five-hour surgery, and then recuperation after—somehow he'd still given thought to getting her a Christmas present she'd love. Not to mention recruiting someone via long distance to place it here. It had to be her mother. None of the males in this household were reliable enough to be trusted to do it or keep the secret. Little prickles of tears pressed at her eyes. God, she loved this thoughtful man.

The door flew open and her mother burst through it. "Sorry, love, I had to see for myself," she said. And then, "Oh, you haven't opened it yet." There was obviously something her mother knew that she didn't. "Here, give me that," she said, snatching the phone and training it on Layla. "He needs to see you open it."

Layla carefully flicked the latch, and the lid sprung open with a firm click. The small tears became a torrent when she saw what was inside. The ring was huge, two gold angel wings supporting a heart-shaped emerald.

"I told him it had to be an emerald," he said. "To match your eyes."

"He made it for me?" She could hardly breathe.

"Yeah, it was a bit of a tall order. Not like I gave the guy much time. But when I told him our situation, and that I needed a stunning one off engagement ring for a stunning once in a lifetime woman—well, he made it a priority." No words came, only the damn persistent tears as the words 'engagement ring' settled on her.

"You need to *ask* her," Sharon hissed over her shoulder. "Go on."

She pressed her hand to her mouth, stifling a smirk of amusement at her mother's impatience. Will failed to suppress his laughter, a guffaw escaping, before he pushed it back down, trying to appear suitably serious.

"Remember what I told my father—that you're my future wife? I meant it. And the future is now. So I'm asking you now. I didn't want to wait till I get back. I love you so much. Layla Angell, will you marry me?"

"You know the answer already, future husband."

"And *you* know it's not a done deal till you say it." He quirked a brow, a grin teasing at his mouth. "You have to say it."

"Yes, I'll marry you. Yes. Yes. A thousand times, yes."

Giggles spilled out of her, carried on a wave of exhilaration. It swept away all the dark thoughts that even now, after the apparent success of the surgery, still cast a small shadow over their future. She wouldn't let them intrude on her happiness.

"I think this is where I'd normally put that ring on your hand..." he said, his voice cracking with emotion, "but perhaps, Sharon, will you do the honours?"

Her mother practically dropped the phone in excitement, but somehow coordinated placing the ring on Layla's outstretched hand, while allowing him to see the moment it settled there, glints of gold and green lighting up the gloomy room.

"Perfect," he said with a satisfied smile. And when their eyes met, his face captured in the small rectangle, she wished that time would speed up, bring him home so she could feel him wrapped around her.

"There's more," he said. "That's if Sharon's done her job," he teased.

Her mother beamed. "Cheeky bugger," she said. "Of course I bloody have."

Layla turned her attention back to the drawer, spotting something else that stood out as new and clean against the debris. An envelope, pristine white, fat with its mysterious contents.

"God, Mum," she said, looking at the mountain of tape her mother had used to seal it, "got shares in a Sellotape factory, have you?"

"You know me, always do a job properly. Here," she said, "you haven't got the nails for it."

Layla's practical doctor's nails certainly weren't up to the job, but her mother's long pointy ones, resplendent in scarlet nail polish in honour of Christmas, were perfect. She pried off the layers of tape and handed the envelope back to Layla.

She shook the envelope, and the contents slipped onto the bed: airline tickets—Auckland to Tahiti—and a brochure with photographs of little bungalows suspended over turquoise waters, a crescent of white sand edging a lagoon, and a perfect curling pipeline on a surf beach.

"Meet me in Tahiti," he said. "When all this is done."

11

Reunion

Papeete, Tahiti - January 2014

LAYLA STARED DOWN AT the serious-faced young woman in the photograph and knew that at this moment, it was not her. That girl was gone, the sad downturn of her mouth evaporated, the shadow in her eyes lifted. Standing in the crowded arrivals processing area in Papeete, knowing that around that winding corridor Will waited for her, it was impossible to prevent a dimpling in her cheeks and a curve in her lips or suppress the great fizzing ball of excitement growing inside her. Surely anyone who looked could see she was a woman transformed from the one who'd sat in the travel agent's booth a month ago, having that photograph taken.

With her pristine passport in hand, carefully open at the correct page, she waited patiently in the heat as the queue inched towards the customs desk. The Tahitian man stationed there with his close-cropped curls and a sunny smile contradicted the traditional image of a stony-faced border official. He offered each new person a warm "Bonjour," while stamping their passport with a cheerful flourish. His friendly welcome made her like this island country already.

Outside the terminal, she slumped on a bench. No sign of Will. God, he was hopeless when it came to time. Beneath her, metal already heated by the mid-morning sun burned through her thin dress. Rummaging in her handbag for sunglasses to ward off the glare of the pavement, she barely noticed when an open-top Jeep roared in behind the row of cabs, ignoring the sign that said 'TAXIS SEULEMENT'.

But when a lanky man with an untidy thatch of golden hair and a pair of Wayfarers perched casually on his nose leapt out, she plunged towards him, her case abandoned. Ignoring the disgruntled glares of the cabbies, Will zeroed in on her, reaching her with two of his long strides. He scooped her up, lifting her off her feet, leaving her dangling from his arms like a small child. She flung her arms around his neck, legs around his waist, and drank in the smell of him. Tears overflowed, relief and joy that their nightmare separation was over.

"I'm sorry, I'm sorry," he said. "I know, I'm *so* late. This island may be tiny, but it takes forever to get anywhere—unless you're prepared to mow down people ambling along in the middle of the road, wipe out stray children and dogs or take out random guys on mopeds."

She laughed through her tears, and then as he set her down on the pavement, felt a flash of annoyance. "You could have phoned, or sent me a text or something."

"But I did. I sent you three texts. The last one must have been less than half an hour ago," he protested.

"No, you did not. *See*," she said, thrusting her phone at him, waving the evidence in front of his nose.

"Ah, I don't suppose it's still in flight mode, is it?" he asked, a little smile playing around his lips.

Flight mode. Fuck, she was such an idiot. Give her the latest bit of medical technology—a flash new heart monitor or a clever morphine pump—and she was great. But no, here she was, defeated by such a mundane thing as an iPhone.

He flicked open the settings and fixed the problem, and three accusatory beeps announced the arrival of his texts. He turned the screen back to her. "Forgiven?" he said.

"You should know I'd forgive you anything." She snatched it back. "Even reminding me of my own stupidity."

"Easy mistake," he said. "I've done it dozens of times. OK, let's get out of here before those taxi drivers turn menacing."

The bright little Jeep may have lacked the Porsche's spectacular speed, but still brought the same smile of exhilaration. Layla leaned back into the headrest while her curls whipped around her face in a lively dance. She sat head tilted towards Will, eyes locked upon him, as if afraid that by looking away it might catapult her out of this moment she had ached for, for six long weeks. He didn't speak, but the grin plastered on his face, and the way he kept stealing glances at her while keeping the vehicle steady on the narrow road, told her all she needed to know.

She said nothing about the surfboard sitting at a jaunty angle in the back, but noticing her surreptitious glances, Will braved the subject.

"I knew you would hate the idea," he said, "but it's an opportunity too good to pass up. There's some world-class surf here that's calling out to me."

"I'd say practically yelling," she said, "considering you were only here two hours before me and still organised both a board and a vehicle to carry it."

"Yeah, when you put it like that." He looked a little sheepish. He knew bloody well that he shouldn't be taking the risk. It was too soon. "Just don't tell Brandon."

"I don't know if I should feel flattered or offended that you're more scared of him than me. Come on Will, a month on from surgery, and it's all tracking well, but really? Surfing?"

Compared to when they'd started this cancer journey, his prognosis was resoundingly positive, so she supposed she should be positive too. But the doctor in her argued for caution.

"I told you," he said, "whatever the outcome, I plan to live big from now on. I kind of thought you realised that's what you'd signed up for."

"Haven't signed up for it yet," she said with a grin.

"I'd argue that the bling on your finger there says otherwise."

She decided, given how attached she was to that beautiful bling, and the beautiful man sitting next to her, she'd let it rest right there. No point in fighting him on this one.

When they pulled into the portico of the resort, valets appeared magically, one taking the keys, another her case. Layla took one last lingering look at the idyllic scene: palm trees flanking the driveway, an azure sea tantalising beyond the edge of the lawn, before following Will into a serene marbled foyer.

"This way," he said, leading her through double doors, along a pathway edged with frangipani in full bloom, their intoxicating fragrance thick in the air. The same perfume followed them as they stepped into the shady interior of their thatched roof villa with its polished wooden floors and tropical accents.

Standing on the small deck off the lounge, she could see jagged peaks of an offshore island rising from the sea in the distance, soaring skyward. With the sharp indigo spires etched against the brilliant blue midday sky, it looked like something out of Jurassic Park, some strange place not quite of this world.

"Moorea," he said, wrapping her from behind, his chin resting on her shoulder. "Beautiful as this is here, that's where I'm taking you in a few days. There's a special place I want you to see. As well as a couple more surf spots."

It was hard to imagine any place more beautiful than this, where the lush tropical gardens encroached on the space, and the world inside and out blended seamlessly.

"For now, come with me."

She followed willingly, longing for a private space where after these six lonely, frightening weeks, they could lose themselves in each other once more.

He led her into a huge bedroom, an enormous bed at the centre, the suspended mosquito netting falling from the ceiling draped across it like a bridal veil. She broke free from him, unable to suppress her child-like glee at the sight. However, knowing it wasn't quite the reaction he expected, she pulled back from the urge to leap on it and bounce up and down as if on a trampoline. Instead, she took in the beauty of the room, the perfect romantic setting for this moment.

Then, slipping the straps of her dress from her bare shoulders, she tugged it down, letting it pool around her feet in layers of sea-foam green. Turning to face him, the thrill as his eyes flickered appreciatively across her body was so electric, the anticipation of his hands on her so great, it was as if his fingers already traced the contours of her breasts, her thighs.

"Oh, my god, Layla. Don't tell me you travelled all that way on the plane wearing no freaking underwear."

The romance of the moment came crashing down, and all her sexy confidence dissipated as laughter spilled from him.

"Nope," she said, heat creeping across her cheeks. She wanted to be mad at him for laughing at her, but then it was so good to hear him laugh, that beautiful spontaneous sound, tumbling from him. "Took it off in the toilet on the plane just before they asked us to buckle in for landing. Thought I'd surprise you."

"Well, you sure did that. Just when I thought I knew all there was to know about you, there you go doing something like that and leave me speechless." He took her in his arms, still chuckling against her ear. "Fuck, lucky they didn't pull you aside for a strip search. Now that would have been a surprise."

She recoiled from him in horror at the thought.

"Relax," he said, pulling her close again, and this time his voice oozed a seductive warmth. "The only person stripping any clothes off around here is me."

She shivered as he stepped back and tugged his shirt over his head. She stood admiring him for a moment, while his eyes roved across her body, and she saw him swallow hard just once, before all possibility of taking this slowly evaporated.

He fell upon her like a man starved. His mouth upon hers was bruising, and she returned the ferocity of his kiss with the same desperation. How had she survived six weeks, without his insistent hands on her body, without her hands twining in his hair?

In the chaos, somehow they found the bed, and he lost his jandals, flicked across the room. Her hands tugged at his shorts, her need for him urgent.

"Give me a second," he said, working them free while she took the chance to catch her breath.

She lay back on the white linen covers, enjoying the crisp fabric against her skin, and let the cool air from the lazy whorls of a rattan fan play across her body. Her thoughts skipped to their conversations about this, planning for this moment when they'd meet again. Six weeks apart had allowed time for taking care of other small but important matters, like tests and birth control. She tingled in anticipation that this time, for the first time, she'd take him inside of her so entirely with nothing to come between them.

He re-joined her, bracketing her body with his, and they waited there for a moment in silence, bodies still, hands clasped, only the rhythmic swoop of the fan and the racing of his heart in time with hers. And then he was on top of her, pressing against her. She guided his thrusts and caught his moan of pleasure in her mouth as he slid with ease between her wet folds. They moved in that perfect exquisite rhythm, hips arched, two halves of one whole, exactly where they should be, together, reunited.

The waves of joy radiating off Will banished any thoughts that she should have done more to dissuade him from the surf. With the board tucked under one arm, he jogged towards the edge of the water, where huge foam-edged crests pounded on the black sand beach. North of the resort, a narrow track dived off from the single road looping the island. At the end, a rough palm-fringed parking area gave way to glinting volcanic sand. And now, after a lengthy walk down the beach, the reward was a secluded surf spot where a hidden reef sculpted towering curves of water.

Layla delayed taking up the book she'd brought to occupy her and simply watched, taking vicarious pleasure as Will made up for six weeks of separation from what he laughingly referred to as the other great love of his life: the sea. This was his secret, the reason he'd always remained so chilled in the face of the pressure cooker world of assignments and exams, internships and evaluations.

She remembered sitting beside him on the school bus in the mornings, even back in that first year she met him, his hair stalky and salt-crusted, his face already alive with the new day while the rest of them struggled to shake off the natural teenage desire to sleep till noon.

And she vividly recalled the weekend when he'd proudly pulled up at her house in that beat-up old van. His board, which was probably worth more than the van, adorned the roof. She still smiled, thinking how much his parents hated that van, but he refused to accept their offer of a more stylish alternative. It was one of the rare times he'd shown any interest in cultivating a certain image. Although school regulations forbade him growing his hair long and shaggy, everything else about teenage Will screamed surfer.

She wasn't sure where he'd stashed that van during his gap year, but the ugly orange vehicle reappeared on his return, accompanying him to university in Dunedin. Not even winter snow down to sea level or the great white sharks that roamed the southern waters had deterred him from mornings riding waves at St Clair Beach.

And more recently, although a slick Audi four-wheel-drive wagon had replaced the van, he and Carson regularly indulged in brotherly bonding while facing the wild surf off Auckland's west coast.

In fact, sitting here on the black sand beach with formidable sets rolling towards her she might have been at Piha, except here the wind buffeting her hair was warm.

Eventually she lay back on a towel, Will's clothes bundled under her head as a pillow, and began to read. Time slipped by quickly, immersed in the pages, with nearly an hour gone before she finally noticed him paddling for shore. She discarded her book and wandered down to meet him.

He emerged from the waves, a lithe golden sea creature, jewel droplets of water glistening on his skin. Land-Will still bore the slightest hint of the lanky teen with limbs grown too fast to control, but Water-Will was a sleek selkie, and the touch of liquid magic lingered as he strolled towards her, the remnants of the waves upon his skin. As she approached, he abandoned the board, scooping her in with salty kisses. Captured by his dripping limbs, she ignored her wet clothes and languidly sank into him, her body responding with electric currents of delight at his damp chest pressed to hers.

His hand trailed down her neck, coming to rest where the shadow of a dark nipple peeked through the now sodden fabric of her t-shirt. He raised a brow and then bent his head down to meet it, his breath warm, his teeth lightly plucking at the fabric. "Aureole," he mumbled against her, the hiss of the word a tantalising exhale against her skin. She moaned in pleasure as one hand snaked underneath the shirt while the other fumbled with the knot of her sarong.

As he leaned in, she saw the briefest flicker as his eyes darted towards something back along the beach, but he swiftly returned his focus to her, capturing her lips in a slow, deep kiss. Hearing voices, she drew back, pulling down her rumpled t-shirt and rearranging her sarong. No longer was this their own private beach; time to damp down their desire.

"Later," she promised, seeing the shades of lust still hovering in his eyes. She pressed one last kiss on his lips, leaving the tangy taste of seawater lingering on her own.

She turned toward the approaching people, thinking to check out who interrupted their romantic interlude. Against the glare of the sun, she could make out three figures, faces indecipherable at this distance.

A tall woman strode towards them, the sun illuminating her white blonde hair. In denim cut-offs and a white singlet, her long tanned legs moved purposefully in their direction. Two men followed in her wake, one on her left small and compact, dark skin and waves of black hair, the other to the right, taller, his hair glinting a rich chestnut in the sun. While they kept pace with the woman, they lagged a few steps behind her, like faithful retainers flanking their queen. She recognised each of those figures, the build, the gait, and even the formation they'd instinctively fallen into. Charlie. Leo. Tristan.

For a moment she paused, unable to process what she saw, her brain questioning the message her eyes relayed. But no, she wasn't imagining it. She looked to Will. His face remained calm, no look of shock to mirror her own, instead a small smile of expectation. He knew. He knew they would be here, and he hadn't told her.

"You knew!" she said.

"Yes," he said. "I did."

"But why? I get you missed them too—hopefully not so much as you missed me. But I'm not sure why they are here. Surely we don't need chaperones the first time we've been together in six weeks."

His smile turned enigmatic. "You'll see. And I promise you—you will be pleased they're here."

Charlie's long strides ate up the distance between them. To Layla's surprise, she caught her in a hug first, even though it was only two days since she'd hugged her goodbye in the drop off at Auckland airport. Then, breaking away, Charlie pushed between Leo and Tristan, fending them off from embracing Will to envelope him in her arms. She pressed a rough kiss on his forehead. Nearly as tall as him, she could virtually look him in the eyes.

"You didn't tell her yet, did you?" Layla caught Charlie's low hiss intended just for Will and became even more confused.

Trapped between Tristan and Leo, she saw twin knowing grins turned upon her. "Oh my god, you guys, what are you doing here?" she asked through a laugh. It was good to see them, always was, but for an entire month she'd looked forward to having Will to herself and after twenty-four hours she wasn't yet ready to share him, not even with this lot.

"Someone mentioned a wedding," Tristan said.

It didn't make sense at first. She scrolled through possibilities and none jumped out at her. Wedding. It was as if she'd woken up this morning a fully functioning person, and then in the last minutes some fog had rolled in off the Tahitian sea, wrapping her brain in tendrils of confusion.

"Don't worry hun," Charlie said, with a droll voice, her face deadpan, "we might be crashing the wedding, but we don't expect to come on the honeymoon."

Layla turned back to Will, who dropped his head to one side with a pleased smile. That cute little boy gesture never failed to grab her right there, in the centre, right around her heart, squeezing it tight with love for him. Recognising her unfurling understanding of what was going on, he moved into her. He tilted her chin up, and she saw mischief dancing in his eyes.

"Layla, I've asked you before, but I'm asking again. I hope you don't change your mind and turn me down. Especially with this lot watching." His eyes became serious. "Will you marry me? On Saturday? In Moorea?"

12

Dr Leroux

Moorea, Tahiti - January 2014

FRUSTRATED BY THE NERVOUS tremor in her own hands, Layla called on Charlie's steady ones to fasten the simple gold pendant at her throat. It was the one piece of jewellery of any value in her family. Granny Angell had known better than to let it fall into her son's clutches. Layla's father would have sold it off in a heartbeat, with no room for sentimentality getting between him and the money needed to support his many vices.

Instead, Granny kept it locked away until the day of Layla's eighteenth birthday. She clearly remembered the discussion around the dinner table that night. Six weeks out of high school, her father had been extolling the merits of her job at the country club.

"Stick with it and you can't go wrong," he'd said. He, who'd never stuck with any job, felt qualified to stand in judgement on hers. "Give it a few months and I guarantee you'll dump all of this university nonsense. Who in their right mind would trade it for a life of poverty while racking up a student loan you'll never pay back? No, my girl, you've fallen on your feet there."

Pressing the small heart-shaped locket into Layla's palm as she rose to leave, Granny brushed thin lips against her cheek and offered a quiet murmur of encouragement. "Happy birthday, love." Her voice had a similar smoky rasp in it as her father's, but with a softer edge. "Don't you listen to a word he says. You fly high. Get yourself out of this shit hole and don't look back."

And she had.

"It's as if she knew," Layla said, laying the hand with the emerald ring against her chest, the two hearts, one green and one gold, each a perfect twin to the other.

"Beautiful," said Charlie, standing back to admire her handiwork. Although her personal style leaned towards simple and casual, Charlie gravitated towards a soft feminine aesthetic in others. The girls she dated were often all curves and curls, floating through her life in waves of bohemian florals and lace. She'd relished the opportunity of the wedding, taking it as a personal mission to help Layla find a suitable dress. And even in these tiny tropical islands, she'd succeeded, spotting this in a small boutique in Papeete.

It was traditionally white, but there the resemblance to a wedding dress ended. The sleeveless muslin sundress revealed every intricate inch of Layla's tattooed arms and shoulders. From her waist its layers tumbled like a waterfall, on her tiny five-foot two the hem brushing the floor. As she made her way out onto the boardwalk from the over-water villa, the breeze lifted it gently, with the fabric billowing behind her like a wispy cloud.

She raised one hand to steady the wreath of tropical flowers in her hair, her touch on the petals releasing a small burst of fragrant molecules to drift lightly in the air. The wooden boards beneath her bare feet were warm in the late afternoon sun as she padded towards the beach.

Will spilled out of a room in the main lodge, followed by Tristan and Leo. She'd banished him there two hours earlier. Now all three emerged barefoot in shorts and loose linen shirts, cuffs turned up, a relaxed, casual look to match a beach wedding. They were a good-looking trio; on one side, Tristan all honed muscle and shiny copper hair, on the other Leo, dark and broodingly handsome, but

Layla only saw the man in the centre, the sun, who outshone them all. And like the sun, she'd felt his intense gravitational pull from the beginning. Now willingly captured in his orbit, there was safety and security, knowing he'd never again let her stray beyond the limits of his blazing golden aura.

He stretched out one hand as she approached, his eyes flicking across her, his mouth dimpling in an appreciative smile. Tristan let out a low wolf-whistle and Charlie stepped from behind her to cuff him lightly across the head.

"Down boy," she said. "You could at least behave yourself for one afternoon."

"You look beautiful, Layla," said Leo. Conflicted by his desire to compliment the bride and his natural shyness, a flush crept up his face.

"No words," said Will, his voice low, catching in his throat. "I won't even attempt to describe how you look. I'll let Charlie's pictures do the talking."

"You should see the ones I already have," she said. "Not wanting to sound big-headed, but they're freaking a-mazing. Of course, it helps when your subject looks like her, and in a place that looks like that." She nodded back towards the thatched villa, crouching low over water of a sheer azure. The setting was idyllic. Charlie had taken a string of pictures in the hazy afternoon sun: Layla wading in the sea, her dress bunched up, the shallow water of the ebb tide lapping around her feet; Layla lying back on the vast bed, shafts of light playing across her closed eyes; Layla lifting the wreath of flowers to breathe in the scent. Charlie had shown her the images, and she was in awe, as if looking through some magical camera lens her friend had captured the essence of her and of what this day meant.

They wandered down the beach, just the five of them. Charlie led the way, toting two camera bags, and holding a Go-Pro in her hand, set to film the ceremony. Tristan, with his ever-present restless energy, jogged along the shoreline, kicking at the waves like an excited puppy. Will and Layla strolled hand in hand, not speaking, drinking in the minutes. And Leo brought up the rear, clutching a small leather-bound book, a page marked with a blue ribbon.

Charlie paused for a moment, scanned the tree-clad sand hills and then motioned them on a little further. When they arrived at the spot they'd chosen yesterday, she tossed a sarong onto the ground and laid out her camera gear as carefully as Will might have once laid out a set of surgical instruments. Satisfied all was ready, the tight five moved into formation.

Leo took up his position facing them, with his back to the sea. He flipped open the book, resting it on his palms. He smiled at them with a quiet confidence, comfortable in this role. It had been a stroke of genius on Will's part, this ceremony so intimate that even the celebrant was a friend. Leo, raised in a family with a steadfast religious devotion, still held to it, not overtly displayed, but quietly observed. In his early twenties, he'd become a deacon in the church and alongside that trained as a celebrant. The maturity beyond his years that he'd always had now found fruition in this desire for service to others.

He'd married three couples at the little country church his family attended in the endless summer of New Zealand's far north. Today, under a Tahitian sky, with sandy seagrass beneath their feet, it would become four. Although not recognised under Tahitian law, they'd do the formalities when they got home. But as far as Layla was concerned, in every way that mattered, this would forever be their wedding day, not the future date registered on a bit of paper.

Tristan stilled his internal perpetual motion machine, standing alongside Will with an uncharacteristically solemn expression. From beneath the joker, the man with a heart for family emerged today, as witness to the beginning of a new family, their family. It would be a few years yet, but they would one day be a proper family. For Layla, children had always been part of some hazy future with some nebulous Mr Right. Uncovering Mr Right in the man who'd been beside her since she was sixteen had crystallised her thoughts: she craved a child with Will, but the certainty of that allowed her to place it carefully a little further on in their journey, like a beautifully wrapped present, the anticipation of knowing what was inside adding to the thrill of the gift. He'd walked considerately around the subject, observing her reactions to his careful questions, not sharing that he was all-in for being a father until he knew it was what she wanted. This way he put her first in everything, simply magnified her love till it seemed to encompass the whole world. It was more than she'd ever hoped for, more than she deserved.

Leo produced the two neat folded pieces of hotel stationery on which they'd written their vows. They'd sat back to back beside the pool, as if by connecting physically they might find the words that would connect them forever. Each with pen in hand and notepad propped on their knees, each alone with a blank page. It was as simple as a promise to love, but the most complex words she'd ever needed to find. She'd felt his spine slump with a sigh as he too wrestled with his thoughts and reached up to stroke his shoulder, pressing reassurance with a firm thumb. He'd heard the dreamy hiss of satisfaction that escaped her as she reread a line she'd written, and his hand snaked around to squeeze hers. Now those words would spill out into the world, an expression of forever, captured forever as Charlie pushed play on the camera she held in her hand.

Tristan, proving himself more reliable than anyone might expect, produced two wedding bands from his shirt lapel pocket. They lay on Leo's palm, glowing with an almost unearthly light, as if already infused with the essence of the love they symbolised. Will took her hand and carefully slid the winged heart from her finger, entrusting it to Leo for safekeeping. She almost gasped when she saw the detail on the etched gold bands, the delicate twining vines and tiny petals, a replica of the lines of ink on her arms. It reinforced two things she already knew: Nik Francovic was a master craftsman and William Leroux the most romantic man she'd ever known. When he replaced the heart-shaped engagement ring, it blended seamlessly into the band, locking the heart in place, as her heart was forever locked in place with his.

She reached for the larger band, recognising it as a twin to her own. "I had it engraved, so I'd always see you when I look at it," he said. "And see this—" he traced the curve in the centre, "—the heart you wear fits into this, just as your heart will always be a part of me."

It didn't need Leo to offer permission for Will to kiss his bride. He swept her into his arms, lifting her off the sand. Engulfed in his arms, his lips warm, their love spiralling around them in waves that were surely visible, she knew what perfect happiness was. Later, when she gazed at Charlie's photographs, she was certain she could see the threads of joy swirling around them.

They wandered back up the beach, chatting in low murmurs, as if not to break the spell, holding tight to the magic they'd woven around the five of them today. However, while they'd excluded the rest of the world from the ceremony, it seemed the entire world was included in the celebrations. As they made their way to the outdoor table, the restaurant manager welcomed them publicly as newly-weds and the other resort guests erupted in delight. The last rays of sun bounced off silver and crystal, and the heady smell of frangipani mixed with the salt breeze off the sea. The bubbles pinging to the surface of the champagne matched the effervescence in his eyes and the froth of her emotions as they toasted their emergence into the real world. Layla didn't want to think about what that might mean beyond today, not prepared to let any thoughts of tomorrow impinge on the perfect moment.

They ordered in dinner the next night, too weary from hours in the sun and sea to venture out. The day had started in a flurry. Bundling Charlie laden with her precious camera gear onto the ferry was a mission. Long-suffering Tristan and Leo simply rolled their eyes, took charge of the remaining luggage, and still found enough of a good mood to offer cheery waves from the deck of the departing boat. Not wanting their own mood to suffer by the sudden absence of the trio, Will had bustled her into a rental wagon and, with a hired surfboard organised, they'd spent the day languishing on a secluded beach with an enviable surf break.

She'd known Will forever, and thought she knew everything there was to know. But since this immutable change in their relationship, it seemed each day he shared other facets of himself. For example, where had he acquired this nuanced understanding of all things romantic? Certainly not from his parents. She could never imagine Hilton, even back as a newly-wed, being as attentive to Ginny in the way Will was to her. Organising a picnic basket and a blanket, a bottle of wine in a cooler, and a couple of books he knew she'd happily fall into, it was the perfect first day of their honeymoon. He surfed the waves for a while, before coming to lay alongside her, damp and salty, all sexy bare skin. She surfaced from the pages and spent most of the day in the pleasant distraction of her new husband, an isolated spot and uninterrupted hours to explore each other.

Catapulted back into reality at the resort, she decided it was time to probe his thoughts about the future, even though it risked opening up a barely healed wound: the loss of his surgical career. Yesterday they'd taken a bold step forward, made promises to each other that whatever may come, they'd face it together. And she wanted him to know that even though his future would not look like the one he'd mapped out for himself from right back in high school, this new future with her by his side could still be amazing. Sitting on the deck over dinner, she decided to make a gentle move to open up that discussion.

"I don't want to think about going back," she said, toying with the little pieces of mango garnish, pushing them round her plate in thoughtful circles. "Sometimes I think I could happily stay here—you and me in a little shack somewhere, living our lives in this paradise, not a care in the world."

"Tempting. But we're not really built that way, are we?" he said. "Sometimes I wish I was. Become a beach bum, have a simple life, no worries, no responsibilities. It's an attractive thought. Especially since—" There it was; the shadow drifted across his eyes. "Well, you know." The resigned expression on his face stabbed at her heart, and she swallowed down the guilt at nudging the conversation in that direction.

"Will, one thing I do know is that we *are* meant to do more than that. You and me, we need our lives to mean something, to contribute something to the world. Give, not just take. "

"Yeah," he said, giving a slight nod, but his attention wandered elsewhere. He stared down at his hands, examining them for that slight telltale tremor, evidence of what he'd lost. Somehow she needed to stop him fixating on what he couldn't have. If she could rekindle his passion—focus him back on the reason they'd both chosen medicine in the first place, and from there explore the possibilities.

Neither had chased it for the money; his family backing meant he had no need of it, and although she would be relieved when she'd paid off her student loan, her humble beginnings had tempered any aspirations of wealth. Nor was it the status; he'd inherited that to some extent with two renowned parents but was mostly oblivious to it, and she just craved good old-fashioned respect, no more than that. Back as idealistic teenagers, she and Will had discovered they shared a simple but consuming desire to help others and leave the world a better place. And there were so many options for that besides being a surgeon. She had to make him see it.

"Anyway," he said, leading her off the deck into the airy privacy of the villa. "What about you Dr Angell? We've hardly talked about how the GP programme is going." He'd neatly deflected the conversation away from himself for now. He sat on the bed, pulling her down beside him.

"I like it. It feels right for me." And now was the right time to give him her other news. "But I'm not planning to be Dr Angell. I'm going to be Dr Leroux." His mouth dropped open, his eyes grew wide. It was unusual for a doctor to sacrifice her name to the conventions of marriage. "I never thought I'd ever want to give up my name. But I do. By taking your name, it makes me feel like I'm yours in every way."

It had been a startling moment of self-realisation, to accept that something had shifted in her so irrevocably that she would take what was certainly a bold step—one that might invite questions, criticism and most likely sniggers from some of her colleagues. But she was determined.

"Are you sure?" he said. "I'd never have asked that of you, or expected it. I mean you could use Leroux for everyday, but keep Angell professionally..."

"Will, I'm absolutely sure. Layla Angell was then. Meet the new me, Layla Leroux. Although," she mused, "sadly, it won't help my image. It's been rather challenging to wear the name Layla Angell. But Layla Leroux sounds even more like a porn star's name."

"Just let me at anyone who even thinks to suggest it," he said.

"Oh no, William Leroux, you certainly will not. Your days of going caveman and hitting people are over. Besides, I can fight my own battles."

He burst out laughing. "God, please let me be a fly on the wall the first time someone makes the mistake of messing with you about it. People think it's Charlie they should worry about, but you are a feisty little hell cat when riled."

She leapt onto him, wrestling his arms up above his head and pinning them against the bed.

"Careful," she said, "this kitty has claws."

"My point exactly," he laughed, rolling her over and trapping her beneath him.

She parked the conversation about his future till morning.

"So... since we agree we *are* getting on that flight home next week..." It had taken her most of breakfast to broach the subject. She'd picked nervously at the fruit platter while downing two coffees to summon energy for what must come. She smiled at him, took a deep breath, and pressed on. "Have you decided what you'll do?"

"No. I've tried not to think about it. Bloody coward, aren't I?" he said with a self-deprecating laugh. That little sound, those words, triggered something inside her. She'd resolved to be gentle, but maybe it was time for some tough love.

"Don't *ever* let me hear you say that," she said. "You've faced down something that no one our age ever expects to have to deal with. Not only that, you took an incredibly brave route to do it. Just think, while saving yourself, you've helped save others too. Every single patient in that research trial contributed something, but no one as much as you. You could have gone down the easy route, but you didn't. So never tell me you're a coward, William Leroux."

"OK," he said slowly. "So I fought the good fight and won. To some extent."

"Yes, and you need to take the win and make something of it." She placed her hand over his, squeezing it tight, willing him to believe.

"I don't know," he said. "There's been a couple of offers."

"There have? And you didn't tell me?" She tried to keep calm, but reflexively withdrew her hand. There was a shrill edge to her voice, a peeved note. And she *was* peeved. How could he think that this information wasn't worth sharing with his wife?

He sighed. "Look, I don't know how serious they are. I didn't want to get my hopes up, and I certainly didn't want to raise yours until I felt certain there was something to be hopeful about."

This was so *not* the old Will she knew. That Will sailed across life's ups and downs with a contagious optimism that had carried them all through. He'd always sensed potential, grabbed onto small hopes and made you believe they'd come true by his own unwavering belief. But loving Will was to accept all of him, even this new side where he let show how his four-month battle had left a part of him battered and bruised. She tried to keep her face neutral and vowed to do the same with her words.

"They probably just feel sorry for me," he said. "I have a sense they might be simply trying to reassure me that there is life after a failed surgical career, but if I show definite interest, they'll come up with a legitimate reason I'm not right for it."

She couldn't help the huff of frustration. "Why should they? You've got so much to give. What were these offers?"

He took a resigned breath, realising she wouldn't let him off the hook now.

"Dad's old golf buddy Ivan—the urologist—messaged me to say he'd heard what had happened and to contact him as they might have an opening."

"And who else?" She knew Will wouldn't take a job with Ivan. He'd never be that desperate to work for a man he despised in a field he disliked. She stared at him, expecting more.

"Mark Tregoweth."

"Mark?" she said. "Well, there we are. Mark would never make any sort of offer lightly. No way he'd get in touch just as part of some pity party. What did he say?"

Mark Tregoweth was the medical equivalent of a rock star. A St Aidan's old-boy, two years ahead of them at med school, they'd met him at an O-week event. In that first year, their first week, back when they were too new to have slotted into the grind of study, they'd ventured to a few university orientation activities. Mark had the illustrious honour of being the winner of that year's 'chunder mile'. The rules were simple: after each lap of the cricket oval, scull a jug of beer, run some more, with brief breaks allowed for 'chundering' (student slang for spewing); last man—or woman—standing, wins.

A veteran of two earlier occasions, Mark arrived at the start line with form, and a keen desire to beat his nemesis from his previous year's second place finish. Achieving that goal resulted in an impromptu victory party, with all the ex-St Aidan's students electing him their hero. Outside the wildness of student orientation, Mark presented as a pleasant, mild-mannered young man with an eye-wateringly high GPA. And he'd become Will's closest friend outside the tight five, and a partner in a specialist cardiology practice by the age of thirty-one.

"He wants to meet for a drink. When we get back."

"But that's great. I mean, you toyed with the idea of cardio-thoracic."

"Yeah—as a surgeon."

"But at least it's an area where you've got *some* interest. And working with Mark. Wouldn't that be great?"

"Yeah. Maybe."

Heat surged in her and spilled over into her cheeks. "You know you're a fucking hypocrite, William Leroux." His eyes widened, and she saw him swallow, preparing to brace himself for further attack. "You tell me how amazing I am, how skilled ED doctors are, that GPs are pivotal in medical care. The frontline troops fighting the battle. But when it comes to you, only neurosurgery will do." The words tumbled out in an angry torrent. "So, does that mean all that other stuff—it's fine for the rest of us mere mortals, but the really important work lies in the hands of the neurosurgeon gods like you?"

"You know I don't think that." His mouth twisted in a scowl.

"Don't you? When you talk about an offer from one of the smartest people we know, like it's the consolation prize? Mark and his team are fucking rock stars, just they're too modest to be strutting around like they've got a stick up their arse saying 'Look at me, folks. The brain surgeon. The only one that really counts.' It seems to me you're letting pride get in the way of finding a way forward here."

The fire blazing in his eyes told her she'd made an inroad. If it took provoking anger at her to jolt him out of this sad limbo he'd drifted into, she was up for it.

"Is that how you see me? An arrogant arsehole like my father?"

"You *know* I don't. But to be honest, right now I'm struggling to *not* see a little of him in you when you refuse to consider anything beyond emulating him as worthy."

That had done it. His face was ashen, eyes wide and disbelieving. She realised this was the first time in all these years that she'd really challenged him. She didn't want to hurt Will; god knows he'd suffered enough. But the single-mindedness and determination with which he'd pursued his dream had an ugly side—a stubborn pride. Holding up a mirror to him, letting him see how this appeared to others was painful for both of them, but necessary. She loved him too much to simply accept this version of him, living a life overshadowed by bitter regrets about something that wasn't his fault and couldn't be changed.

"So," he said, the words little more than a whisper, "if that's what you think, where do we go from here?"

"We go forward, together. No more sitting around hoping things will go back to how they were." She reached for his hand, tracing the sweep of the long fingers, before lacing her own through them. "Promise me you'll have that drink?"

"OK—I promise," he snapped at her, with a frustrated wave. He closed his eyes, resting his head in one hand, brows furrowed, then gave a deep, resigned sigh. "You're right," he said with an impatient shrug. "I shouldn't be so surly about the idea. Whenever Mark and I have talked work, it's been interesting stuff. And with him, I know he wouldn't piss me around."

She couldn't help a small smile of triumph. "No, he would never do that to you."

"So," he said, "as long as *you* agree to drop this subject so we can enjoy the rest of our honeymoon, *I* promise I'll call him when we get back."

"Thank you," she whispered, squeezing his hand again. She felt a surge of relief; she'd risked damaging this thing between them with her harsh words, but the risk was worth it. Hearing his agreement, despite his obvious reluctance, her heart pulsated in a wild, hopeful dance. Sure, he'd simply agreed to please her. Talk of working with Mark didn't bring the same sparkle to his eyes as when he spoke of surgery. But one day it might. It was a small start, from which something good could flourish.

13

Collusion

Five years later, Auckland, New Zealand - February 2019

WILL'S EYES FOLLOWED CHARLIE'S enormous backpack as it lumbered towards the conveyor belt. He stood ready to launch himself should the dangling straps catch in the machinery. God, it had been heavy, and on the lengthy walk from car to airport terminal, he'd regretted offering to carry it for her. He had no idea how she'd manage single-handed at the other end. Visions sprang to mind: her outside Heathrow, over-balancing with it on her back, cast on the pavement, arms and legs waving in the air like a furious upended insect. He hoped there might be someone strong and chivalrous in that eventuality to rescue her from the indignity. Not that Charlie appreciated chivalry. Any helpful Pommie bloke thinking this might get him an 'in' with a stunning blonde would get a rude surprise.

At the end of the belt, her bag toppled backwards with a resounding thunk onto the next carousel, before disappearing into the dark cavernous depths of the airport check-in area; in the same way as Charlie was about to disappear from their lives for months, possibly years. Their house was going to feel empty. While technically he and Layla owned it, his wedding gift to her five years ago, it still felt like they were living those nostalgic student years. Sure, things had got a little quieter since Tristan's latest relationship took a serious turn, with him often at his girlfriend's house as they tested the possibility of moving in together. And Leo seemed to be away more often than not lately, flying to every corner of the country, his legal advice in demand by various tribal authorities. But it never seemed quiet, not with Charlie's huge presence filling the space left by their absence.

Charlie hefted two large camera bags onto her shoulder, not trusting any baggage handler enough to let her precious photographic equipment out of her sight. While none of it was irreplaceable, she'd insisted on hand-carrying it, not wanting its potential loss en route to London to jeopardise an immediate start to her new job.

And it was a brilliant job. As a photographer for the hottest new entertainment magazine in the UK, Charlie would soon cover assignments she could only have dreamed of stuck here way down at the bottom of the world in little old New Zealand. They were happy for her. This was her ticket to the top.

"The house won't be the same without you," he said. "Shit, think of what Tristan's going to get up to in your absence: food six months out-of-date in the fridge, dirty undies left in the laundry tub and manky towels germinating toxic bacteria in the bathroom."

She rolled her eyes at the thought. It was ironic that she, not one of the two health professionals, had become their unelected health and safety officer. Tristan remained the bane of her life, seemingly untrainable in the niceties of cleanliness and order.

"Yeah, he's a fucking lost cause. Failed in my role there, I'm afraid. Just remember to have a throw out once a week, otherwise you might end up with a nasty superbug."

She grinned at them, and Will could see she appreciated his attempts at levity. Charlie's eyes hinted at the wrench they all shared at her leaving. They'd been apart before, but this time there was a finality about it. And London was a long way.

He wrapped her in a hug. "You know we're going to miss your stroppy ways and potty mouth, don't you?"

"I'm sorry to be the one to break up the tight five," she said, pulling back and looking up at him with a rueful smile. "But it had to come sometime."

"Don't be sorry," said Layla, flinging an arm over Charlie's shoulder, stretching up to crush the taller woman in a hug. "None of us begrudge you this chance. Even if it means the five will become four. Besides having you over there—well, maybe it's a good excuse for a trip over to see you."

She tried to sound positive, but he knew that inside Layla's heart was melancholy. The thought of the house without Charlie's tinkling laughter echoing in the hallway unsettled her. These two were bonded so tight, practically joined at the hip.

"Oh, god," said Charlie. "I'm not sure even London is ready for the tight five."

"No, perhaps not," said Will with a grin. "It could get messy."

"But you two should come over. Really. Think about it. Layla's never been further than Australia. It's about time you showed her the world, Will."

She was right; apart from their Tahitian wedding, the east coast Australian cities were the total of Layla's travel experience. Even her Aussie trips had been for work, spent inside a hotel conference centre or a hospital. Charlie's comment triggered guilt. He felt bad that he'd never considered how limited Layla's exploration of the world was, compared to his own.

The thought came back to him as they barrelled up the airport motorway. Layla's tear-stained face and red-rimmed eyes were another reason he toyed with the idea. He decided to test it out. Maybe it would cheer her up.

"You know, I was thinking, once Charlie's settled—you should go over to London."

"Me? Just me?"

"Yeah, why not? The timing is great. You're finishing that locum position in a few weeks."

He knew she was grateful for the end of that job. Layla hadn't done all her GP training to be trapped in a Remuera practice where most of the wealthy patients who came in weren't particularly unwell. On top of that, they were inclined to have a thinly-veiled distrust of doctors who didn't agree with their self-diagnoses courtesy of Dr Google. She was determined to work somewhere where she felt she made a real difference, where people's needs were great and a doctor's input was significant. And an opportunity for that would be hers later this year.

"It would be a great way to fill in the four months till the Clendon position comes up."

"Yeah." She spoke slowly, but he could see her mind racing. She knew the job at Clendon was hers, and the offer for her to buy into the practice at some future date was genuine. And he knew she wouldn't want to spend four months sitting around doing nothing in the meantime. The idle wife of a well-off cardiac specialist would never be Layla's role. "But what would I do in London? I mean, Charlie will be working, not available at my beck and call as a tour guide."

"She'll be travelling for work. So you could tag along with her. Carry her camera bags." Now a plan crystallised in his mind. "And in between, maybe you do some temping. I bet their hospitals always need people to pick up shifts in the ED." He saw her face screw up in a less than-impressed grimace. She'd been pleased to leave the ED behind. Bad suggestion. He backtracked a little. "You could pick and choose. Work when and where you want. Turn down the ones you don't like. I mean, it's not as if you'd need jobs for the money. Just something to do when things don't work in with Charlie's plans."

He felt her hand slip across to lie over his. "But it would be four months without you."

Her voice was small and uncertain. It surprised him to hear doubts about her travelling without him. It wasn't often he discovered things outside Layla's comfort zone. In that case, nudging her towards it was a very good thing. Although, to be honest, they'd never been apart more than a few days these last few years. Both of them had an acute sense of how precious time was. Once the threat of loss had come calling, you never really trusted that it wouldn't show up again.

"Yeah, well, it would have to be without me, I'm afraid. With Mark off to the States soon, we can't afford the team to be another person down. But the time will fly by when you're seeing all those things." Her expression suggested she wasn't buying that one. He tried another angle. "Once he's back, I could come over. Maybe near the end—and we go somewhere together. I'd love you to see Italy. Or the Greek Islands. The south of France?"

"Hmm," she said. "I'll think about it." That was a good first step.

A month later, on the morning of Layla's departure, he seriously regretted how effectively he'd enacted his plan. Enlisting Charlie was, of course, the master stroke. One phone call two weeks prior had swept away any insecurities Layla had felt about imposing on her.

"Hey, Layla."

Charlie's wide moon-face filled the screen. Holding the phone at chest level, it was most unflattering. You'd never suspect what a stunning-looking woman she was in real life. For someone with an impeccable photographic eye, Charlie had appalling FaceTime skills.

"Charlie, it's so good to see you," Layla gushed. Her face glowed with delight at the opportunity to see her friend and confidante for the first time since her departure. "How's it going? What's your flat like?"

"Work's going great. And the flat—see for yourself." She talked them through an impromptu virtual tour of her London home. A three-bedroom terrace house in Camden.

"Nice." Layla cooed at the stylish interior, all white walls and trendy art works. "But I bet the flatmates aren't as good as us. No—don't answer that. I'll be crushed if you've found some new besties."

Charlie's laugh echoed off the sparsely-furnished minimalist lounge as she sprawled on a large couch.

"It's actually the 'flatmate' now. Singular. DeeDee's company transferred her to Munich. Moved out yesterday. Banks, I don't know how anyone can stomach working for them when they play with people's lives like pawns on a chessboard. She's not happy. But Reed is staying on."

Charlie's emails revealed she thought Reed was a model flatmate in the ways that counted most: clean, tidy, didn't leave laundry littering the shared bathroom and maintained a vigilant attitude to keeping the fridge fresh-smelling and free of mouldy food.

"So," Charlie said, pausing meaningfully, an enigmatic smile spreading across her lips. Will knew what was coming next. He just hoped Charlie didn't fuck up and let Layla know they had set her up. While it was for a good cause, in fact, for her own good, he knew she would be pretty pissed off if she suspected he'd manipulated things behind her back. She would forgive him, but it might be enough for her to dig her toes in and reject the whole idea. "You know how we talked at the airport—about you coming over?"

"Ah, yeah," Layla said, not yet joining the dots. God, he was relieved. Please let it stay that way.

"Well, we've got this room free. And there are heaps of rooms to let at present. With spring coming, it seems everyone's on the move, so getting a new flatmate isn't so easy. Plus, it's a little pricey here for many people. If you were to come over, take the room for a few months, you'd have the chance to spend some time in London, maybe see some of Europe. I've got a whole heap of work coming up and it's all over. And it would buy us a bit of time to find someone else more long-term for the flat."

The battle in Layla's brain spilled onto her face. Part of her desperately longed to spread her wings; some compensation for the hand life had dealt her where overseas travel was a luxury. But part of her clung to him. It wasn't in Layla's basic nature to be clingy, an aspect of their relationship he would never have predicted. But something about his illness, the way they'd come together and then forced to separate while he flew to the States for treatment, had undermined her trust in the world. She'd never admit it for fear of upsetting him, but deep down she held a suspicion that if she let him out of her sight, some evil dark force would snatch him away from her.

Layla looked at him, her eyes wide in question, seeking reassurance. Now it was his turn to hold his poker face, attempt to show a little surprise but not seem unhappy.

"Well, why not?" he said, waving a nonchalant hand in the air. "Sounds like it would help Charlie out."

"But could you come too?" she asked, a small note of hope in her voice, even though she knew his schedule for the next couple of months was both busy and inflexible.

"I could, but not straight away. You could go first, suss things out. Do a few things with Charlie that you know I'd hate."

"Yeah, can you imagine the Tate Modern with this philistine traipsing around behind us, whinging that he could do better than any of these artists?" Charlie had really thought this through. He didn't mind her dissing him to help their cause.

Layla choked down a laugh. "Oh my god, yes. And sparing him the V&A would be a smart move, too."

"But promise you won't do the British Museum without me," he interrupted. "I want to reconnect with my mummy friends in the Egyptian hall."

"OK," Layla agreed. "We promise. No clandestine visits with the mummies before you get there."

And with that, without realising it, Layla had agreed.

He'd only had one moment of doubt since. A stupid doubt triggered by an unlikely source, Layla's father, Terry.

Last weekend's visit with her family had largely played out as expected. Her father and brothers, excited that she would get to walk the hallowed streets of London, gave her a list of rare vinyl to scavenge for in the markets and a request for a picture of her on Abbey Road. Sharon simply wanted something from Harrods, preferably emblazoned with their name so her friends would be in no doubt that her daughter could shop in posh places.

But as they set to leave, Terry had sidled up to him, his voice low. "You're a good man, you know. Letting her go. Letting her have this."

"Thanks Terry. I just want her to be happy."

"I know you do. And that's why you're a braver boy than me. No way I'd have let her mother go gallivanting off like this without me, hanging out with her single friends on the other side of the world. I mean, you wouldn't know it now," he said, casting a surreptitious glance at his wife, "but Layla's the spitting image of her mother back then. No, no fucking way I'd have risked all those guys thinking she was there for the taking, itching to get their grubby hands on her." He choked out a bawdy laugh. "Oh, well, you make sure you tell her to keep that wedding ring front and centre." And with a clap on the back and another throaty chuckle, he ambled back into the house to watch the rugby league.

It was a ridiculous comment. And it was even more ridiculous that it had stuck in his mind. He had not even the slightest glimmer of doubt about Layla. They'd come by their love the long hard way and having fought for it, he knew neither of them was prepared to lose it. But again this morning, perhaps because inside he too struggled with their imminent separation, it lurked there, an ugly lie taunting him.

She stirred beside him, and his body stirred in response. God, how she did that to him, the slightest ripple of her body and he was desperate with need for her. He let his hand wander across her breasts, cupping each one, the pale almost translucent skin, the small veins, the strong contrast of the dark nipples, mesmerising. His mouth sought one out and he sucked on it, lapping it with his tongue, slowly increasing the pressure.

She came fully awake with a groan, almost a growl in her throat. He let one hand trace the shape of her, the petite curves, the soft thigh, the sleek triangle of hair and the already slick crevices beneath. Their lovemaking was often languid and sensual, delighting that, because of luck and Brandon de Luca's skill, they had all the time in the world ahead of them, years to discover the vast repertoire of melodies they might elicit from each other's bodies.

But today it was raw and hungry, almost brutal in its intensity. She rode him hard, head thrown back in ecstasy. It took every ounce of control not to leave her behind as she arched her back, mercilessly rising and falling upon him. But as her last shuddering gasps echoed across him, as the sound of her name on his lips faded with the release of his own orgasm, she fell forward onto his chest, her hot tears flooding his skin, and her sobs tearing at his heart.

He stroked her hair, let his hands soothe her taut shoulders, while all the while wondering what had reduced her to this. It was as if something inside her had broken, and he feared it was something he'd done. For this to be happening, right now, when in a few brief hours he'd be putting on her plane, with twelve thousand miles and four months separating them, it was breaking him too. Her father was right—he must have lost his mind.

When she stilled, he continued to stroke her, slow calm strokes, hoping that comforted by them, she might tell him what had provoked this emotion.

Eventually, he spoke. "Layla, honey, what is it? What's wrong? What can I do?"

She sniffled against his chest, wiping her nose roughly with one small hand. "It's hard to explain. You know I really, really want to go. And I know you'll come over, and the time will go fast, and I'll have a great time. But I worry about leaving you here without me."

"But why? I'm fine. You know I am."

"I know that," she said. "But my heart's not listening to my brain too well at the moment."

"Is it you think Tristan's going to let all the wild women into the house the moment you're gone and I won't be able to fight them off?"

She laughed. "Tristan's too scared of me. He knows I'll be back to deal with him if he causes any trouble, or brings any your way."

He said the words into her hair, hoping by getting his fears out there, it would banish them. "Your father told me if he was in my shoes, he wouldn't let you go. Too many predatory men out there looking to catch your attention."

She looked up at him. "And does that bother you? Me out there with all these unknown men?"

"No," he said. "Is this weird? It bothers me that I'm not bothered."

"I don't know whether to feel relieved or offended," she snorted. "It's nice to be trusted, but I kind of think it's nice if you still want to protect me, too."

"So we're good then. I'll agree to still worry a little that some guy might hit on you. And you'll agree not to run off with anyone who does."

"Deal," she said, her little laugh tickling the hairs on his chest.

"But by God I'm going to miss you," he said, already feeling a small stab of pain at the thought of her not being here, in their bed, waking up to her.

"Good," she said. "I'm going to miss you, too. Let me show you how much." Her small hand fumbled between his thighs and a sly smile pressed against his throat. He wasn't about to argue with that.

14

OE And Over It

London, England - July 2019

DYING HER NATURALLY BOMBSHELL blonde locks might help. Even pulled back severely in a taut bun, the very hue seemed to scream slutty. It was as if a hint of the bed-hopping, no-strings-attached woman she'd once been still lurked in the tumble of her hair. Will would never forgive her a dye job. He loved to run his hands through those golden curls; told her how much it made his heart sing when he saw her unruly mane bobbing towards him across a crowded room. But perhaps it would wash out by the time he arrived. Yes, maybe she would book into that hairdresser two doors down from the apartment. What would she go for? Maybe a brunette, the most drab shade they could find, so she could hide behind it.

But there was no way to disguise her eyes, the same unusual green as her mother's, that hinted of wild places, not the seriousness of a hospital ward. And of course, the tattoos that wound their way down her forearms into a full sleeve didn't help matters. They were part of her though, an expression of what she felt inside, the soul of her on display to those who cared to study them rather than write them off as a youthful excess.

She might have changed her name. Perhaps gone by her middle name. Elizabeth, after her grandmother. It may have been preferable to this one. Teasing about her name was nothing new, but this drunk tonight in Cubicle 3—his jibes had gotten to her.

"Layla Leroux, eh?" His lecherous wink made her nauseous. "That's a hooker's name. Or a porn star. Which one are you, love? Bit of moonlighting after hours, doc?" And then he'd tried to check for himself, his hand straying dangerously close to her chest.

It was times like this she wondered whether she should have gone with Will's suggestion and not taken on his name. But she always rejected it immediately. She loved his name. She loved him, and god, especially stuck here in this central London ED, she missed him. It was pride that had got her here. She didn't need to work. They had plenty of savings and the weekly rent on the room in Charlie's flat made only a small dent. They owned the Mt Eden house outright, thanks to Will's inheritance from his grandparents. It still thrilled her to think it was theirs, so many great memories in that house and so many more still to make. With Tristan and Leo paying rent and Will's income, there was no issue if hers was patchy. But she had never wanted to be reliant on him, and so in between trailing behind Charlie as her unofficial assistant on assignments, she picked up shifts in whichever ED needed staff.

This week she'd flown in overnight from Berlin, where Charlie had covered a concert, and gone straight to work from the airport. Two day shifts and now two extended night shifts and she was exhausted. If she'd been less so, she would have put Mr Cubicle 3 in his place. But tonight she let out a surprised "No!" left the cubicle and stepped over to her colleague.

"Patrick, could I ask you to look at this patient, please?"

Patrick, who'd overheard the exchange, and perhaps was already on his way to intervene, simply gave a sympathetic nod and slipped past her. She left him with the jerk, pulled up her protective cloak of self-assurance, and grabbed the chart for the next patient.

New hospital, new city, new country, same shit. It simply defined for her more clearly why she'd moved out of being an ED specialist, why she'd signed up for the GP training. Right now, she questioned the wisdom of acting on Will's suggestion to follow Charlie to London. More than a suggestion, he'd encouraged her.

"Do it, honey. There's no time like the present. Let's face it, once you get yourself into a practice, an OE like this will be out of the question. You'll be head down, working to get established."

"But without you…"

How could she tell him that having spent those years denying what they felt for each other, they'd already wasted too much time apart? It would only make him feel guilty for being the one who'd kept her at arm's length, even if in his misguided way he'd had her interests at heart.

And how could she say that having nearly lost him, it scared her to let him out of her sight? No cure was guaranteed permanent. Remission was often temporary. Each year, that check-up would mean a week of waiting and wondering for both of them. Wondering if this would be the year that someone told him "It's back". She knew he pushed those fears right down deep and she wouldn't be the one to drag them back to the surface.

Soon he would be here. He'd promised, and he was true to his word. She was having an amazing time outside of these shitty ED shifts and in a few weeks he'd arrive, too. She was relieved to hear him confirm it.

"Haven't booked the tickets yet, but it will be soon, I promise. Mark's organising for me to do a few weeks with an old colleague over there from later this month. Then we'll have a holiday in Europe before we come home to Auckland."

She knew his enthusiasm was partly because he felt guilty. He'd travelled the world from the time he was a kid. When Will was ten, the family had moved to Belgium while Virginia took up a lucrative year-long research position. They'd followed Hilton to conferences all over the globe. And then, while she'd been slogging it out at

Summerfields Country Club, scrambling to build up funds before starting university, Will had been on his gap year.

This was one reason she knew she loved him. It would have been easy to envy the spoiled rich kid he'd been, let it stand in the way of recognising the beautiful human being he'd also always been. It was no more his fault he'd been born into privilege than it was hers she'd landed on this earth in a family of no-hopers. With a smile at the thought of that beautiful human being joining her soon, she pulled aside the curtains to Cubicle 4, where yet another patient waited. And smiled some more because this was her last shift. It had been a relief to refuse more offers of casual work. She had other plans for these last weeks of her OE.

Tired as she was, Layla still chuckled to herself at the sight of Reed perched on the couch shooting anxious glances at the pile of bags and boxes stacked in the lounge while the final episode of *The Great British Bake Off* blared from the television. It was hilarious to discover someone more particular than Charlie existed. Tomorrow, the offending pile would be gone. They would load that stack into a rental car and head off on a road trip to what would probably be their last gig together before Will arrived. Charlie had been excited about this one for ages.

"Have you heard of Slane?" Charlie had asked during one of those first phone calls a few months back. Of course Layla had heard of it. *U2 Go Home: Live From Slane Castle* was her brother Jimmy's favourite, and he'd punished the family with it repeatedly. Not that she disliked U2, in fact she was a fan, but it was possible to have too much of a good thing, especially played at enough volume to cause the neighbours to call noise control.

"You're going to Slane? Wow, that will be amazing."

"No, not Slane. But it is a castle—Dallblane Castle. In Scotland. And it's not just a one-off concert but a whole five-day festival. A mini-Glastonbury. The line-up they've got suggests it could become as big one day."

And now it was here; tomorrow they were off to Dallblane. The romance of a castle, the allure of Scotland, and five days of music that made her the envy of her family. She already had a list of merchandise to purchase for her brothers. But no amount of band t-shirts was a substitute for actually being there, as she would be.

"How long will it take? The drive?" she asked as they shovelled mouthfuls of curry. They'd appeased Reed somewhat over the jumble in the living room by buying takeaways, the best Indian food Layla had ever tasted, from a little shop one block over.

"Eight hours if we go non-stop."

"Holy shit, Charlie. I don't think I can survive that long in a car. Not coming off the back of those last two night shifts."

"Don't stress, I've got one of those Shewee things so you can pee while we drive."

Seeing the look of horror on Layla's face, Charlie doubled over with laughter. Reed almost choked on a piece of Chicken Madras, and Layla knew she'd fallen once more for Charlie's evil sense of humour.

"Right, Charlie Christensen, I can tell you now, if anyone's going to use the Shewee thing, it will be you. Between coffee and a whole heap of Red Bull, I think *I'll* do the driving, and *I'll* control the stops."

"Hey, chill babe, you know I'm messing with you. We'll drive till we've had enough, grab a place for the night and carry on the next day. Campsite won't be open till then, anyway."

Campsite? Layla wished she'd paid a lot more attention. And doubted that anything in the pile of stuff Charlie had assembled would get them through a week of camping. Charlie had never camped in her life. She could imagine them freezing cold and hungry in a tiny tent with wind and rain battering the thin walls, while around them seasoned campers laughed at the two clueless girls from New Zealand.

"Campsite? For real. You're telling me *you* are prepared to spend almost a week in a tent. This must be some assignment." She shook her head in disbelief.

"I'll show you something." Charlie calmly picked up her phone and scrolled lazily before thrusting it in front of Layla's face. "Not camping—glamping. I've booked us one each."

"Oh, yeah, they look great. I *knew* there'd have to be something I was missing." The circular tents were really rather gorgeous, a proper big bed, a small couch, rugs on the floor. OK, they'd still have to go cross-country to the loo and showers, but at least freezing to death was unlikely. "One each? Not prepared to share with me? Will assures me I don't snore."

"Just being prepared." Charlie shot her a wink. "After all, in a crowd of thousands, there's a lot of opportunity."

"Well, happily married me has no need of that opportunity. When Will encouraged me into taking a few months to try out the OE thing, I'm fairly certain it didn't extend to pretending I'm single." Not that she'd want to. Five years of marriage and no regrets about her choice. 'Happily married' was exactly what she was. "I don't think even single me would hook up with some random guy at a festival. Remember, I've watched *Bridget Jones's Baby*. We all know where frolicking with strangers in yurts leads to—trouble."

"And why do you think this is all about you?" Charlie tossed back. "Wouldn't look too great if I invite some gorgeous woman back to my tent and we find you in there, all pouty lips and big eyes. That wouldn't help my love life one bit. And as I seem to have been in a bit of a drought lately, I definitely want to keep my options open. Remember, we're not all thirty-three and married to the love of our life. Some of us are thirty-four and still looking. And getting worried about it, too."

Layla wrapped her arm round Charlie's shoulders. "You shouldn't worry, hun. She's out there somewhere."

"Yes, and hopefully on her way to Dallblane," Charlie offered with a smile.

Driving into Dallblane was a relief—they'd easily covered the miles over two days and not once had either of them needed the Shewee. Here on the edge of the Highlands, the green of the countryside gave way to golden hues of tussock and heather coating low hills, interspersed with the deep green of forest. Brooding mountains loomed indigo blue in the distance. The towns grew smaller and more sparse until finally they reached the postcard-pretty village of Dallblane. Charlie stopped in the main street, a cluster of little shops and cottages, some natural stone, others with glowing whitewashed walls.

"God, it's good to be out of the car," she said, unravelling her long legs.

"Yeah, well, I did say I'd cover the cost of a larger vehicle, but you insisted on the economy model," Layla said. "Best we don't think about the drive back."

"I'm even dreading the last bit to the castle. I'm not sure I can wedge myself back into that seat."

"Let's grab some food first," Layla suggested, nodding towards a small pub. Its jaunty, red-painted door and inviting blackboard menu propped outside suggested a warm welcome inside. "And then next stop—Dallblane Castle."

She cast her eyes towards the castle perched on a rise overseeing the village, perhaps a mile or so away. From here, they were looking at the back of it, with clusters of outbuildings and gardens sprawling away from the main building. Even this less attractive face looked impressive, with walls of soft honey stone rising skyward.

An hour later, stomachs bursting with a pub lunch, they took the road to the main entrance. Two heavy iron gates flung open in welcome, framed by massive stone pillars obviously designed to inspire awe. The dark, foreboding tree-lined driveway, guarded by ancient oaks, gave way to a broad expanse of green. To the left, a cute two-storey cottage nestled against the trees, and above them the castle stood in proud Victorian splendour. The central structure, with an arched stone doorway, was flanked by two narrow towers. In perfect symmetry, two further wings to the east and west each sported their own larger tower. Layla half expected to see uniformed soldiers patrolling the crenellated battlements atop each.

One vast stage partly obscured the front of the castle. In the distance, other smaller stages sat on the crests of hills. Lighting towers pointed stark black fingers at the hazy summer sky. People scurried ant-like between the structures, intent on the final preparations for five days and nights of music.

Ahead of them, a thicket of signs pointed off along a warren of narrow roads and laneways. Charlie, following other cars in the slow-moving line, headed for the one that said 'Camping Section A'.

The cute bell-shaped tent did not disappoint. Flicking off her flip-flops by the door, Layla cast her eyes around the room, taking in the cosy couch, dropping her tote on the comfy chair, before flopping across the inviting bed. The creamy, sun-washed walls glowed with a welcoming ambience. Above her head, the pleasing symmetry of the structure's curved ribs met a central pole. A string of fairy lights spiralled down it. Layla reached for the small switch near the base of the pole and they blinked into life, lending the space a festive air.

This was certainly not camping as she knew it. It was a world away from her memories of a claustrophobic nylon pup-tent pitched next to her uncle's old caravan with a leaky air mattress, dodgy zippers and a lingering mustiness from not being aired properly after the previous summer holidays. This tent made her old university dorm room look like a prison cell. In fact, the only improvement she could think of was that Will would be here to share it. But he was still two weeks away, expecting to arrive a couple of days before his first morning at the London cardiology clinic. She counted down the days and they moved with painful slowness. Perhaps caught up in the excitement and bustle of the festival would be the perfect antidote to time's dawdling progress.

With a flash of white-blonde, Charlie's head poked through the doorway. "What did I tell you?" she said, her face smug. "Happy with your accommodation, Dr Leroux?"

"Very," Layla smiled back as she rose to her feet. "I mean, who wouldn't be—look cushions, throw rugs, candles," she said, pointing to the unexpected accessories scattered artfully around the tent.

"I think the candles are for the bugs," Charlie said, picking one up and sniffing at it. "Yes, citronella, but you'll be glad of that. Especially if the infamous Scottish midgies decide to invade."

"Well, bugs or not, it's beautiful. Thank you Charlie. You did good."

"Ahhm, well, there was a fair bit of self-interest involved. But it's my pleasure. Enjoy. Meanwhile, I need to get my butt over to the media centre. It's easy to get lulled into thinking this is a holiday. But I've got work to do I'm afraid. Hope you don't mind me abandoning you so soon?"

"No, honestly, it's fine. It's me who feels guilty. While you're working, I intend to curl up in that bed and catch up on some sleep."

"If you can," laughed Charlie, nodding towards outside where random booms of music issued from speakers as the army of sound techs tuned the banks of equipment in front of each stage.

"Oh I can," she replied. "Once you've learned to sleep in the day, you don't forget."

Within minutes of Charlie's departure, she'd shucked off her shorts and t-shirt, pulled the sheet over her head and drifted off into the heavy dreamless sleep of the perpetually overtired shift worker.

15

Opening Night

Dallblane, Scotland - July 2019

As the sun finally lowered, plunging them into glorious Scottish twilight, Layla made her way to the front of the media pit. The music enveloped her, the musicians so close if she'd stretched out a hand she might almost touch them. Although not quite. Being short had serious disadvantages, with the massive main stage looming above her. But it was better than out there in the midst of the crowd, where every person was a giant blocking her view. And there were thousands of them, a surging sea of people swaying to the beat, upturned faces alive with the thrill of live music.

Instinctively, her own body moved in time to the sound, a catchy pop tune, but she couldn't really dance properly. Not surrounded by photographers jostling to catch the shot; the one that would be the moneymaker. They wouldn't take kindly to being elbowed by some tiny chick bopping next to them. Charlie stood further back, fiddling with her gear, analysing light, and selecting lenses with a practised eye. She already had enough shots of this boy band. They might be the darlings of thousands of teen fans, but not to the audience Charlie's media clients catered for. Like Layla, she waited for the next act, apportioning her time to preparation.

The Destitute had rocketed up the charts and seemed destined to wrestle with the likes of Coldplay and U2 for the title of biggest band in the world. Playing two sets over the five days, bookending the festival with their star power and musical genius, they were the real draw card here. Charlie was determined to leave with their magic captured on film. Tonight she'd do stills, and on the final night video. That's where the really big money was now. And Charlie had shifted her skills effortlessly from the photography where she'd cut her teeth to film. Despite her success, she was never satisfied that she'd truly made it, always seeking her next goal. Right now, it was to make music documentaries. And she'd chosen this festival as the subject of her potential debut.

When the set ended, Layla made her way back to where Charlie stood, now calm, a camera slung over each shoulder, that aura of quiet confidence surrounding her. She was ready.

"They weren't too bad were they," she said, nodding at the stage, where crew scurried removing the band's gear, making way for the real stars of the evening line-up.

"No, they certainly got the crowd warmed up," Layla replied, looking out at the sea of people clustered ever more closely as more poured into the area in anticipation of the next act.

At first she thought she imagined it; as if by wishing he was here with her, enjoying this experience, her crazy brain had conjured him. She watched as the man weaving his way purposefully through the crowd got closer. He paused here and there to offer polite apologies to some who questioned the right of a latecomer to aim for a place near the front. One man took an aggressive stance, and looked like he might stand staunch in blocking the way, but then gave way as the sandy-haired man gave a nod in her direction, waved and smiled at her. Will threaded his way through the crowd.

She turned to Charlie, understanding the smug smile plastered across her friend's face. She expected him.

"Surprised?" she said. "Now you know why you needed a separate tent. Hearing you two going at it through the walls is bad enough, but sharing a tent after you've been apart for months, well…"

After what seemed like forever, there he was, only a metal grill separating them. He grinned at her, clasping her hands tightly across the barrier fence. It was like prison during visiting hours, close enough to make contact, but unable to fling herself against him with all the joy surging in her veins.

"So, when you phoned last night…"

"I was at Heathrow," he said. "Caught the train up today. Don't be mad at Charlie. I swore her to secrecy. She made all the arrangements at this end." She was still speechless. Will, here. The delighted shock stretched her mouth into a wide smile. "So, the rest of the week here, I have two weeks in London at the clinic and then I'm going to make good on that promise and take you to Europe. And after that…" He looked at her a little sheepishly, as if unsure of her reaction. "Well, they've offered me a couple of months at another specialist cardiology clinic in London. They're doing some really innovative stuff. Mark thinks I could learn a few things to take home with me."

"But, what will I do?" she said, feeling a small surge of panic coupled with immediate guilt for focusing on herself rather than his opportunity. There were times like now that she saw a return of that old glimmer of excitement in his eyes. She wouldn't deny him anything that might arouse his passion once more. And there was no longer any urgency for her to get back to New Zealand.

It had disappointed her when the position down at Clendon evaporated, and she was saddened by the reason. Layla had planned to take the place of a lovely GP, but a miscarriage had rocked the woman's excited plans for maternity leave. That phone call had been heartbreaking, and Layla's own thwarted plans seemed trivial in comparison. But she shuddered at the thought of more shifts in a frantic London ED. No, last Monday night's hideous stream of patients had hardened her resolve to put a full stop on emergency medicine for good.

"Well, what's wrong with taking a couple of months off? God knows you've earned it being back in the ED again." Even from a distance, he understood how this stint had really taken it out of her. No amount of bank holiday weekend jaunts to France, or a week in Greece with Charlie, could erase the exhaustion or take away the frustration of working in a busy London ED. "Besides, the idea of making you a kept woman has always appealed." Seeing how her face blanched at that, he quickly added, "Sorry, just joking, love." Yes, he should know better than to joke about it. Virginia and Hilton had always harboured the screwed-up idea that once she'd married Will, she'd revert to her base nature, living an idle life on the strength of his money.

She brushed it aside, desperate to be with him, feel him wrap those strong arms around her from behind, protect her from the crush of the crowd.

"I'll come through," she said, already freeing her hands from his as she prepared to head for the security gate. "The Destitute are on next."

"Glad I got here in time. No wonder all those guys were pissed off with me pushing my way through."

There was a tap on her shoulder. Charlie's long fingers appeared. "Hate to break up your happy reunion, but Layla, there's been a message passed along through the stage crew. They're looking for a doctor. Backstage."

"Go on," he said. "I know you want to. Who knows, maybe Mick Harrison needs a bit of personal attention. This lot will riot if he's not on stage as scheduled."

Well, tempting as that was to get up close and personal with a rock legend that sent women all over the world to mush with his oozing sex appeal, there was only one man she wanted to be with right now. And he stood on the other side of that barrier.

"But surely there's someone over in the camping area they can call. After all, they've got a full medical centre set up there?"

"Don't know," said Charlie. "All I know is they said it's urgent. That guy over there came from backstage and I overheard him talking to security. I told him I knew someone."

"It's OK," Will said. "Go. I'll wait for you here. We've been apart almost four months, I can hold out another hour. Just." Those months had been so hard she didn't know if she could survive another hour. Not now he was here. She was torn. She wanted to do more than hold his hand across the fence. To tuck in underneath his shoulder, to press herself against his familiar body would be a balm to heal the scars of all those demoralising shifts. And if she was honest, she wanted to stay and listen to The Destitute as well. Although they had another set on the final night and that would be the big one, they were the sort of band that no one in their right mind would pass up an opportunity to hear.

"Go," he repeated softly. "I'll be here."

"OK," she said, placing a kiss on her finger and touching it to his lips. "Don't go away. I'll be back as soon as I can."

A young man in stagehand uniform of black jeans and t-shirt led her along the side of the stage and then off into a plywood tunnel lit by bare bulbs. When they emerged into the open air, she realised they were now up against the wall of the castle itself. She stopped for a moment, raising her eyes to the sky, thinking how pretty the first stars were, like tiny brave candle flames trembling with the effort of holding back the creeping darkness. The light breeze caressed her face, and she closed her eyes, drinking in its refreshing touch after being in the huddle of the pit. And on that breeze, also came the low thrum of the massive crowd, like the buzz of an industrious hive.

But beyond that was yet another sound—one she couldn't identify. At first she wrote it off as feedback, a gremlin in the massive sound system. However, rather than from the stage area behind, it seemed to come from the direction of the dark trees that fringed this side of the castle. She peered towards them, as the young man, not realising she'd halted, disappeared around the curve of the wall. It was an eerie noise, as if some stray musician, on discovering an ancient instrument, now experimented with the sounds he might coax from it.

It grew in intensity; the sound magnified to where it assumed physical presence, a giant hand propelling her forward, her body a tiny plaything powerless against its force, pinning her against the castle wall. Blood rushed to her head. The frantic pulse throbbed with violence in her temples as the sound intensified to the point of pain. And all the while, the relentless assailant pressed her harder against the brutal stone. She tried to scream back a challenge, refusing to submit, but no voice came. And at that point, when she had lost all hope of fighting this invisible enemy, an unexpected ally intervened on her behalf. The deafening cacophony announcing the arrival of the loudest rock band on the planet boomed from the speakers, the almighty roar of the crowd obliterated by its power, at the same time swamping the thunder surrounding her. Layla slumped to the ground, letting the familiar music wash over her, welcoming its rough caress.

Part Two

THERE

16

Drugged

Dallblane, Scotland - July 2019

"Oh, God, that's all we need. Another passed out druggie."

Layla recognised the pissed off tone in the man's voice, despite it almost being drowned out by a sudden angry explosion of drums. The wave of sound was familiar: The Destitute. She'd recognise that beat anywhere. The loudspeaker boomed a welcome to the band. She pictured them striding onstage, with low-slung jeans and bare muscular arms; the very picture of rock-gods. Powerful guitar riffs echoed across the valley as lead singer, Mick Harrison, launched into the opening song of their set. The sheer force of the music drowned out any last remaining threads of the other hideous sound that had momentarily held her in its disturbing grasp.

"Hey. You. Wake up." The man, closer now, crouched low, leaning over her. A hand clasped her shoulder, shook her roughly. Her mind still whirled in confusion. She lay there for a moment, unsure of what had happened, uncertain of how to respond. Seeing her lack of movement, he stood up, leaving Layla lying on the hard ground, paralysed by her tangled thoughts. She heard other footsteps approach, a click of female heels that stopped beside her.

"Shit. I suppose we'll have to do something about her, too." The woman's voice sounded equally unimpressed. "As if we haven't got enough problems."

"God knows how she even got past security." He was Scottish. Not the broad accent of some she'd met. You almost needed a translator for the nurse from Glasgow she'd worked a few shifts with. No, this was a softer, rolling cadence, almost soothing.

"Yeah. So much for all their promises: 'we can assure you there will be no public beyond the barriers'. That's what they said, and here it is day one, and already they're getting through." This woman was seriously pissed off. Perhaps it would be wiser to pretend to be unconscious. "Can't be much of a barrier if a tiny thing like her can just waltz on by. Especially in her state. You think one of them would have noticed."

"Any sign of that doctor?"

"No. She should be here by now. Vic said they'd found one in the media area. A woman. Not sure why a doctor was in there with the journos. But where the hell is she?"

A doctor. A woman doctor. That was her. Layla opened her eyes with a start.

"Me," she said. "The doctor. It's me."

"Sorry love. The doctor's not coming for you," said the woman. She stared down at her, arms folded across her chest. Layla's eyes met hers and read a total lack of concern there.

"No," she said, dragging herself into a sitting position. "I don't need the doctor. I *am* the doctor."

"Yeah and I'm the Prince of Wales." His smirk was unkind. It marred an otherwise attractive face. Dark eyes. A tumble of shoulder length hair to match. Sweet, full lips, but such a mean tone.

Anger flared, and she found the strength to leap to her feet.

"Look, you pompous little prick. You said you need a doctor. My name is Layla Angell. *Doctor* Layla Angell."

He grinned at her now. "Layla Angell... come on, no offence, but it sounds more like a film star. And you don't look like one of those either." He cast a pointed glance at her inked arms.

Layla felt her tiny body physically grow as a crescendo of anger surged through her and came crashing from her mouth.

"Well, fuck you!" she said and turned to walk off. But the niggling thought of that sworn oath, the oath she'd never taken lightly, wouldn't let her go. She reeled back to face him. "So sorry that my name doesn't fit your narrow-minded view of the world. But I can assure you that I'm not only a doctor, but a bloody good one. I'm an ED specialist, but hey, if you'd rather look for another more stereotypically satisfying one, that's fine by me. I'd much prefer to be back with my friend enjoying the concert than having this unpleasant conversation with a jumped up little creep..."

"OK, OK," he said, raising his hands protectively as if he thought she might hit him; a good call on his part because she really felt like giving him a slap. "I'm sorry, but you'll have to forgive me for assuming otherwise. After all, when you send for a doctor, you don't expect to trip over them passed out on the ground." His eyes flickered across her tattooed arms. "Nor do we normally see such, ah, extensive art work on our doctors around here."

She hesitated a moment. He had a point. What the hell had she been doing on the ground? She knew it must have something to do with the sound that had swamped her as she stepped out of the exit from the backstage tunnel. And the fear and disorientation that had seeped out of the air, joining with the noise, surrounding her, twisting and turning to ensnare her. She remembered falling to the ground, seeking to escape the noise and the sickening sensations. But they were gone now. She was needed. And she must get a grip on herself. She couldn't lose face in front of this man.

"Look," he said, his voice taking on a conciliatory tone. "I really am sorry that we got off to such a bad start. But if you are indeed a doctor, then I can assure you, you are very much needed. Please, I'm Finlay McGill. Finn. This is my sister, Star."

The woman inclined her head a little in a polite, even respectful nod. A look of curiosity had replaced her previous disinterested expression. Layla had seen it before. It intrigued Star that someone who looked like her could be a doctor. Layla was equally intrigued that someone dressed like Kate Middleton could be called Star. But she'd seen almost everything, so allowed her doctor's face to mask her surprise.

"If you'd be so kind, Doctor—Doctor Angell, come this way." He was all charm now, but she also sensed an undercurrent of agitation. She followed him, the glow of his white UB-40 t-shirt making it easy for her to do so in the semi-darkness. They made their way around the outer wall of the castle, the woman shadowing her.

"So what's the emergency? What am I needed for?"

"It's our brother," said Star. "We don't know what's wrong. He's not doing well. We need you to help him."

Layla had absolutely nothing with her. Just her hands and her experience. And the rush of adrenaline that she knew would come in the face of a tricky situation.

The young man, Finn, led her through a low wooden door in the stonework. Its aged appearance gave it the look of something from a fairytale. The creaking sound as it swung open and clanged shut behind her grated on her still jangling nerves. In here, beyond the thick walls, even the sound of The Destitute was muted.

Finn guided them along a series of narrow wood-panelled passageways, dimly lit by small tapered wall lights; electric, but cleverly made to look like wall sconces from hundreds of years earlier. It was as if she'd stepped onto the set of a horror movie and she felt uneasy at the thought, ridiculous as it was. With Star still close behind, there was no option to turn and run. The only way was forward.

Layla let out a breath of relief as they finally stepped into an enormous hallway. A massive chandelier suspended from the centre of its cavernous ceiling gave off a brilliant glow, lighting every corner of the space. A wide central staircase at one end disappeared upwards into the gloom beyond. Doors and more passageways surrounded them.

"This way," said Star. She turned a highly-polished brass knob and pushed open one of the tall wooden doors. Layla stepped into a room to find three walls completely covered with shelves. Each shelf was filled with books, some old, others newer, all jostling for room in the crowded space. It was the most books she'd ever seen in one place outside of the university library. A heavy set of drapes suggested windows in the other wall.

Finn looked over his shoulder before quickly closing the door behind them. Leather furniture clustered in the centre of the room, wide armchairs and comfortable sofas. On one sofa, a man lay sprawled, one arm hanging over the side. Long, slender bare feet poked out stiffly from under a throw rug. Like Finn, his hair was shoulder length. But whereas Finn's wild locks had the careless grace of a model from a *Men's Health* magazine, this man's hair hung lank. A few long strands lay plastered over his brow. Beneath them, his face had a sickly grey pallor. Even from a distance, she could see the sheen of sweat on his skin. His breathing came in short pants, like a woman in labour.

An older woman sat on a chair pulled up next to him. Her dark hair, with its prominent strands of steel grey, hung in long loose waves almost to her waist. The bohemian-style dress of flowing black hung loosely on a thin frame. A chunky crocheted shawl of undyed wool sprawled over her shoulders. Now, if *she'd* said her name was Star, Layla wouldn't have been the least surprised. It was as if the music festival organisers had somehow transported her through time from Woodstock to lend an air of authenticity.

The man on the sofa let out a low moan. Only the one and he appeared to slip back into unconsciousness. The woman reached for his hand, clasping it in her own. Layla noticed the bands of silver, some plain, some ornately engraved, a stack that made its way up the length of her forearm, and jangled as she moved. There were definite hippie vibes radiating off this woman, alongside palpable waves of distress. She turned her head to acknowledge Layla, a pleading look in her eyes.

"This is my mother," said Finn. "Patti McGill."

She could see it before he'd even said the words. Star, Finn, the man on the sofa, the woman on the chair, their resemblance to each other was striking; the same almost heart-shaped face. And the three sets of eyes studying her confirmed it; all the same deep mahogany, but at this moment there was no warmth in their depths. Rather, each wore an identical look of fear.

"Mum, this is Layla. She's a doctor. She's going to check out Euan for us." His voice was soft as he took his mother by the hand. He led her gently to one of the generous armchairs, leaving Layla to take a closer look at her patient.

"Mrs McGill, I'm afraid I haven't got my things with me, but I've worked a lot of years in an ED, so I can at least assess what might be the next steps needed to help your son."

"Thank you," said the woman. "Thank you for coming." She forced the words out between tense lips, her voice barely a whisper. Even so, Layla detected the distinct and surprising trace of an American accent. It made this woman seem even more out of place in the library of a Scottish castle.

"Can you perhaps tell me a little about what's happened here? Anything you saw? Anything you know that might have led to this?"

Layla caught Finn's slight shake of his head as his eyes flashed a warning in Star's direction. But she'd missed it, her focus totally on her mother.

"When I found him," said Patti McGill, "he was on the floor having some kind of seizure. I was so frightened. His eyes rolled back in his head, his legs and arms rigid. And his body was shaking. Out of control. I know they say you shouldn't do anything if someone's having a seizure. Just make sure they're safe. So I moved a chair aside, stayed with him. Called for help."

"That was exactly right," said Layla, her voice reassuring. "You did the right thing."

Layla methodically checked the man. His pulse raced. His temperature appeared elevated. But otherwise, there didn't seem to be any obvious signs of anything like a stroke or heart attack.

"But your son's not epileptic?"

"No, no. Well, not that we know."

"Any other medical conditions?"

Patti hesitated a moment. "He's recently been diagnosed with a heart condition. Inherited. It's what caused his father's death."

"HCM—hypertrophic cardiomyopathy," said Finn. "There's a fifty-fifty chance of it being passed on. But Euan had some tests. He's positive for it."

"I know of it," said Layla. "But I'm fairly sure that's not what's going on here."

And she was also fairly sure she knew what had caused Euan McGill's seizure. She'd seen enough people come into the ED with these symptoms to recognise it. Maybe an addict, or given the woman's revelations, perhaps his attempt to numb the pain of a terrible diagnosis.

She'd lived that situation and understood it. She remembered her friend Will's struggle, back in those first days of his brain cancer diagnosis, the excess of alcohol, an attempt to block out the unthinkable. Thinking of his out of character behaviour, a cry for help to summon his friends to rally around him, she felt slightly more charitable towards the man in front of her.

"No." Star confirmed it. "It's *not* the heart condition. And it's about time we stopped wasting your time and come clean. It's drugs. Euan's taking drugs."

Patti hung her head, eyes closed, rocking forward on the chair, as if she'd considered that possibility, but had been in denial. Finn's eyes flashed angrily in Star's direction. But then, seeing Layla's gaze on him, he pulled the mask of composure back over his face and sighed in resignation. *Idiots*, Layla thought. *As if I wouldn't find out, anyway.*

"So then I have to ask, if it's drugs, why did you call me?" she said, loosening the man's shirt. "Why? When the medical centre over there is well-prepared for patients suffering drug overdoses. It's one of the first things they set up for a music festival."

"Look," said Finn. "For reasons which you won't understand, we can't take Euan over there. Or call their medics over here. So, can you help him?" He lifted his chin, his expression challenging—challenging her to put her judgement of them aside, and help his brother. And she must. She'd taken an oath to do exactly that.

"I can help him, but not as well as they can. Must be some pretty big reason that you'd put your brother's life in jeopardy for it." Layla's disbelief turned to anger. "And believe me, while I think he'll pull through, and I will do my best to make that happen, it's a stupid decision to not seek more specialised assistance."

"Only stupid to people who don't know what's behind it."

"Right," she said, ignoring his retort. There would be time to sort out Finn McGill later. For now, she had his brother to deal with. Fortunately, while the seizure had obviously been frightening for his mother, Euan was in reasonable shape. His pulse was already more regular, his breathing settling. She'd like to get that temperature down, though.

"I need something to cool him," she said. "Ice pack, a bag of ice, anything frozen will do. Maybe a few facecloths, tea towels, even a pillowcase. Chilled water maybe?"

"I'll go," said Star, placing a reassuring hand on her mother's shoulder as she passed.

Layla assessed the man lying before her. Fortunately, the sofa was enormous, so there'd be no need to move him for now. But she didn't like him lying there like that. His head thrown back meant the airway was already partly blocked. And if he was to vomit, things would get ugly very fast.

"Finn, you can help me. I want to get him into the recovery position. In case he vomits. Aspirated vomit and we'll be needing the ambulance, no matter what."

She could have done it herself, but Euan was tall. It was all in the technique, but help would be welcome. Together, they adjusted the big man's position until she was satisfied. She placed one hand on his forehead. It was still too warm. With relief, she turned to see Star, arms filled with a selection of items. Layla grabbed a pillowcase, tore open a bag of ice, and poured it in.

"Finn," she said, "any chance you can crush this a bit?"

"Not with my bare hands," he said. "But this will do it."

He grabbed a heavy iron poker from beside the enormous fireplace in the centre of one wall, took the pillowcase, laid it on the hearth, and bashed it with strong rhythmic strokes. Now more malleable, he handed it back to her, and she folded it carefully, laying it across the still unconscious Euan's brow.

"Do another," she said.

She wrapped the second bag of ice underneath his neck. His colour was already improved. The panting had subsided and his breathing, although a little raspy, was regular. She placed a finger along his throat. Euan McGill's carotid artery throbbed, the pulse strong but measured. He was bloody lucky that whatever he'd taken, he'd likely have no lasting effects. Despite his family's lack of commonsense.

As if they too contemplated this, the room fell silent, no sound except Euan's breathing and the crackle of a fire in the hearth. Not ideal for bringing Euan's temperature down, but welcome for the rest of them. Although the sun lingered late in this part of the world during summer, the evenings were chilly the moment it disappeared.

The door swung open and a tall, thin, soberly dressed woman entered. She balanced a large tray, and the tantalising smell of coffee drifted across. The aroma alone reminded Layla that she'd had nothing to eat or drink for hours. They'd had a snack in the media area around five o'clock, but now it was nearly ten. She was pleased to see a plate of chunky sandwiches, looking oddly out of place surrounded by a silver coffeepot and dainty cups.

"Thanks Isabel," Finn said as the woman arranged the things on a side table, and deftly poured the coffee without spilling so much as a drop. "Mum, here, take this," he said. Patti, slumped with her head in her hands, looked up at him with a grateful smile. The cup rattled against the saucer as she took it in her unsteady hand.

"Milk? Sugar?" he said, picking up a second cup and offering it to Layla.

"Yes, to both." She needed this caffeine and sugar hit.

He passed it to her, along with a delicate plate dwarfed by the thick sandwich he'd placed on it. Between two crusty white bread slices, Layla glimpsed golden pungent-smelling cheese and a generous slice of ham, and her stomach growled in anticipation. She had just swallowed one large mouthful, washing it down with a slug of coffee, when coughing sounds from the patient caused them all to turn and stare. Euan was stirring.

She dumped the cup and plate on the side table, moving closer to her patient. He moaned a little, his head twisting towards the light, eyelids flickering. This was a good sign. Consciousness returning. It seemed he'd had a lucky escape. Thank god. If his condition had worsened and it had forced them to seek proper medical care, she would have had some embarrassing explaining to do. They'd have rightly questioned her competence, having treated him herself, alone.

She leaned in a little closer, hoping he'd open his eyes fully and she might observe the pupils' reaction to light. One hand reached for the phone in her back pocket. Its torch app would be perfect for the job.

Afterwards, she cursed her lack of caution. It should have been instinctive, drilled into her throughout long hours of clinical practice in the ED. It was the mantra of every text written for first responders: think about yourself first, don't put yourself in the way of danger. But somehow, here, in these most unusual circumstances, perched on leather armchairs in a library straight out of a period drama, drinking coffee from stylish cups and eating sandwiches served on expensive china, she forgot to keep herself safe.

Euan, without warning, flung one huge arm into the air as he rolled himself onto his back, catching her unawares. She had no time to react as his tensely clenched fist caught her on the temple. For the second time that night, Layla found herself lying on the ground. This time, the only sounds she heard as she slipped into black oblivion were the gasps of the stunned family.

17

Guardian

Dallblane Castle, Scotland - July 2019

LAYLA AWOKE TO THE sound of snoring. Not loud, aggressive snoring that shook the room. More of a rhythmic snuffling. Still, it felt disturbing, hearing the noise but not having the least idea who it came from.

Just as disconcerting was her discovery that lying here, the one visible part of the room was an unfamiliar dark wood-panelled ceiling above her. She was trapped in a strange cocoon. When she twisted her head to either side, heavy curtains obscured the view. And that simple act of turning her head triggered awareness of a dull throbbing ache in one temple. She drew one finger across it, tracing the extent of a large lump and noting a sharp stab of pain despite her gentle touch.

She sat up, finding a door of the same heavy wood as the ceiling centred in the distant wall. This was the largest bedroom she'd ever seen. And this was possibly the largest bed she'd ever slept in. But she recognised neither.

The snoring noise came from her right, and she whisked back the curtains. Sitting in a large wing-backed armchair, feet propped on a velvet ottoman, was the sleeping form of Finn McGill. The name came unbidden, but she was still hazy as to why she would even know it. His chest rose and fell in time with the whistling intake and exhale of his breath. Her brain whirled; words, images, people and she struggled to sort out the reality from the possibly imagined.

Lying back, she closed her eyes, took five deep calming breaths before going through the previous night methodically, starting from the last thing she remembered: leaving Charlie behind in the media area as she responded to the call for a doctor. From that recalled moment, the rest tumbled forth. Trailing this man and his sister around the castle walls and into the dark passageway; in a library, the distraught Patti McGill near to tears over her other son; and drugged out Euan McGill unconscious on an antique leather sofa. Bloody Euan McGill who'd repaid her care of him by knocking her down with an elbow to the head.

She sat up again, surveying herself and her surroundings with renewed interest. Still dressed in the singlet top she'd been wearing yesterday, she found to her distress she was missing her jeans and the cotton overshirt. God, had Finn undressed her and put her to bed? It surprised her how much it bothered her that a virtual stranger might have lifted her unconscious body, removed her clothes and tucked her into bed. After all, many of her patients had endured exactly that. But they'd suffered this fate at the hands of trustworthy medical professionals, not the second son of some Scottish landed gentry.

The least embarrassing solution would be to collect her things and leave. She slipped lightly onto the vibrant Oriental rug, creeping towards her clothes with careful steps, while keeping one eye on the sleeping man. That was her downfall. Just as she extended a hand to retrieve her jeans, she stumbled. Glancing down, she saw she'd tripped over her burgundy Doc Martens. The noise was enough to startle Finn from sleep.

She had to admit his tousled curls and velvet brown eyes were rather handsome. As was the smile that spread across his boyish face, a promising warmth radiating from it, like the first brush of morning sun on her skin. Attractive enough that, although right this minute he had her at a disadvantage—he fully clad, having slept in his clothes while she stood there in little more than underwear—somehow she relaxed and let it go.

She struggled to understand how this man, who she should really have despised on sight, could so easily disarm her with only a smile. After all, her own upbringing had cultivated a serious distrust of the moneyed classes. Time spent in the company of some of her wealthy friends' families had reinforced it. And here in the UK it was even worse: these people held their wealth and titles simply by virtue of their birth, prosperity built on the backs of people who for generations had worked that land, even fought for the owners. While it must be Euan who was at the top of the pecking order in this household, still Finn was a part of it.

But god, if there wasn't something about him that was absolutely, unequivocally enchanting. She shouldn't even be flirting with such thoughts about a man she'd barely laid eyes on. Fine, she was quick to appreciate a good-looking guy, but there it was, something way deeper than that: a high possibility that Layla Angell was already smitten with him, despite their rather rocky introduction last night.

"Good morning," he said, the smile broadening into a cheerful grin.

It was contagious. She found herself smiling in return, his natural charm overwhelming both the awkwardness of the situation, and the part of her that desperately wanted to dislike him, to hold last night's tense stand-off against him. That part of herself she was very familiar with. Charlie banged on about it all the time: "Give the man a chance Layla", "At least get to know him before you write him off".

It was her armour—assume the worst and you won't get hurt; and if by some chance you're wrong, it will be a pleasant surprise—and that armour had served her well. It had stopped her from repeating past mistakes. Like thinking guys cared for her, when all the time she was destined to remain firmly planted in their friend zone. Or plunging into unhealthy relationships where the risk of damage was high.

But now, with just one look, this man had shredded it. No, worse than that, he'd not even given her a chance to put it on. This was why she felt vulnerable—it wasn't simply because she stood here scantily clad with those velvety eyes upon her; the protective shield was out of reach, her defences were down, and while that should really disturb her, it didn't. She wanted to like this man and wanted to give him a chance. It was if she already knew enough about him to know he deserved it.

"Good morning," she said, grabbing at her jeans and shirt.

"Sorry," he said, looking a little bashful. "I thought you'd be more comfortable without those. Star helped."

"Yeah, I sort of remember."

She did now. Remembered walking slowly up the huge central staircase, supported by a person on either side. Remembered sitting on the side of this enormous bed, observing the top of Star's blonde head, as she crouched to unlace Layla's boots.

"So how come you slept here?" she asked, already suspecting the answer.

"Didn't want to leave you alone. Thought it was the least I could do. Given that you came here to help us out, not to get hurt. We put you in the recovery position." He looked at her hopefully, seeking approval at his application of his new first aid knowledge.

She peered into the mirror of an antique dressing table. Brushing back her curls to reveal a rather nasty bruise, she chastised herself for her stupidity. She should have been more careful with a semi-conscious patient still under the influence of drugs.

"That's a rather spectacular bruise," he said, standing behind her and observing her reflection. His stance appeared almost protective, but she tried to shrug it off. It was just that she barely reached his shoulder. Tall, dark and handsome—cliché, but damn if it wasn't true.

"Yeah," she said. "He got me a good one, that's for sure." She turned to face him. "How is your brother? Do you know?"

"Doing fine last time I saw him. Decided to leave him there in the library. We brought a bed in for Mum. She spent the night there. Checked in around three a.m. and they were both asleep."

She had a sudden horrible thought. "Oh God, what about my friend? Charlie? She expected me to come back to my tent. She might be worried."

"All taken care of," he said. "Sent a message back with the security guys. Said you would stay the night. And for breakfast. Which will be about now," he said, glancing at his chunky wristwatch.

"Thank you," she said. "The last thing Charlie needs is me getting in the way of this assignment. Particularly after she begged for an extra pass so I could hang out in the media area."

"You've got a good friend there," he said. "Came to check on you just after dawn, but I convinced her all was well, and she went away happy enough." His guarded smile suggested more lay beyond the "happy enough" and knowing that for Charlie, being sent away, it was probably just "enough". She'd not have been happy leaving Layla in the hands of strangers. It was best not to probe further.

"So she's a journo?" he asked.

"Photographer."

"Nice. I dabbled myself, but never good enough to make it more than a hobby."

"She started way back in high school. She's good. Even after a few months here in the UK, her work is in demand."

"Look," he said, "it's almost ten. How about I leave you to shower? There's a bathroom through there," he said, nodding at a door to the left of the bed. "Help yourself. And downstairs, opposite the library, you'll find the dining room."

"Thanks," she said, unable to summon the energy to be anything but agreeable.

A voice in her head told her she shouldn't be acting so damn nice to him. He'd dragged her away from a concert she was enjoying to make a house call on his drug-dazed brother when any normal person would have simply called the medics. But he wasn't a normal person. This wasn't a normal family. After all, they lived in a castle on a vast estate. They must be loaded. And that was what money did for you: gave you a sense of entitlement, a right to things that normal people would never dream of expecting.

After a shower and something to eat, she was going to tackle him about it. And then, to her surprise, she realised she wasn't. Yesterday's Layla was silenced, this new one dictating her moves. Maybe the bump on the head was messing with her judgement.

"See you soon," he said, pausing at the door to toss her another of those infuriatingly attractive smiles. "We can catch up some more over breakfast."

"We sure will," she said under her breath.

Feeling more human after a shower, Layla made her way down the staircase, following the rise and fall of voices and clattering cutlery. Already, the strains of music drifted from one of the side stages. Through the tall sash windows, a watery sun poked through the cloud cover. It looked like the forecast of another fine day was accurate.

Finn rose from the table as she entered the dining room, pulling out a chair and fussing to settle her at the place set. He'd changed too, the rumpled looking earlier outfit replaced, the dark freshly-washed hair hanging in damp spirals. With a loose denim shirt open over a white t-shirt and grey cargo pants, he exuded the same casual sexiness as the musicians who commanded the festival stage.

Opposite, Star greeted her with a smile, a warmth in those brown eyes that she hadn't seen last night. "Sorry, I was a bit frosty last night," she said in between nibbles of an English muffin dripping with butter. "To be honest, it was all too much—Euan being a dick on top of all the hassles with the festival."

"Hey, it's OK," Layla said, grabbing a muffin for herself, while the trusty Isabel appeared at her shoulder and poured tea into a floral cup. "It's not easy being the family of someone who's unwell. And I can only imagine what it's like having thousands of people camped on your doorstep for five days."

"Yes, well," said Star, with a pointed look at Finn. "Some of us didn't listen when others suggested it might *not* be a good idea."

"You know as well as I do why saying no wasn't an option." Finn's voice was weary, his eyes darting everywhere except to face his sister. "You see Layla, the truth is—"He took a deep breath and faced her directly. He licked his lips, swallowed, and pressed on. "—despite what you might see here, this family is broke. And unlike some people in this room, I'm trying to be creative in how we deal with that fact so we don't see our mother have to move back to the village with her tail between her legs."

Star crossed her arms and glared at him. "I guess you weren't creative enough." And with that, she left the rest of her half-eaten muffin and stomped out of the room.

"My apologies for my sister. You'd never guess that she's ten years older than me having seen that toddler tantrum."

"Families always have their differences."

"Yes," he said with an exasperated sigh. "And with Star not on board, and Euan incapacitated, seems like it's down to me to sort it out."

"Look, you don't have to explain," she said. After all, their business wasn't her business. "But I am curious—why didn't you just send for the regular medics last night? It seemed so odd, and I suppose I owe you an apology too as I let that question colour my handling of the situation. My bedside manner was a bit off and you deserved better."

"Well, I have no issue with what you did for us last night. We're—all of us—very grateful. But I agree on the other point. I do owe you an explanation." Finn glanced at his watch. "And I'll give you one. Give me quarter of an hour. I have the head of security coming to discuss the breaches yesterday and tell me what they've put in place to be sure it doesn't happen again. Finish your breakfast and we'll catch up after."

Mouth full of muffin, she nodded a mumbled agreement at him, and then sat surveying the room with its antique sideboards and heavy rugs underfoot.

He'd only been gone a moment when the dining-room door opened and the drawn face of Patti McGill appeared. The bruised skin under her dark eyes and their dull expression suggested she'd had little sleep. But at the sight of Layla, she summoned a smile.

She really was the most striking woman, even with the lines of age that creased her face and the streaks of silver in her hair. She still wore the same flowing dress she'd been in last night, reminiscent of Stevie Nicks, with its bell sleeves and layers of chiffon. The pointy toes of black suede boots that peeked from beneath it completed the picture.

"And how are you this morning?" she asked in a melodious voice, with American and Scottish vowels rolled into a sweet, lilting cadence. She stretched one hand to Layla's hair, gently revealing her bruised face. "If you like, I have something for that—a little tincture of arnica root. And I'll ask Isabel to make you some yarrow tea. That's if you aren't averse to alternative remedies. I know some doctors are not at all trusting of such things." She looked at Layla with a half-smile, quirking one eyebrow expectantly.

"Oh, no, I'm fine with all of that," said Layla. "You'd be fairly short-sighted not to recognise how many of our modern drugs originate from plant lore. But don't feel you have to go to any trouble."

"It's no trouble," said Patti, looking pleased at Layla's answer, and patting her hand. "It's the least I can do, my dear, after all you've done for us." She stood and called through a door opposite, "Isabel, have you got a moment?" and the willing Isabel appeared with a ready smile. "Do you think you could organise Layla some yarrow tea, please?" Patti asked. "I think there's a new packet in the pantry."

Finn returned as Layla downed the last of the mild-tasting tea, reminiscent of cucumber. There was also a greasy patch of hair hanging limp over the spot where Patti had smoothed arnica on her forehead.

Finn rested his arm gently on his mother's shoulder and placed a light kiss on her cheek. "Morning Mum. How are things upstairs?"

"Better than expected. He's awake and ordering people around, so I suppose that's a good sign. Star's up there now."

"Rather her than me," he said. "Mum, I'll take Layla for a walk out back. Show her the gardens."

Patti smiled up at him, not seeming to think that an odd thing to be doing rather than getting Layla back to her accommodation. "Nice day for it," she beamed while rummaging inside a pocket of her voluminous dress. "Perhaps stop by the herb garden? Cut a little of the yarrow for Layla to take with her," she said, producing a small pair of scissors that she pressed into his hand. "Just chop it up a little and steep it in boiling water for a few minutes," she told Layla. "Twice a day for the next few days."

Outside it *was* a beautiful day, the earlier cloud cover having burned off and the sun now high in a clear blue sky. The jaunty beat of a reggae band flowed from the main stage, and Layla was sure she caught a predictable whiff of marijuana accompanying it. She raised her nose like a deer sniffing the breeze. She'd always found its grassy smell pleasant, perhaps because it reminded her of home. Neither her father nor brothers were averse to the odd joint while kicking back on the porch on a summer evening.

Layla and Finn strolled on once-manicured lawns between unkempt topiary hedges and straggling roses in full bloom. Finn motioned to a stone summerhouse that faced a small fountain. The babble of water gushing from it was a pleasant counterpoint to the rhythmic music.

"So," Finn said with a weighty pause, "you must have thought you'd landed in a madhouse last night. But there is some method in the madness, I can assure you."

She couldn't help the smirk that slid across her face. "Yeah," she said. "It wasn't quite what I expected of my first invitation into a castle."

"Mmm," he said. "Yeah, the castle. That's sort of at the centre of the problem. Well, not so much the castle itself, but the title and the lands that go with it. Believe it or not, your patient last night was none other than Lord Euan McGill, the 15th Earl of Dallblane." Seeing her raised eyebrows, he added, "Yes, not very lordly behaviour."

"So, what does that make you?"

"Nothing special. If you were to bother with a title, I'm officially 'The Honourable Finlay McGill'. Not that I ever use it."

Layla couldn't help but let loose a giggle at that. "Sorry," she said. "It's not that I don't think you deserve to be called honourable. I don't know you well enough to make a call on that."

He smiled at that. "Well, I hope when you do get to know me better, I don't disappoint."

Was he flirting with her? It seemed like it and it wasn't unwelcome. He was definitely good-looking with those deep-set dark eyes. And that unruly bed hair falling over his face, begging her to stretch out her fingers and brush it back, or bury them in its depths. With that smooth unlined forehead, only the merest hint of laugh lines around his eyes, and small dimpled creases bracketing bowed lips, he was obviously young—not much more than twenty-five, definitely less than thirty. She hadn't dated younger men. And why was her wayward brain even putting Finn McGill into the potential date category?

"It's just kind of odd to meet young people with these big weighty titles," she said. "Remember, I'm from the colonies. We don't have any of your sort—hereditary titles don't exist in New Zealand. To be a 'Sir' or a 'Lady' you usually need to be over sixty with an illustrious career or a friendly politician cheering you on."

She thought of her friend Will's obnoxious father and his recent OBE for services to medicine. No doubt Hilton had his sights set on a knighthood before he was finished.

"Anyway," she went on, "I get it. You didn't want the papers getting hold of any stories about the Earl of Dallblane and his drug habit. Very honourable." Although she'd tried, she couldn't help the derisory note in her voice and she immediately felt bad, seeing him flinch at it.

"Yes, and no," he said, embarrassment blooming on his face. "Look, if it was only about Euan, I'd have no qualms about letting him take his chances, live with the consequences, but it's not as straightforward as that." He hesitated a moment and licked his lips before allowing them to relax in a nervous smile.

"Because?" she asked gently.

He took a deep breath. "To understand, you need to know a bit about us. My father—and Euan's—the 14th Earl died last year."

"The hereditary heart condition."

"Yes. If Dad had known, he might have made some lifestyle changes, had a few years more, but he didn't have the luxury Euan has in that respect. I'm sure he would have done a lot of things differently if he'd known. My father was very good at making money and even better at spending it. Hence the financial bind we find ourselves in. But it's not just the lack of money for upkeep of the place. He adored Mum, and he'd hate how his death has left her vulnerable. Now, without him here to care for her, it's fallen to us."

She frowned, confused at why his mother might need care. Patti had an innocent fragility about her, but she seemed perfectly capable of caring for herself. And capable enough to care for others too, such as organising herbal remedies for Layla's injury.

"No, she doesn't need that kind of care," he said, noticing the question in her eyes. "She's sixty-seven and fit as can be, a walking advertisement for all her healthy eating and herb lore. It's more protection she needs." She couldn't help but look even more surprised. Was there some shadowy Scottish underworld that wanted to harm Patti McGill? It sounded like a plot from a BBC crime drama. Things seemed to get stranger by the minute with this family.

"You see, when my mother arrived in the village, back in the eighties, a single mother with a wee girl, but even worse, an American, she was already a target for those who might judge her. We're way behind the times here. Close-minded when the rest of the world has moved on. These people will fight for you fearlessly when you're one of their own. But they're merciless when it comes to outsiders who don't fit the mould. I'm sure they thought they would drive her away. They made life difficult for her and anyone who helped in any way."

"So it's 'If you're not with us, you're against us' around here?"

"Exactly. They even made things very uncomfortable for the woman who gave her a job in the tea shop and let her a room upstairs. They never forgave her for providing Mum the means to settle here. But when the young Earl happened to fall in love and marry her, making her their countess, they were outraged. I'm sure some of them thought she'd put a spell on him."

"Well, your mother does have a touch of that 'Witchy Woman' vibe about her."

"For sure, but if she had the ability to enchant people, I'm sure she'd have used it to tame the villagers. She can do no right in their eyes. And they basically considered Euan and I to be devil's spawn. Oh, nothing to our faces. They are too respectful of the Earldom for that. Our family has a long history in this area and it's always been one of mutual respect. The Earls from way back always saw the village as their responsibility and the villagers mostly loved them for it. Growing up, we weren't bad kids, but like all kids, we made our mistakes. And any time something happened, the gossip always focused on Mum. Bad blood, tainting the noble Dallblane lineage."

"So, they'd blame her for Euan's sudden descent into drug use. If they found out."

"Yes, and there are too many locals who've picked up jobs around the festival. Too many eyes and ears. If we'd taken him to the medical centre in the festival grounds, word would have spread in minutes. And then by today, Mum wouldn't have been able to walk through that village without pointed stares and gossip behind hands. And she doesn't deserve it."

"Wow," she said, marvelling at this young man, admiring his devotion to his mother. This morning he was gentle and kind, but last night she'd seen another side of him: hard, determined; now she understood why. But this openness, the fact he'd shared all this so willingly with her, a virtual stranger, remained a mystery. Was it he felt the same odd sensation as she did—this inexplicable feeling they weren't strangers at all? "Finn, why did you tell me all this? You didn't have to."

"Lots of reasons," he said, swivelling to face her directly. She read nothing but honesty in that innocent expression. "Because you went out on a limb for us last night when most other doctors would have run a mile. You took a risk for us. I'm taking a risk with you. Because I trust you."

"That I'm not going to run off and tell all to the first journalist I meet in the media pit?"

"You wouldn't do that." He shook his head. His eyes, all-knowing, met hers.

"No," she said softly. "I wouldn't."

"When we sent them out looking for a doctor last night, I'm glad they found you." His lips dimpled in a small smile.

"Me too," she replied.

"OK," he said, breaking the gaze. He stood and extended a hand to help her from the seat. The brief connection sent a small arc between them. She felt it. Had he? Did he let her hand fall gently from his because of its presence? Or because of its absence? "A quick detour to the herb garden for that yarrow, and then we'd better be getting you back before that formidable Viking shield maiden comes banging on the door again, demanding your release."

"Oh, that's right," she said with a grin, "you've met Charlie." Of course, Charlie would have wanted more proof of life than a message from a security chief. Thank god for friends like her.

"Yes, when they summoned me to deal with her at six-thirty this morning, I must say it took all my charm to convince her we weren't keeping you prisoner for our own nefarious purposes, and she should let you sleep."

"No surprises there. I can assure you Charlie would have been completely immune to your charms." She tried to suppress a small smile, thinking he might have been better off sending Star out to hit Charlie with a charm offensive. However, as for herself, he'd totally charmed her with no effort on his part. In fact, she had to admit that she found Finn McGill rather bewitching. Maybe he'd inherited a little of his mother's skill and was drawing her to him with a spell. Or maybe it was more that she was a sucker for the kind open expression in those mahogany eyes that she could imagine losing herself in; or those spiralling curls a dark mirror of her own that begged her to twine her fingers in them; and sensuous lips—lips speaking to her right now.

"Layla, are you OK?"

"Yes, yes," she said, while still lingering in her dreamy reverie. "I'm great." And she was, considering there were five more days to find excuses to come back to the castle. "Just thinking about what I'll do today." It wasn't a complete lie.

18

Rhythm Of My Heart

Dallblane Castle, Scotland - July 2019

Finn's chest thudded with wild beats, as he lunged for the door. He'd managed to keep it together during the late morning meeting but now there was no holding it back. Droplets of sweat pearled on his upper lip, and he smeared them away with the back of his hand. He punched his code into the keypad and the unlocking mechanism replied with a familiar hum and click. The modern faceplate with its lit buttons in a bed of stainless steel was incongruous with the two-hundred-year-old door surround. So was the way the door swung open of its own accord, a faint whir providing a hint of the discreet motor driving it.

He plunged downwards into the bowels of the castle, the vicious teeth of his anxiety snapping at his ankles. Even the touch of the smooth oak panelling trailing under his fingers as he navigated the tight spiral staircase provided some immediate relief. But the small studio, behind a second door, was the refuge he sought. All would be well inside.

As he heard the quiet 'thunk' of the automatic door close behind him, the sounds of the main stage disappeared. No mean feat given the abrasive din of the heavy metal band out of Manchester that commanded the lunchtime slot. He felt a surge of pride at the way the line-up of bands was rolling out. He'd created that musical montage across five stages, from blues to punk to pop to metal, and a bit of reggae thrown in; as well as the main course of solid rock. He and Eric had assembled the team who had brought this crazy dream to life. They'd been ultimately responsible for fifty thousand people descending on this tiny corner of Scotland. And he'd been the one with the vision that this might manage to drag his family back from the edge of ruin.

But the source of his pride was also the trigger for this raging bout of anxiety. He'd expected it would happen. It would take a rare person to not experience even a little worry about how it all might play out. And for someone like him, who'd spent most of his life in this wary dance with the traitorous half of himself, moments of overwhelm were guaranteed. It was surprising he'd got this far before needing a quick trip to the underworld to still his mind. If it hadn't been for bloody Euan and his antics last night, he might have held out longer.

Thoughts of Euan, of course, compounded the tightness in his chest, as the nagging question pushed to the forefront—were these sensations simply the angry black dog that had pursued him all his life, making its snarling presence felt? Or did he too bear a ticking time bomb in his chest like his father and brother? Well, very soon he'd know the answer to that. Once the festival wrapped up, a visit to the London clinic would tell him, and hopefully, whichever way it went, there'd be more peace in knowing.

As he stepped through a second door, his presence triggered an automatic bank of LED lamps that illuminated the studio in a warm glow. He breathed deeply, the soothing wisps of sandalwood and lavender drifting in the air with each whispered puff from the diffuser in one corner.

As Finn settled at the drum kit, he offered his usual silent prayer of thanks to whatever god had delivered a small, scared teenager to a dour Scottish boarding school at the same time as Mr Anthony

Burrell. And that same god who had kept Anthony's seditious ideas about music under the radar for the entire five years of his time at Elsdon. Under a cloak patched from trombone and trumpet, violin and cello, Anthony's clandestine teaching of rhythm and bass guitar, pounding drums and wailing saxophone had fed boys hungry for a diet of music that would have appalled the conservative board of Elsdon School For Boys. By the time Anthony's deceit was uncovered, it was too late—a cohort of students, Finn amongst them, graduated from the school with the expected exemplary marks and an underlying passion for music that would change their lives. For Finn, it had saved his life.

He took up his drumsticks and, as always, with no conscious thought as to what he would play, he began. The ball of raging emotion that had gripped him started to unravel, its threads writhing around him, twisting and twirling, and then reforming, the beat of the drums directing them and shaping them into a thing of beauty, a glistening sphere of pure happiness. He tossed it in the air, an invisible plaything bouncing in time to the music.

With relief, he succumbed to the calming effect of the familiar rhythms, every part of his body, arms, legs, head, in blissful motion, while the frenzied thunder of his powerful strokes worked their magic, bringing stillness to his mind. And there in that quiet centre, the eye of a storm whipped up by the sound, the drumbeats swirling around him, was her. Layla Angell.

After the first little ping of surprise at seeing her there, he let himself relax with her image, taking time to explore it: the neatly formed contours of her face; full lips curved in a smile but also hinting of a determined edge; green eyes projecting kindness but a knowing competence; and a tumble of golden curls wildly at odds with her rather serious demeanour. He'd had moments like this before, when he'd pushed all the world aside, driving away the troubling thoughts to leave him with a calm singular focus. But it had always been an idea, or a place, or maybe a feeling of something he should do; never a person. What that meant, he wasn't sure; but later, as he switched off all the gear and made his way back up the stairs into the daylight, he was sure that he needed to spend some more time with her to find out.

It shouldn't be easy to find one tiny woman in a crowd of thousands. Especially as it seemed blondes outnumbered all the rest two to one. But using intel stored away from their conversation on the way back from the gardens, Finn was fairly confident where he might start. He'd enjoyed it when their discussion had diverted from his family woes to the subject of music. The light in her eyes when he'd broached the day's lineup shone brightest when he'd mentioned Dervla McBride. He headed for the Meadow Stage where, at this moment, the Irish singer's soulful voice wailed above the tight melodies of her band.

There must be hundreds of blonde women dotted in the crowd on the hillside, but only one had those distinctive tattooed arms, currently pillowed behind her head, as she lay back in the grass, eyes closed, a slight smile on her lips. With the afternoon sun playing across her face, her body relaxed in joyful appreciation of the music, it felt wrong to disturb her. And it was certainly no hardship to stand there and gaze upon her. It was as if some delicate exotic flower bloomed in the ordinary grass of a Scottish meadow, outshining the common wildflowers around it.

Standing sentinel while she slept last night had awoken something in him. The protectiveness he felt towards this angel who had dropped into his world, was more than concern that she'd been damaged by it. Yes, it had been his responsibility, as the only one in his family capable of watching over her, to stay by her side. But even if it hadn't been, he would have fought to be the one. The tenderness towards her that crept over him as he'd studied the tousled blonde curls and the curve of her small body under the sheets was unexpected. The relief at hearing the gentle hum of her breathing, a soft steady rise and fall, was not. And the thought that Euan had hurt her, although unintentional, still angered him. Perhaps more than it angered Layla herself. She seemed to have forgiven his great stupid lump of a brother.

Thinking of the previous night's events prompted a niggle of doubt. Her warmth towards him this morning had surprised him. Particularly since they'd got off to such a rocky start. What was it she'd called him? *A pompous little prick.* That was it. Fair enough. He deserved that. He'd certainly been acting like one. He hated that side of him that slid out at times. It was the anxiety talking, of course. But it didn't excuse it. And he had apologised this morning, explaining why he'd been so agitated. That didn't excuse it either. Maybe she was glad to put all that behind her and enjoy the rest of the festival. Maybe she'd be pleased if she never saw him again.

He replayed her last words in his mind, capturing how she'd looked at him as he pressed the carefully wrapped bouquet of yarrow into her hands: "Thank you, Finn. I suppose I'd better get back before Charlie has a meltdown." *Was there a hit of reluctance? Was she only leaving because she had to pacify her friend? Would she prefer to spend more time with him?* "But I'll see you later." *Not goodbye. Not see you tomorrow. Not sometime. See you later. As in today.*

But that only left him wondering if she'd merely been nice to him this morning out of habit, the politeness cultivated in her profession.

However, two things urged him towards her to find out. The first was the odd looks people cast his way. Seeing him standing there fixating on a woman lying on her own, unaware of his presence, he must look like some weirdo seeking an opportunity to prey on solo women. If he didn't move, someone might call security. The second reason was the bizarre way she'd found her way into his quiet place at the drums when no one ever had before.

As he wove his way through the maze of bodies towards her, this moment felt significant. He didn't want to stuff it up.

Others had left a respectful space around her, and he lowered himself to the grass. Sensing his presence, she opened her eyes, squinting up at him between the dark lashes.

"Hi," he said. "Thought I might find you here."

She rolled onto one elbow. "Finn," she said, a smile drifting across her face. "Yeah. Wouldn't have missed this one. She's freaking amazing."

"She is that," he said. "Couldn't believe my luck when she said yes."

She sat up at that. "So you mean you were a part of all that? Signing up the acts? Talking to people like Dervla?"

"Yeah," he said, feeling colour rise in his face. Admitting he was on first-name terms with known musicians provoked awkwardness in him. What if she saw this information as him grabbing an opportunity to brag? "Some of them. When it was people like her who we hoped wouldn't hang up on some random Scottish guy with an invite to a new festival, we tried to keep the costs down by going direct. With the big guns, it was all promoters and agents hammering it out. And sending us large bills for doing it."

"It's pretty ballsy," she said. "Aren't there easier ways to make money?"

"For sure. But when Eric came to me with this idea, I knew that it might not only be a good earner, but we could also create something special, something enduring. Call it vanity, I suppose, but yeah, we took a risk." She was right. He wasn't stupid. He'd had other options and now he felt a sudden need to explain why he hadn't taken them. "It certainly would have been easier to find some well-paid job and funnel money back into the estate. But, this—it feels like we're not just taking, we're giving something back."

"Nah, I get it," she said. "What you do in life, it has to mean something. That's why I became a doctor."

Their attention turned back to the stage as Dervla McBride launched into another song. He could feel the waves of enjoyment rolling off Layla, a genuine passion for the music evident in her intense focus.

"So you've actually spoken to her? Dervla?" she said, as the last haunting notes of the song faded.

"Yeah," he said. "I did."

"Wow," she said. "Not that I want to sound all fan girly. It's just that she always seems so nice in interviews and stuff. And so the fact she'd speak with you, give you a chance, confirms it. I like that."

"Yeah, me too. She's lovely. In fact, I'm supposed to meet up with them later. At the village pub. Would you believe they insisted on staying locally? Wanted to feel the local vibe."

He'd been running around like a blue-arsed fly so much, he'd actually almost forgotten about the softly-spoken Irish woman's invitation. She and her guitarist husband and the rest of the band had rented a cottage for a few days, rather than dropping in for their set and heading straight out of town after. He'd appreciated the invitation and wanted to go, but not for the reasons anyone else might expect. It was simply that talking music with musicians was like a drug and he'd been so busy with the festival organisation these months; he hadn't had a fix for ages.

"You want to come with me?" He saw the immediate flash of interest in her eyes. "As long as you don't tell anyone. Like your photographer friend. I'd hate Dervla's down-to-earth approach to her growing celebrity result in an impromptu media scrum."

She looked at him thoughtfully. "I'd love to. And yeah, no worries about Charlie. She'll be staking out the main stage tonight. Already over there now, playing with ideas and angles. I don't expect to see her before midnight."

"OK," he said. "It should be fun. And seeing the chemistry between Dervla and the band, to get behind the scenes with them will be fascinating." But not as fascinating as spending more time with this riveting woman. He felt a thrill of pleasure at having found an excuse to keep her in his company.

They may not have spoken during the last few songs, but there was a constant current of communication between them. Instinctively, they turned to one other with shared smiles of delight as Dervla's guitarist husband Brendan launched into a powerful riff. When the crowd sang along to a chorus, they joined in, their eyes meeting, the words of a song about finding unexpected love seeming eerily prophetic. Ridiculous really, to link lyrics about love to someone he'd met less than twenty-four hours ago. But it was as if the music had the power to strip away the layers from two strangers, forging a connection not bound by the normal rules of time.

When the band disappeared into the wings with their most famous song not yet played, they chanted and clapped "More! More!" side by side, their voices blending in strident demand. And during the inevitable encore, they both sprang to their feet and danced facing each other, their faces wearing identical grins of pleasure, immersed in the spontaneity of the moment. Finn had to make a conscious effort to lose himself in the music, otherwise he might have stopped and stared, simply to appreciate the sight of her lithe body captured by the relentless rhythm and the soaring lyrics raining down on them.

As Dervla McBride strode off the stage with a long "Thank you-uuuu Dalllblannne, see you next year!" they cheered and whistled in unison. He felt a surge of excitement. He wasn't sure if it came from the words "see you next year", echoing his belief that there would be a festival next year, or from this tiny woman with seemingly boundless energy leaping around beside him.

"Hungry?" she said, snatching up a denim jacket from the ground and arranging her cross-body bag. He tried not to look at the way the strap defined an enticing valley of cleavage between two pert breasts, and fixed his eyes on her face.

"Yeah," he laughed. "I haven't had a thing since breakfast."

"Me neither," she said. "God, those muffins were good, but I'm starving."

"So, nearest food?"

She laughed. "I thought you'd have every inch of this site memorised."

"No," he said. "I had a fairly long list of jobs, but food wasn't on it."

"Follow me. There's a whole row of food trucks down by tent city."

She led him on a winding pathway between legs and bodies and rugs, and it was certainly not an unpleasant task to keep his eyes focused on her neat little butt in white cut-offs swaying enticingly ahead of him. Down on the level, he fell in alongside her, realising how tiny she was. He wasn't exceptionally tall; at five-ten, even Star could look him in the eye. But Layla's head barely reached his shoulder, encouraging her to turn that pretty face upwards towards him as she spoke.

She chattered away, pointing out the path to her glamping tent, enthusing about the comfortable bed and her surprise at how clean the facilities were. In his position, he should have been taking in all this information, noting it down in the feedback files, storing it away for next year's planning. But all he could think of was how relaxed she was in his company, and how grateful he was that she seemed to have forgiven him for being such an arsehole last night. Grateful enough that he didn't attempt to dissuade her from the notion that ice cream was a suitable substitute for lunch.

"Mmmm, that is good," she said, arching her neck, eyes closed in rapture. As if that wasn't bad enough, watching her small tongue lapping at the ice cream while squeezing the giant Danish waffle cone in that dainty wee hand was doing something very dangerous to parts of him that were thankfully under the wooden trestle table. "I haven't tasted ice-cream that good since I left home."

"Tell me about home," he said. If he could distract her from the sensual pleasure of good ice-cream on a hot afternoon, it might ease the torture of observing it. "Auckland, right?"

"Yeah," she said. "What do you want to know?"

"Everything. New Zealand is an exotic destination to me," he said. "Apart from Europe, because it's basically on our doorstep, my travels have been pretty limited."

"You and me both," she said. "Thirty-three years old and first time away from home."

At that, she dropped her head, and he caught the faint blush of embarrassment. She might be over thirty, but outside her doctor persona, she seemed younger. Perhaps it was this lack of worldly experience.

"OK, but New Zealand's meant to be a must-see country. So when you take me home with you, what will I see?" It was a leading question, but the slight raise of her brows coupled with a flirty smile made him glad he'd dared to step outside his initial cautious approach.

"Well," she said, playing along, "we'd rent a beat up old camper and do a road trip from north to south: volcanoes, mountains and lakes. And then I'd take you out to Piha Beach. I'd borrow a board from a friend and you could go surfing—some amazing waves."

"That would be quite the adventure. I can swim, but not being the most sporty person, I'm not sure how that would end. Possibly badly."

"OK, so if I didn't manage to drown you out surfing, we'd have a fish and chip dinner or a barbecue beside the beach with a cold beer to end the day. And then we'd turn in for the night listening to the sound of the sea." The thought of sharing a camper with her heightened the prickles of imagination he'd hoped to quell. "I'm sorry I can't offer a guided tour of the flash tourist spots or fine dining restaurants," she said, "as I've never been to them. But we'd have more fun my way."

"I've no doubt we would," he said, desperate to fix his attention anywhere but the lips that were now delicately slurping the melting mound of ice cream. His eyes drifted to her arms. Up close, the tattoos were visually stunning. Intricate foliage spiralled upwards from her wrists, morphing subtly into tangled ribbon swirls that echoed Celtic knotwork, before transforming back into delicate sprays of flowers and leaves that brushed the contours of her shoulder and neck.

"Yeah, I know," she said, noticing the direction of his gaze. "You told me last night—you're not used to doctors with extensive art work."

He grimaced. Fuck, his mouth had run away with him last night, in a most unattractive fashion. It was his turn to flush. "Yeah, sorry about that. I was a right arsehole. I can't believe you're even sitting here with me after that. Not a great first impression."

"It's not a problem. I'm used to dealing with highly stressed people. It goes with the job. And it's pretty usual for people to wonder why someone like me would be a doctor."

"Someone like you?"

"Well, yeah, all the tats for a start. But, also my family background isn't exactly fertile ground for producing professionals. Hell, most of them aren't even employed, let alone qualified. Even my parents suspect I might be a cuckoo in the nest. They're totally mystified that anyone would choose to do all those years of study."

He had been right about the determination he'd seen in her, and felt both admiration and a sense of camaraderie—bucking the trend, going for what she wanted. He could relate to that.

"At least they can't complain about its lack of usefulness like my family." That familiar morose assertion dropped out of his mouth without thought. He saw the immediate sharp arch of her brows, and her intense look of curiosity shifted to understanding.

"I gather they weren't impressed with your choice?"

"No. Neither of them." He already regretted airing more of the McGill dirty laundry in front of her. Now she'd expect an explanation.

"Which were...?"

"Conjoint degrees, BA in Music, BSc in Mathematics, then followed on with the MSc. The maths won in the end. Minimally more applicable to real life." He was proud of it; he'd worked bloody hard, maintaining a top GPA all the way through. Of course his mother had been effusive in her praise, but his father—well he'd expressed pride in Finn's achievements, beamed along with all the other families at his graduation, but beyond that moderated his opinions by the lack of obvious practical use of either maths or music beyond university.

"Ahh, I see," she said. "Looks like the music's still come in handy." She was right. This had been a chance to make something of the thing that meant more to him than anything. It was a shame his father hadn't lived to see it. "So you play, obviously?"

"Yeah, guitar, a bit of keyboard, but mostly drums." He saw her face spark with interest.

"Bonham or Moon?" she fired at him with a grin.

"Bonham," he shot back without hesitation. "I mean Moon was impressive, flashy, compelling; but Bonham gave every song that feel of motion. He—" He stopped for a moment, worrying he might be boring her with the details, knowing how his fervour on certain subjects wasn't always well received, but she looked as if she was hanging on his words, nodding in approval. "He carried the song and played his instrument as it was meant to be played."

"*Rolling Stone* and my dad would agree," she said. "Dad's kinda hung up on the axemen, as you might have guessed, given the name he insisted on for me, but John Bonham is one of his idols. As our entire neighbourhood would know."

Layla—of course, he understood—named for the mesmerising woman of the Clapton song. And how he could relate to that; her green eyes alive with a passion for life, he could lose himself in those eyes.

Her gaze flicked down to his chest, casting an appreciative look, and he felt a flush of pleasure at her scrutiny. As well as the drums, he'd thrown himself into the gym this last year, part of his self-imposed therapy. It was a pleasant thought that maybe all that lifting weights, beyond giving him a physical escape from his problems, had made sufficient difference to have an attractive woman notice.

"But it seems your loyalties might lie elsewhere," she said with a downward nod. He dropped his chin to his chest. It was the t-shirt, the huge Foo Fighters logo drawing her eyes, and he chided himself for his brief moment of vanity. "Dave Grohl, what a musician. I grew up addicted to Nirvana. Now—he's a man I'd love to see live."

He quickly recovered from the misinterpretation of her gaze, pleased to find another thing they had in common. This is how normal people built a relationship: found shared interests, established a friendship and grew it from there. Not through a sudden overwhelming connection with a stranger.

He'd been down that route before with his girlfriend, Niamh, and it had ended in disaster. So while he sensed he teetered on the edge, knowing how easy it would be to fall into something wild and unpredictable with this beautiful stranger, his newly emerged sense of self-preservation advised caution. He took a long moment, summoning enough control to lend a casual air to his next words, despite the thrill of possibility that gripped him.

"They're in Glasgow in August. Perhaps we could go together?"

The snug bar's dark interior, while cosy in winter, felt equally welcoming in the summer. With only one tiny bank of small high windows, it kept the heat of the day at bay, and now in the evening it remained pleasantly cool. The few locals clustered in the front public bar were oblivious to the fact that an X-Factor finalist and her band had taken up residence out back. And given that anyone young enough for that to mean anything was probably over at the festival, either taking up the discounted tickets for locals or in a paid role, Dervla was safe to relax and enjoy the evening.

Seeing Finn and Layla approach, she whispered to the two people opposite her and they made space in the booth.

"Finn," she said with a genuine smile. "So glad you could spare the time. I can only imagine how insane it is keeping all this under control."

"Yeah, but I'm grateful for an escape from the madness. I've been hanging out for this drink." He placed the handle of lager on the table and slid into the booth. Layla slipped in beside him.

"And you brought your lady with you, too. Hi there, I'm Dervla," she said, extending a hand in Layla's direction. He was about to correct the mistake, but caught a little tug of amusement as Layla threw a smile his way while taking Dervla's hand, and took it to mean he should let that misconception lie.

"I'm Layla," she said. "It's so great to meet you."

"Ah, another Kiwi," Dervla said, her eyes merry. "Well, wouldn't you know it, such a small world it is? See that big hairy brute over there—that's Josh, our lighting technician, all the way from New Zealand too. Picked him up at the Edinburgh Fringe a few years back and he's been with us ever since. Be sure to go over and introduce yourself. He's tamer than he looks."

Finn watched the two women naturally fall into conversation and was happy to take a back seat for a while. He sipped at the beer; the welcome freshness and hoppy aroma soothed his parched throat better than Layla's ice cream had. But as he sat, letting Dervla's Irish singsong voice wash over him, he drifted between the pleasure and pain it evoked.

An Irish accent would forever be wrapped in memories of Niamh. It was two years since they'd parted, but still the ghost of her velvety voice, the rhythm of the rounded vowels, a counterpoint to his own, still echoed in his brain. He'd loved her Irish lilt as much as she was captivated by the Scottish accent he maintained despite Elsdon's attempts to repress it. It was one way he'd fought back at school, holding tight to that which made him who he was. And with that, keeping the unexpected added charm he could wield with women by simply opening his mouth.

But as always, the pain of losing her quickly overran good thoughts of Niamh. She'd gone the way of the rest, burned by his searing intensity, unable to withstand being the sole object of a love so sudden and deep it had scared her. Only twenty, she was young, of course, too young to cope with such big emotions. It had scared him, too. Even the memories were still raw.

And now he sensed it might be happening again. He pushed Niamh back into the past where she belonged and focused on the delicious warmth of Layla's bare shoulder under his arm. In the crowded booth, it seemed less intrusive to loop it there rather than drop it to his side where it would brush the taut line of her waist, and trigger dangerous thoughts of allowing it to roam across the dainty curves above and below.

The slight sheen of sweat on his neck wasn't simply the heat of the crush. The small zap of electricity that teased each nerve in his body each time she moved against him, adjusting her body in time to the beat of her conversation, confirmed it: this petite New Zealander, her voice with its soft syllables, a hint of a drawl and a slight upward intonation at the end of each sentence as if posing a question, had him in her thrall. Even just listening to her captivated him. Yet he'd known her less than a day.

But if it was happening, if that crazy, all-encompassing need was about to consume him, this time it felt less risky. She was older. There was a core of something there, an inner strength, a worldliness. Sure, she claimed she had little experience of the world as a traveller, but she had experienced life and perhaps love, too.

She wasn't a naïve kid straight out of school like Niamh, twenty, briefly charmed by a twenty-six-year-old who'd seemed a man to her, so much older and wiser. In reality, he'd been just a kid, too. Now he certainly was older and wiser. Tempered by her loss, his father's death, the ensuing family turmoil and Euan's abdication of all responsibilities, he had become the de facto head of his family and stepped up to sort it out. Could this older wiser version of himself risk falling suddenly and irrevocably for a woman again? This woman, who now spoke to him while he stupidly gazed at her, hearing only an impression of the words.

"What? Sorry?" he asked, unsure of the question, but pretending he simply hadn't heard above the chatter of the group.

"I said, what do you feel like for dinner?" She waved a menu at him. "Apparently we need to order soon, as the kitchen closes at eight. Unless you're up for ice cream as a main meal twice in a day."

He took the proffered menu with a laugh. "I think some real food might be required to sop up the alcohol." It might have been the residual effects of the afternoon heat, but the beer had gone straight to his head.

"I don't know if some of this *is* real food," she said, her brows knotted in a cute frown that made his heart skip a beat. "I mean, what the hell is cullen skink? Where I come from a skink is a small lizard. I can't imagine there'd be much nutrition on one of those. You'd need a dozen for a meal."

As he laughingly explained that it was, in fact, a Scottish variety of fish soup, he marvelled again at the unexpected ease between them. Particularly considering their less than auspicious meeting last night. Anyone observing the way Layla leaned in to him, her face upturned, asking his opinion on the options, or noticed the casual way her hand slid over his and her playful smile as she informed him that she'd not hold it against him if he sat next to her with the haggis but she'd draw the line at tripe—well it would be easy for them to draw the same conclusion as Dervla: that this was a couple, relaxed in each other's company, at least a little backstory of mutual experiences, not two virtual strangers.

If there was already this sudden unexpected promise of something between them, it was far removed from the brutal lightning crash of connection he'd experienced with Niamh. This felt more like the lighting of a fuse, that was now burning relentlessly towards a point of ignition. And if it continued towards that end point, would it be a bright, beautiful burst of fireworks between them? Or an explosion where someone might get hurt? He knew his damaged heart couldn't take that hurt again. He'd barely escaped with his mind intact from the last. And such was this odd protective tenderness Layla evoked in him, the thought of seeing her hurt—or worse, him hurting her—was abhorrent. This time he would try to damp down that fuse, to a safe slow burn that would buy them both some time.

19

Rock My World

Dallblane, Scotland - July 2019

It would be difficult for a woman to resist the charm of Brendan McBride's Irish accent, except for one such as Layla, already under the spell of the Scottish man next to her. She felt powerless against the magic of Finn's easy smile and self-deprecating sense of humour.

And then there was the comfortable but thrilling pressure of his body alongside hers. In the confines of the leather-seated booth in the back bar of the village pub, she was acutely aware of how his arm casually draped across the back of the seat brushed her bare shoulder. The little tickle of the hairs as he moved slightly, sent a small ripple of electricity. Despite his attempts to appear casual, each time she noted how the contact between them triggered a similar tension in him. Although he didn't miss a beat in the conversation, she knew he was attuned to her every movement.

And the deep velvety rumble of his voice mesmerised her. Its mellow tone suggested Finn had more in common with their mutual idol, Dave Grohl, than his drumming. She'd love to hear him sing, watch him play, see other sides of the man who, for some indefinable reason, had caught her attention in a most unexpected way. The beguiling purr of his accent in her ear was simply one more item on a long list of Finn McGill's assets that she couldn't ignore.

Tonight, this asset was on full display during a lively debate as he and Brendan argued the merits of Irish whiskey with an 'e' and Scottish whisky without. They'd requested the bartender provide the means to settle this argument in a blind tasting, with Layla and Dervla obliging the two men by agreeing to act as the official tasting panel.

"I'm not sure I'm qualified to judge," she said, "given my experience is limited to Kentucky bourbon with a hefty dash of Coke." In fact, that had been her first encounter with spirits. In the Angell household refrigerator, RTDs lined up in neat rows, either JDs or Woodstock, always took priority over space for food. Her father's big old fridge in the garage held sufficient back-up supplies that he never missed a few when Layla and her brothers helped themselves. Assured that being a whisky virgin wasn't a drawback, she settled to the task. She and Dervla sipped at each sample thoughtfully, while Brendan and Finn watched, eager for the women to reach a final verdict.

"This one," Dervla said, carefully placing the tumbler back into its assigned place in the lineup.

"Yes," Layla agreed, "it's a no-brainer." There was no doubt the gold-hued contents of that glass, with their smooth warmth, were easily the winner.

Brendan waved the bartender over and he and Finn waited with bated breath for him to disclose the brands he'd poured in order.

"Of course," said Finn with a triumphant smile, when he revealed the victor was a Scotch. "Even better—it's practically a local. Mac-Farlane's is about forty minutes from here. You should take a drive over. Take some decent whisky home with you."

"Well," said Brendan, looking to the bartender, "looks like it's a round of MacFarlane's we'll be requiring."

Sipping at the alarmingly half full glass that appeared in front of her, Layla was enjoying it against her better judgement. Her advice to any patient knocked unconscious less than twenty-four hours ago would be to lay off the alcohol. But Layla ignored that advice. There was an undercurrent of something tonight that made her feel reckless. And it wasn't merely that she was already slightly tipsy from two beers and a sampling of whisky.

She already sensed she'd veered into dangerous territory. Aside from the sensual appeal of his attractive body with its musky masculinity tucked around her, Finn exerted an emotional pull, the unavoidable gravity of the person within drawing her into his orbit. And all the unfavourable memories of their first encounter last night—the instant flare of animosity towards him when he'd treated her so rudely while she lay sprawled on the ground at his feet, her irritation at finding his drugged out brother was the reason she'd rushed to their aide, and the frustration at his refusal to seek proper medical care—all that had evaporated with the dawn.

The sight of him there beside her bed, keeping vigil despite his limbs and body contorted like a puzzle ring to fit in the chair, had prompted a flood of gratitude. This was a thoroughly decent man thrust by others into situations he probably didn't want and trying to do the best by them. For someone who'd spent her life dedicated to caring for others, his tenderness towards her, a virtual stranger, was a rare and unexpected kindness that tugged at her heart, pulling it in strange new directions.

But that natural instinct to help ingrained in her very DNA also detected other dimensions to Finn. Under the laid back charm he let flow so readily, there were undercurrents, vulnerabilities, even a fragility that he tried to shield. Behind those smiling brown eyes, she read fleeting thoughts and emotions that told a different story.

And that was where the real danger lay. That drive to heal what was broken had got her into trouble before. She'd learned the hard way that while her skills of observation, of diagnosis, and the healing magic she might weave with her hands were first-rate, to fix someone emotionally, particularly someone you cared about—well, that was something totally different and possibly beyond her. Her mother was living proof of the adage that you shouldn't hook up with someone thinking you'd fix their flaws And Layla had ignored that wisdom once before with near disastrous consequences.

She'd met Ben while sharing a few beers with her brothers in a dingy South Auckland bar. He'd sauntered up to the leaner, a brave move as she sat dwarfed by the three burly young men, and struck up a conversation about her tattoos. He was charming in a rough, brusque way, and captivated her with his laconic humour and the bold way he lived life, drawing her out of her serious and cautious shell.

But he was like a comet. He'd blazed across her life for a brief time, before she'd had to let him go, and now small remnants of their relationship brushed her thoughts from time to time. At first she'd felt a failure, abandoning the damaged man she'd fallen for before he damaged her. Fighting his demons with drugs and his fists, Layla had realised that not only could her infatuation with a 'bad boy' wreck her career, she felt unsafe. The simmering threat that he might go beyond punching walls and doors, to punching her, undermined any chance of a future, much as she'd wanted one.

But Finn wasn't Ben, she reminded herself. From what she'd seen, he was more of the mould of her friends—Tristan, Leo, Will—good men, caring men who looked out for her and loved her in their own way. That was the kind of man she'd longed for. Life hadn't delivered one who longed for her in the same way yet, but maybe this time... She shook off the niggling worries. Whatever troubles Finn McGill had, it seemed like he handled them. It was simply her fixer-upper tendencies leaping to the fore. She snuggled back under the comfort of his arm and took another sip of the whisky, sending a pleasant warmth down her throat, to match the warm glow she felt from his nearness.

Two hours later, the bartender reluctantly called time. "I'm sorry folks," he said with a genuine look of regret, "but I'm not prepared to risk going beyond my licence tonight. Too many out-of-town coppers up there," he said with a nod towards the castle. "Our local bobby would probably stop in and join us, but those city boys are a different breed."

"Probably won't catch you tomorrow, I imagine," Dervla said, releasing Layla from a hug, "but it's been fun. So glad we got to meet you, Layla. The four of us should get together sometime. Get that man of yours to bring you over to Dublin, perhaps?"

"That's if he's up for a rematch of whisky wars." Brendan chimed in with a grin.

"Any time, mate," Finn said, "even though you know the outcome will be just the same."

They followed the rest of the band and crew to a row of three cottages off an alleyway behind the pub, leaving Finn and Layla to consider the way back to the festival. Outside, the lingering Scottish twilight held back the night, painting the western sky in trails of green and indigo. From the castle grounds, music drifted down from the day's final act on the main stage, with the sound of the crowd singing along to a much-loved chorus smoothing the jagged edges of the lead singer's growl.

A trail of solar lights edged the road leading uphill from the village to the back of the castle, as if marking a magical pathway. The powerful stage lights pulsed in time to the music, while others swept in wide arcs across the sky, bouncing off an approaching bank of cloud that loomed in the east.

"Looks like they'll finish just in time to beat the rain," Finn said. "That song's their usual encore. But as for us..."

She looked at the road stretching ahead of them. The castle, picked out by floodlights, looked almost close enough to touch. Although she wondered if the nearness was an illusion conjured by the creeping darkness, like a blanket pulling the world close under its shelter. The thick cloying air pushed ahead of the storm seemed to draw the night even closer. A faint exhale of breeze brought tantalising relief from the sultry heat of the evening, but there was a tang of ozone in its breath. The anticipation of the approaching storm echoed the flutter of anticipation in Layla's stomach. Walking back to her tent with Finn McGill felt like conscious steps towards as yet undefined but irresistible possibilities.

"It doesn't look far," she said.

"About a kilometre. Uphill too. I can call for a car to come down for us."

So there were the options: brave the threat of a drenching and have him escort her right to the privacy of her tent; or spend a few minutes in the confines of a car with a stranger observing their every interaction, then dropping her at the campsite pathway with their night cut short. The choice was simple.

"Nah," she said, the recklessness still pulsing in her veins, "we can outrun it if we have to, can't we?"

"I dunno. You look a little wobbly on your feet there, Layla. Running might not be an option."

"It's OK. I promise you won't have to carry me."

She *was* a bit wobbly, and her words slurred. But she was determined to walk up the road to prolong their parting and keep other opportunities open.

"I'll hold you to that," he said with a grin, taking her hand as he set off with brisk strides. She thought how ridiculous they must look: Finn, in full possession of his faculties despite the whisky, moving forward with a graceful ease; she, like a child struggling to keep up, adding a little skip every few paces to stay level with him. This thought bubbled over into giggles, then a hiccup, and finally a plaintive "Finn!"

He stopped and turned to her with a bemused grin. "You promised I wouldn't have to carry you."

"And trust me, you won't," she said. "I just need you to slow down for chrissakes. My legs are half as long as yours. I can't bloody keep up if you haven't noticed."

The first drops peppered the surrounding ground, a black polka dot pattern on the grey asphalt. Small wisps of steam drifted up as the road gave up the day's heat, soothed by the cool water from above. Squeals of surprise from the dispersing crowd on the hill above accompanied the first flash of lightning. The bass note of thunder followed quickly.

Finn glanced up at the sky, and then back to where a pathway led to the camping area, eyes narrowing as if calculating the distance and the time needed to beat the full onslaught of the storm. Then, in one swift, decisive movement, he whisked Layla off her feet and flung her over his shoulder. She screamed, half in shock and half in delight. Considered the serious one of her group of friends since high school, the 'tight five', in fact, she thrived on this sort of craziness. It was so freeing to let all those inhibitions fall. All she needed was a little encouragement. And with a bit of alcohol on board and this playful man egging her on, she was all in for some fun.

Finn jogged along the path, weaving in and out of other campers flowing in brisk-walking streams. Layla felt her flailing legs make contact with one as they passed. She offered a breathless "Sorry" and an apologetic wave. She wondered if Finn was as conscious of the press of her breasts against his back as she was of his large hand splayed across her butt. She angled her head to look at his expression and could see the smirk on his face.

"Comfy back there?" he called.

"What do you think?" she flung back, giving his bum a playful slap.

He stumbled the final few steps, and she nearly lost her grip. He'd come to an abrupt halt right outside her tent.

"This it?" he asked.

He had a great memory, since she'd only casually pointed it out on their way to the food trucks earlier. Either that, or he'd made a particular effort to mark out which was hers. That second thought gave her a little happy buzz of pleasure, that even in the afternoon he might have already picked up on the spark of attraction she sensed between them.

"Sure is," she replied. And with that, he lowered her to the ground. She slid down the length of his body before feeling solid earth beneath her feet, and the absence of space between them. Her bare nipples under her singlet, already aroused by the friction of his broad back, were now more pronounced. She saw his downward glance flicker towards them and felt his keen awareness of her interest and his response as he hardened against her.

They stood for a long moment, each taking the other in, as the now insistent rain ran in rivulets, soaking their hair, droplets rolling down their cheeks like tears. Taking in the sight of him, his hair hanging in wild spirals, his eyes an intense, almost black, Layla decided Finn McGill was a most beautiful man. His face, with its soft dimpled curves and glowing olive skin, emphasised his youth. But the masculine shadow of stubble on his chin, and the commanding way his hands slid over her hips, left her in no doubt—this was no boy. This was a man who right now looked like he had definite ideas of what he'd like to do to her—ideas that she wouldn't hesitate to encourage.

Then, with a start, as if those very thoughts had stung him, he took one deliberate step away from her. Freeing her from the circle of his arms, he lifted a hand to wipe a damp lock of hair away from his eyes. The movement appeared forced, as if he looked for some excuse to create this sudden distance between them. He broke their gaze, and stood, appearing unsure of what to do or say next.

Oh no, she thought, *you don't get all flirty with me, make me all hot and bothered and then turn it off like a tap.* She took his hand.

"I think we'd better get inside," she said with a nod towards the sky. In the distance, a violent squall progressed across the open fields, slashing at the trees edging the valley. Unzipping the door, she dived inside, dragging Finn behind her. She secured it again, moments ahead of the torrent of water already hammering on the trees beyond. She turned to face him. He stood his back against the centre pole as if it had leapt out to prevent him from fleeing further from her, the halo of fairy lights glistening off his wet hair.

"You're drowned," she said, and pulled a towel from the small drying rack in one corner.

Ignoring the small awkward flinch, she tousled his damp, shiny hair with one hand, dabbing with the towel in the other. The whole time they stared at each other, her trying to project a steady reassurance coupled with quiet determination. And while his face remained a mask of calm, it couldn't hide the whirling thoughts that tumbled across the background of his eyes. She trailed one hand down his damp neck, coming to rest on the saturated t-shirt. He'd worn most of the rain, her body sheltered by his larger one.

"That needs to go," she said, her voice soft and low, as if not wishing to spook a flighty horse. There was an answering shiver under her touch. She fumbled at his waist, and finding the edge, lifted the shirt carefully, her fingers tracing the pattern of dark hairs, lingering a moment at his navel before continuing along the pathway. He closed his eyes, and she heard the faintest groan as she allowed one fingertip to brush a nipple, before tugging the shirt over his head.

She stood for a moment, admiring the sight. The bronze skin stretched taut over a lean, slightly muscled torso was far from the stereotypical Scot. Her brain was so hazed over with desire, she was unable to retrieve the name for those beautifully defined muscles that plunged down into the low-slung jeans. Whatever they were called, it didn't matter, just the fact that the thought of tracing her hands along them and exploring in that direction sent her stupid. Realising she was staring, the lust probably plain on her face, she broke away with a flush of embarrassment, draping the sodden t-shirt over a chair.

What was it about this man standing here inside her tent that made her feel like living dangerously? Right now, there were two things going on with her that were totally unexpected. First, despite her protestations otherwise, she was a little drunk. And she was never drunk. Second, she was about to invite him to make love to her after having known him less than twenty-four hours. And that wasn't because she was drunk. It was because when she'd woken up this morning to see those brown eyes staring back at her with a look of tender concern—in that moment, the world had tilted and sent

Finn tumbling into her life. But perhaps he didn't feel it, this intense connection. Maybe she had gone too far.

When she turned back, she knew she hadn't. His hand reached for the towel. She let it fall from her grasp and held her breath in anticipation of his touch. He lifted his arms, and then it came, long fingers weaving through her hair, careful hands guiding the towel gently in its work, his eyes never leaving hers. It was the most erotic gesture she'd ever experienced, triggering her heart to flail so wildly in her chest she thought it must be audible above the slap of the rain on the canvas roof. There was something both terrifying and thrilling in the intensity of his eyes, knowing that he felt it too.

A small spontaneous gasp hissed from deep inside her, as discarding the towel, his hand now reached for the hem of her singlet top. His slight hesitation elicited another gasp, and her hand acted as if it had a mind of his own, seeking to rest over his, and then slowly guiding it upwards, edging the top with it. With her other hand cupped behind his head, she drew him lightly towards her.

His head tipped forward at the invitation, pressing a trail of butterfly kisses along her stomach. A small hum of pleasure rose in the back of her throat, the delicacy of his lips teasing her nerve endings till they sang with a sweet high-pitched note. He peeled the top higher and higher, revealing fresh territory for his relentless lips, kissing, and nipping and tasting while her unsteady legs wavered to hold her upright.

Now revealing her breasts, he brushed each with his tongue, before pausing to remove the damp bunch of fabric. The absence of his lips, even for those few seconds, induced a searing flash of heat deep in her centre. She craved their return, desperate for him to taste her skin once more. And her wish was answered, as now his warm mouth explored her neck with tiny grazes of teeth and lingering caresses of lips before finally finding home, his insistent tongue parting her lips as their bodies blurred together. She sank into him, lost in the shared breath, the warm press of skin to skin, the all-encompassing presence of him.

His gasp caught her by surprise as much as the sudden jerk of his mouth away from hers, his eyes frantic. "God, Layla," he said. "This is too much, too fast."

Her confusion whirled. One moment he'd totally given himself over to her, and she'd accepted that, prepared to gift him all of her in return, a gift she never gave lightly or often these days. Now he threw it back at her, unwanted? He must have read the hurt on her face, and he bent to kiss her again, this time light, consoling, soothing.

"It's not you," he said. "It's me." He sighed, looking down at her, and she saw hurt there, too. Another woman's hurt. Her instincts had been correct. Finn's past hadn't been kind. Love had chewed him up and spat him out. "God, you are the most amazing woman," he said. "But I think we should take a little time, get to know each other. Before we plunge into this. Because I don't do casual sex."

"Hey," she said, reaching a hand to those beautiful dark spirals framing his face. "It's OK. Believe it or not, despite what just happened between us, I don't do casual sex either."

She caught his short exhale of relief. It spurred a small flurry of relief in her chest too, that she could say those words with honesty. While the idea of falling into bed with Finn so quickly tempted her, it came with a quiet niggle of worry that she'd reverted to what had been her modus operandi for relationships for most of her adult life.

There was only one man she'd considered worth saving herself for, but while he'd never hooked up with anyone else, he'd also never shown any sign of wanting more than friendship from her. And so, weary and disillusioned, she'd lived up to the expectations of her looks—a slutty little blonde from the cheap streets of Auckland who gave herself cheaply, too—and simply given up on finding anything more.

A year ago, casual sex was all she did. But one morning she'd woken up to the empty space beside her, sheets still pungent with the sweat of the latest man who'd slipped out early rather than face waking up next to her, and decided she was over it. She'd drawn on the wisdom of her dear Granny Meredith: *If you do what you've always done, you get what you've always got.* This was the reward for doing something different, the chance to do it right, to only give that part of yourself to someone who'd still be there in the morning.

"You're right. We can take this slower, spend some time together, and if we still feel this way, then... we can explore where that takes us," and then despite her sadness that accompanied the thought, "or we can not go there at all, if you want."

His laugh was low and throaty. "No, I want," he said. "But this is sudden, surprising. I don't want to overwhelm you or risk what might be, by being greedy or impatient." She saw the shadow behind his eyes and silently cursed whoever had hurt this kind man.

"OK," she said. "So, how about we start again? Perhaps if I make us a coffee and we can sit and talk."

She retrieved a t-shirt from her bag. Fully-clothed would be a good step towards cooling down the situation.

"I really should go home," he said. She saw his nervous glance at the bed and heard the pummelling rain on the roof. The storm seemed to have settled itself on Dallblane and wasn't inclined to move onto other victims anytime soon.

"It's hideous out there. Why don't you stay until it stops?" His gaze found the chair. "And no, I'm not going to be the reason you sleep in a chair for the second night in a row. The bed is huge and I absolutely promise not to leap on top of you. As long as you promise the same." She arched a brow at him, and his face dimpled in amusement.

"I think we both deserve to sleep a little more peacefully than last night."

Seeing her light tone had the desired effect, she set to brewing up a coffee each in the little Nespresso machine, a bonus of Charlie booking them flash glamping tents. She tactfully kept her back turned. Hearing his damp jeans hit the floor, she almost weakened, wanting a glimpse of what lay beneath them, but the rustle of sheets as he slipped into the bed ended this test of her willpower.

When she turned to see him propped up there against the mound of pillows, bare-chested and those brown eyes all molten, she kind of regretted her promise, but pushed down thoughts of snuggling in alongside. This was the sort of man she'd lacked in her life. If she was to make the most of this gift the universe had bestowed on her in a most unlikely fashion, she must retrieve her more cautious self.

She delivered his coffee on the little nightstand and carefully slid in on the other side, leaving a large conspicuous gap down the centre of the bed. She flicked off the main light, leaving him just a warm-voiced shadowy form as they sat like two kids on a sleepover, making small talk and sipping coffee, until both faded into sleep, lulled by the hum of the rain.

When she woke in the half-light of dawn, his eyes were the first thing she saw. And her first thought was a question—what might it be like to wake up to those soft chocolate brown eyes each morning? To see that expression of simple delight triggered in another simply by the mere act of waking?

"Good morning," he said, his voice a half-whisper. "Sleep OK?"

"Good morning. Yeah, I slept really well." Even the flapping of tents and the distant rumble of the thunder as it edged away hadn't intruded on a deep dreamless sleep. The constant rain provided a soothing white noise, and she'd drifted happily until the rising sun lit the tent's roof with a glow. It was like she'd been as a kid, no need for an alarm, her body in tune with the rhythms of the day.

"Was it the whisky—or me?" he said, a little smile tugging at his mouth.

"A bit of both," she said. "There is something nice about sleeping with someone. And I mean sleeping," she said, seeing his brow quirk up, and the smile morph into a grin. "Perhaps it's something primal, you know, a feeling of safety. But yeah, I'm glad you stayed." So they'd agreed to take it slow, but after being awake less than two minutes, neither could help but flirt a little. This going slow might be a challenge.

"Yeah, glad I didn't walk home in that downpour. I suppose I'd better get up and go see if there's any damage to report. Can't dodge my responsibilities by hiding out down here with you."

"Do you think you might be able to dodge them a bit later in the day? Maybe go watch a band or two?" She'd pencilled in a couple of possibilities on the main stage and there was an intriguing country/metal fusion band on the Valley stage in the late afternoon.

"Oh for sure," he said. "Unless there's been a total disaster, I'll be done by lunchtime. How about I meet you at the food trucks at one? The proper food," he said with a grin. "I'm not having ice cream for lunch again."

She stood at the door of the tent, watching him meander along the path, dodging the few other early risers and the maze of puddles. Considering the scale of the deluge, and the squally winds preceding it, the tent city looked reasonably intact. He stopped and looked back at her, his hair all wild and tangled, just as hers must also be, and with a quick smile and nod, headed up the hill.

"Woo-hoo! You go, girl!" Charlie launched herself from the tent opposite and flung her arms around Layla's shoulders, crushing her till she could hardly breathe. Layla felt the giggle rising in her chest and pushed it down.

"Shhh," she said, bringing her finger to her lips. "You'll wake the neighbours." She bustled Charlie inside and prepared for the interrogation.

"Now, aren't you glad I got you your own tent?" Charlie said with a sly smile, eyes gleaming across the top of her mug of coffee. "I know I sure am. It's been way too long, Layla honey. Thank god the man drought is over. I can stop worrying about you so much."

"Don't get too excited. What happened isn't quite what you think."

"No? Come on, don't tell me you had him in there all night and nothing happened. This is me. You don't have to be all coy about seducing some guy you've just met."

"Well, yes, something happened, but *it* didn't."

"OK, well, I suppose there's no surprise there. Great to see Layla's new approach is paying off at last—hold him off for a bit, then reel him in nice and slow so he's got no chance to get away."

"It's him who wants to go slow. In the light of day, to be honest, I'm not sure where I see this all heading. Or if it's heading anywhere at all. After all, he has responsibilities here. And me, I'm supposed to be going home. Maybe he wants to go slow because he's not sure it's worth pursuing. Or maybe there's someone else."

"For real? Well, maybe I need to add you as an agenda item when I meet him at ten o'clock. Put him straight. He should consider himself lucky to have even caught your attention."

"What?" Layla turned on her. "Explain. Please. Now."

Charlie laughed. "Calm down. I booked a meeting with his partner and him yesterday because I have a little proposal for them. Nothing to do with you. I promise. It was all set up long before you enticed him into your tent."

She could be so infuriating, this love of being enigmatic, keeping you hanging on every word. Layla rolled her eyes and waited, knowing Charlie would reveal all. You had to let her enjoy the drama.

"Well, you know how I've been slowly building up my film work? But it's hard to find an inroad, to really make something happen. Anyway, I've got an idea. This festival is a trailblazer. It's caught lots of people's attention. But believe it or not, *nobody* is making any lasting record of it on film. I think it's because the organisers are all newbies. So busy getting it off the ground, they haven't thought about what they need to make it live on, and hook people into the next one. That's where I come in. I'm going to make them a doco."

"Oh, that's bloody brilliant, Charlie."

"I thought so," she said with a Cheshire cat grin. "And Finn will too. And while he's basking in the sheer brilliance of it, while he thinks I'm the best damn thing that's walked through his doorway, I'm going to tell him he's wrong. You're the best thing that's walked through his doorway. He needs to wake up and get his arse over here before some other guy swoops in and grabs you while he's still stuffing around deciding. Go slow! What the fuck's wrong with him?"

"Charlie, please promise me you won't. Look, whatever the reason behind it, I don't want anyone railroading him. If he's just not that into me, then that's how it is."

She huffed a little at that, but Layla could see the thoughtful expression on her face.

"OK," she said. "I won't do anything to stuff it up. I promise to be gentle with him where you're concerned. But if I see an opportunity to nudge him in your direction, I'm going to take it."

20

Big Love

Dallblane, Scotland - July 2019

A STEADY STREAM OF parched festival goers sought out the cool enclave of the outdoor bar at this time of day. Lured by the promise of frosty drinks and a comfortable seat, people scanned for vacant tables, and Layla congratulated herself for securing one by arriving early. It was a pleasant oasis from the dust that, despite the ground staff's constant attention, rose from the pathways under the tread of many feet.

The tang of her lemon, lime and bitters soothed the heat, but she was far from calm, swirling the annoying ice-cubes against the sides of her plastic cup in a restless rumble that mirrored the tumble of emotions, her unsettling constant inner companions all morning. For about the tenth time since she'd sat down, she checked her phone. 12:58. She wondered if Finn McGill was a punctual man.

It seemed he was. As the time clicked over to 1:00, she caught sight of him, his gait casual, but his eyes darting left and right, a searching expression on his face. It sent a light flush of pleasure to observe him amongst a crowd of thousands seeking her. She leapt to her feet, the cup teetering, almost toppling over as she flung an arm up in careless excitement. She waved madly at him. "Finn!"

A smile of boyish delight lit up his face, and her heart leapt that merely catching sight of her should be the reason for this expression of joy. Even from here, she could see the small crinkles bloom around his eyes and mouth as he retraced his steps to the entrance.

He sidestepped the line of thirsty punters waiting for admission. She caught a few annoyed looks thrown his way. But then, seeing the dangling lanyard with its purple card, most of them relaxed, having surmised he was some sort of official, not a rude man deviating from the unwritten British rules for queuing.

It seemed natural to walk into his embrace, and in the secure sweep of his arms, all the nervous tension she'd battled since her conversation with Charlie seeped away. He slid onto the wooden bench seat opposite, and picked up her cup, sucking up a mouthful of the drink before bumping it back down onto the table.

"Please tell me this isn't your idea of an alternative to ice cream for lunch," he said, his cheeks creasing in amusement.

"No, I don't think a liquid lunch would be a great idea after last night. I'm definitely in the mood for some solid food."

She still felt a little queasy, the aftereffect of alcohol. For the daughter of a hard-drinking man, with three brothers following in the same footsteps, she herself had little recent experience. She enjoyed a wine with a meal, an evening at the pub, even the odd party, but Layla and alcohol were not close friends. Now her stomach reminded her why. Although she'd appreciated that little shot of courage the whisky had provided where Finn was concerned.

Remembering last night's events had provoked a slight flutter of unease in her stomach this morning. Once fully awake, she'd taken them out, examining them in the harsh light of day, and felt no regrets.

Yes, she'd invited Finn into her tent, unashamedly undressed him and enticed him to reciprocate, before coaxing him into staying, even though the sleeping arrangements had been chaste. But no, she wasn't sorry that she'd attempted to move things along with a sweet and decent man that she liked and who actually seemed interested in her, too. Those had been even less frequent in her life than alcohol. Charlie's description of the man drought was wholly accurate.

It didn't hurt that those deep brown eyes looking at hers in amusement, or the tumble of dark wayward hair coupled with a knowledge of exactly what lay under that t-shirt made her feel more than a little weak at the knees. The only nagging question was the one she couldn't come right out and ask him: why was he holding back? If there was already someone else, surely he wouldn't be sitting opposite her right now, unless she'd totally misjudged him. Whatever the answer, it seemed patience was the only way she was going to get it.

"Bacon butties?" he said. "I'm told they do a pretty tasty version over there." He nodded towards a nearby food truck. The sign said 'GRUB' in jaunty red lettering, flanked by two Union Jack flags. Beneath it she read 'Traditional British Pub Food'.

"Sounds good to me."

After politely waiting their turn in the short queue, they soon emerged laden with thick bacon sandwiches in brown paper bags, a thing called a 'Yorkie Pud Wrap', safe in its pizza box, which Finn assured her she would love, and steaming English Breakfast tea in takeaway cups. They found a space at one of the long wooden picnic tables and spread out their feast.

"Well, I survived another encounter with your extremely scary friend," he said with a grin, before biting into one of the bacon butties. "No scars to show for it. But the festival office staff agree with me she bears a strong resemblance to a certain Viking warrior queen. They've nicknamed her Lagertha."

Layla nearly choked on her sandwich, as the laughter spilled from her. "Tell them they're not that original. It's not the first time. Much as she protests otherwise, I know for a fact Charlie loves *Vikings* and secretly enjoys the comparison. But for god's sake, don't let her hear it."

"Thanks for the warning," he said. "Because it seems she and I are going to be seeing quite a bit of each other. So I don't want to get in her bad books."

"Oh," she said, "so you liked the idea?"

She'd thought he would. Knowing how much this festival meant to him, with his desperate attempt to turn around the family's downhill decline, of course he'd jump at an opportunity like this.

"More than liked it. It's a stroke of brilliance." His eyes glowed with excitement. "I can't believe we were so stupid not to think of doing it ourselves. Sure, we've missed capturing all the lead in and set-up. But I've snapped a fair few stills along the way that she can use, and we can recreate mock-ups of other parts. I doubt anyone will know the difference in the end. And my god, her footage is impressive. She has this incredible eye, a knack of focusing you in on small details that have a tremendous impact visually. It's magic."

She was used to this awestruck reaction to Charlie's work. To gaze on it was like stepping through a portal into a parallel world where the one you knew became amplified, reimagined in Charlie's own unique vision.

"The talent was always there. Even when we were teenagers, she always had a camera in her hand. Which wasn't always a good thing," she said with a wry grin. "A few parts of my life I'd prefer she *hadn't* recorded on film."

"Worse than embarrassing baby photos?" He threw her a knowing smile.

"Way worse."

"Hmmm," he said. "I wonder if she'd show me if I pay her enough." He paused, eyes thoughtful and a hint of a cheeky smirk.

"Remember, she's been *my* friend long before she met you. So no, I don't think throwing money at her will work."

"A shame," he said. "I guess I'll just have to leave it up to my imagination."

"You will," she said.

"And make a note to check she's not lurking when I'm doing something I'd rather not have captured by her lens," he grinned. "No—joking aside, she's talented, and obviously very driven."

"Yeah, Charlie didn't rest on the fact she's got an eye for it. She's worked really hard for a long time. I hope this gives her the attention she deserves. And helps you out too."

It was a genuine sentiment. She'd been forced to put aside her assumptions about a man who lived in a castle. While to an outsider Finn looked like the definition of rich and privileged, it was clear from the single servant, the opulent but tired furnishings, and the beautiful but poorly tended gardens that money didn't flow easily for them. And the McGills themselves, perhaps except for Euan—she'd reserved judgement on him and she wasn't particularly hopeful—were a fairly ordinary family of modest means, with the castle a modern day white elephant they couldn't afford to maintain.

"It was a great meeting. I have a really good feeling that both of us will get what we want out of this arrangement."

Layla moved on to devouring the newfound delight that was 'Yorky Pud Wrap'. The tender strands of gravy-drenched beef and soft chewy batter were as delicious as promised.

"Sit still," he said. She paused mid-chew as he reached across, dabbing at her cheek with a napkin. With a few deft flicks, he removed a large drop of gravy from her cheek. "It's good to see you're enjoying it," he said with a satisfied grin. It was a strangely intimate gesture, sending another little tingle of electricity across her spine.

"Messy, but delicious," she said, mustering an unaffected tone. "You win. I have to concede this is far better than ice cream for lunch."

But while the food felt good settling in her hungry stomach, there was a returned twinge of nerves as she wondered whether Charlie had slipped any mention of her into the meeting. While part of her cringed at the thought of what Charlie might have said—she was renowned for having no filter—another part gave a hopeful flutter. She needed Finn to know that she was interested in more from him than this friendly banter back and forth over lunch, or as part of a group of friends drinking at the pub, or the companionship of dancing side by side at a concert. She sensed that the next twenty-four hours would determine one way or another: would she gain a friend or a lover?

They agreed that the first band they watched on the main stage, despite being much hyped, was a tad lacklustre. Their next stop, the Valley Stage, lay beyond a thick, forested area. It wasn't far, and they had over an hour to cover the distance. They strolled hand-in-hand, following a winding path that wove around the perimeter of the woods.

Layla was about to suggest a detour for a cold drink when Finn came to a sudden halt at a bend in the path. He studied the high mesh fence beside them. Its obvious purpose was to keep festival goers out of the forest. But Finn had other ideas. With a quick glance sideways, he chose this moment when no one else was in sight to lift the hinge between two partitions, and slide them apart, creating a narrow gap.

"Come on," he urged, and Layla followed him through. He slid the fence back into place and disappeared down into the trees. The slope was slick from the previous night's rain. She slipped and slid her way to the bottom, where Finn stood waiting on a small track.

"Don't worry, we won't get lost. I know this place well. We used to play here for hours when we were kids. Dad was always so busy, and well, you've met Mum—she was totally comfortable with free range children. Never worried what we were up to as long as we turned up home for supper."

"Wow," Layla breathed, her eyes drawn to the towering oaks, with broad ancient trunks topped by dense leafy canopies that blocked the sun. The air was cool and the hush of the trees filtered the distant music until it was simply a faint hum like busy insects. "It's kind of magical," she said, in whispered awe.

She and her brothers had been free range children too, but this forest playground was so far removed from the suburban cul-de-sac where they had played. An untidy street, un-mown grass verges and tired houses in need of a good coat of paint bordered it. Neighbours discarded unwanted broken furniture on the front lawns. Every yard had a dog, some sad chained prisoners who barked hopefully at their approach, others aggressive guardians who flung themselves at the fence with threatening snarls.

The children had ridden rusty bicycles up and down, or played cricket in the street with a piece of wood for a bat and an old tennis ball, making their own fun with what little they had. Her childhood resembled the film set for some dystopian sci-fi movie. This was another world altogether, more like they'd wandered into a fairytale. She stood mesmerised by the beauty, immersed in a green wonderland.

"Come on, you need to see the most magical bit," Finn said. He walked on, peering carefully between the trees, until finding what he sought. He stepped off the track, weaving through the undergrowth, leading her deeper into the forest. It felt like any moment the Big Bad Wolf or Hansel and Gretel might appear from behind a tree. That sense was heightened when he parted some bushes to reveal a tiny secluded clearing, a secretive space huddled under the ever-present oaks.

"My thinking spot," he said, lowering himself to the ground right where an inward curve in one trunk made a comfortable space to lean. He reached up a hand, drawing her down to sit between his outstretched legs. To her surprise, the ground was dry, perhaps protected from the previous night's onslaught by the dense canopy that now today fought off the sun.

One tanned arm slipped around her, his fingers resting lightly on her collarbone as he pressed a kiss to her hair. It felt so tranquil here, surrounded by calm green, and his comfortable presence. But it seemed these feelings of peace had yet to find Finn. The fingers of his free hand drummed out a restless rhythm on the ground.

"And what are you thinking in your thinking spot?"

She probed delicately, sensing the tension in him. At first he said nothing, the single sound the staccato of his fingers vibrating in anxious time beside her. She was acutely aware of his breathing, the press of his chest rising and falling, and the caress of his breath on her hair. When he spoke, his voice was steady, as if he'd rehearsed this.

"I want to be honest with you," he said. "But this is a risk for me. I don't want to scare you off by the things I'm going to share. But I know I need to do this. I've tried the other way, and it led to disaster."

"OK," she said, curious but also a little fearful. "You can tell me anything. And I don't scare easily. Unless some great hairy spider comes marching out of the undergrowth." She felt the curve of his smile against her neck.

"OK," he said. "And if one does, I promise to flatten it."

"Deal," she said. She felt his deep inhale, and then the words tumbled out.

"So, even when I was small, I kind of knew I was different. But it was when I got to school that I started to understand that fully. I think I was about six when I first heard the word 'gifted', when the teacher met with Mum and Dad. At first, it didn't really mean much to me. But I slowly realised that there were things in the world that spoke to me in a way they didn't for other people.

"Right from when I was little I loved music, but it was when I got older that I noticed the sudden looks, some surprise, often delight, when I'd just pick up something and play. It hadn't occurred to me you had to 'learn' those things. And when I started school, for the first time I had a word for the whirl of patterns and numbers that seemed to surround me wherever I went: mathematics. Up till then, I had no idea that these things that fascinated me weren't readily obvious to everyone else."

"Ah," she said, "so that explains the double degrees."

"Yes. I couldn't choose between them. Like choosing your favourite child. And university was heaven for me. I met other people there who were as obsessed as I was. It was a safe place. I didn't feel like a freak. To be honest, I might have stayed there forever. But the real world came for me, in the form of my father, insisting that I make something of myself. That I owed the world, and him, to *do something*."

She turned her face up to him. "I have to tell you, the fact that you're some sort of mathematical and musical genius isn't the least bit daunting. I've spent a lot of time in the company of some seriously smart people. But I'm not intimidated by it. I love the fact that the human mind is capable of so much. And that you can tap into it."

He smiled down at her. "I'm grateful for that part of my mind, too. It's served me well. It's the other bit that's problematic." Another deep inhale filled his chest and then came out as a sigh. "You see what none of us understood—and thankfully there's been some progress since I was a kid—is that many gifted people have other things that are like, supercharged. It's as if there are parts of you that are on steroids. Some people are incredibly sensitive to stimuli: light, sound and stuff."

"Yeah, I've heard that," she said, having vague recollections of lectures in human development and psychology from her early training.

"Well, others, like me, have these big emotions. You know when you see toddlers and it's all drama. And the teen years. Teenagers live so intensely, like everything matters so very much."

"Yeah, I remember," she said. Those years weren't so far away. She could recall falling suddenly and hopelessly in love. And being outraged at almost everything her brothers did or the times when she'd lectured her parents on the latest cause she was passionate about. Becoming a teenager was like being swept up by this huge emotional tornado that carried you along for a few years before running out of power and dumping you back to earth, a rational, grown human being. "It was pretty wild. Made worse by all four of us being close in age. Poor mum, I don't know how she survived a household of teenagers."

"Well, that's how it's always been for me. And to some extent still is, although I've learned to manage it better. Small things escalate into big things quickly. Little worries become massive anxieties."

"Wow," she said, intrigued. "But you seem so relaxed. Honestly, except for these last few minutes, I'd have taken you for a really chilled guy."

"You know the analogy of the duck—gliding peacefully on top of the water, but underneath, those little feet are paddling furiously? That's me."

Realisation dawned on her. She turned herself around, sitting cross-legged, grasping his hands in hers, eyes locked onto the dark turbulence of his.

"So, was that what last night was about? When you wanted to leave? You and I, things are going along fine on the surface, but underneath, there's trouble?"

"You're a fast learner, Layla Angell. But yeah. Not trouble exactly, but something troubling. Big feelings like a tidal wave about to sweep me away. Feelings for you."

"So, you have feelings for me." He didn't need to tell her that. She could almost see them in the air, soft warm tendrils radiating off him, wrapping her in a tingling caress. "After last night, surely you know that I have feelings for you, too. I don't just invite guys in on a whim. If I gave you that impression—well, I can understand it might seem that way. But it's not. So admitting that to me, us admitting that to each other—it's still not scaring me off."

"Well, we're about to get to the scary part." He grasped her hands once more, tightening his grip, as if preparing that she might actually get up and run. But she wouldn't. She felt things for this guy. Although she wouldn't admit it to him, the sudden onslaught of feelings did kind of scare her, too. But whatever he revealed, she was going to fight any urge to run.

"I've only been in love once before in my life," he said.

That word 'before' leapt out at her. Before what? Before now? Before her? She felt him swallow, as if even the memories choked his words.

"Almost three years ago, I met a girl named Niamh. Irish, from Belfast. She was twenty, about to start her second year at uni. And I was almost twenty-six, just about to leave and come home. I stayed on at the end of the semester, did some tutoring in a couple of summer school maths papers. It was a chance to do what I love a bit longer and delay the inevitable: come back here and search for something to do that wouldn't drive me mad but was acceptable to my father.

"Anyway, we met one night at a student bar. From the moment I saw her, I knew. And I fell for her so damn hard. Of course there'd been girls before, girlfriends." Of course there had been—sweet guy, definitely easy on the eye—of course he'd have had girls chasing him. He swallowed audibly once more, his struggle obvious. "But nothing like this. I ignored Dad's demands, cancelled my trip home, stayed on. And for six months, she was my life, my whole life." There was a tremor in his voice. His body slumped as if the air had been sucked out of him.

"But you weren't hers." She understood.

"No. To me, she was the only girl. The one. She was forever. But to her, I was simply one of many possibilities. I know she cared for me, but that was part of the problem. If she hadn't, she might have told me straight. Kicked me back into the friend zone. But she thought that not being honest was kinder. I don't blame her. She was young and dealing with me, and this big, crazy love projected onto her—I think it simply overwhelmed her."

"What happened?"

There had to have been something more than a girl calling it off to leave him so deeply scarred, this hesitant, this scared to risk another relationship. Even this gentle man surely could have come back from the broken heart of a first love. God knows she had.

"We were at this stupid party. She was still at the stage where student parties were a big deal. Insisted we go to them every damn weekend. So it's a different night but the same thing—we're at some house bursting at the seams with drunk people, bad music playing loudly with everyone pretending they're enjoying it."

"Yeah," she said. "I know the ones."

"She disappeared and after a while, I started to worry. I mean, it's not always students at those parties. Glasgow has a pretty seedy underbelly. By that time of the night, there were all kinds of people drifting through. So I went looking—and I found her. Upstairs in a room with some scrawny little shit from her chemistry class. It was fairly obvious they'd been screwing. And she just sat there and looked at me as if it was no big deal."

"Oh, Finn, that's bloody awful."

She had known it would be bad. A flare of anger battled with a surge of protectiveness. How could this Niamh have been so heartless as to do that to this beautiful, sensitive man?

"I honestly think she wanted me to find her. Knew that there'd be no coming back. And she was right. I realised for all my so-called intelligence, I was too dumb to see what everyone else must have. It was my own stupid fault for making it into something it wasn't."

He hung his head, the heat of shame creeping up his neck. He blamed himself. Unbelievable. Now she had a name for the cause of his pain and caution, she wanted to hit back at this gutless woman, but she was out of reach. She couldn't undo what had happened to him, but she could help him bury it in the past. She pried one hand free and tilted his head to look at her.

"Finn, no one deserves that. Not you, not anyone. You seem to think there's something wrong with you, for loving hard, for loving fiercely. But that's not right. From what you've said, it seems to me that there was only something wrong with *her*. A girl of twenty is old enough to know you don't treat someone like that." His dark eyes were serious, and he swallowed audibly, but no words came. She summoned a reassuring smile. Who knew where this was going, but she vowed no matter what, she would not hurt him like he'd been hurt before. "And you still haven't got to the scary part," she said, with a questioning look.

He took another slow breath and she could feel the pulse throbbing where her fingers wrapped over his wrist.

"The scary part is that while I sat in that chair beside you, watched you sleeping, I recognised those same feelings I had for Niamh, bubbling up from somewhere inside of me. I kept thinking 'I've only just met her. I don't know her. But god how I want to.' The scary part is needing to tell you that, but not knowing what comes next."

21

If You Know

Dallblane Castle, Scotland - July 2019

AT TODAY'S MEETING, LIKE most others, Finn looked across at Eric Walters and shook his head in wonder that he'd found this unlikely friendship with someone who was his polar opposite.

Finn McGill: twenty-eight-year-old son of Scottish nobility, no claim to fame of his own, and no major achievements except two Masters Degrees with First Class Honours in Music and Mathematics, and a hankering to plunge back into academia when schemes to bail this family out no longer consumed all of his time. Although lately he was questioning that, given the success of the festival beyond his wildest dreams. And also having admitted to himself that despite all the stress, and the doubts, and the downright exhausting work, he'd pretty much loved every minute of the last seven months. Here they were, the morning of the final day. They'd done it. But he wasn't sure where to next.

Of course, his world had flipped itself on its side five days ago when Layla Angell walked into his life. Not to mention her sidekick, the force of nature that now sat in his father's study just across the hallway. If Charlie Christiensen had her way, he'd soon be embroiled in her get rich and famous scheme, which he had to admit was not only intriguing, but seemed to have a high likelihood of success. Suddenly, chasing a PhD didn't seem half as attractive as it had before.

Sitting opposite him, Eric slouched in an untidy heap that overflowed the tub chair—why the hell the guy always insisted sitting there he never understood—his head a shiny dome atop what was left of his spiky grey hair, the fifty-something eldest child of five, born to a plumber and a nurse, growing up somewhere in Clapham, who'd never finished high school but had an education in life, and more specifically in music promotion. His success was the product of his ballsy determination, an inherent likeability and a fuck-you attitude towards anyone he couldn't win over with his other qualities. The man was an absolute legend. And yet he'd seen in Finn more than a business proposal.

Sure Finn had other friends. Most nerdy introverts like himself who'd be more likely found playing WarCraft online or writing songs that no one else would ever hear in their back bedrooms. The only exception was Dexter Woodham, who for some unknown reason that he'd never elaborated on, took Finn under his wing on his arrival at Elsdon, saved him from the worst excesses of the ubiquitous bullies, and didn't seem to mind that he was rubbish at cricket and rugby, both sports Dex excelled at. He must call him, meet him for a drink down in London. And what a surprise he had for Dex: Layla, a Kiwi girl who knew all about rugby and cricket. God, she was something. He smiled to himself at the thought of introducing them.

There he went again, projecting a future for him and Layla, something beyond this perfect bubble. He wanted it—badly. He wanted her. And although she hadn't come right out and said it, he was sure she wanted him, too. But was it enough? Enough for her to rethink her whole life, her career, the country she called home, and hitch her future to his? It was a big ask, and he was afraid to explore the question in case her answer broke his heart.

"For chrissakes, Finn!" Eric leaned forward, his paunch pressing tight against the business shirt, an unattractive sliver of white skin pushing between the buttons. While other promoters his age tried to impress by dressing like their clients, uber cool suits, or leather jacketed with designer sunglasses, Eric was old school, neat shirt, often a tie, and a pair of Bill Gates glasses balanced on his sharp nose. Which he was currently peering over the top of with a frustrated frown.

"Sorry mate," Finn said with an apologetic smile. "Zoning out a bit there. Blame it on being overtired."

"Not surprised by that," Eric huffed. "Oh, and here's the cause right now." Layla appeared, two coffee mugs clutched in one hand, in the other a plate with a precarious biscuit stack.

"Special delivery courtesy of Isabel," she said, placing them on the desk, finding a space between the stacks of papers. The smell of warm baking wafted up, merging deliciously with the spicy perfume that he'd come to associate with her. Even after this short time, he could find Layla in a crowd while blindfolded. He'd have no problem locating the intoxicating blend that was uniquely her.

"Looks bloody marvellous, thanks love," Eric said with an approving glance. "By god it's time I went home while I can still squeeze through the door."

"You and me both," Layla laughed, helping herself to one, biting down with those neat, even little teeth that hardly three hours earlier had nibbled on Finn's neck. Cocooned in that tent, it was becoming increasingly difficult to get himself across here to work each morning. Waking to her cute curvy arse tucked in against his thighs, him spooning her protectively, was bliss. The only difficulty was this 'taking it slower' idea. Fuck, what was wrong with him to have suggested that? His cock stiffened at the thought of just how he'd like to put an end to that stupid notion. Just as well he'd chosen the chair behind his desk. He didn't want to confirm that Eric's suspicions about Finn's lack of sleep were ninety percent correct. And as for the other ten percent—it was this self-protective boundary he'd placed around their relationship that was causing him to lie awake next to her, weighing up when he should tear it down.

"Can't say I blame you for not mucking around there," Eric said, as she left them to their work. She'd taken to hanging out in the kitchen with Patti and Isabel each morning. Their chatter provided a tantalising hint of future idyllic possibilities: Layla, here, all the time.

"Yeah, well, sometimes I still worry about the wisdom of that. Rushing things."

"Oh, you can stop that bloody nonsense right now," Eric scoffed. "I can tell you firsthand—all this crap about getting to know each other first—it's a load of bollocks. Met Livvy in a club in Soho back in '96, came home with me that night and never left. Buggered if I was going to let some other bastard get his grubby hands on her."

Finn tried to hide his smile. He'd met Olivia Walters, and she was pretty feisty, but also besotted with Eric, even now. He couldn't imagine any other man laying a hand on her and getting away with it. She'd probably knock the guy down herself while Eric was still thinking about it.

"If that's the case, you two are a good advertisement for just jumping right in."

"Too bloody right. If you know, you know," Eric said, wagging a finger at him for emphasis.

And he knew. This was it this time. He just hoped she knew it too.

He quickened his pace as he caught sight of her waiting for him on the path below. Leaning against the fence, under the midday sun, her gilded hair glowed in a shining halo. She shucked off a shirt, the singlet top beneath revealing slender arms, the intricate ink patterns reminding him that only hours earlier he'd trailed kisses along them.

He'd never been a fan of tattoos, but on Layla, the flowers that bloomed on her body were a thing of beauty. She tied the shirt around her waist, drawing his eyes to her slim legs. She might be small, but no one would ever fail to notice her. And people were noticing. Men were noticing. Those in the company of other women tended to check her out surreptitiously, although the occasional one was crass enough to be blatant. And it seemed every damn unattached male gave her a good once over. When one stopped, her gestures indicating directions that the bastard could have read for himself on one of a hundred fucking signposts, Finn fought the urge to run. As well as pushing back a savage need to punch the man. He'd always chosen flight over fight, but his feelings for Layla were upending even his most basic instincts. Including the ingrained lack of trust that had tarnished every possibility of forming a relationship since Niamh's betrayal. He didn't trust women. He didn't trust himself to make good decisions about women. Until now.

"Hey." She waved at him, turning her back on the man. The light on her face at seeing Finn was enough to tell the guy he was wasting his time, and he wisely ambled off. He bent to kiss her, not just for the sheer pleasure, but to mark her out as his for all those other bastards to see. His appetite for those lips—rosy, and always curved in a sexy pout, even when she smiled—was insatiable.

"Shall we?" he said, taking advantage of a brief lull in the traffic to edge open the gap in the fence. They slipped through straight into the cover of bushes and he eased the fence partition back, covering all traces of their passing. Hand in hand they skittered down the slippery bank, clutching at slender trees to slow the descent. Down on the forest track, it was like entering some strange parallel world, the sunlight and music of the real world muted by the dense trees.

Sitting in the hollow of the tree in the hidden glade, it struck him that this was the first time he'd entered this place in a state of calm. For sure, he'd often left that way. Letting the peace of nature work its magic, moulding his troubled thoughts into a more bearable shape, had been his only refuge aside from music. But now he'd found refuge in her.

So much had altered in mere days. Going into the festival, he'd not expected things to play out like this: dodging the need to belt the anxiety out of him in the studio; not requiring escape from the pressure of his responsibilities in this forest hideaway. It was she who'd insisted they come here. He hadn't slowed down enough to ponder the reason for her request, and now, at the thought of the unknown, a familiar wrench of fear gripped his chest.

"So beautiful," she murmured, leaning her head back against his chest, the soft brush of her curls tickling his neck. Her eyes were closed. A stray beam of sunlight forced its way through the canopy, illuminating the pink flush of the day's heat on her cheek. So beautiful.

"That's why you wanted to come here?"

"Sort of. Thought it might be a chance for us to have some time, just you and me before the madness of final night." She nuzzled against his neck, languid in the heat of their joined bodies. "It's peaceful. Like you said, a good thinking spot."

"So, what are you thinking?"

"Oh, I dunno. Just about being here, at this festival. It's like some amazing alternate world we're living in, and then with one tick of the clock, it will be gone. It will all be over. It's kind of sad." She tipped her head to meet his eyes, and a little melancholy lurked there. "Does it make you sad? That it will be over?"

"Yeah, I suppose it does. I've put my heart and soul into this, my entire life directed towards these five days. I'm not sure how I'll feel when it's over. Sad. Probably. Empty. Maybe. But then there's still lots to do."

"Yeah, like the documentary. You do realise once Charlie moves into your place tomorrow, you might never get rid of her?"

He wanted to ask her right there. Come with her. Move in too. Stay. Don't go back to London. Don't go back to New Zealand. But he stopped himself. He needed it to come from her—if it did. He focused on his reply, pushing down the nauseating uncertainty.

"She'll have to move onto other assignments, eventually. I reckon a week or so and she'll have what she needs to move forward without actually being here. Let's face it, Charlie will find this place pretty boring once the music ends and the crowds go home."

"She will. She's no small-town girl. Not enough here for her. And she enjoys life on the road too much. Must be the Viking blood in her," she mused. "All those ancestors voyaging around the world."

Again, he wanted to say something. Could she be a small-town girl? Would living a life here be enough? Would he be enough? The doubt twisted painfully in his gut, but he kept the conversation flowing, diverting his mind.

"Eric thinks we need to go for it again. Rock The Castle 2020. That's what he wanted to talk about this morning, a firm commitment, in principle. Announce it tonight. Confirm in a couple of weeks when we see how the final accounts look."

"Finn, that's amazing," she said. "You should. It's too good not to. All these people, they'll be back."

"Will you?" He couldn't hold back any longer.

"Wouldn't miss it," she said, and he wanted to read so much into those words, and the sparkle in those forest-green eyes.

It wasn't a commitment to stay. It wasn't a commitment to him. But it was enough to give him a shred of hope that come the dawn, Layla Angell wasn't walking out of his life forever.

22

Dancing In The Dark

Dallblane, Scotland - July 2019

THE PRESS OF THE sweaty crowd around them was almost suffocating. Layla stood in front of Finn, his large frame protective, his arms caged around her upper body, shielding her from the jostle of sharp elbows. He made her feel so tiny and safe. Not only physically, but like nothing could ever truly hurt her again if he was around. It wasn't something she'd realised she either needed or lacked. She'd made it this far on her own, fully prepared to take on the world single-handedly. But now she didn't have to. Now there was Finn. And he needed her too.

Not to fix him as she'd worried in the beginning. He didn't need fixing; he was beautiful and whole in her eyes, but like a moody sea, captivating in all its deep and complex shades. No, what Finn needed was someone who could love him as he was. And that was easy for her. Love had breezed into her life, unannounced and unexpected, but undeniable. There were the two of them now.

It was kind of crazy, squashed down here near the front of the main stage, but the atmosphere was electric with anticipation. There was only one place to be on the final night of the festival, and this was it. Although if he'd suggested they leave, right this minute, walk away from the promise of seeing these rock gods live mere metres away, she'd have done it without hesitation. Especially if leaving came with the promise of Finn, all to herself, just the two of them in the shelter of the tent that had become their de facto home for the last four days—nothing could compete with an offer like that.

On stage, Phoenix Alferez warmed up the crowd with her set. Well, it was more like whipping them into a frenzy. It was hard to believe that raspy voice could come from deep inside a tiny eighteen-year-old who looked more like twelve. Although the pure sexual energy as she danced and wriggled her taut young body, barely covered by a bra top and denims so scant that they could hardly be called shorts, shouted all-woman. She was nothing short of spectacular, a fitting lead up to the main act due on next.

After missing The Destitute's set, on that disastrous opening night five days ago, while she tended to the unconscious Euan, Layla was excited. She wouldn't face returning to New Zealand without seeing them. Her brothers would be so jealous, perhaps even her father too, although he still argued that the next generation would never outdo the old rockers. Of course, that first night had eventually turned out to be a windfall rather than a disaster. But she absolutely knew that if she had to choose between Finn and The Destitute—well, Mick Harrison might think he was irresistible, but she wouldn't hesitate to turn her back on him and follow this sweet Scottish man wherever he led.

"You OK way down there," he yelled in her ear, over the tumultuous blend of voice and instruments that engulfed the crowd.

"Yeah," she yelled back, "I'm OK, although I wish I had longer legs."

While being small had its advantages—she'd managed to weave her way through gaps in the crowd, edging closer and closer to the front, creating a space and then dragging Finn behind her—now she felt like the entire LA Lakers team had somehow wedged their way into the row in front and she had no choice but to take snippets of opportunity to peer between the giants blocking her view. Her neck ached from craning upwards.

Finn gave her a slight nudge, and she followed the direction of his gaze.

"You up for that?" he shouted. Was she ever? A few sardine-squeezed people to their left, one guy had lifted a woman onto his shoulders. The sheer exhilaration on her face was contagious.

"If you can, I will," she called up to him.

Within moments, he'd hoisted her high above the crowd, tossing her as effortlessly as a feather. She sat with her legs draped over his chest, his strong hands securing her. And the broad shoulders she'd delighted in nestling against in her bed now provided a stable base. Spontaneous laughter bubbled up inside of her. She relaxed with the sway of his body beneath her, and the faint tickle of his breath on her thigh as he sang along with the music. His voice wasn't audible. The power of the massive sound system took Phoenix Alferez's throaty roar and magnified it almost to the point of pain, blotting out all other sound.

He hadn't sung for her yet, but he'd promised he would. Tomorrow, while the army of workers swarmed in to dismantle this world they'd inhabited for a week, she and Charlie would move into rooms in the castle. And she hoped he would take her to his special place, deep in the depths where normally it was Finn, alone with his thoughts and his music. He'd already trusted her enough to share parts of him he didn't share easily, let her in far more than she could ever have imagined a few short days ago. Now she wondered if he was prepared to take that trust further, let her step beyond the barriers, take her with him to places no one else ever got to see.

After the last notes faded away, they rode the wave of the surging crowd pouring out of the main stage area. Underlying the hum of elation, each person knowing they had witnessed something truly special in The Destitute's thundering full stop to the festival, ran a tiny thread of melancholy.

As bare-chested Mick Harrison flounced off stage, tossing out a final foul-mouthed farewell—"Thanks for coming, you can all fuck off now, see you next year!"—his words popped the magic bubble surrounding them. Protected by its fragile walls, for five days of summer a world of music and laughter existed in this rural Scottish backwater. Now they must all head back to their lives, mourning its loss, but perhaps hopeful of the possibility of recreating it in the future.

Layla trailed behind Finn, the man on whom she'd pinned her hopes for the future, as he now used his superior size to navigate the streams of people. For the first time, her desperate need to prove herself in her career took second place to another need: to prove to him she was worthy of his trust and he was worthy of her love.

Strangely, practical tell-it-like-it-is Charlie stood firmly behind this crazy notion that it was possible in the space of a week to meet someone, fall in love and have certainty that from this moment on, your lives would be forever intertwined. Without that support, Layla might have let her earlier doubts win. But now she'd abandoned those. All that was left was to coax Finn to leave his doubts behind, too.

She didn't doubt that he loved her. But she could see in his eyes the lingering hurt of Niamh casting a shadow, clouding his view. She needed him to believe she loved him back in equal measure, and that he hadn't got it wrong. She hoped in all the hours spent together he'd seen sufficient proof she was all in.

No light spilled from Charlie's tent opposite hers. She would still be over at the castle, buried deep in the workspace Finn had set up for her in what had been his father's study. Charlie had become a creature of the night, inhabiting this quiet room, her eyes studying miles of video footage, while around her festival goers slept off the heat and excesses of the day. So she wasn't there to note with approval that it was Finn who opened the door to Layla's tent and led her inside. She smiled in quiet satisfaction, remembering his reluctance that first night as she'd dragged him out of the torrential rain.

Tonight he led the way, and she followed him willingly. And tonight no haze of whisky clouded her senses, and she was glad of the clarity. Without either of them expressing it verbally, there was a mutual feeling they were ready to revisit that moment when he'd pulled away from her. They'd backed off physically in the intervening days, an unspoken agreement that there was no need for haste, and instead explored with words. But tonight, Layla craved the chance to let Finn possess all of her.

She flicked a switch by the doorway, flooding the tent with golden light. But he stepped over to it, his eyes meeting hers knowingly, and turned it off. In the half dark, his fingers fumbled with his phone, before he placed it on the small table, a glowing rectangle, its light reflecting off the canvas ceiling. As he drew her in close to him, sounds of an acoustic guitar drifted up from the phone, the melody and words familiar: "Dancing in the Dark". But the haunting vocals and stripped back guitar were far removed from Springsteen.

A bell-like woman's voice controlled the melody, letting it roll and flow around them, while occasionally hinting at a restrained power. They swayed in time, the darkness blocking out all but the press of his warm body against her length, his arms protective around her shoulders and the rhythm of their hearts, playing in unison.

"Beautiful," Layla murmured. She wanted to imprint this moment on her brain forever: the featherlight fingers ghosting her cheek, the weight of his chin resting on her shoulder, the soft steady breaths caressing her neck, and his fingers buried in her hair.

"Amy Macdonald," he said, his voice a whisper, "a wee Scottish lassie. I'll take you to see her one day." One day. A day in the future. Their future together.

As the music faded into silence, he released her, standing back as if they balanced on the edge of a cliff. Even now, it seemed he teetered between taking her hand and leaping together or imprinting the moment before backing away. In the faint glow of the fairy lights, she tried to read his expression.

"A day was enough for me to know," she said. "After five, I'm absolutely sure. Are you?" She feared his answer, but the absence of any wariness in his eyes gave her hope.

"Oh, I'm sure," he said, pressing a kiss on her forehead. "I just wanted to look at you first. To remember you like this for all the time that's still to come."

It was her turn to step away. "And like this," she said. Eyes locked on him as she pulled the top over her head, discarding it on the floor. She stood and let him observe a moment while she drank in the small smile that tugged at his lips.

"Definitely like this," he said. "Come here."

He held out a hand, but instead of reaching for it, she took control of it and placed it on her breast. She shuddered at the touch as he cupped it firmly, bringing his large thumb to caress her nipple. The firm rolling motion sent little jolts of pleasure rippling downwards. Now an urgent hand tilted her jaw, his mouth meeting hers, her sharp inhales of breath stifled by his lips, his answering moan muted by her kiss.

Hungry now, he thrust her back against the tent pole, his free hand busy at the waistband of her denims, deftly popping the row of buttons. She gasped in anticipation as a finger dug inside the lace panties, before sliding smoothly down into the hot wetness between her legs. He moved it back and forth with careful strokes, while a thumb found what he sought and began to circle the heat at her centre. His other hand twined in her hair, insistent as he dragged her mouth against his, his tongue teasing.

Her own hands fumbled at his jeans, and he slid his hands away from her, although the echo of his touch remained, all her nerve endings still raw. Two sets of hands flew, hastily dispensing with their remaining clothes. He lifted her to him, and she wrapped her legs around his waist.

Folding his arms around her, he lay her back on the bed with the utmost care, like she was a fragile butterfly. "My god," he said, "I feel like I'll crush you." He lay alongside her, trailing one hand from the hollow of her neck, flickering between her breasts, before seeking the spot that once again caused uncontrollable little gasps to escape from her lips. He stifled them with kisses, finally drawing back with an amused smile.

"How soundproof do you think these tents are?" he asked. While freed from the insistence of his hungry mouth, his hand continued to circle and tease and thrust.

"Not very, I imagine," she gasped. "But I think I'm beyond caring," she huffed out as his hand remained relentless, and she arched her hips to meet it.

"Good," he said. "Because I can't stop all that noise you're making at the same time as I do this." He dropped his head to her breasts, his tongue nipping and tasting, before tickling at her navel. As it flickered across her stomach, she squirmed in pleasure, while the gasps became moans.

"And this," he said. She stilled for a moment, as he removed the finger that had so skilfully amped up her pleasure, and instinctively let her thighs fall open, making way for his head between them. His tongue found its home, and each wave of pleasure brought her closer to orgasm, as she twisted a hand in his hair.

"Finn, oh my god, you're going to make me come," she puffed out.

"That was the objective," he hummed against her thigh. "Making love to you has been on my mind all night." He planted delicate kisses against the skin there, through a self-satisfied smile.

"Wait," she said, as his mouth made its way back to its centre of attention. She struggled to get the words out between her still ragged breaths. "Finn, I don't want you to just make love to me, I want you to make love with me."

"Oh, I think that could be arranged." His voice was thick with the promise of mutual pleasure. He slid his body up the length of her, taking most of his weight on his elbows. Even so, the press of skin to skin, the exquisite feeling of his solid presence against her, and the hard shaft pressing between her legs, caused her to shudder against him in anticipation. "Give me a moment."

He dotted a playful kiss on the tip of her nose before rolling onto his side. One long arm reached down to the floor, retrieving his jeans from the tangle of clothes. He sat back with the small foil packet in his hand.

"Want to help me out here?" he said, offering the condom on his palm.

"Oh, I want," she said, taking it and straddling him. His erection stood between them, and she thanked her deft doctor's hands, as she tended to the task swiftly. Easing herself over him, his moan of pleasure sent a ripple of heat through her, and with arched back she gave in to the rhythm, their bodies matched perfectly in the motion of the dance.

Waking up in the tent that first morning to sweat-soaked sheets and Finn's limbs entwined with hers, she'd felt exhilaration. The soft glow of a four am dawn through the canvas roof announced a new day and a new chapter in her life. Two days later she lay in an equally blissed-out doze, having slipped easily into the comfort of that new life, already writing beautiful words on each page.

The sweet satisfaction of waking up in his bed for a second morning, knowing this could be every morning, was enticing. Cocooned in his room, the heavy curtains kept the new day at bay for as long as they wanted. The faintly snoring man beside her snuffled, turned over, and shuffled into wakefulness.

"Morning, beautiful," he mumbled. He rolled onto one elbow, a tumble of sexy bed hair falling across his face. "God, I love waking up to you," he said. "Can we do this forever?"

"For as long as you want," she replied, enjoying the mellow Scottish voice that skimmed across her, like a soft caress.

He stroked her hair, while with eyes closed, she thought about what that promise meant for her. Two days ago, she'd tossed all her plans aside. Not that it was difficult. When she faced it squarely, she knew two things she didn't want to do.

Number one, she never wanted to work in an ED again. She was done. ED, ER, EW, A&E—whatever the acronym, this was no longer her happy place. She needed more from her career than negotiating a never-ending stream of faces and cases. The GP role sat well upon her, so that was what she'd look for. But if it came to a choice between a GP job and Finn, to her surprise, her gut instinct told her she wouldn't choose the job.

Number two, she wasn't going back to New Zealand. Distance from her family worked well for all concerned. That way, they didn't have to deal with the huge divide between their lives and hers. It was easier not to confront their entirely different outlook on the world, viewing each other's choices from a safe position of curiosity that didn't require real understanding.

"What the hell are you thinking about?" The amusement in his voice pulled her out of her serious thoughts. "I see your little face all screwed up." His hand cupped her cheeks playfully, as if she was a child. "Your brows meeting just here—" He placed a kiss in the centre of her forehead. "—in a frown." Relaxation spread through her in an instant, soothed by his tenderness. "It looks like you're about to renege on that 'for as long as you want' statement."

"Absolutely not." She curled towards him, sealing her reassurance with a light kiss that quickly descended into mouths clashing and tongues dancing. "Believe me now?" She came up for air for a moment, before, with a nod and the flash of a mischievous smile, he pulled her into him.

"I do, but it wouldn't hurt you to convince me some more."

"You promised to do the convincing today. Remember?" He'd told her that he'd take her somewhere that would prove there was no going back for him. However, despite her teasing and pleading, he had then stubbornly refused to be drawn on it any further. She hoped that perhaps this was the day he would trust her with an invitation into his studio, the quiet haven where he found stillness in a turbulent world.

"OK, if you'd rather we do that, time to get some clothes on." There was a note of disappointment in his voice, but an edge of anticipation, too. "Attractive as that body is, I can't have you wandering around the house with it on full display. Even though Euan's still 'recuperating' down in the bloody south of France, there's still Mum and Isabel. They might be open-minded, but that's probably one step too far, even for them." And with a playful slap on her naked butt, he turned and rummaged for his own clothes on the floor.

The sole feature of the small passageway that led off the main hall was a solid steel door resembling a bank vault. It was an odd contrast to the weathered timber frame and ancient stonework surrounding it. Finn's fingers tapped a code into a keypad and the door gave a gentle hum before swinging open.

A series of small lights leapt into life, revealing dark wood-panelled walls and roughhewn stairs of golden stone disappearing downwards. An aura of suppressed energy surrounded him, like a coiled spring, wound tight. He motioned for her to go ahead of him, while he secured the door behind. The well-lit stairs appeared benign, but even so, they gave the impression of stepping into a Bond movie, or perhaps an episode of *Game of Thrones*.

"Dungeon? Or dragon's lair?" she called back to him.

"Just *my* lair," he said. His voice came husky in her ear, having caught her up in his eagerness. "And I promise I won't detain you against your will."

"I don't mind you detaining me at all, Mr McGill," she said, tossing him a flirty smile. "But seriously, how come all the security?"

"I know. It's a bit weird. After all, there's nothing top secret in here," he said, opening a second door, this one neither formidably solid nor locked like the first. "I guess when Dad gave me the money to set it up—about six years ago—I had the feeling this could be one place that was totally mine, where I determined everything from the décor to the contents, and controlled who might gain access. When you're an adult still living much of your life in close quarters with your family, your every move scrutinised by them, not to mention a swag of household servants—we had a full complement of them back then—and of course you can't even take a casual stroll to the village pub without someone noting your presence; it's as if nothing is private. I suppose this was my small way of striking back."

That distinctive fragrance, with notes of lavender and sandalwood, met them at the entrance. She inhaled it, the familiar smell already etched in her brain as that of Finn. It marked his spaces: his bedroom, his office, and here at his studio. With a smile, she remembered how now it even marked her; when she took off her clothes, if she brought them to her face, this was the smell that teased her senses.

The windowless studio was huge, but despite that had a cosy feel, buried down here in the depths of the earth and bathed in a warm glow from banks of lights that ran its length. They nestled within a ceiling of a dimpled pale material; the same material also lined the walls. Layla presumed it was necessary for the correct acoustics. The wooden floor was barely visible, tucked beneath a patchwork of Persian rugs.

But the real stars of the show were the instruments. In a rack, a rainbow of guitars in an array of shapes and sizes stood waiting, flickers of light reflecting off their shiny lacquered surfaces, as if each one hoped to catch Finn's attention. A gleaming saxophone merited its own stand. Two keyboards stood along one wall, and between them an odd instrument, barely more than an s-shaped skeleton on a metal stand.

"Electric violin," he said with a grin, noting her frown. He whisked the strange instrument off its stand, propped it under his chin, and with the flick of a switch launched into a frenzied version of a piece of classical music that she recalled from her dreary compulsory music classes at St Aidan's. It bore little resemblance to the original, and its new appeal was generated simply by the sight of the man playing, eyes closed, a look of sheer bliss on his face and his whole body engaged in the task.

She was in awe at the speed and skill of his hands, the bow rising and falling, his fingers deftly navigating the frets. Yet it appeared effortless; he and the instrument, perfect partners in an elaborate dance. The music carried her along, building faster and stronger, and then finally dropped her back to earth, as he finished with a flourish.

"I thought you might like that," he said, meeting her grin of delight with one of modest pleasure. "And now you can see it's not all about the rock and roll."

"But mostly," she said, pointing at the two drum kits that dominated the space.

"Yeah, mostly." He placed the violin almost reverently back on the stand. "Take a seat," he said, while he arranged himself behind the more traditional looking kit. "Any special requests?"

"You choose something for me. For us."

"That's easy," he said, with an enigmatic smile. He swivelled around, fingers flying across the keys of the computer set up on a table behind him, adjusted levels of a soundboard to his right, and twisted microphones into place. He sat, his body tensed in readiness, eyes locked on her, waiting for it to begin.

Layla knew what he'd chosen the moment a faint teasing single guitar riff emerged from the speakers behind her. Her eyes widened in delighted recognition: "Everlong". Of course, it was iconic Foo Fighters, but it was also a love song. He got it—that singing about love didn't have to be all sweet and plaintive. He got her.

Layla couldn't help but move with the familiar music as the sound of a second guitar crashed over top of the first. Now Finn's body sprang into action, layering the drums' insistent rhythm across the recorded track. The mellow voice that she had suspected poured from him, as he launched into lyrics she knew by heart, but sung as she'd never heard them before. He sang them to her, each word imbued with the rawness of his feelings. When he kicked into the chorus, letting loose the full power of his voice, the intensity overwhelmed her. She closed her eyes, her senses unable to deal with it all at once.

As the last notes faded to silence, she opened her eyes to his shy smile, projecting a quiet pride that he'd elicited so much emotion in her. She couldn't help the tears that sprang to the surface, and she leapt up behind the drum kit to wrap him in a hug so tight that surely he could feel her heart pounding out a rhythm that said "I love you, I love you, I love you."

23

Journey

Dallblane Castle, Scotland - July 2019

"A PITY REALLY," FINN said. Above their heads, the bluest of skies stretched in a vibrant canopy. Scotland had defied its reputation as the land of endless rain and gloom this past week. They stacked their bags on the front steps of the castle, waiting for Euan. He'd agreed to be their driver to the train station, where they'd make a short hop to Glasgow and then beyond to London. "Would have been a good day for us to spend time with my other favourite girl," he added, with a cheeky smirk.

"Are you keeping secrets from me, Finn McGill?" she teased.

"Well, yes, but I don't think you'll mind the other woman in our relationship. Come on," he said. "We've got time. How about I introduce you?"

She followed him around the path to a series of sheds that crouched low behind the main castle. He produced a bundle of keys from his pocket and pointed the fob at one of the doors. The smooth mechanism glided up to reveal a lineup of vehicles.

On one side languished a moss green Range Rover well past its prime; on the other a large sedate silver BMW sedan sat prim and proper. And nestled between them a bright scarlet convertible smiled at them. Centred between its two glassy-eyed headlights was a deep chrome 'V', not a marque that Layla recognised. While she loved cars, she'd not delved into anything pre-1980, and this one was certainly much older than that, a classic, or possibly even vintage.

"Oh, Finn, that's adorable," she said. "I have no idea what I'm looking at. But definitely old, and in beautiful condition, I bet she's worth a few pounds."

"Yeah," he said, "isn't she pretty? Another reason I hope when all the accounts are settled, there's enough money to see us through for a while. I'd be gutted if it came to—" He let his voice drop low. "—selling her. I can't even talk about that in front of her."

Layla caught his teasing tone, but behind it she could see how the thought genuinely pained him.

"So tell me all," she said. "If I'm going to share you with her, maybe it's best we get acquainted."

"She's a Daimler SP250, 1962. I've owned her for almost ten years. But in this condition—" Again he slipped into a theatrical whisper. "—I'd probably get at least fifty thousand pounds."

"If I'd known sooner, I think I might have scrapped that train ticket."

"To be honest, there's one small reason why it's best you didn't." They walked around the side of the car and Layla peered into the black leather interior. She could see it straight away: no space for luggage.

"OK, but when we come back, you are definitely taking us both out for the day."

Those words felt good: 'when we come back'. Because soon they would. In the space of ten days, he'd turned her world upside down. Her plans for the future—return to London, maybe take a brief jaunt back to France and then head home to New Zealand to find a GP position with possibilities—all now swept aside, for what she wasn't sure, except for the fact that it would involve him.

Her parents would have plenty to say on the matter. After years of arguing that this path she'd chosen was perfect, now she might have to admit to them she may have been wrong. There'd be sarcastic comments for sure, maybe some smugness, but she'd tough it out. She'd long ago learned how to put a buffer between herself and their opinions.

Her friends might struggle to understand. She, who they'd only ever known as someone wedded to a medical career, was for the first time in her life making that a lesser priority. And her biggest hurdle was to break the news to Will. With him, it felt like a betrayal after the years they'd supported each other on that single-minded journey through med school and the highs and lows of becoming fully-fledged doctors. But by choosing to keep her in the friend zone and nothing more, he'd abdicated any right to expect her life and his would continue to move forward in tandem. He'd made it clear she was his best friend, so now he could prove it by supporting her new choices.

She'd always needed to prove herself, desperate to earn respect for her knowledge and skill as a doctor. Now the single thing she needed to prove was her loyalty and love to Finn. That prospect offered blissful freedom. It was ironic that committing herself to someone could make her feel like a bird escaped from its cage, testing its wings as it soared above the world with a dizzying new perspective. Soaring high beyond the clutches of doubt that sought to bring her crashing back to earth below.

"I promise," he said as he led her back into the bright sunshine, "that you and I will do many miles in that car. So many things I have to show you."

Hearing the crunch of footsteps on gravel, she turned to see Euan's scrawny legs appear around the corner. "Take the Beemer?" he asked, jangling a set of keys.

"Yeah, might as well ride in comfort."

"No other option then," said Euan, casting disparaging glances at both the Daimler and Range Rover, before unlocking the BMW with a beep. While they loaded up cases, Charlie appeared, taking a brief reprieve from the work she'd been buried in since breakfast.

"See you in a couple of days," she said, delivering one of her usual rib-bruising hugs. "I think I'll have everything I need by then. Just want to capture a few more background pieces. I can splice them into the main footage and we have a winner." Her face glowed with enthusiasm. Layla couldn't recall ever seeing her friend so happy. "Make sure you tell Reed he'd better not have lapsed into any bad habits while we've been gone."

"For sure," Layla said through a laugh, "and even if he has, I'll knock him back into line for you." After a few months living with Reed, who was as pedantic as Charlie over household organisation, she doubted any reprimand would be necessary.

Charlie moved on to Finn, who'd stood observing the two of them with an indulgent grin. "And as for you," she said, offering him an equally powerful hug, "make sure you look after her. You know I'll come for you if you don't." Her wink was playful. Finn had certainly won Charlie over. "And look after yourself too. You might have your own personal doctor, but I want you to be careful. I don't want you dropping dead on me when this project is just getting off the ground." In her rough, unsentimental fashion, Charlie offered her hopes that the outcome of this trip would be good news.

They dropped the subject as Euan approached the driver's door. It seemed insensitive to state it outright in front of him: they had their hopes pinned on the visit to London. If all went well, the barrage of tests at a high calibre cardiology clinic would reveal Finn as a winner in the family genetic lottery, the one who lacked the ticking time bomb Euan harboured inside him, the one that had killed their father. And if it didn't go well, if the news was bad—it still needn't be a death sentence. She was determined that either way, she'd support him. She wasn't about to lose the best thing that had ever happened to her.

They drove in virtual silence. After Euan's rebuffs of her first attempts at polite conversation, she pulled out her phone and scrolled through messages, followed by firing off a quick text to Reed to remind him they would be in London that afternoon. It was a relief to think of zipping along through the British countryside on the train, rather than a reverse of the chaotic roadie with Charlie that had brought her to Scotland.

After a short hop on a tired local train and then trailing behind Finn as they navigated the bustling Glasgow station, at last she snuggled up beside him, soothed by the rolling motion. The rhythmic flicker of the landscape was like watching a movie on fast forward. This time to sit in comfortable, silent companionship or to talk without the intrusion of his busy life was a gift. He deftly balanced a Bowie biography on his lap, turning the pages with one hand while resting his other on hers.

Meanwhile, she let her mind wander with Emily Brontë across the haunting Yorkshire moors. She sat, legs curled up beneath her. The cloth-bound book plucked from a shelf in the castle library weighed heavy in her hands. She wasn't familiar with either the physical weight of this sort of reading material or the weight of the words, but ignored both, captivated by the tragedy of *Wuthering Heights*.

She'd never read these classics of English literature before. In high school they'd forced her as close as she'd ever dared to cheating—finding summaries online, 'borrowing' notes from friends, in a desperate attempt to avoid failed assignments. As a teenager in far off New Zealand, they'd felt too remote, so beyond her experience. But now immersed in this country, she'd read three in a week and was hungry for more.

She let the book fall closed for a moment and at the motion, he turned to her. "All good?"

"Never better," she said. "How about you? Nervous?'

"A little. But either way, I know it's going to be fine. I mean, this thing doesn't have to wreck my life? Right?"

"Absolutely right. Look, I knew a bit about it already, but I have to admit I did some reading up about it the last few days."

"And?" His eyes took on that intense expression he got sometimes. How could she ever lie to a man in the face of a look like that?

It was like he saw right into her. It could be unnerving, but there was also something beautiful in the feeling of being seen so clearly and being known so intimately by another person.

"A person with HCM can generally live a pretty normal life. And has a normal life expectancy. Hell, most people with it don't even know they've got it till later in life. So you and Euan have a tremendous advantage. If there's one good thing to come out of your father's death is that you knew to get the tests. To be honest, the only drawback for someone young is that you should avoid competitive sports."

Laughter spilled out of him. "I've been doing that all my bloody life. Now I know why I'm so shit at virtually every sport I've ever tried. Explains my natural aversion to PE at school."

"The universe was telling you something?"

"Looks like it," he chuckled. "So just stick to lifting a few weights in the gym and I'll be fine?"

"Or playing online games with those nerdy mates of yours you mentioned."

He grimaced. "They may be my friends, but there are some things I refuse to do, even in the name of friendship."

Layla hadn't expected she'd get to meet any of Finn's friends, nerdy or otherwise, but here she was preparing to meet his best friend Dexter Woodham. She sat before the mirror, trying to apply makeup, flustered from the rush to meet their five-thirty appointment with him.

The leisurely start to the day had ended in a flurry of activity. Arriving at Euston, it was only a quick trip on the tube to the flat, but long enough for Finn to spring his surprise on her. She was to do the obligatory check in with Reed so she could report back to

Charlie, grab another bag of clothes more appropriate to drinks and a dinner out, while he called a cab to whisk them off to a hotel in Regent Street.

His impulsive decision to interrupt her shower, slipping in under the cascade of water to press that beautiful but demanding body against hers, knowing full well what her own response to the slick wetness of him would be, had cost them another half an hour, but it was a price worth paying. Even now, the memory of it stirred desire low inside her.

"You look stunning," Finn whispered in her ear as they made their way through the lobby to where a taxi awaited them. It was, of course, the first time he'd seen her in anything but singlet tops teamed with shorts or jeans. It wasn't hard to improve on that, though she suspected she had done rather well in her choice if the approving sweep of his eyes when she'd appeared in this dress was anything to judge by. She knew the emerald dress suited her well, with its body-hugging shape and deep v-front. The sleeveless design and the cut of the neckline aligned with the path of her tattoos so harmoniously that from a distance it looked as if intricate sleeves of indigo lace covered her arms.

She was acutely aware of those designs tonight. Hovering while she attempted to tame her hair and apply a brush of make-up, it was the first time he'd asked about them. Until now, he'd simply accepted them as part of her. But today the questions had surfaced.

"How long have you had these?" His fingertip trailed from wrist to elbow, and she shivered at the lightness of his touch.

"Since I was eighteen. Just after I left high school." She continued to blot foundation on her chin. The next question hung in the air between them—why? It was hard to ask that without the further implication—why would you?—as if no one in their right mind would choose this. Why would she take the clear unmarked skin of her youth and embellish it to this degree? Why would she allow these indelible marks that would stay with her for a lifetime?

"To help you face the big bad world out there?" No one had ever worked it out on their own before. Not even Will. Or Charlie. She'd patiently explained, and they understood. But here was a man who didn't need an explanation.

"Yeah, a bit like putting this make-up on," she said with one last dab of the sponge. "Putting on my armour before I plunge into battle." She swept some blusher across her cheekbones. "Or maybe issuing a challenge? Somehow it made me feel braver, a way of saying 'fuck you' to anyone who dared to judge me by how I looked."

"And did it work?"

"Sometimes. But often not." She paused to make two deft sweeps of eyeliner. Her steady hands came in useful for less frivolous tasks than doctoring. "People are going to judge you whatever you look like, or whatever you do."

"No regrets?"

"Nowadays—never. I figure if people don't like them, it's their problem, not mine. As they say, 'the people who matter don't mind, and the people who mind don't matter'—good old Dr Seuss wisdom."

"They're stunning," he said, as he lightly kissed the line of her collarbone, his lips leaving little hot tingles of desire along its length. "I can't imagine you without them."

That gave her confidence as she strode towards the cab, hoping to make a good impression on his closest friend. After all, while she was now part of Finn's life, she was still a stranger to many parts of it.

The expensive private clinic was in the upmarket district where all the high-powered specialists clustered, and within walking distance of the hotel Finn had booked, but Layla insisted on a cab that morning.

"Not a good idea to get your heart rate elevated," she said, sliding into the big bench seat beside him.

"Then stop fussing," he said. "You're as bad as Mum and Isabel." A small laugh broke through his grimace.

"I thought you appreciated having your own personal physician." She let her lips fall into a pout. He loved it when she tried to act sulky, seeing it as a challenge for his own mouth to seek out hers, coaxing a kiss and a smile.

"Mmm," he hummed, "especially when she offers to kiss it better."

She broke away with a playful shove. "We are not making out in the backseat of this cab on the way to the clinic either," she warned. "One, this cabbie is already giving us the look. And two, that will definitely elevate your heart rate."

"Whatever you say, Doctor Angell," he said, falling back from the kiss, but still resting a casual hand between her thighs.

The protective feelings that surged in her as she left him in the elegant reception area were far removed from those of a doctor for their patient. She knew better than he did—whatever the outcome of the tests, this thing was manageable. Despite that knowledge, it took a focused effort to damp down her nerves and farewell him with a smile. No matter what information this day provided, he had a future. They had a future. The thought brought a flush of optimism as she set off for the shops of Oxford Street.

A whole day to kill in London's upmarket shopping district would be a welcome luxury for plenty of her old schoolmates, but for Layla, it was merely a diversion and not a successful one. By three o'clock she languished on the pavement outside the clinic, pondering if it was too early to go inside.

Spits of rain pushed her through the door to sit on one of the broad modern couches in the waiting area. With relief, she noticed that one of the floor to ceiling windows overlooking the courtyard garden was in fact a door. Not wanting to be one of those anxious family members hovering in reception, she took the cup of coffee provided by a smiling staff member and made her way into the walled space. Large pavers bordered by neat topiary hedges enclosed an unlikely explosion of lush tropical plants, a vibrant contrast to the severe grey stone bounding them.

While the threatening drops of rain had abated, the sultry humidity of the afternoon remained, an unpleasant reminder of the unexpected heatwave stalled across the city. Low overhead, a thick wedge of clouds loomed, and Layla could almost physically feel their pressure, pinning her within the enclosure.

A high-pitched sound caused her head to flick back to the glass door, despite her mind rejecting that as the source. At first it seemed like the tone of a heart monitor flatlining, a noise that never failed to stir dread in her. To a doctor, that was the sound of failure. But this sound was different, an underlying malevolent drone harmonising with the higher range. At the same time, it was as if the noise was directed through some sort of amplifier, but not an external one, rather a device hard-wired into her brain. The accompanying excruciating pain caused Layla's fingers to lose their grip on the coffee, her hands useless except to clutch at her ears in a futile attempt to block the sound.

The iron fist of the overhanging clouds pressed from above at the same time as the waves of sound dragged her body downwards against her feeble protests. She crashed onto the warm grey pavers of the pathway, the low topiary hedging at their edge, catching her hair in its prickly fingers, cushioning her head on the way down.

Part Three

HERE

24

Back To Earth

London, England - July 2019

HER FINGERS LAY IN a puddle of warm liquid. A slight flex of her hand suggested it wasn't blood, not viscous enough, and lacking the pungent metallic odour she could always recognise from the tiniest drifting molecules. Instead a green smell, like crushed leaves overlaid with dampness, the earthy fragrance of nature, wafted around her head.

She lay wrapped in a blanket of silence. As her awareness reached out, making a tentative brush against her surroundings, she noticed the benign chirping of a lone bird, a tiny repetitive sparrow-like cheep. Its hesitant sound mirrored her own reluctance to explore further, but she was unable to prevent the intrusion of the muted but still raucous blaring of a car horn. It subsided, making way for the faint background hum of traffic. Its normality soothed her, and she made no attempt to do anything more but lie there, lulled by the even buzz.

With a crash, a door flung open, and an avalanche of sound descended upon her. Raised voices, running feet, a call for help. In the midst she isolated a familiar voice, repeating her name over and over, in time to a painful rhythm as sharp fingers tapped out a coded message on her clavicle. Her eyes flew open, and the pain receded.

"God, Layla."

A pair of dark eyes met hers. She knew those eyes but squeezed hers shut, focusing on the thought, the name, but unable to retrieve it from the tangle in her head. When she blinked them open again, she saw the eyes weren't dark at all. They'd drawn back a little to reveal irises of bluest-grey, the darkness simply pupils dilated wide in fear. And the name flowed into her mouth, scraping across her tongue, escaping her lips; a faint query delivered with a small hiss of breath.

"Will?"

"Hey, baby." His voice was low and steady now. "What's all this about then, huh?" A tender hand swiped at her curls, tucking them behind her ears.

"I dunno," she said, squinting at the sky, where a hidden sun illuminated the clouds with a punishing silver glare. Her breath came out in small huffs.

His hair fell forward, a gilded halo above her. Beyond him, other faces gathered, still hazy, but for the tense lines of their mouths. She let her eyes close again and did as he asked.

"Just breathe baby, nice and slow. Just breathe."

The examination room was no different to dozens of others she'd been in, except for the fact it was her lying on the bed, beneath the sheet a web of leads feeding the sticky sensors attached to her body. The monitoring equipment beeped quietly, and she cast an approving look at the readings scrolling across the small screen.

"See," she said to him, as he perched next to her, fair brows still knitted in a frown. "Now please get me out of here."

To Will's dismay, the first thing to surface once she'd arrived back in a fully alert state was her rebellious streak. Channelling the intractable attitude of some of her most stubborn former patients, she'd presented him with a succinct but pithy argument why she should be already out of this clinic and in a cab back to the apartment. She wasn't about to reveal that at this moment her knowledge of that apartment was at best sketchy.

For now, she only clearly recalled the moments from when Will had pounced on her lying in the garden of the cardiology clinic, drumming on her collarbone with sufficient force to not only rouse her, but leave a painful residual sensation. It was so at odds with how she normally felt about him touching her there, with butterfly kisses he knew could strip away all her barriers in seconds. She shuddered a little at the remembered force, his urgency removing all finesse in his hands.

With a sigh, he powered off the monitor and methodically peeled off each sensor. "Overheating, huh? That's your story and you're sticking with it?"

"It's not a story," she replied with a snort. "It's a fact. You've seen it on the news, even back in New Zealand. The slightest sign that the Brits are in for something that might actually pass for summer weather, it's worldwide headlines, and all over London people are keeling over with the heat." He rolled his eyes, but didn't attempt to interrupt the barrage. "And I, dressed in jeans, stupidly leave an air-conditioned area, go into an enclosed garden with no shade and not a breath of wind to offer the slightest reprieve, while drinking a hot coffee instead of the iced water I should have chosen. No wonder I passed out. I'm not sure why you're all being so bloody dramatic."

"I'm not going to argue," he said, in a tone that indicated he still wrestled with that vow as he spoke it. "Let's do what you want, get you out of here, and hope that your self-diagnosis is right."

"I bloody know it's right," she said, unable to suppress a final irritated huff for emphasis. "And I'm sorry," she said, guilt at what she'd put him through, mellowing her tone a little. "The first time your wife appears here, and this happens. Not a great first impression, I know."

"That's the least of my concerns, believe me," he said, with a grimace, indicating that she and her unexpected argumentative mood was his number one concern. "Anyway, you'll be able to make up for that with a better impression at the dinner party on Friday."

She was grateful he was still busy winding up the snaking leads and stashing the trolley of equipment in a corner. Otherwise, he would have seen the shock that flared on her face. Dinner party on Friday? Yet another thing that, for some reason, she could recall absolutely nothing about.

The ringtone was the one she'd been dreading. Charlie. With Will she'd had the advantage of reading his body language, as well as blithely following a few steps behind him, cueing off his actions so she might hide this veil of vagueness that overlaid all of her thoughts and memories of the past two weeks. Her rational mind urged caution, whispering in her ear that Will was right—something strange had happened to her in that garden. She tried to fend off the idea. Her doctor brain supplied strident admonishments. It disliked how she had deliberately chosen to ignore her years of training and experience. But there was some odd tenacious voice deep inside that insisted she should just move on, let it go.

Now Charlie was calling, and she summoned all her energy. How strange it was that it should take so much effort to appear normal. Charlie was as bad as Will, taking the role of personal bodyguard, sworn to protect her, not only from others but from herself. She needed to act like this was just a regular evening, doing whatever they did in the evening here in this London apartment.

"Oh my fucking god, Layla." She screeched the words, her face looming large. "What the fuck is going on with you?"

So Will had told her. Damn him, but it wasn't surprising he'd enlisted a supporter in the face of her deviation from common sense. He kept his eyes fixed on the BBC news, while listening in on the havoc he'd unleashed.

Layla deployed her years of experience at steering difficult conversations in the right direction. Once she'd diffused Charlie's explosion of concern, it took a few simple nudges and they were soon deep in discussion of a far more important subject—the festival documentary that looked set to consume Charlie's attention for the foreseeable future.

Layla nodded and tried to appear as if she knew all about it. But Charlie's meetings with the young festival organiser, her staying on to tidy up the footage before returning to London—they too were consigned to that vague part of her life that she'd given up on trying to understand for now. Perhaps, when Charlie returned, she could make use of the photographs and film to fill the yawning gaps in her memories.

Lying in bed that night, his limbs entwined with hers, Will conceded defeat. His chin rested on her head, as he cradled her in his arms, his body a protective parenthesis around hers.

"I know I've been a pain in the arse," he said. "I shouldn't have questioned your judgement. I'm sorry. It was disrespectful of me, Doctor Leroux." He murmured his apology against her hair.

"You are forgiven, Doctor Leroux. And you are still my favourite pain in the arse." She pressed a kiss against his chest, inhaling the comforting familiar smell of him, enjoying the tickle of his chest hairs beneath her cheek.

"It just stirred up all those bad memories of when I was unwell. The worry that this time there might be something unknown lurking there inside you, waiting to take you from me. I can't lose you, Layla. You're everything to me."

"You're not going to lose me," she said.

"I felt what life was like without you these past few months. I know I encouraged you to come over here with Charlie. But god it's been hard. I didn't realise how much I need to wake up with you in the morning. Have you come home at night. It's completely selfish, but if I had my time again, I'd never have let you go. Not without me. I never imagined how hard it would be to not have you in my life physically for so long."

"It's OK," she said. "I'm back now."

25

Parting

Three years later, Auckland, New Zealand - March 2022

SHE WAS BEREFT AT the thought he was leaving her. And that was crazy. How had it come to this? After all, three years ago she'd instigated a four-month separation so she might have a taste of travelling the world. But now, the threat of a mere week apart and she was teetering on the verge of tears.

Will had taken many such jaunts, a week or two here and there, often with Carson, indulging a love of snow that she didn't share. She'd never begrudged him the time away, not only for the sport, but an opportunity to do something he enjoyed with the only member of his family he cared for. This had to be yet another after-effect of two years of a world turned upside down, where they'd endured months not only trapped inside the country, but locked inside this city. The intensity of the experience had messed with everyone's heads. It seemed she wasn't immune.

Layla lay with her face buried in the curls of pale hair on his chest, quietly weeping. The salt tang merged with the sweet scent of him and the heady sweat of their lovemaking that lay thick in the air. It had been so long since they'd spent time apart that the wrench of his imminent departure had triggered crazy emotions she'd thought long buried.

"Oh, baby, don't cry," he said, one hand a caress on her shoulder. "It's only for a week. You know I'll be missing you every moment I'm away." His lips murmured against her hair, the gentle whisper of breath across her head like a kiss.

"I know," she said, the words muffled against his chest. "It's stupid. I'm sorry, but it's just—"

How did you put into words this unbearable tearing feeling, knowing that this man whose body mere moments ago was buried deep inside her, its rhythm matching her own in exquisite time, would not be there tomorrow, or the next day, or the next? Seven days, a blink of an eye to some, but to Layla it felt like forever.

"It's the prospect of not waking up to our recent daily ritual, isn't it?" he said through a throaty chuckle. "Me too. This interest in making a baby has definitely upped the game another notch."

She laughed through her tears. Neither of them could complain about a lack of sex at any time in their relationship. She loved making love with Will. Somehow, they continued to discover new dimensions to their intimacy, each still having the capacity to surprise the other. But since a couple of months ago, when she'd employed a bit of medical technology to confirm that nothing stood in the way of pregnancy, the thrill of potential new life each time they came together added a surprising layer of intensity. Now the tantalising possibility that soon they could be a family danced before them. And theirs would be a family unlike either of their own. On that, they were in full agreement.

She lifted her head, kissing him through a smile. "Oh yes, I fully intend to meet you at the airport next Saturday—no matter that the flight lands at a ridiculous time. I plan to whisk you home to our bed without delay. Make sure you get some sleep on the plane because there won't be any time for sleeping once you land." His flaccid penis unfurled a little against her thigh at the suggestion. She glanced down at it, a wicked giggle squeezing out. "Oh, looks like part of you thinks we might have time now, before Carson gets here?"

"I'm sure we have." He stiffened a little more. "He's paranoid about missing the flight. No way we need to leave as early as he intends." He flipped her onto her back, his knee nudging her still sticky legs apart as he fitted himself between her thighs while the heat bloomed inside her. "My brother can wait. This can't," he said with a growl.

Carson wasn't exactly pleased with that line of thinking when he arrived. He grumbled at Will for his tardiness until she appeared behind him in her robe, hair tousled and face still flushed. Guessing at the reason, he exchanged his frown for a knowing smirk.

"Looks as if even the chance of wilderness skiing in Utah can't compete with you," he joked, while Will checked through the cards in his wallet.

"Can't say I didn't try to persuade him to stay."

"You could have come with us."

"Well, I am rather envious of you two swooping around in a chopper. But you know I don't care about skiing one jot. Cold and I are not good friends."

"How many times do I have to tell you," Will interrupted, "you don't feel the cold. Why do you think we have all this gear?" He waved his hand at the oversized case propping up his skis in their bag and his ski boots in another.

"Well, make sure you protect these, too. Plenty of sunblock," she said, moulding her lips to his in a deep farewell kiss. "I have plans for them when you get back."

"I think that's my cue to head for the car," said Carson, sweeping up one case. "Please, don't let her tempt you back upstairs. We're late already," he added, with a theatrical roll of his eyes, before giving her a cheeky wink.

Layla loved this time of day, a golden interlude between the heaviness of sleep and the frantic bustle of her day. At least the commute south wasn't too bad. Driving against the worst of the traffic, and with the companionship of her favourite radio jocks, she usually arrived at work unfrayed. But the moment she stepped foot in the clinic there'd be no letup.

While most of the country breathed a huge collective sigh of relief that the worst was over, in South Auckland with so many large extended families, often living in crowded conditions, the long tentacles of the pandemic hadn't yet relinquished their grip. The five GPs faced a relentless stream of patients. Her day was always overbooked, but how could you turn away people in need?

The early morning autumn sun slanted across the broad oak kitchen table. She sipped her coffee, savouring the richness of a new blend of beans the enthusiastic owner of a deli down the road had persuaded her to buy. Picking up her phone, she tapped through to the world clock. One pm in Utah. By now, Will and Carson would be out on the snow. She envied their time off from the grind of work, and that they'd escaped New Zealand, a paradise turned prison for the past two years. But she didn't envy them plunging into the remnants of the American winter. It would be here soon enough without preempting it. Will's suggestion of going back to Tahiti in June was far more tempting.

She loaded her breakfast things into the dishwasher, as well as those Tristan had left scattered on the bench as he hurried out the door complaining about an early meeting. Some things didn't change. She picked up his half-eaten piece of toast and tossed it out onto the lawn. Watching the unruly group of sparrows scrabbling over their windfall, she caught a flash of navy blue. Two uniformed police officers made their way along the path.

She knew the moment she opened the door. They always came in pairs, caps in hand, faces wearing bland expressions of kindness. She'd seen it time and again when she'd worked in the ED: the stiff stance, the unnatural stillness, carefully fixed expressions of deathly calm in place as they prepared to unleash a storm. It took only a few pounding heartbeats for the dread to take hold.

"Leo!" she called before they could even speak. Her strangled voice came out as a high-pitched squawk.

She pushed a fist against her mouth, trying to suppress the guttural sobs welling up from deep inside. The officers' mouths moved, but Layla didn't hear the words above the roaring in her ears, the blood pulsing in her temples with painful throbs.

Leo appeared beside her, and seeing the blue uniforms, wrapped an arm across her shoulders, pulling her back from the doorway, as if by doing so he could place her beyond the clutches of this monster, while shielding her against the pain that was coming.

"Layla," he said. "Come and sit down."

With firm hands, he steered her into the lounge and bustled the officers onto a sofa. She sat gazing at them, willing them not to be real. Willing this not to be happening.

"Mrs Leroux," the older man began. His hazel eyes were so kind, but his words, cruel beyond anything she might have imagined, slammed into her. "I am afraid we have bad news. We've been contacted by police in the US. Your husband, William, and his brother, were in a party of seven caught by an avalanche. A rescue team was on the scene almost immediately. They located all of the group." He paused for a moment, swallowing as if it pained him too. "There were no survivors. We're still waiting for our US counterparts for official confirmation of the identities of those who died, but it's only a formality. I'm very sorry for your loss."

A howl of indignation at the platitude tore at her throat. Leo clasped her to him, his hand stroking her back as shuddering shockwaves rolled across her body.

"We'll be in touch when we know more. In the meantime, I'll leave my card here. Anything Mrs Leroux needs, just call."

She felt Leo's nod of assent, heard the officers rise to go, their footsteps strangely quiet for two large men, even their leaving an attempt at gentleness in the face of her overwhelming grief. And then he just held her, stroking her hair with warm hands, making small soothing noises, while she lay keening against him. Sucking in deep breaths of his pristine white business shirt, the clean smell so ordinary and reassuring, she might almost pretend this wasn't happening.

But it was. She'd seen other people clutch at small shreds of hope in this sort of situation, but she had none. There wouldn't be a phone call saying they'd got it wrong, that it wasn't Will who'd died, that it was someone else. They'd had one chance to sidestep tragedy nine years ago. They wouldn't have another.

She sat on their bed as the last light of the day frittered away, wearing one of Will's t-shirts she'd retrieved from the floor. She remembered watching him pull it over his head, his gaze never leaving hers, the promise of his body lean but muscular. Discarded on the floor as unimportant, now it became a treasured possession. It was a favourite; she loved its shade of blue, the colour of his eyes, with the cresting wave of the Quicksilver surf logo rolling across the front. Her hands moved of their own accord, scrunching the fabric, wringing it between her fingers as if she could squeeze the essence of the man from the fibres, conjure him before her eyes. She lifted it to her nose, inhaling the smell of him. How long would it linger? How long before even she, so attuned to each tiny nuanced part of him, would be unable to detect that he had once been in this place, touched these things, touched her skin?

She lay back on the bed rehearsing the script. *My husband and his brother were killed in an avalanche while on a ski trip in Utah.* These were the lines she would need to repeat over and over for the rest of her life, explaining his loss to other people, seeing their expressions of pity, and resenting it because they could never truly know what it was like to live without him.

She couldn't bear to dwell on the details for a second. The thought of the avalanche swallowing him and Carson within its terrible mouth left her gasping in distress, the physical pain in her chest so gripping she couldn't breathe. It was as if her panicked brain sought to further torture her, forcing her to live Will's last moments with him, the pressure crushing his lungs, the impossible lack of air, his limbs bent like matchsticks within the powerful tonnes of snow. Once again, she fought back, pushing the dark thoughts away, offering the only possibility for her survival. Once more her fingers traced the outline of the wave on her chest, allowing it to transport her to another happier place, the relentless sea carrying her back to where he waited on a tropical beach.

She perched on the deep leather couch, feeling like Alice in Wonderland having eaten a mushroom, now shrunk to child size. Her feet barely touched the ground. Next to her, Kirsten veered wildly within moments between soundless whimpers and small choking sobs. Their clasped hands felt natural, each drawing and giving support from this small gesture.

Hilton had dispatched a car to collect Kirsten, delivering the girls to her own parents before whisking her to Whitford so the family might plan what would happen next together. He'd done the same for Layla. But to her, the Leroux's attempt at kindness felt more like a summons, and the suggestion of her having some say in the matter a token offer.

The churning nausea rose again in her stomach, and she tried to swallow down the sour taste. She had visions of throwing up on Virginia's fur throw rug, or, if she made it that far, puking on the base of the fan shaped palm that sat in a huge black Morris and James pot on the deck outside.

A sickly smell of vanilla hung in the air, urging the nausea on. Locating its source, an enormous candle on the sideboard, she pried her hand from Kirsten's sweaty grip and, in two steps, snuffed out the flame between her fingers, uncaring of the black mark and instant blister that appeared on her singed skin.

They sat in silence and waited for the grieving parents to join them. She should pity these people, their two children gone in the blink of an eye. But she couldn't feel the slightest empathy. They'd made no effort to accept her into the family, preferring not to be reminded that their son loved her, instead, as far as possible, making her invisible.

The family photographs clustered on the wide mantelpiece opposite were proof. Will had given his parents one of their wedding photos in a gilt frame. This particular one of the hundreds Charlie had reeled off on the beach in Tahiti, capturing their love in stunning clarity, was her favourite shot of them. It was tucked in behind one of Carson and Kirsten's wedding, so Will's face laughing down at her was visible, but she, with her wild hair and tattooed arms was obscured. Now Hilton and Virginia had the opportunity to excise her from their lives completely. She wasn't sorry. After this was all over, she never needed to visit this house again, never had to see them again. She was adamant nothing could change that.

Layla moved mechanically through the funeral and the hours beyond, until once more she was standing on the verandah of their home, mute and numb. It was partly from the drugs—a colleague had called in one day, pressing the prescription into her hand, her eyes quietly insistent—and partly from the surreal feeling of breathing the crisp autumn evening air that Will would never breathe, while staring out on the back yard, empty of the children they'd hoped for but would never exist. As she inhaled, she detected an undercurrent of mustiness. It drifted from a mound of damp leaves ripped from the cherry tree in a weekend storm, the damp smell of death and decay infiltrating her lungs.

Inside, her father and brothers knocked back tequila shots. Her mother chain-smoked, a drooping roll-your-own cigarette pressed between her lips, with a glass of the cask wine she'd brought along in her hand. At times like this, Layla regretted her lack of the vices her family used to ease their passage through life. She wished she was the sort of person who found nicotine a balm for jarred nerves, or could drink until blessed oblivion took the sadness away. But she would need to find other ways. What those were, she had no idea.

The small group gathered in her home comprised those who had gladly peeled off from the huge formal function. She'd only gone to the reception lounge at the insistence of the Leroux family. But after fifteen minutes there, her grief had overwhelmed the dictates of funeral etiquette, and she'd fled under Tristan's protective arm. Her other friends and family had followed, Layla's escape giving them permission to do the same.

She still felt Tristan's concerned gaze upon her from where he stood in conversation with Charlie. She'd never imagined that she'd come to lean on him as she had this past week. His carefree and often downright irresponsible persona stripped away by loss, he'd revealed an unexpected reliable inner core. Doing all the heavy-lifting with practical matters—placing forms in front of her to sign, providing gentle advice on details of the funeral, acting as her intermediary with the Leroux family, negotiating with them on her behalf so at least she had some small say in how the world would farewell Will—he'd done it all with a quiet tenderness.

Lending his support in the way he knew best, Tristan had also navigated the legal maze that confronted her. It had almost broken her to hear him quietly explain the plans Will had made, plans Tristan had never thought he would need to enact so soon. She saw Will's love in that provision. She had no cause to worry about anything materially in the future. But with his love gone, the future remained bleak. She was uncertain how she'd even endure today, let alone all those days ahead without him by her side.

Charlie sat hunched on a couch, clutching at her girlfriend's hand. Her face was wretched, eyes sunk back in their sockets, underlined by the deep bruise-like hue of someone who'd barely slept for days. There were times since her arrival from the UK a few days ago that Layla swore the only thing keeping Charlie upright was the stunning woman she'd brought with her. They were like night and day, Charlie a pale shaft of Nordic sunshine, while Safiyah's skin was as dark and lustrous as a starless Sahara sky.

They'd met at a WOMAD festival, Charlie unable to focus her lens on anything but the striking lead singer of a Sudanese band. Engineering a meeting hadn't proved difficult, and with Safiyah equally smitten, the two had been virtually inseparable ever since, except when the demands of work required, which fortunately had been few. Two years of a severely damped down music scene hadn't been great for either woman's career, but had given them time apart from the world. They'd emerged from the lockdown with an unassailable bond, and an all-encompassing love that was immediately apparent to Layla the moment they'd walked into the international arrivals hall hand in hand. It was the one bright spot in this time; Charlie had finally found happiness.

Leo appeared with a mug of tea and a bulky cheese sandwich. "You should sit down," he said, nudging her towards the tatty sofa. "You've been on your feet all day."

Dear Leo. He had been her constant shadow since that first terrible morning, attentive to all the small daily needs that she was incapable of managing for herself: placing food in front of her, sweeping discarded clothes and towels into the laundry, and guiding her to bed with kind hands, nudging her to take the rest that her body desperately needed but her mind protested. He stood now with a firm hand on her back, still putting his own grief aside to support her through her own. She did as he asked, taking the cup and balancing the plate on her knee. Her hand traced the knobbly nylon cushion.

"He hated this couch. I don't know how many times he went to throw it out, then changed his mind," she said, a sad smile finding its way to her lips.

"Like all of us, he was too scared at the thought of facing Charlie. She'd have been extremely pissed off to come home and find her favourite couch had gone to the dump," Leo replied with a grin. "Just as well he didn't biff it, otherwise it would have been us left to explain."

"Thank you Leo," she said. "Somehow you've known what I needed these last two weeks better than I did."

"Hey," he said, his hand cupping hers, "it's what we do for the people we love." His brown eyes projected a calm that soothed, and she stared into them again, drawing on his quiet strength. "There's something else I'd like you to do," he said. "Something I think might help."

"Whatever it is, I'm sure if you think it's a good idea, it will be."

"I'll start moving this lot along soon," he said, nodding at the small group inside, who even now had returned to the world of normal, a faint laugh drifting across now and then, voices less hushed as they engaged in mundane chatter. "And while I'm doing that, I want you to go upstairs. Don't worry," he said, seeing the look of concern on her face. "I'll make the polite excuses. Tell them you're having a lie down. And maybe you should for a bit. But then I want you to pack a bag. I want to take you home, to my place. It's where I go when the world gets too much for me. The others will come too—Charlie and Safiyah, and Tristan. It's all organised."

If it was anyone but Leo, she might have pushed back at the suggestion. But she trusted this quiet man, and so after weaving her way through the small crowd, brushed by a consoling hand, accepting a sympathetic hug, she climbed the stairs on weary legs and set about packing.

26

Refugee

Northland, New Zealand - March 2022

There was a comfortable feel about the tired weatherboard house with peeling paint and a creaky front porch that crouched on the sand dunes fringing the bay. Leo's family had occupied this land from back before anyone could remember, their origins vaguely recalled in the oral history passed down from generations long past. Dotted in the gentle contours of the coast were a variety of small houses from different eras built by various family members as the need arose.

Those of his extended family who still lived permanently in the tiny Northland community had largely overlooked this one, constructed by Leo's great grandparents in the 1920s. The family consensus was they were happy for Leo to be its caretaker for as long as he wished. This was where he escaped to, leaving the bustle of the city behind, returning refreshed with a renewed energy to face the world. She felt its quiet magic too from the minute she walked up the rickety front steps. He'd been right to bring her here.

At this moment, he and Tristan were a little way along the beach, testing their luck with two tall surfcasting rods. Both men were immersed in the rhythm: hurling the line with a deft flick, hoping to land it as far out past the small surf break as possible, and then with a click of the reel, winding it back in with smooth constant turns. They were yet to hook anything tonight, but this morning's catch on the early high tide was now in Safiyah's deft hands.

She'd returned from a brief foray into the nearby rural service town, delighted with her successful mission to find suitable ingredients. Tonight she buzzed with excitement at the opportunity to showcase the North African cuisine she loved. Undeterred by the prospect of cooking on the wood-fired Aga, Safiyah leapt into filleting fish and chopping vegetables as she sang to herself. Her deep melodious voice and fragrant smells wafted from the kitchen, promising to tempt even Layla's jaded appetite.

There was a sudden pause, and Layla couldn't help but smile.

"For god's sake Charlie. If you lift that lid one more time, I swear I'll strangle you. And all that pacing back and forth is driving me bonkers. Get out of the kitchen. Outside would be even better."

It was definitely love between these two. No one else would ever dare speak to Charlie with such bossy candour. And no one else would cause Charlie to submit and meekly do as asked. She arrived with a thump on the old rattan couch next to Layla.

"She's something else," Layla said, summoning a smile.

"Oh yeah," Charlie said. "But she's my something else and I intend it to stay that way."

"I'm really happy for you, Charlie. You deserve this." It was true. Seeing this relationship firsthand was the only thing that had given her any small sense of happiness in the past two weeks.

"Yeah, I had to kiss a few frogs before I found my princess." Her tinkling laugh matched the dreamy expression in her eyes.

"I'm sorry Will never got to meet her. He would have loved her. Especially seeing her bossing you around and you trotting along meekly doing it." So many things Will would never get to do. The hurt surrounded her every thought, every word.

"As they say, 'happy wife, happy life'—well, not a wife yet, but she will be. We wanted to wait for this whole stupid pandemic thing to be over. Although she's been in London since she was a kid, she's still got family back in Sudan. We want to fly her grandmother over. And—"she paused, a slight awkwardness in her posture, "—well, you know, we'd love our friends from all over to be there too."

"I promise, I'll come," Layla said. She made the promise, already knowing how hard that would be, watching another couple pledge their love, knowing that her love was gone. But everything was hard.

"Well, leading on from that thought, honey, there's something else I wanted to ask you. Now, I know you thought you'd probably go back to your clinic, but there's an opportunity in the UK that might be worth considering. I had an email from a friend a few days ago, and I can't stop thinking about it, and about you."

Layla slumped in the seat. Typical Charlie, trying so hard to help in her no-nonsense practical way. You had to love her for trying. "OK," she said with an encouraging nod, even though she couldn't imagine it being anything she'd care to pursue.

"So, you remember when you were over in 2019, and we went to Rock The Castle, at Dallblane?"

Layla remembered it more because Charlie's footage from the festival had morphed into the great little documentary that had opened doors to her current work. Her actual memories of the festival itself seemed distant. She had recollections of the glamping tent, dusty pathways through meadows and gyrating crowds clustered around stages under the Scottish twilight. So much had happened since then, two and a half years of the entire world turned upside down.

"Yeah, I remember. After I finished that awful ED stint and when Will came up to spend time at the London cardio clinic."

"We're going to make a second doco following the progress of the festival this year. You know 'Rock The Castle rises above the pandemic' sort of thing, and so I've been spending quite a bit of time up there."

"You said it's to do with a friend?"

"Yes, Finn McGill. He's the guy who runs the festival, and who backed me on the first documentary. I mean, you wouldn't believe it, but he's about five years younger than us and he's a fucking Earl! Inherited the title, the castle and the whole frigging estate. Don't screw your nose up like that," she admonished, seeing the look of distaste flash on Layla's face. "He's not the least bit snobby. He's a good guy. But you know what they say about an heir and a spare? He was the spare. Never expected his brother to die young and leave him to hold it all together."

She hesitated a moment; her gaze sliding away, an uncomfortable flush creeping up her face at the words so innocently dropped into the conversation.

Layla leapt in, moving on from talk of dying young before it sent her plummeting back into the darkness, and saving Charlie from the awkwardness of the moment.

"So, I'm not quite sure how this relates to me?"

"OK, so in between working to resurrect a festival that's only been held once before, not to mention how hard that is after the whole live music industry has been royally fucked over by Covid, Finn's trying to fulfill his responsibilities to the locals. This Earl business means he's drawn into all sorts of local issues and they look to him to sort them out."

"And what local issue could possibly involve me?"

"The village GP wants to retire. Her elderly mother down in Dorset isn't well, and she wants to relocate to care for her. Which leaves Dallblane without a GP in the middle of a massive shortage."

"Oh, Charlie, I'm not sure about that."

Her instinctive reaction was that it was too big, too soon. She still had a couple more weeks left before they expected her back at the South Auckland GP practice. At least there everyone knew her situation. There'd be no awkward explaining. She could take refuge in the familiar.

But then she *had* considered not going back at all. She'd realised fighting Covid in one of the city's most impoverished and vulnerable communities had left her burnt out. And now losing Will on top of that. Maybe it was time for a change. In the perfect life they'd mapped out, she would have been leaving her job anyway the moment she got pregnant. Of course, *that* perfect life was gone, but in her mind perhaps she'd already moved on to other options.

"Look, just think about it. It's a 'bonnie wee place', as the locals will tell you. Apparently, the people adored Doctor Jean, and they're really worried. There are quite a lot of younger families in the area now, moved to the country, a great place to raise their kids. But without a GP, especially one with paediatric and obstetric experience—which you have—they're nervous. It's forty minutes to the nearest hospital and over an hour to Glasgow." Charlie tugged at her professionalism now. She'd always enjoyed working where there was need. There was a definite appeal to the suggestion.

"I remember it being pretty. Postcard pretty."

Whether it was the memory of the relief she'd felt at Will's surprise arrival at the festival, calling an early end to their four-month separation, or something deep within the place itself, either way she felt a fondness at the mention of Dallblane. The long days of an uncharacteristically warm Scottish summer, the soaring music surrounding them, nights making love in the soft glow of fairy lights in their bell-shaped tent, wandering past small stone cottages down to the friendly pub—just the name of the place took her back to a time when she'd felt blissfully happy, wrapped safe in Will's love—back before this living hell of existing without him.

"And Finn's keen to help. I mean, he genuinely wants to do good, but in the past, the locals haven't been so warm towards the younger generation of Earls. Not surprising, as his brother was a right tosser. So this is another chance to show he has their interests at heart. There's a nice little furnished cottage on the estate and a vehicle. You wouldn't need a thing. And it would put some space between you and all that's happened."

Was that what she needed—space? Something totally different? A new life to take her mind away from the life that would never be? A safe place to spend some time while she figured out what her future would look like? Whatever she needed, to her surprise, she found herself not writing off the idea Dallblane might provide it.

"All right," she said, "I'll think about it."

"Good," said Charlie. "OK, at serious risk to my life, I'm going to check on Safiyah. The singing's stopped—which is usually *not* a good sign."

Movement on the beach below caught Layla's eye. Even from this distance, she could see the triumphant gleam in Tristan's eyes as he wrangled a good-sized kahawai from his hook. Leo crouched beside him, offering advice to his novice fisher friend. They'd be firing up Leo's smoker tonight, and delicious smoked fish pie would be on the menu tomorrow.

Further along the bay, where a rocky headland trapped a curling wave, surfers bobbed in the water, necks craned in anticipation of the next ride. There was an agonising punch to her gut at the sight. She would never again sit and watch those sleek wetsuit-clad bodies knowing one of them was hers, or vicariously live the sheer exhilaration of the surf through him as he emerged with a grin as wide as the sky, shaking his blonde hair like a wet labrador. When they were strong enough, she and Kirsten had agreed to brave Piha and cast some of their husbands' ashes into the waves they had so loved.

But for now, the thought of confronting the rolling surf was unbearable. Whereas, the prospect of a quiet Scottish village, far inland from the melancholy taunt of the sea, was surprisingly attractive. She gave Tristan a thumbs up and headed inside to see Charlie. She needed to check out this email for herself.

After dinner, they insisted Charlie and Safiyah leave the cleanup, a show of gratitude for the meal. Although Layla struggled to eat much despite its alluring spicy flavour, she appreciated others taking care of her needs by tempting her to try. Dishes done, while Tristan and Leo headed back to the beach to check a long line they'd set earlier, she joined the two women on the verandah.

She'd developed a painful aversion to other couples this past two weeks. Seeing people so in love, hand in hand with their favourite human being, triggered an unpredictable cascade of emotions. Sometimes it was a searing anger at the unfairness that she should be robbed of her husband while they basked in love and a belief it would last forever. Other times a passionate envy flared then passed, leaving guilt that she should begrudge others their happiness because her own was gone. Mostly despair washed over her as she wondered how she could endure what lay ahead, alone, without him by her side.

But none of these feelings ambushed her when she caught sight of her beautiful friend and her lover, lying with limbs entwined on the old couch. After so many failed relationships, seeing Charlie with someone who loved her so completely, treasuring her endearing qualities and good-naturedly tolerating her annoying quirks, brought a small spark of joy in an otherwise dark time.

Safiyah curled back her long legs and patted the space beside her with a jangle of the gleaming bracelets on her wrist. "Layla, sit down," she said, with her East End accent coated in soft caramel, a hint at the singing voice that enchanted crowds.

"Tell me more about Dallblane," Layla said. "I remember the castle, and the village, of course, but it would be quite different living there compared to camping out at a music festival." She saw the immediate enthusiastic spark in Charlie's eyes. "I'm a long way off from any decision," she warned, "but I'm curious enough to want to know more. Being here these few days has shown me the possibility that a change of place might be the least painful option for me for a while."

A place with no memories, and no reminders of his absence until she was strong enough to bear them was the idea now taking up residence in her mind.

"It's changed a bit since you were there. Not physically, but the mood of the place. Largely because of Finn."

"Ah, yeah, he's a doll," Safiyah said. Her eyes lit up at the mention of his name. "And his mother, Patti; such a sweet woman," she mused.

"They are the only reason I suggested it," Charlie said. "To be honest, hun, I'd love to just take you home with us. But we'll both be away a lot for work for at least the next six months. And if you wanted to work, well, that ED stint in London wrecked you. This GP spot is much more your sort of thing. And I know the McGills would look after you like one of their own. They've had it rough themselves the past couple of years. They don't need too much explanation to understand what you need right now."

"They've been through it." The words caught in the back of her throat. She grasped at equilibrium by keeping her focus on the wavering candle perched beside them. Locking her gaze on the flame and watching the faint smoke straggle skyward calmed her. The pungent smell of citronella masked the troubling tang of salt in the breeze off the sea.

"Yeah, first Finn's dad in 2018, then his older brother in 2021. Some hereditary heart thing. Although his brother Euan was an idiot. What sort of person with a heart condition pisses around with drugs? And then of course he got Covid. Didn't need to become a statistic, but you can't save some people from themselves."

"Tough on their mother."

"Yeah, at least she's got Finn. I tell you, Layla, they would really take care of you. And they wouldn't hesitate to have you. Patti would go all earth mother, but I guarantee you'll love her. Finn can come across as a bit uptight at first, but once he knows you... God, we've had some good times with him, eh, Saf?"

Safiyah added her endorsement with an enthusiastic nod and a broad grin. "Oh, man, once you get him started on music, there's no stopping him. Wish I could coax him across to some world music. He's the sort of guy who would hold his own in the band."

"So what's the village like? The people?" Layla was curious about the type of community she'd be part of. As the sole doctor, she'd need to win their trust and earn their respect.

"Typical small rural community, can be slow to warm up to new people, apparently. But with the McGill's endorsement, they'll be fine. Finn and Patti got alongside Dr Jean during the lockdown. Did a brilliant job of making sure people were OK. When you're in the village, if you say you're staying up at the castle, they'll bend your ear for half an hour singing their praises. I don't think it was always that way, but some good things came out of the bloody pandemic."

The three women sat in companionable silence, punctuated by the mournful call of a morepork. The lament of the tiny owl echoed from deep in the small tangle of bush behind the house. Lulled by the distant hiss of the waves and the warm, comfortable presence of Safiyah's knees against her thigh, Layla dozed. Charlie and Safiyah planned to head off in the morning, a seven-hour drive and then thirty on a plane. Their imminent departure added another layer to the weight of loneliness that threatened to suffocate her life. Dallblane might not be the solution, but nor was hastily ruling it out.

27

No Going Back

Glasgow, Scotland - April 2022

LAYLA SPOTTED ONE AVAILABLE stool at the counter of the tiny coffee shop in a corner of the terminal. Summoning her last flicker of energy, she zeroed in on it, fearful someone else might win the race. She dragged one unwilling suitcase in each hand, cursing this country she'd only been in for half an hour. Not only did you have to pay for a baggage trolley, by some miracle they expected you to have British coinage handy in your pocket to pay for it; which is why she'd wrangled these two unruly beasts from the baggage carousel and through customs, leaving her arms aching and wondering if all her possessions stuffed inside them were necessary. She flopped at the counter, tired shoulders slumped, her head a heavy weight resting in one hand, defeated by her luggage.

Scottish accents swirled around her; many were the broad Glaswegian so thick it resembled a whole different language. She scanned each new wave of people pouring through the busy electronic doors of Glasgow Airport. Pulling up his picture on her phone, and checking those standing in anticipation by the arrivals door, just in case Finn McGill had somehow walked past without her spotting him, she decided that wasn't the case. He was late.

Part of her wanted to trust Charlie on this one. She had a reliable gut instinct about people. She wanted to believe this man Charlie had forged a relationship with as a business partner and now considered a friend was everything she'd been told: pleasant, genuine, and fun once you got to know him. The photo was incontrovertible evidence that he was also extremely good-looking in an untidy sort of way. The tumble of dark hair fell in spirals rather like her own. He wore faded jeans, a Lou Reed t-shirt and a shy smile.

But she had reservations. After all, he was an Earl: the 16th Earl of Dallblane. Young to hold such a lofty title. Young to hold the family fortune in his hands. Layla prickled at the thought. Despite all the evidence to the contrary, provided by the people she loved most in the world who'd all come from a background of wealth and privilege, she'd never overcome the mistrust of money instilled in her by her own family. And Hilton and Virginia Leroux had finally extinguished any possibility of that.

Finn was pictured standing next to Charlie, a casual arm across her shoulders. Not an overly tall man, hardly taller than Charlie. He might be difficult to spot in this crowd where hulking red-haired Highlander types seemed to dominate. In the photo, Charlie was definitely the centre of the fun, head thrown back in unbridled laughter, with Safiyah on one side gazing at her with liquid-brown lovelorn eyes. And on the other side Finn looked relaxed and happy—not at all how he appeared when, hearing a soft voice behind her, she turned to find him standing at her shoulder.

"Layla?" His voice held the lightest touch of Scots, a gentleness in the vowels. "Oh thank God," he said, with a gush of breath as if he'd been running. "I'm so sorry. Bloody car troubles."

It seemed a lame excuse. It was hard to imagine a man who lived in a castle would be forced to suffer unreliable transport like mere mortals. But she plastered a forgiving smile on her face. After all, he didn't have to collect her; they might have left Dallblane's new GP to find a taxi. And that would have made a sizable dent on her credit card, given the distance from the airport to the village. She didn't lack money, but it still irked her frugal nature to run up unnecessary costs.

"It's fine." She placed a soothing hand on his arm. The man seemed genuinely distressed. "I've been here less than five minutes. Honestly," she said. "Don't stress. After thirty hours flying, a few minutes more is nothing, believe me."

She slipped from the stool, finding her feet. He stepped towards her, then hesitated, his apologetic expression replaced by an awkward smile. His hand hovered between them for a moment and then, with a decisive lurch, he chose to clasp her in a stiff hug.

"Anyway, welcome to Scotland, Layla."

The gesture was rather sweet, and Layla returned the embrace with genuine warmth. She'd had the odd sense even from studying his picture that she was going to like Finn McGill. There was a guileless look about him, an openness to his expression as if he had nothing to hide. And of course, Charlie had encouraged positive thoughts towards him; the constant litany of Finn's good qualities she reeled off at every phone call left no doubt she was a fan.

Layla had suspected it might be a ploy to ensure she didn't renege on the deal to take on the GP's position for a year. Totally unnecessary, of course: one, she'd signed a contract, and two, she trusted Charlie's judgement on this.

It was a new and uncomfortable experience, relying on others to make calls on your behalf because you were incapable of doing so for yourself. But she'd accepted that in the wake of losing Will, for a time she might need to trust the people around her while her own brain recovered its full functioning. How long would that take? Maybe here in Dallblane, cocooned from reminders of the life she had lost, she'd find the strength to do that.

Now, meeting Finn, she decided this friend of a friend might easily become hers too. And that would be a good thing. Surrounded by strangers, her old friends far distant, building some new friendships might also help her heal.

"Thank you Finn, it's good to be here."

"Right," he said, pulling away, his face flushed but looking pleased that she'd not held his tardiness against him. He turned to the two enormous suitcases, grabbing one in each hand. She cringed at the thought of their weight. He had no idea what his chivalry had let him in for. But apart from a small puff of effort to get the beasts rolling, he showed no sign of struggle, striding ahead of her.

She was having difficulty putting one tired foot ahead of the other, so it was a relief to find the car parking building was handy and had a lift. However, on the third floor of the multistory park, her thoughts that this was all going smoothly came to an abrupt end when they came to a halt in front of two large SUVs. Crouched between them was an odd little sports car. Finn's car.

The perky red vehicle might have been lifted straight out of an old Bond movie. It sported shining wire wheels, a chrome grill with a wide-mouthed smile, bug-eyed headlamps and a fin-shaped body that suggested an ability to cut through the air at speed. Layla's first thought was that it was really quite enchanting. But the charm of the little car evaporated as she dragged her eyes away from its cheeky grin to inspect the interior.

Tucked in behind two black leather seats, sheltered by the soft-top that lay in neat folds, was a narrow bench seat only suitable for a person who didn't possess legs. Or maybe a small dog. Beyond that, she saw the slope of a tiny rear boot. For a couple to take a jaunt in the countryside on a spring day, a small picnic hamper and a bottle of wine, it was perfect. To transport Finn and Layla, and two massive suitcases, it was not.

"Ahh..." he said, running a hand through that thick mop of hair. "... shit, maybe the universe was trying to tell me something when the car wouldn't start."

"I think it was," she said, wondering if she'd be going to Dallblane minus her luggage. Sweaty and smelly from thirty hours of travel, that wasn't an acceptable option.

"Oh, I am *so* sorry," he said, an embarrassed flush flooding his face. "I have no idea what I was thinking."

"Ah, maybe you weren't?" she offered. She should have tried for a more charitable tone, but she was, frankly, exhausted. She wanted nothing more than to get to the promised cottage at the estate, have a shower and go to bed, even if it was only eight o'clock in the morning. Right now it felt like she'd arrived in a Scottish version of *Virgin River*, lured here by false promises. She feared this shambolic start was an omen of worse awaiting her in Dallblane.

"OK," he said, parking the bags, and leaning back on the car bonnet, where he sat, chin cupped in thought. In moments, he was back on his feet. "Wait here." He took three purposeful steps towards the lift before thinking better of it and turned back to the car. "You should have a seat." Unlocking the door, he settled her into the surprisingly comfortable passenger seat. She lay back in the neat leather cockpit, closed her eyes, and waited.

Layla dozed rather blissfully until the door of the car swung open, launching her back into wakefulness with a shock. For a moment, she couldn't recall where she was or why she was there. And no recognition of this good-looking stranger who beamed down at her with a satisfied smile. Then it was there: Glasgow, airport, waiting in a car, Finn.

"This is more like it," he said, pointing at the bulky Range Rover idling in front of them.

"But what about your car?" she said. "You're just going to leave it here?"

"Well," he said, "can't be helped. I'll drag the roof up, lock her up, and hope she's still there when I bring the rental back later. Though I'd be pretty pissed if someone stole her. She's my pride and joy, even if she can be a temperamental bitch sometimes. But I suppose she's sixty years old, so she's allowed to be a little moody."

"Wow," Layla said. "A classic."

"Yes, 1962 Daimler SP250, four speed synchromesh transmission. Nice Hemi V8 under the hood there—" He stopped short, and looked at her apologetically, no doubt expecting Layla's eyes to have glazed over as he detailed the specs of the little car. "Sorry, I got a bit carried away. I love this car."

She laughed. "You don't have to apologise, Finn. I'm a V8 girl from way back. Tell me," she said, "what sort of brake horsepower did they get out of these babies back then?"

With a surprised smile, he launched into a list of details, hardly pausing for breath except to heft the two suitcases in the back of the Range Rover. Layla decided that despite the slightly bumpy start, Charlie was right: Finn McGill was a good guy. And she herself was right too: there was a strong possibility that they'd be friends.

After that, conversation flowed easily. She regaled him with tales of Holden car club runs and days spent at Pukekohe Motorsport Park watching V8 supercars eat up the racetrack. Will had indulged her love of petrol and rubber, buying them VIP tickets with access to pit lane and taken a quiet pride in his wife's knowledge as she conversed with drivers and mechanics.

Finn reciprocated, his stories describing classic car rallies where he'd navigated miles of Britain's highways and idyllic country lanes. She couldn't suppress a small flash of envy when she discovered he'd once driven his nifty little sports car with a massive heart at the Goodwood Festival of Speed. Her father and brothers would love this guy—as long as she didn't introduce him by his weighty title.

He neatly skirted around anything too personal in his questions. No doubt Charlie had filled him in on her background so he might tactfully avoid it. But she didn't have the same advantage and was curious to know more. Although, odd as it was, she had a strange sense of already knowing quite a lot about Finn McGill. Maybe it was the immediately easy banter stemming from their common love of cars. And of course, his face was familiar; she'd studied the photo on her phone during the flight, noting the high cheekbones, the dark eyes and sensual lips, fixing them in her mind so she'd recognise him at the airport. Perhaps it was just that she'd heard about him so often in conversation with Charlie over the past few weeks that made it feel there was already something between them, a mutual friend acting as the conduit. She'd certainly done a hard-sell on the idea of Layla coming to Dallblane, offering Finn's support as an added incentive.

"So your mum is the only family still at the castle?" Charlie had told her Finn's mum, Patti, was a great lady, and not at all what you'd expect of a woman of seventy who bore the title 'Dowager Countess'.

"Yes, just the two of us rattling around for now. My sister, Star, is married to a guy from the Isle of Lewis, of all places. Way up in the Outer Hebrides. They've got a baby on the way in a few months, so she's planning to come and stay here for the birth. I know the Daimler can get us from home to the hospital in Glasgow fairly quickly if need be."

Star. It was a rather unusual name, quite exotic compared to the traditionally Scottish sounding Finn. Layla had a fleeting vision of a heavily pregnant woman stuffed into Finn's tiny Daimler, her skin pale with pain and long hair streaming behind her as he raced towards the city.

"Oh well, if it happens too fast for that, I've got my Diploma in Obstetrics," she reassured him. "I've delivered quite a few babies, although only in a hospital. But if the baby decides it doesn't want to wait, I'm happy to help."

"Mum will be relieved to hear that. She's quietly stressing, although she doesn't admit it. First grandchild. She's been spending hours with her head buried in her herb books and following up with more on the internet." Layla pictured his mother, an older female version of Finn, with dark hair, head down, studying pages of some dusty herbal medical encyclopedia. "But despite her faith in natural remedies," he said, "and with no midwife anywhere near, I think she's hoping Star delivers in a hospital. Having you there if it doesn't go to plan is brilliant. Thank you."

"You're very welcome," she said. "Bringing babies into the world is special. I love it."

And now that was the only way she would get to experience the joy of a new life. She swallowed hard, pushing down the grief that still reared up. All it took was a word, or a look, to bring the fragile future she was building for herself crashing down in a million painful pieces.

The tree-lined driveway to Dallblane Castle was rather gloomy, the thick woods on either side letting in little light. She remembered this from when she and Charlie had entered the grounds nearly three years ago, smugly taking the route for media and VIPs, unlike the thousands of cars, campers and busloads of festival-goers sent the long way. The more cheerful spring sunlight as they emerged from the woods was welcome. It picked out the golden-hued stonework of a small building to their left. Finn eased the rental in beside a haphazardly parked van hogging the driveway to the cottage. A small brass sign by the door read 'Darach Dubh'

"It means 'Black Oak'—for obvious reasons," he said, following her gaze. The cottage looked warm and welcoming in contrast to its backdrop of looming oak trees. "I hope it's going to be OK." This was the promised refurbished gamekeeper's accommodation. It looked pretty decent, considering it must be old. "It's cosy." He pointed up at the chimney. "Don't worry, no fire lighting required. Gas so you can have heat at the flick of a switch. You'll need that for a bit. It's still a little cool in the mornings and evenings. Won't really warm up till the end of May. "

"I'm sure it will be fine," she said, climbing out of the vehicle. "I hail from a fairly modest background, so I don't expect to be treated like a princess."

"Oh, prepare to be treated exactly like that," he said with a laugh. "The people in the village are very relieved you're coming. There's a desperate GP shortage and not too many want to come out here into the wilds. Pulling off success in finding a replacement for Dr Jean has certainly upped my credit with the locals. Thanks to you and Charlie," he said.

"It sounds like Dr Jean might be a hard act to follow. I hope they don't find the change too confronting."

Replacing a sixty-year-old much-loved village doctor with someone nearly half her age, from the colonies no less, and not to mention having extensive tattoos—certainly there was potential to shock the locals. Layla suspected she might need to work extra hard to gain the trust and respect of the villagers. Dallblane was so different from the impoverished but appreciative Polynesian community she'd worked in back in Auckland. But she was up for the challenge. It would provide a diversion from the dark thoughts that took over her mind whenever she left it free to roam.

An overall-clad man with a Santa Claus beard and the physique to match stepped out of the cottage doorway. He broke into a broad grin at the sight of Finn and crunched across the driveway towards them with heavy-booted feet.

"All good in there, Finn," he said, giving them a cheerful thumbs up.

"Pleased to hear it, Rabbie," Finn said. "And I'm sure Dr Leroux is too. A functioning bathroom and loo is definitely part of the package. Layla, meet Rabbie Wallace. Officially here as a plumber, but can turn his hand to just about anything."

"Pleased ta meet ye Doc." Rabbie extended a large paw. Layla tried not to wince as he crushed her hand inside his larger one, jerking it up and down with enthusiasm. "Finn, ye didn't let on the lady doc would be so easy on the eye. No offence ta Dr Jean, but I think some of the blokes might be in a hurry for an appointment. In fact, I can feel some sort of lurgy already coming on."

He let out a theatrical cough before tossing Layla a wink. She couldn't help but return the grin. She expected he wouldn't be the last to offer a bit of cheek. But at least she seemed to have won over her first local; that was a good start.

Inside the cottage, a small but cheerful lounge and dining room took up most of the first floor space. The promised gas fire occupied an old stone hearth. While an open fire definitely had a touch of romance about it, Layla was grateful that fetching and carrying wood wouldn't be necessary when the inevitable winter snows arrived. A bulging sofa and two matching chairs faced the hearth, while to one side an exuberant bunch of frilly peonies spilled out of a glass jug in the centre of an old but serviceable dining table.

To the left mid-morning sunshine filled the kitchen. Layla peered in and saw another less formal dining table, white-painted with matching cushioned chairs and a second bunch of flowers, these a tumble of delicate wildflowers in an old green bottle. She could already imagine breakfasts here each morning before starting her day. Perhaps coffee with a friend, once she'd made some connections.

"The fridge and pantry are well-stocked," Finn said. "Mum and Isabel have been busy."

"That's so kind of them," she said.

"Yes, I forgot to mention Isabel. She has quarters in the castle too. Technically, she works for us, and has done for years. But she's practically family, like a sister to Mum, and a second mother to us kids. She takes real pride in her job of caring for everyone, so expect her to do the same to you. You'll like her. And Mum's bound to swoop on you, too. She'd happily have a house full if she could."

Layla looked forward to meeting these kind women who had gone to such trouble to make the cottage welcoming. Without even knowing them, she already felt their motherly touch on her new life.

Finn successfully wrestled the two cases, one in front of him and one behind, up the narrow staircase without becoming wedged. Following below, Layla expected any moment that one would wrest itself free of his grasp and plummet down the steep stairs. Being mowed down by one's own overstuffed suitcase wouldn't make for an auspicious start. Fortunately Finn proved up to the task, leading her past two smaller bedrooms and what she presumed to be the bathroom, to where a door stood ajar.

When she stepped into the room, she was overcome with a contradictory tug of emotions. The king-sized bed sported a heavily patterned floral cover and a profusion of pillows in shades of pink and ruby with small touches of gold. It was warm and inviting, feminine without being fussy, and Layla wished she could crawl straight into it and steal back the hours lost to broken sleep on the flight.

But in the cream-painted tongue-and-groove panelling, a patterned frieze above it, the wooden floors with natural fibre rugs and the wide bay window that no doubt overlooked the garden below, all Layla could see was a mirror of the room she'd left behind, Will's room, that had become their room. Her heart broke at the thought that she'd never again stand in front of that bay window, with his arms clasped around her shoulders, his breath on her neck, his lips pressed into her hair. She inhaled a sob, her lungs filling with the ache of emptiness that stretched before her.

"Layla, are you OK?"

She turned to meet Finn's concerned frown and nodded, despite the tear that edged slowly down her cheek. She wiped it away and forced a smile.

"Yes," she said. "The room is lovely. Your Mum and Isabel again?"

"Yes, they wanted it to be nice for you."

As if mentioning his mother had summoned her, a click of footsteps on the stairs announced her arrival in the house, followed by her soft voice. "Finn?"

"We're up here Mum."

When Patti McGill entered the room a few moments later, she was much as Layla had envisaged her. Hair once dark, now streaked with silver, hung in loose waves down her back. She wore a long skirt of purple muslin, and a flowing black velvet and lace top. Neat pointed boots poked out from beneath the floaty layers. But the erect posture, unmarked skin and bright keen eyes were unexpected. Perhaps the secret to such youthful beauty lay in Patti's herbal knowledge.

She didn't hesitate to envelop Layla in a cloud of grassy perfume overlaid with spice. A tall slim woman, Layla felt childlike in her arms, and a sense of safety in her embrace.

"Welcome, my dear," she murmured in her ear, the lingering trace of an American accent colouring her words. Releasing Layla, Patti took a step back and appraised her with a knowing stare. "And how are you after that punishing journey? Not too exhausted, I hope?"

"I'm doing fine, thanks. My friends bullied me into going business class, and I'm thankful I wasn't too stubborn to push back." It was another sign of how crushed she'd been after Will's death, giving in to things she'd have fought in the past. She'd always thought it ridiculous for someone of her stature to be paying double the airfare for unneeded extra leg room. Sitting in the spacious seat on the way over, guilt about insisting Will and her always fly economy had surfaced. He'd always laughingly tucked his long legs in as best he could and endured it, humouring her ingrained leaning towards thriftiness. So many regrets haunted her, things she might have done differently, little ways she might have loved him a little more.

"You look like some sleep might still be in order," Patti said.

She was right; even in the comfortable seat, with a cosy blanket, each tiny movement of the staff no matter how considerate, any slight change in the engines' drone as the plane changed course, every soft murmur between one passenger and another, had impinged on her rest.

"Yeah, I definitely need sleep." She raised a polite hand to stifle the yawn that rose automatically at the thought.

"These should do a good job of keeping out the light," Patti said, drawing the heavy curtains.

"I'm sorry about that out there," Finn said with a nod towards the sound of distant hammering, the grind of a saw and the odd clatter of machinery. "Less than three months out from the festival, it's a building site at every turn."

"Oh, I'm looking forward to it," Layla said. And she was looking forward to it: the music, and the fact Charlie and Safiyah would be up, Charlie to work and Safiyah to provide practical and moral support for Charlie's next big film. As for the memories—Will surprising her by arriving early, the long lazy days lying on the grass listening to music in the sun, dancing in the crowd under a magical Scottish sky with stars sprawled above them, and nights in their tent, their own private universe—she wasn't sure how she would survive those. But she was pleased for Finn and for Charlie that Rock The Castle 2 was without a doubt happening. "I was at the first one. It was amazing. I'm so pleased you've resurrected it after damn Covid."

"Covid? What's that?" he said with a grin. "Yeah, we are certainly happy to put the last two years behind us. I think the rest of Britain is too. Tickets sold out in an hour."

"OK, enough talk of the festival. Plenty of time for that. You can take Layla on a tour sometime. But for now, the poor girl needs us to be out of here. There's a number on the kitchen table," Patti said. "Just phone me if there's anything you need."

She bustled Finn out of the room, leaving Layla to sit as the door whispered closed. She was here. No going back now.

28

Peace

Dallblane Castle, Scotland - May 2022

THE IRRITATING SOUND STARTLED Finn from sleep. He'd thought the Darth Vader ringtone funny when he'd downloaded it, but at this time of day it was bloody annoying. Who the fuck was calling him this early, anyway? He was no morning person and six am was way beyond his idea of acceptable. No one was due on the festival site for at least another hour, so there shouldn't be anyone bothering him with problems yet.

He scrabbled for the phone and, seeing the name lit up on the screen, a grin fought with a grimace: Charlie. The woman was the very definition of spontaneous. No matter what hour of the day or night, when an idea pushed itself forward in her crazy creative overcrowded brain, she didn't stop to think about whether it was an appropriate time to unleash it on others.

"Morning, Charlie," he sighed down the line.

"Finn, I suppose your lazy arse is still in bed?"

"For chrissakes, Charlie, it's six am. Not everyone is a workaholic insomniac like you." Her burst of laughter, that delightful bell-like sound, worked its magic. There was such a pure joy in Charlie's laugh that once she let it loose, you couldn't help but forgive her anything.

"It's not about work," she said. "I'm off to Spain in a couple of hours. Just making sure everything's OK there before I catch the train to Heathrow. How's it going with Layla?"

How was it going with Layla? From his side, it was going better than he could have imagined. As ordered by Charlie, he checked in on her each day. But in that newly established afternoon ritual—meeting her at the clinic, encouraging her to have a drink with him at the pub, maybe stay on for dinner—he'd found his own refuge. In her presence, the daily barrage of problems that had the potential to send his anxiety off the radar simply seeped away. But he wasn't about to tell Charlie that. She wasn't calling to hear about his selfish perspective on the situation.

"Layla's doing great," he said. "Handover with Dr Jean went smoothly. Waved her off on Monday with a smile on her face. She still felt guilty about leaving, but with Layla here, she knows everyone is in good hands. And Layla, well, she's just one of those people you trust. After four days, the village has pretty much adopted her as their own."

"Yeah, I never had any worries about that. She's a brilliant doctor. They're lucky to have her. But what about outside the clinic? Is she holding up? You're checking in on her?"

"Every day. Without fail."

Finn was embarrassed to admit it, but from lunchtime onwards he found himself counting down the minutes to the end of the day. Layla Leroux was a balm for his soul. He was so thankful Charlie had made the connection, catapulting her into his life at exactly the right time.

Not that Charlie had done it for his personal benefit. Not even for Dallblane. It was her overwhelming concern for a friend battling a tragic loss that led her to push Layla in their direction. But god, he was glad she had. The instant calm he felt around Layla was the strangest thing. In providing a safe harbour for her, protection from the storm she'd sailed through, he'd found his own peace.

Maybe it flowed from this ritual he'd created on her behalf. Numbers, patterns, rhythm, order, routines: these were the scaffolds that held his life together. They minimised the risk he'd crumple under the stress of existing in the world's intensity. Someone like him, hyper sensitised, hyper vigilant, who felt too much, who felt too deeply, found challenge in the very act of existing. And if life broke through the defences and he began freaking out, these were the weapons he deployed to save himself.

But the oddest thing was, smack in the busiest part of the festival prep, an insane time when he should have been most vulnerable to overwhelm, he'd never felt more secure, more even. He hadn't once this week needed to hide out in his studio. He hadn't taken a single puff of the calming herbal spray prescribed by his mother. The aromatherapy candles tucked in his office sat unlit, forgotten, their soothing smell unrequired. Staring into the calm of Layla's green eyes anchored him in the present. He forgot about the past, was happy to let the future sit lightly ahead of him, and just focus on the woman in front of him.

"So, how do you think *she* is, really?" Charlie demanded. "I've known her for almost half my life, Finn. I know Layla. She'll try to be staunch even if underneath things are falling apart. You need to tell me if that's happening. I'm responsible for her being there, and I'm the one who should front up if things are going wrong. If they are, I'll come."

He could see that about Layla. Despite her fragile appearance—tiny wee thing that she was—there was an inner toughness, the ability to mask what was really going on. He supposed, being a doctor, you developed that if you didn't have it already. She didn't know him. Had no reason to let him see what lay beneath. But for some unfathomable reason, there was trust between them.

Even on the journey back from the airport, she'd let him in a little. Maybe she'd instinctively responded to his own vulnerabilities, sensed they had that in common—for both of them, the world only saw the tip of the iceberg, cool and calm, with no hint of the depths beneath. Maybe it was because she had no one else. She needed to trust someone. He was a friend of Charlie's; he could be trusted.

And on Monday, that first evening at the pub, he'd also seen the mask slip just a bit. It was always the little things that seemed to stab you right in the heart. Like when he'd rummaged deep in a desk drawer the other day, hunting for a pen that actually worked, and he'd found his father's backgammon set tucked away down the back. He'd been gone years, but still the reminders of time spent together, father and son banter over a board and a beer, had made him tear up. Absence of someone you loved held far more power to hurt than the presence of someone you hated.

For Layla, simply placing a large glass of lemon, lime, and bitters on the table in front of her triggered tears. She'd wiped them away on her sleeve, bravely offering an explanation: Layla hated ice in her drinks. Ridiculous as it might sound, the rattle of frosty cubes emphasised her husband, Will, was gone. No longer there to inter-cept the bar staff, making sure her glass arrived just as she liked it. To have someone who knew you so well, understood all those tiny idiosyncrasies, took care of you in big and small ways—that must be special. He'd never had that sort of relationship with anyone, so while he could appreciate it, he didn't miss it. But to have had that level of intimacy with another, and then to lose it—even the smallest reminder would be painful.

"She's sad, Charlie. You can't help but see it. But like you said, she's a strong person. Broken, but working to keep it together. Down, but not out. I promise if I think she needs you, I'll call. But for now, we're doing OK."

"Thank you Finn. What you're doing for her, for me, it's…" He heard the hitch in her voice. "She's precious to me."

"It's not a problem, Charlie. Happy to help. Now get on that train and don't worry. Everything is fine."

He'd lied, of course. There was a problem. One that should trouble him, but he shoved it aside. He harboured more than concern for Layla. The moment he'd seen her picture emailed through, there was a jolt of attraction. Disturbing for sure, given her situation, but also thrilling. Looking at those startling green eyes framed by an explosion of blonde hair, he'd felt recognition, a warm familiar current of knowing. It was weird, and he'd brushed it off until the moment he'd seen her at the airport. Despite his embarrassment at turning up late, it had pushed its way forward again. Now a week later, there it was, a definite need for her that fuelled his days, getting him through till late afternoon when he had a legitimate reason to see her.

He and Charlie had long ago moved beyond business partners. They were friends. But that wouldn't save him if she knew. Luckily, Charlie wasn't the most perceptive person. If she had any hint he had more than protective feelings towards Layla, she'd tell him in no uncertain terms: back off. And if he hurt Layla, she'd have his balls.

29

Wish You Were Here

Dallblane, Scotland - May 2022

LAYLA ENJOYED THE STILLNESS of the village clinic in the late afternoon. Sun still poured through the window, promising hours more of daylight, the advantage of being at a latitude where at this time of year night came late and was brief. She sat scrolling through the day's notes, reviewing the parade of patients who'd come through her door that day. There had been a steady stream of them from the moment the village grapevine carried word the new doctor was in residence. Today's clientele was much the same as those she'd seen most days so far: two young mothers with grizzly babies needing reassurance; a distressed woman with a toddler who'd stuck a bead up his nose; a teenager suffering from painful heavy periods; another wanting to go on the pill; four people with colds that thankfully weren't Covid; and the usual string of older people who, as Rabbie Wallace had predicted, had simply come to check her out.

However, Rabbie was wrong to some extent; it wasn't the men that mostly made up the group of the curious. Lots of the older women seemed keen for an appointment to revisit their numerous ailments, nod in agreement when she dispensed the same advice as

Dr Jean, and leave happy knowing they could now knowledgeably contribute their two-cents worth to the gossip about the new doctor when they gathered at the village store.

Her capable nurse-come-receptionist, Raylene, had tactfully let her know that while most of this chatter was harmless, the odd villager was unimpressed with her. Their judgement was no surprise: her age, her tattoos, and definitely her looks apparently deemed her unsuitable for the role. She'd brushed it off, knowing there were far greater things to hurt you than the nasty gossip of small-minded people. The one surprise was that the worst of them all, a woman who'd been openly hostile, was Rabbie's own wife, Jocelyn. It was ironic that jolly Rabbie, with his Santa smile, should be married to a frosty Mrs Claus.

The opening clinic door triggered a small electronic ding, announcing a new arrival. The only patient at this time of day would be an emergency, but the steady footsteps across the vinyl waiting room told her this was no emergency. She was already familiar with that sound. She'd been here two weeks, and Finn McGill had come every day for two weeks, determined to keep his promise to Charlie that he'd look after her. And she was glad of it. He had more than lived up to Charlie's expectations, and exceeded hers.

"Hey, how was your day?" he said, appearing in the doorway, crinkles blooming around his eyes. "Have those old battleaxes from the village given up on reconnaissance missions yet?" He'd heard the talk too, and reassured her it would pass.

Layla admitted she looked forward to him popping in around six each evening, with his mellow Scottish voice, an easy smile, and a genuine concern for her wellbeing. It was a welcome end to her busy days. In fact, she dreaded the time when he no longer stopped by as presumably would happen soon enough, once he saw she was settled. Although she liked to think maybe they'd forge enough of a friendship to still meet up like this now and then. Their stroll to the pub, the bartender lining up the predictable choice of drinks the moment they stepped through the door (his always a Tennent's lager and hers a lemon lime, and bitters), and then conversation over dinner, had become a safe routine that delayed her return to the cottage and the inevitable loneliness of the space in her bed.

"Down to two today," she laughed, "and both seemed to have a valid reason for an appointment, so perhaps the novelty of me is wearing off."

"Well, not on me," he said. His words sent an unexpected hopeful flutter in her stomach that he saw this growing friendship as she did. "Come on then, I need a drink." She closed the laptop with a decisive click. He sighed. "You wouldn't believe the day I've had. Started this morning with some fuckwits who attempted to bring an enormous truckload of scaffolding through the south gate." He shook his head in exasperation. Although he confessed to having few practical skills, Finn proved capable enough, stepping up to help the site foreman when needed. "Anyone could see that there was no way they could turn a truck of that length there, but no, they had to try, and then it took about two hours to get it out again. Meanwhile, traffic's stalled behind them and the guys onsite are screaming for the scaffolding. But yes, it was all downhill from there."

"Sounds like you definitely need a drink."

"Probably ten, but I'll restrain myself."

They settled into their usual booth in the back bar of the pub. It was a comfortable routine, making this quiet spot their own, with most of the locals perched at the leaners out front. Here they were isolated from the raucous conversation of the regulars. Although they too might be classed as regulars, since each night for the past two weeks, they'd carved out their own space for two, buffered from the buzz of the rest of the world.

She enjoyed Finn's upbeat company. She'd honestly reported back to Charlie that yes, he was taking good care of her, and yes, Charlie was right, he was a great guy. But these evening debriefs of their respective days held yet another of the small sadnesses that dogged her wherever she went, whatever she did. It was like someone had a voodoo doll with her face on it, and, when she least expected it, a vicious stab would catch her, the pain sharp and paralysing.

The nightly conversations with Finn reminded her of the pact she and Will had made: that they'd always take time together, no matter what time they arrived home from work; they'd check in with each other, take the opportunity to offload. It had been her sanity through the hard days that inevitably came to anyone working with people in need. And now here was Finn, doing this kindness in Will's place, and doing his best, although he could never really understand the intensity of her work.

"Are you really OK?" he asked after dinner, as Lenny whisked away their plates, the remnants of a huge roast meal she couldn't finish heaped to one side. Finn was too damn observant, seeming to spot the sadness in her face, no matter how hard she tried to hide it. "I mean, you say work is going fine, as much as can be expected with this motley lot. And we have fun here each night. I see you smile and laugh. But this is a new place. You don't have your friends and family around. Are you really doing all right?"

Was she? Probably as well as could be expected. Whether she was in Auckland or Dallblane, going home on her own each night was always going to be hard. But it would be harder without him.

"You know, I'm not sure. I've got nothing to measure this against. My old life is gone. But, I am really grateful that in this new life I decided to come here. Your mum, Isabel, and you, I couldn't have asked for more caring people. I feel like I have friends. So, thank you."

He reached across, laid his hand across hers, and gave it a gentle squeeze. "Anything you need, you let me know. And in the evening, if you ever want to come across to our place, just come."

"Oh, no... I couldn't impose on you. You're already giving up so much time for me."

"I mean it. In fact, why don't you come over for a bit tonight?" She saw the flicker of an idea in his eyes. "Tell me, what music do you like?"

She thought for a moment. Her tastes might best be described as eclectic. She'd grown up immersed in her father's favourites, the big rock bands from the 60s and 70s, but as a child of the 80s, a teen in the 90s, she'd ventured off in all kinds of directions.

"Big question," she said, "no simple answer."

"OK," he said, "give me a list. If I pick up your phone, what will I find?"

"Clapton."

"Of course," he said with a grin. "Which version?"

"I like the original "Layla" best. And there's some Led Zep, a lot of Pink Floyd. Ummm, and The Stones, quite a bit of U2, thanks to my brother Jimmy's obsession. Coldplay, who I love. Saw them live and they were incredible. Florence and the Machine—saw her in Auckland too." She saw his eyes light up at that.

"Working hard to get her here next year," he said. "Amazing."

"Any chance of The Foo Fighters?"

"Also on the wish list. But who knows, with Taylor Hawkins gone..." His voice trailed away, his expression awkward. She saw untimely death was a subject he regretted broaching even in this roundabout way. She saved him from his obvious discomfort, turning the conversation to other still dead but less raw musical losses.

"Yeah, I wish I'd been old enough to see Nirvana. You know I think my Kurt Cobain poster is still on my bedroom wall? So yes, you'd better add the Foos and Nirvana to my playlist."

"Right, well, I think that's enough to work with," he said. "Drink up, let's go."

Intrigued, she followed him and, as they did every evening, strolled up the hill to the castle grounds. But instead of veering off to her cottage, they headed straight up the main steps. It seemed bizarre to walk in the front door of a castle, and hear Finn call out "Hi, Mum," like a kid coming home from playing in the streets of a normal neighbourhood.

But this was the odd thing about the McGill family—an Earl and a Countess, a noble house—yet they were so ordinary, so incredibly normal. Layla wondered at what differences in the shape of their lives had created this family for them to be so at odds with her past experience of wealth and privilege. Whatever it was, she was grateful. These were the sort of people she needed in her life. Not people like Hilton and Virginia.

"Hi, darling." Patti appeared in the doorway of a dim lounge. "Oh and Layla, too. Good," she said with a satisfied nod. Behind her, the very ordinary sound of television blared in the background. Isabel waved at them from a chair facing the tv, a smug smile on her face. "We hoped you might spend some time here. Isabel and I were just saying how nice it is to have people besides us rattling around in this big house."

"We'll just be downstairs," he said.

Patti's eyebrows shot up. "Oh...well enjoy yourselves," she said, patting Layla's hand.

Layla, mystified as to exactly what lay downstairs, and confused about Patti's reaction to Finn taking her there, followed him into a small passageway. The heavy metal security door that blocked their way should have surprised her. But an odd sense of recognition emanated from both the door and the wood panelled flight of stairs that descended beyond it. It reminded her of somewhere she'd been before. Perhaps it was because following Finn mirrored a scene from *Money Heist*, as if they approached the entrance to some secret bank vault. Maybe the McGill family jewels or precious antiques lay inside.

But beyond the second door, all was modern. She shivered as another uncomfortable prickle of déjà vu rippled across her. A pair of suspended JBL speakers, vaguely like those that were her father's pride and joy, were the only familiar items in the room. She stood in what appeared to be a hi-tech music studio. Amps, speakers, and a sound desk with several mixers jostled with guitars both electric and acoustic, drum kits, keyboards and some instruments she couldn't even name, bearing only a passing resemblance to those she'd seen in the music classes at St Aidan's.

"Finn, this is incredible," she said. This explained his passion for the festival, the way his eyes lit up when he spoke about it. It wasn't only about making money. Finn was a musician. She felt a twinge of shame that for all their conversation, she really knew little about him. It was time to stop being so self-absorbed and pay more attention to other people's happiness instead of wallowing in her own misery.

"Yeah, I don't usually bring people down here. But I thought you might enjoy it." His hands flew across a computer keyboard while his eyes scanned the screen. "Won't be a minute. Sit there if you like."

She took up her position on a tall stool. A pleasant odour hung in the room; a calming hint of lavender layered across that woody fragrance she had come to associate with Finn as he stepped into the clinic each afternoon. She watched him flick switches, adjust the sliders on a mixer, while in between scrolling through lines and lines of text on the screen in front of him. With a last decisive tap on the 'Enter' key, and a satisfied smile, he leaned back in his chair as sound enveloped them.

"This OK?" he said as Florence's powerhouse voice filled the room. She didn't answer with words. The sound washed across her, causing something deep inside to burst open with delight, like a flower unfolding at the first rays of the sun. Music had always unleashed her inhibitions. She took to her feet and danced, at first eyes closed, creating a dark solitude where she might lose herself in the music. But then when she opened them to find Finn's eyes fixated on her, his pure joy at seeing her enjoyment written there, his smiling pride as each new song on the playlist he'd created for her rolled out, she found herself not wanting to break his gaze.

He himself, although seated, was in constant motion. In between tweaking the soundboard, his head nodded in time, feet tapped, hands played rhythms on his knees. And finally, when he couldn't contain the music inside any longer, he rose to his feet and danced with her. It was the first moment in the past two months that she could say she'd felt any real happiness. The simple pleasure of the music allowed her to abandon all else and simply exist. No past, no future, just a beautiful moment of now. Song after song of her favourite musicians captured her in a warm hug.

"One more for the road?" he said, when the room finally fell silent.

"Sure," she said.

"One of my favourites."

As the distinctive plaintive notes of a guitar filled the room, he moved towards her, tentatively at first, preserving the space between them. But the music took over, his hands seeking her waist, hers drawn to his shoulders. She pressed her cheek against his chest, finding solace in the smell of him, its earthiness so grounding, so re-assuring. And as they moved quietly together in time to the melancholy melody, Layla wondered whether her own lost soul might have found another equally bereft.

"Wish You Were Here"—who was he wishing for as they swayed to Roger Waters' moody lyrics? His father and brother had died to make him the Earl. But he didn't really speak about either. Was it this loss that had created the yawning gap that she sensed inside him, one that mirrored her own? Or had someone left and broken Finn's heart? Was it a blameless crime, like Will's, having no choice but to go? Or had they turned their back on him and walked away? She sensed he'd been damaged by life, but nothing she knew about him provided answers.

Perhaps it should have felt wrong, her body pressed against that of another man, but somehow his solid presence allowed her to feel alive once more, not trapped in some grey limbo of space that delineated the end of her life with Will but offered no vision of what lay on the other side. Tonight offered a first small glimmer, that in this time after, her life stretched ahead of her for what—forty, fifty, even sixty years if she emulated her great-granny Meredith—she wouldn't always be alone.

He insisted on walking her home afterwards, even though the sky was still not fully dark and the distance short. They had spoken barely a word, as if neither wished to break the spell of the encircling music. Stopping on the stone steps, they stood bathed in the golden glow of a porch light while moths circled in lazy spirals above them.

"See you tomorrow?" His phrasing it as a question surprised her. She thought it went without saying that he'd continue to come each evening, drag her away from the work, create a pleasant interlude before delivering her gently back to the lonely night. But there was an awkward set to his stance, as if he feared in their final intimate dance he'd crossed a line. She wanted to reassure him. She realised she couldn't bear the thought that he might not walk into the clinic tomorrow at six.

"Of course," she said, and on impulse stepped towards him, placing a chaste kiss on his flushed cheek. "Good night Finn." Relief washed over his face. "And thank you."

Now his expression morphed into modest pleasure. She unlocked the door, and he leaned around her, stretching a hand inside to flick on a light. She'd always valued her independence, but this gesture of seeing her safely into the cottage was welcome. It was only after she'd closed the door with a firm thud and turned the lock that she heard his brisk footsteps head back up the driveway. She might be lonely at times, but even here on the other side of the world, she wasn't truly alone. Even in this tiny rural backwater was someone who enjoyed her company, appreciated eliciting her smile, and cared enough to see her home safe at night.

30

One Step Too Far

Dallblane, Scotland - May 2022

YOU STUPID PRICK. YOU stupid prick. You stupid prick.

Finn's footsteps beat out the four-time on the driveway as he strode towards the castle. His arms swung in an angry counterpoint, balled hands punching the cool air in frustration. Jesus Christ, he should have known better than to take her down to the studio, the one place in the world that was truly his, all him. By going there, it was always going to end up being about him.

The basic reason for breaking the rule was an unselfish one. Seeing the spontaneous sparkle in those green eyes when their conversation turned to music was addictive. He had so desperately needed to see more of that unbridled happiness replace her guarded sadness. It was always there, an undercurrent to the sense of normalcy she worked hard to project. And he'd succeeded at blotting it out, even if only for a brief time. To watch her dance, losing herself in the music, was the most beautiful thing he'd ever seen.

But he'd turned his selflessness at opening up the studio to her, letting her simply be in the moment, to his own ends. Dancing alongside her, feeling the joy radiate from her like a warm wind off the desert—he'd done that for him. And he might have got away with that. But revisiting that totally selfish gesture with the last song triggered a shameful heat that overtook the remembered pleasure of her body pressed to his.

This was a woman still grieving, a deep profound grief at the loss of a man who was her world. Charlie had told him about Will and Layla. Until a few months ago their life read like the script of one of those Hallmark movies that Isabel was addicted to: friends since their teens, years of denial that there'd be anything more and then catapulted by the trauma of Will's illness into acknowledging love, sealing it with marriage, getting their happy ever after. And then a few months ago, a tragic accident leaving her alone and broken.

That wasn't how movies were supposed to end. Layla deserved a happy ending. And now he knew he wanted that to be with him. But as in the past, where his heart was concerned, he'd gone in too hard, too soon, taken one step too far.

The next day moved slowly: he snapped at people; his lunch prepared with Isabel's care sat untouched to one side; a dull ache threatened to take up residence in one temple. He'd slept fitfully, his thoughts churning, his gut unsteady, and although the day had presented a never ending list of problems, he was almost grateful that finding solutions had occupied his mind.

If the events on site yesterday had been a comedy of errors, today was beyond funny. He'd started off dealing with a contractual dispute with an obnoxious agent—a cocky little shit, representing a minor act who now wanted more money as their new release went viral. It irked him he'd had to give in to the demands. The risk of disappointed fans was too great, and the long-term viability of the festival rode on the reputation of this one.

By noon, he had a foreman seated in his office outlining problems with the supply of materials. A flurry of phone calls to every damn building supplies place in a hundred-mile radius and he'd solved the problem, but his mood hadn't improved.

But despite all the distractions, his mind hadn't been on the job. Thoughts of Layla Leroux subtly wound themselves through the minutiae of his day with the same delicate beauty as the ink that embellished those slender arms and disappeared into the hidden depths of her body. The physical ache to trace those lines, trail his fingers along them, explore what lay beyond pounced on him at the mention of her name: his mother's gentle query, Rabbie's grinning question, Charlie's email today to check up on him, reminding him in her own direct manner that it was his job to take care of Layla. And he was, but from that responsibility, unexpected but familiar emotions grew inside him.

When he sat across from her each day, conversation flowing easily, he saw more than friendship. In small ways, a reassuring smile, a soothing placement of her hand over his, she recognised his anxieties and responded to them with a calm acceptance. The recognition wasn't new. He'd had other women with whom he'd let down his guard, allowing him to see the struggle that sat behind the face he presented to the world. That intensity of feeling that might so easily tip the balance between coping with life and allowing it to swamp him always lurked just below the surface, threatening to rear up and knock him down.

With some, it had scared them off. Whether it was they were too fragile to deal with his own difficulties alongside their own, or as was more often the case they were uncomfortable with a man who had dared to let slip and show what sat behind the expected masculine bravado, either way they left.

Others had seen him as a challenge, to allow them to act out some romantic notion of fixing a damaged man. With those, he'd walked away. He could never be with a woman who saw him as less than whole, who needed him to be other than he was.

Just as Charlie had ensured he was fully aware of Layla's personal battles, he was fairly certain she'd have briefed Layla about him. But there was no hint she saw the need to do anything but listen and reassure, when each evening they unburdened themselves of the worries of the day, and more often lately explored their bigger life dilemmas over a drink at the pub.

And he didn't feel the need to fix Layla, either. How could you piece someone back together after that level of damage? All you could do was be there for them, a quiet support while they rebuilt their life. Nor could he ever replace Will for her. That would be a naïve and utterly stupid ambition. But he could be someone important in her life, a friend for now, but eventually...that's if he didn't totally fuck it all up as he'd almost done last night. He cursed his impulsivity for the hundredth time that day and forced himself back to answering the stream of emails that had poured into his inbox in the space of less than an hour.

When Finn glanced at his watch, it was 5:40. Once more, he bent his head over the latest report from their accountant, scanning rows of figures, seeking to lose himself in the numbers. Although spreadsheets of costs and projections were a poor second to the beauty of algebra, or the elegance of trigonometry, normally they were enough to soothe him. Today, they only increased his irritation with the world.

When this type of mood descended on him, his usual next step was to head for the studio, sit at a drum kit, and immerse himself in the calming rhythm. But he knew the studio was no refuge today. When he'd let Layla in there last night, he'd also let something else loose in his world, and both she and his total infatuation with her couldn't be pushed aside. Not there, not here, not anywhere.

There was a soft knock on the door, and his annoyance flared. Which idiot had done something mindless this time? His frown melted away as his mother edged through the door, tucking into the tub chair opposite. He knew what she was about to say, but he wouldn't let her sway him. He was not going to the clinic tonight. He wanted to protect Layla. At the moment, staying away was the best way to do that. Otherwise, he risked overwhelming her with the buzzing sense of possibility he saw in their future.

"I know what you're doing, love."

His mother's insightfulness was both curse and blessing. So was her directness.

"I acted like an idiot last night. What sort of man makes advances on a woman whose husband died only a couple of months ago?"

Shame bloomed on his face at the admission. Even here in his mother's presence, he wished he could turn back time, do things differently and free himself from this embarrassment.

"Do you think she sees it like that?"

"No, thank god." He recalled her farewell, a chaste kiss on the cheek, no more than a thanks for his kindness. "But I dare not go near her. I can't guarantee I won't overstep the line. And I couldn't live with that. I need to give her some space, and give myself some space. Try to get myself in hand."

"You cannot abandon her like that, Finn. You're making this all about you. You've offered that girl friendship and looked after her. And now you think you're going to retreat to your own safe space and things will magically sort themselves out?"

"I'm not abandoning her." His mother's accusation of neglect irked him. "Mum, she doesn't need me holding her hand every step of the way. She's doing well."

"So it obviously hasn't occurred to you the reason she might be doing well is *because* of you? Finn, without you, what has she got?" His mother's nostrils flared and her dark eyes flashed like lasers. "What happens at the end of the day if you don't turn up? She sits by herself in the pub. Or after a day of caring about everyone else's problems, walks up the hill to an empty house without another human being bothering to ask about her. Stop making excuses, Finn. You *are* going down there, even if I have to march you down there myself."

The image of his mother herding her wayward child down to the pub provoked a small smile. But a second wave of shame engulfed him as what she'd said sank in. How was it that no matter how well-intentioned he tried to be, he seemed to have an emotional ineptitude that made all paths lead back to him? His mother was right. He'd have to man up, carry on like nothing had happened—because for Layla nothing *had* happened—and hope things might develop between them like they did for normal people. He owed them both that.

"How is it you, who is so damn wise about these things," he said, offering her a rueful smile, "could have three children with such a pathetic level of emotional IQ?"

Euan had blazed through the world like a comet focused solely on where he was going, leaving everyone else behind in his wake. Star kept her feelings firmly confined beneath a prickly exterior that only the brave and gregarious Gary had found a way beneath. And then there was him.

"I have one who doesn't," she said. "It's more that he feels things too deeply, and fights to control his feelings, and sometimes they win."

Without bothering to close the spreadsheet or place the accountant's report in its proper place in his meticulous filing system, he rose and grabbed his wallet and phone, stuffing them into his jeans. As he placed a grateful kiss on his mother's cheek, he could feel it crinkle into a satisfied smile.

Ignoring Isabel's surprise as he launched himself out the door, Finn took off at a sprint. Despite his fitness and the road down to the village being all downhill, he arrived at the clinic in a sweat and panting. He pushed back lank hair from his face, attempting to look less like someone who'd just sprinted a frantic kilometre in the accumulated heat of a summer's day, and more like a person with a perfectly valid reason for being a little late, casually sauntering in. But the door was locked, the blinds pulled. Assuming she was already at the pub, he dialled back his haste, not wanting to look a complete fool by bursting into the bar in a panic.

Their booth sat empty. Her tall glass was empty too, only melting remnants of ice and a sagging mint leaf in the bottom, evidence he hadn't been there to prevent Lenny's heavy-handedness with the ice. As usual, a straw lay discarded on the table. She despised the soggy eco-friendly examples Lenny insisted on in the mistaken belief they made even soft drinks look classy.

She'd gone. He stood rooted to the spot, unsure of what to do. Surely if she'd wanted him to come, she'd have waited. It was only 6:15, and she had already given up on him and left, leaving the lingering hint of flowers, her perfume drifting in the air. He must have missed her by a moment.

He noticed his pint of Tennent's waiting on the bar. One sip of the cool liquid was enough for him to decide that sitting to drink it would allow him to rehydrate after his frantic run down the hill, as well as give him time to think. He would no longer act on impulse. He would mull over each decision about Layla and do the right thing by her, not let his need for her dictate. This time he'd play the long game, no matter how contrary that was to his impatient heart. So here was his first test, his first decision to make: should he go to her at the cottage, or should he read her absence as a sign for him to go home? He didn't really like the sound of either option.

A small hand slid onto his shoulder and the sudden, more strident smell of that familiar perfume with it.

"Thought you'd stood me up," she said with a grin, sliding into the seat opposite.

He swallowed hard, pushing back the guilt that standing her up was exactly what he'd intended to do until ten minutes ago.

"Crazy day," he said, sticking to the truth. "Sorry I'm late."

"Nah, I should have been less impatient to get over here and waited for you. But I'd finished up, and guessed you'd know where to look for me if I wasn't at the clinic. After all, we've got our routine now, haven't we? I couldn't go straight home and miss our daily debrief."

"Yeah," he said, suppressing the relief from spilling onto his face. This time together was important to her, too. Not yet as important as it was to him, perhaps, but give her time. "Days like today, I definitely need it."

"You must do. Look at you. Looks like you ran all the way. I thought my father was the only one who could need a beer so bad he'd sprint to the pub."

"It wasn't the beer, it was you," he said, then realising how that might sound, even though it was the truth, added, "after all I already know what happens if I dare to keep Charlie waiting, so I wasn't taking any chances."

"Another one, Layla?" Lenny called from behind the bar, saving him from any further explanation.

31

Panic

Dallblane, Scotland - June 2022

As the ambulance pulled away, Layla sank to the ground. The need to look after her patient, the single thing keeping her upright, was no longer there. Handing his care to others, she lay back on the grass, eyes closed, the weight of exhaustion exerting physical pressure on her body. But overlaying the wash of weariness was a sense of satisfaction.

Two months of consistent hard work had won the trust of most of the locals, but it was Rabbie's unfortunate accident today that had got her over the line. She'd proved once and for all to the people of this village that they were in capable hands. The murmured admiration of the men, the gruff thanks of the site foreman, and the grateful hands of Jocelyn Wallace clasped over hers before she'd climbed in the back of the ambulance next to her husband; all spoke of doubts doused by her actions this afternoon. Those who'd questioned the competence of a young woman doctor from the bottom of the world would have to eat their words.

The unmistakable roar of a V8 engine dragged her from her smug reverie. Finn, of course. He'd been down in Glasgow for a meeting with a PR company, promising he would be back to meet her as usual. Who knows what they'd told him when he'd arrived at the clinic? When the call had come, she hadn't stopped to explain much to Raylene; just that there was an accident on the festival site, and it was Rabbie. There'd been no time for anything but grab her bag and run. God, he'd be frantic.

Under heavy braking, the Daimler stopped with a lurch. He leapt from the sports car, hair a tangled mess, eyes darting wildly. Seeing her sit up, he was at her side in two strides.

"Layla, is it true? Rabbie's injured?" His words came out in a burst.

"Hey, Finn," she reached a hand to his shoulder, offering reassurance. "Yes, he was, but he's going to be OK. It's all under control."

"What the fuck happened?" His face was a pale mask of worry.

"Rolled the digger. Tried to jump clear but ended up pinned."

"I knew I shouldn't have let him do it." He ran his hands through his hair, shaking his head. "But Rabbie, the old bugger, he's always so bloody keen."

"He's driven one before?"

"Yeah, yeah. Heaps of times. But he's getting on a bit. Time I pulled him off that sort of stuff."

"I don't think it was his fault. Your foreman—Scott?" He nodded. "Scott says that rain last week altered the runoff in that area. Destabilised the ground. No one could have predicted it would give way like that. So it wasn't Rabbie's fault. Finn, it wasn't your fault." She clasped a hand tightly over his.

"Yeah, but it doesn't stop me feeling responsible." He huffed out a frustrated sigh.

"I get that. It's only natural when you want to be so hands on with everything." He was intensely invested in every detail of this festival, treated the workers like family, but it wasn't healthy for him to wear this huge responsibility on his own. "But you have a good team. There's a group of them already gone up to the site office for a meeting. They've got this. You don't have to deal with it all by yourself."

He gave a shrug, another sigh, and she felt him relax a little. "Yeah, you're right. They probably see me as a control freak. I just want them to know I care about the work they do. People need to feel valued."

"They do, Finn." She'd seen the respect every time his name came up in conversation in the village. The locals, the workers, they all saw how seriously he took the role he'd inherited as Earl, as well as the role he'd created managing a festival that brought a hefty income stream to the village.

"I still need to get up to that meeting. Scott will have it in hand, but he'd appreciate me showing up to support him." The rasping sound of Darth Vader cut in; his ridiculous ringtone, and he retrieved the phone from his back pocket. "This is him now," he said, putting the phone to his ear.

He moved back towards the car, leaning against the side of it, deep in conversation with the site foreman. She watched as the emotions played out across his face. Concern turned to worry, worry turned to fear.

"Finn, what is it?" she said, as he fumbled the phone back into his pocket, his hand shaking. Beads of sweat peppered his skin, his face covered by a grey sheen.

"Got to sit down," he said, stumbling to the low stone wall bounding the driveway. "Fuck," he said, the word pushed out between gasps for air. His eyes scrunched shut as he struggled for breath. One hand clasped to his chest, he slumped forward over his knees.

"Finn, what is it?" She knelt in front of him and swung into the practised routines of those years in the ER. A rapid pulse pounded in his wrist. Taking in the symptoms, her experience told her this could be a heart attack. Not likely in most people in their early thirties. But Finn wasn't most people. He had a family history. According to Charlie, an inheritable heart condition lurked in the background. "Has this happened before?" His eyes flashed wide in panic, and he gave a slight nod. Nausea rose in her stomach. Sinister thoughts of the possibilities battled against her professional calm. "OK," she said, fumbling for her own phone. "I'm going to call for help."

As she watched him struggle for air, the lines of agony creasing deeper with every laboured breath, and the clenched hand on his chest right at the source, her own heart lurched with the painful realisation she could lose him, too. She could lose Finn. This couldn't be happening. Not so soon after Will. Dread crippled her and her fingers refused to function as she sought the three numbers on the keypad.

"No," he blurted out. "No ambulance."

"Finn, I can't just sit here and do nothing. This is serious."

"No," he said again, more insistent, huffing out the words between scant breaths. "It's not what you think. Not heart attack."

"We don't know that."

"But I do," he said. "Go to the car, in the glove box, spray bottle. Get it."

Against her better judgement, she did as he asked. It was better than doing nothing. But if it wasn't his heart, why the hell did he want the spray? It was standard issue for angina. She leapt into the passenger seat of the Daimler, wrenching open the small pocket in the black leather dashboard. Her hands scrabbled inside, finding a brown glass bottle; unlabelled. Not angina spray. It didn't make sense—unless, as he said, this wasn't heart related.

"Here," she said, pressing it into his outstretched hand.

He sprayed two puffs into his mouth, then discarded it on the ground. Almost immediately, his face relaxed a little. She let out a ragged breath. Relief surged through her. He was going to be OK.

"Thank you," he said, reaching for her hand. Moments passed and his laboured breathing subsided into a more regular rhythm. "Just sit with me?"

He gave a gentle pull, and she obliged, joining him on the wall, noting the breathing slowing further and the hand that had been clutching his chest now dropping to rest on his knee.

They sat in silence for a couple of minutes, while her brain raced to take the pieces of this confused puzzle and put them together into something that made sense. His hand gave hers a squeeze.

"Feeling better?" she said.

"Yeah, better." His voice was surprisingly normal. "Sorry you had to see that."

"Don't be sorry. Believe me. I've seen far worse than that. Remember who you're talking to here."

"It's a panic attack," he said. "Just my stupid brain. Anxiety blown up out of control."

"Do you have them often?"

"I used to. Now, most of the time, I manage them. If things are ramping up, I have stuff I do to head off an attack."

"Like the spray?"

"Yeah. Mum found it for me, some online herbal store. Works bloody well. I have no idea what's in it. Could be just a placebo. But I'm not going to argue the science. It does what it needs to."

"Sure does. It was amazing how quickly it worked."

"Yeah," he said with a wry smile. "That's what makes me wonder if it's all in my head. But it does the job, and I can carry it with me."

"What else helps?" she asked.

"Music," he said. "The drums mainly. Something about the rhythm. It takes over your body, doesn't leave any room for all that other shit."

She'd seen his restless tapping surface from time to time when they were talking. Thought it was just music bubbling up inside of him that had to come out; but it was more—a type of self-soothing mechanism.

"How long since you last had one like this?"

"Months," he said. "There hasn't been one since you've been here, not till today. Surprising, really, given the heap of problems on my desk on any given day right now."

"That's great, that you've got it under control. And while it can't be easy to live with, at least it's not your heart."

"Yeah, thankfully I'm sure of that," he said grimly. "Have you heard of HCM?"

"Yeah, I have. It's in your family?" So this was the condition Charlie had mentioned. She knew of it.

"My Dad. My brother. But not me. After Dad died, Euan and I both got tested. He had it. I didn't. The lucky one, that's me."

"Tough on him."

"Yeah. More than it had to be, though. He decided he was going to live each day like there was no tomorrow. But the silly bastard did some dumb things. Made sure there wasn't a tomorrow."

She felt a pang of understanding for poor dead Euan. She'd lived that time with Will, a young man confronted with the possibility of his life cut short. There'd been potential for him to spin out of control like that. He'd certainly started down that path. But he'd stopped himself, and she knew why—because of her. Their love for each other had given him something to live for, a reason to fight, a reason to take care of himself. And how they'd lived. They'd had more years than he'd dared to hope for back then. But it wasn't enough. No amount of time with Will would ever have been enough for her. She gulped back the sob that rose in her throat, the rawness of her loss rising up to swamp her. There was no choice but to go on without him.

"Anyway," Finn said, turning to her with a weak smile. "How about we indulge in our usual end of day stress relief? You look like you could do with it, too." She swallowed, trying to push back the prickle of tears. Her emotions were in turmoil. Thoughts of Will wrestled with this near-miss with Finn. She cared about this guy and only minutes ago she'd thought he might die right there in front of her. Now he was the calm one, reassuring her, "Let's go down the pub for a beer and some dinner? I'll even let you drive," he teased.

"You don't need to see Scott?"

"Nah. You're right. He's got it in hand. Anyway, nothing I can do tonight will make any difference. He's meeting with a worksite safety investigator who's driving up from Glasgow in the morning.

He was just calling to let me know the guy is coming. That's what sent me into a spin."

"Shit, they're onto it that fast?"

"Yeah," he said. "Someone called them. Not sure who. But nothing we can do except answer their questions and hope we haven't stuffed up." He stood and grabbed her hand, pulling her gently to her feet. "Come on. Get your butt in the driver's seat before I change my mind."

She slipped in behind the wheel, thinking of other days, another sports car, another man handing his pride and joy into her care. As the motor came to life with a throaty rumble, she tried to take pleasure from the moment, let go of the past, and not dwell on the future.

32

Resurrection

Dallblane, Scotland - July 2022

LAYLA COULDN'T MAKE OUT the features of the two tall figures that strode through the door into the back bar. Silhouetted against the sudden blaze of late afternoon sun, she could only see they were tall. Leaning on the bar talking to Lenny while he poured their next round, Finn had a better view. A wide smile slid across his face as a loud familiar voice rang out.

"Hope those are our fucking drinks you're lining up there Mr McGill?"

"That's Lord McGill to riff raff from the colonies like you Ms Christensen."

Charlie's bell-like laugh rang across the bar. "Not fucking likely," she said, crashing against his chest.

"Did I tell you mine's a vodka and tonic?" Safiyah pushed past Charlie into Finn's welcoming arms.

Layla was on her feet by now. "So, no welcome hugs for me, huh? Never mind that I'm your oldest and best friend."

They immediately pounced upon her, the breath nearly squeezed out of her between the two women.

"Finn, what are you doing hiding her away down the back there?" Charlie released her grip on Layla's shoulders a little to glare at him.

"That's how she likes it Charlie," he said. "Stops us having to put up with randoms who cruise in here from time to time."

Charlie held her at arm's length, scrutinising her with a frown of those arched pale eyebrows.

"We expected you tomorrow."

"Well," Charlie said with a reproachful glance at Safiyah, "Saf here has a bit of a lead foot. No doubt the speed camera tickets will roll in next week."

"Are you sure it's not because of her aversion to that damn She-wee? Maybe Safiyah wanted to get here without having to use it," Layla quipped.

Charlie choked with laughter. "Oh, come on, I never ever made you use it."

"What the hell is a Shewee?" Finn asked as he deposited her usual tall glass and his beer, while behind him Lenny poured a gin and a vodka.

"Work it out Einstein," Charlie said. "She. Wee. Basically, a girl's way of fighting back against a design flaw in our anatomy."

"The fact you even still own it is a worry. Anyway, sit down." Layla sank back into the depths of the booth while Charlie and Safiyah climbed in opposite her. Now two pairs of eyes surveyed her face, one question on their minds.

"I'm good," she said, preempting the words. "I know you want to ask. To be honest, I'm way better than I expected. The people here have been great. But mostly it's thanks to Patti and Isabel, and him." She nodded at Finn, who was throwing notes on the counter in exchange for two glasses of clear liquid.

"Good to hear this useless bastard is doing his job then," Charlie said, throwing a sharp look at him as he dropped the glasses on the table and slipped in beside her.

"Nice to see you too, Charlie," he said. "God, how I've missed you and your foul mouth."

"Knew you would," she said with a wink. Her voice softened. "Knew you'd look after Layla, that is. Good man. So, tell me," she said, taking a slurp of her gin and tonic, "what's been happening here in the bustling centre of the universe?"

Knowing that Charlie and Safiyah were a few hundred metres away kept Layla's mood bright as she prepared for bed that night. When she stood, hands poised on the curtains, ready to shut out the full moon, it was easy to spot the room Finn had set up for Charlie. Lights burned even now,at almost midnight. There, over the next three weeks, she'd take raw footage of the festival, and work her film-making magic on it. She and Finn's little production company had already signed a contract with Netflix. The first festival had launched Charlie into a new era in her career. This one would cement it and make her a substantial amount of money.

Similarly, Finn had laid everything on the line the first time round. He told her how back in 2019, only he and Eric Walters had believed it could work. She'd met Eric when Finn had asked if he could join them one night at the pub. He was larger than life, and, if she was honest, at first sight appeared a rather sleazy character. But she'd found herself liking the man despite his less than favourable first impression. When she sat beside him and Finn while they talked, their overwhelming optimism was contagious. A business partnership had grown into friendship, Finn deferring to the older man with a quiet respect. Outside work, childless Eric veered from treating Finn like a younger drinking buddy who allowed him to relive a little of his youth with much rehashing of hair-raising tales from the music industry, to an indulgent father. Two men, both so different, but both better for having the other in their life.

For her too, whenever she was around Finn, life seemed that little bit better, the challenges a little easier to bear. She understood now why he and Charlie had also become firm friends beyond a business arrangement. He reminded her a lot of Leo. It wasn't just the dark curls, or those soulful brown eyes. While there was a restlessness inside Finn, not at all like Leo's zen-like calm, the two men shared an innate selfless kindness. Each took the time to attend to the small things, noticing the details of others' idiosyncratic little preferences and remembering them.

Finn knew she loathed ice in her drinks, berating Lenny for forgetting that one day last week. He encouraged her love of chick flicks, inviting her over to share telly nights, sitting through replays of classics like *Notting Hill*. She swore he even enjoyed them. He wasn't embarrassed to be seen browsing through the little free library outside the village store, grabbing all the Regency romances. She blamed lockdown for that addiction. Bingeing *Bridgerton* was just one of many extreme measures she'd deployed as a doctor struggling to maintain her sanity during a pandemic. He'd show up at her door with a stack of them most weeks. It was all she could do to prevent herself pointing out the irony of the situation: the Earl of Dallblane offering stories of feisty heroines and lusty noblemen to the woman who lived in the cottage by the castle. She didn't want to deter him and his gifts.

But above all, Finn, like Leo, and of course, like Will, made her feel she was in safe hands. And she needed that right now. Severed from Will's easygoing take on the world, where no problem was insurmountable, she might easily have plummeted back to being the girl she'd been before she met him. Even now, thoughts of those uncertain nights where her drunk father and enraged mother warred in the lounge, sometimes spilling out onto the front lawn or even the street, brought an uncomfortable prickle. She never again wanted to be that girl: living life on high alert, continually scanning for hidden threats, taking swift sidesteps around the real dangers lurking in their dodgy neighbourhood and all the time suppressing the fear that with one more episode this family might implode.

She'd come here with an uncertain future, but as she pulled up the covers, tonight it seemed like the days stretching before her held a tiny seed-like crystal of hope. And with these people around her, day by day she was already adding new layers, the tiny sparkling facets reflecting a new life growing slowly but surely out of the old one ripped away from her.

It wasn't only the castle caught up in a whirl of activity in the weeks leading up to the festival. The presence of increasing numbers of workers saw the village bursting at the seams. Some canny locals abandoned their homes, realising the potential of renting them out for a few weeks while escaping the madness. Others set up spare rooms as Air BnBs, and reaped the benefits of additional income, while looking forward to using the free event passes provided for 'locals'.

Hers had arrived that morning and sat propped on her desk in the clinic. Finn came at six as usual. He'd not wavered in his commitment to their nightly pub sessions, insisting he needed it as much as she did. Only once had he called to cancel, dealing with some minor emergency. Occasionally he brought Safiyah; Charlie just once. The irony wasn't lost on Layla. Charlie, the girl who'd berated her and Will for their workaholic ways, had become a woman determined to succeed even if it meant insane days and little sleep.

"You don't need that," he said, whisking away the yellow lanyard with its dangling card.

"Here. For you." He lifted one of the purple lanyards from around his neck and placed it over her head.

"That there," he said, pointing at the plastic swipe card hanging off it, "will take you anywhere on site. From tomorrow, that includes your place and ours. They're fitting security mechanisms to the doors. No one should get in that close to the cottage, but just in case."

"Wow, I hadn't even thought of that. Of course."

"And there's a room for you at ours if you need it. I mean, you're not going to get any more sleep there than here, but to be honest, we'd probably all feel better if you were safe with us at night."

It hadn't occurred to her what might need to change in her life as thousands of strangers descended on their little patch of paradise less than a week from now. A full medical team arrived soon, so her doctoring skills wouldn't be needed up there. She'd presumed she would still see a few of her own patients, but proactive Raylene was already pulling in some earlier and fobbing off others till it was all over. There was no way Layla would miss out on a five days of music right on her doorstep.

"Thank you," she said. "I might take you up on that. Probably have to if it shuts Charlie up."

"And appeases Mum. You know how she fusses over you."

Layla smiled. "I've become rather attached to her mothering. She's so good at it. Not to mention Isabel."

While she loved her own mother, Sharon's parenting reflected her rough-and-ready approach to life. The warmth and nurturing of these two women was another unexpected treasure she'd found in Dallblane.

"Yeah, and you're rather attached to their food too, I've noticed," he said with a laugh. She could never suppress her enthusiasm when he arrived at her door bearing food parcels from the castle kitchen.

"God, yes, it's lucky I don't own a bathroom scale. And at work, I resist the urge to hop on those." The dial of the large scale sitting beside her desk always seemed to wear an accusing expression. "Too scared of the number. I have gained so much weight."

"You look great," he said. She flushed a little under his appreciative glance. "Healthy. Well," he said, relieving the slight awkwardness. "Right, let's attend to our mental health across the road."

She couldn't help but cast a similar appreciative glance at the man leading her out of the clinic. Finn, despite his punishing schedule this close to the festival start, maintained a boundless energy, and positively glowed with the excitement of seeing his dream resurrected, not another victim of Covid as he'd feared. There was something incredibly alluring about a person who lit up like that. She found herself staring at him sometimes as he talked, and then would force herself to drag her eyes away. It was like looking at the sun even though you knew you shouldn't. And as he strode across the road, making a beeline for the back bar, she couldn't help but think how damn attractive the outer package was too. And that she shouldn't really be looking at that either.

Layla surveyed the lounge, thinking it incongruous that a vast room in a castle could feel so homely. Patti's touch was evident, with feminine throw rugs and soft floral cushions relieving the rather grim wood panelling that surrounded every room. Equally incongruous was the small gathering of family and friends celebrating the opening night of a music festival. No high-powered industry moguls, no fawning wannabes, no desperate hangers-on with false sentiments. Only a group of people who truly understood what it meant to have survived a worldwide disaster to bring this magic to life again.

There was the traditional celebratory champagne, but Layla only sipped one obligatory glass. The stifling air pressed in close, the heat unexpected for a Scottish summer. She intended to hydrate well with plenty of water before she and Finn made her way over to the main stage. With their purple lanyards, they might have watched

The Destitute from the media pit. But while physically closer to the stage, they knew it would lack the electricity. That tantalising burst of contagious energy that came from immersing yourself in a group of thousands, all sharing a common purpose, was addictive. Once you had experienced it, nothing else measured up.

The plan was to arrive during the warm-up act and make their way through the crowd to get a spot as close as possible to the front. Layla was damned if she was going to waste another opportunity to see this band stuck behind rows of people, ninety-nine percent of them taller than her.

Charlie headed in her direction, placing one empty champagne glass on the table and swiping another on her way.

"How fucking amazing is this?" she said, her face glowing as bright as her snowy braids. "Who'd have thought three years ago that this would be happening? Who would have thought even a year ago?"

The first wailing guitar riff sailed through the open window. It really was happening. A bustling tent city. A sprawling campervan park. Seventy thousand people. And a group of the best musicians on the planet, some famous, some yet to be, but all there to share their art.

"You guys should be really proud of yourselves. You and Finn, and Eric. Pulling all this together."

"A long way to go still," she said. "There's money sitting in my bank account for a doco I haven't even made yet. Getting an advance is great for the cash flow, but totally fucking frightening. Sometimes I'm literally shitting myself that I won't be able to deliver."

Safiyah, who'd come to lean on Charlie's shoulder, wrapping one long braceleted arm around Charlie's waist, placed a clumsy kiss on her cheek.

"You always deliver, my love. You are amazing."

"And you, my love, sound like you're a little bit pissed." Charlie turned and cupped her face, returning the kiss.

"Oh hey, just a little," Safiyah laughed. "Besides, there's nothing wrong getting a little bit pissed on a night like tonight."

"Says a person who doesn't actually have to work on a night like tonight. Speaking of which, it's time I got over there. Tess and Brayden are handling this first bit, but you know me, can't help but want to lean over their shoulders. See you later. Have fun."

Charlie had been itching to get over there for the past hour. She'd endured the party for the sake of everyone else, but Layla could see relief on her face as she headed for the door, Safiyah trailing behind, with her tall frame wavering ever so slightly.

She turned, thinking to join the group with Eric at its centre. One of those guys who was the life of the party, she'd started to enjoy his company. But a hand slipped over hers and Finn was there.

"Time to go? Might take a while to find a good spot."

"Yeah," she said, "now is good."

They slipped out of the party, heading through a side entrance that took them down to a high fence and a set of security gates. A press of their swipe cards and they merged into the stream of people pouring towards the main stage.

Now *is* good, she thought. A party with friends, a warm summer evening, the anticipation of great music, walking hand in hand with Finn. Happiness had crept up on her, shadowing her on stealthy feet, and tonight she felt ready to turn and face it, and welcome it back into her life.

33

Crush

Dallblane Castle, Scotland - July 2022

IT BEGAN AS A small pulse through the crowd, so subtle most wouldn't have noticed; just a quiet undercurrent subsumed in the heightened anticipation of that night's audience, as the montage of background music used to fill the gaps between acts faded out. The second ripple, triggered by the stage lights darkening, had the sensation of a gentle wave carried through the press of bodies, causing those in the front row to lap softly against the barriers. And then a voice through the speakers announced the band to the answering roar of the crowd and an accompanying surge.

The excited thudding of Layla's heart as the members of The Destitute ambled onto the stage, switched to a pounding fear as a wave of motion broke against her, sweeping her with it. She flung her hand towards Finn, in a desperate attempt to catch his, but unable to reach him, the inescapable forward momentum carried her away. Although the distance between them wasn't great, she could see the look of panic on his face. He realised what she knew: she was drowning in a human tidal wave.

She screamed, but no one heard as the powerful guitar riffs poured over them. She struggled to remain upright. Already smaller than virtually everyone around her, it would take only one brief stumble for her to fall and be crushed underfoot. Seeing what appeared to be a small gap near the steel mesh barriers, she used all her strength to elbow her way towards it. Arriving there, she breathed a sigh of relief having found this small refuge.

She held tight to the fence, in an attempt to stay on her feet. But when the next wave of bodies descended on her, she realised too late that her refuge had become a prison. Crushed against it, there was no escape with the weight and heat of the crowd pinning her in tight. She could feel herself losing consciousness, whether from fear or the lack of air, when a hand reached over the fence and grasped hers, holding her upright. She'd never in her life been so pleased to see that braided white blonde hair.

"Charlie," she gasped, but no sound came as she faded in the crush of people. They locked eyes with Charlie's fierce and determined, willing her to channel the strength offered in the firm grasp of her hands. She clung to them, even when Charlie broke the gaze, distracted by something beyond the space they occupied.

"Finn!" Charlie bawled across the crush behind them. "Over here!" It seemed unlikely that anyone might hear the lone voice of a woman above the all-encompassing sound of the loudest band on the planet in full flight.

But Layla knew her call was answered when his large body replaced those behind her, and his two strong arms pushed underneath hers. Wedged against her, Finn became a protective shield, holding off the still surging crowd. If there'd been more room, he might have boosted her over the top to safety, but there were too many people for that possibility.

"I've got you Layla. Just relax. I've got you." Finn's voice close to her ear and the slight reprieve from the writhing press of those around them, gave her the small glimmer of hope she needed to maintain awareness.

Charlie's voice bellowed out again, this time across the group in the media pit.

"Help her," she roared, and heads flicked towards them. "Fuck! We need help here."

The sheer desperation in her voice somehow carried above the thunder of the band. On the other side of the fence, people appeared, running towards them. A man in a security uniform gave a jubilant cry as he spotted a joint in the panels to Layla's left. Another man joined him and they worked in unison, frantically bashing on the connectors between the two panels, using their heavy torches like hammers.

"Hang on, Layla," Charlie screamed, her grip fierce. But she didn't know if she could. The lack of air, the weight of the people behind, and the pain of her body jammed against the metal bars was all too much. Her eyelids fluttered as she felt consciousness ebbing away. "Layla," Charlie screamed again. "Stay with me, damn you."

"Layla, hold on, hold on, honey." She wanted to do as Finn asked, but it was so very, very hard.

Layla couldn't help it. Her eyes drooped shut, and she felt herself start to slump. While around her was a whirl of noise and activity, an inner eerie stillness descended on her, as one single thought took hold: *I'm not going to make it.* And then, just as she'd calmly accepted that as a fact, Charlie's hands released their grip. With a groaning of metal against metal, the panel beside her crashed to the ground.

Her eyes jerked open as her rescuers scattered. Those watching the scene from the media pit reeled back. But amongst it all, Charlie stood her ground, unafraid for herself, all focus on Layla. Layla cascaded forward into her arms, thankful for the tall safe frame of her friend. Finn plummeted through the space after her, catching her between them, safe in their embrace.

As air flooded her lungs, her awareness once again reached outwards, bringing all her senses back online.

"Here, let me help." She heard Finn's voice again. He looped one of his arms under hers on one side, while Charlie took up a position on the other. "We're going to get you out of here, Layla," he said. His voice was calm, but when she turned to meet his eyes, she saw fear. Not for himself, but for her. "Do you think you can walk a bit? Just a little way so we can get you somewhere to sit you down for a moment?"

"Yeah," she said. Her voice came out as a wheeze, but her legs already felt stronger. "Yeah," she repeated, this time the word completely formed. "I can." She attempted to convince herself as much as them.

They supported her to the side of the media area, where one of the numerous little golf carts was parked. Sitting in the cushioned seat, Charlie by her side still propping her up, Finn leaning on the other, their conversation swirled across her.

"She needs to get checked out," he said. "God, there has to be some bruising, at least. But there could be more." A tentative hand tugged at her t-shirt, and she felt their scrutiny of her bare stomach and ribs.

"Amazing, though," Charlie said. "No redness, not even a scratch. Finn, I think we should just get her back to the castle."

"I'd feel better if we had some more expert eyes on this."

"No, you know what?" Charlie's words had a resolute tone. "I think the less eyes on this, the better."

"Because?" he said, confusion in his voice.

Charlie's reply was low, "Because, if this gets out, that someone was almost crushed up here tonight, well, you might have all the health and safety inspectors descend on you, and before you know it—shut down. The whole fucking lot. And that would mean disaster—unless you've got a few spare million kicking around to pay everyone and refund your ticket holders. They could sue you. And I'm not sure your insurance company will cover your arses if they find negligence on your part."

"And you think that doing nothing is a good idea?" he hissed back. "What about if there is a real problem? What if it happens again? And we've got a frigging Hillsborough on our conscience?"

"Look, I'm not saying do nothing. I'm not that bloody stupid. But maybe what happened with Layla tonight was a one-off, a small bit of bad luck. It would be crazy to risk all of this, if there is no risk."

Even to Layla's hazy mind, Charlie's thinking sounded like common sense. After all, the absence of any major pain suggested she was fine, only the residual fog from the shock of it all still cast a disorienting cloud over her thoughts. And it seemed with no one else caught in the wave, perhaps it was just a case of 'wrong place, wrong time'.

"OK, so tell me, Charlie, what do we do? Because although the idea of this whole thing exploding in my face is like my worst nightmare, it would be nothing compared to people getting seriously hurt. I couldn't live with that. And I don't think you could either."

"So three years ago, you had five days, a huge crowd in an untested set-up and nothing went wrong?" Charlie was like a machine, processing the situation in calm steps.

"Yes, you're right. It was a dream run, really. Apart from a couple of security breaches, a few couples shagging in the castle gardens, and an impromptu drunken rave in the woods one night, yeah, nothing. Certainly not in the crowds by the stage. Even on that final night with these guys."

Although they were now positioned behind the speakers and at a distance away, the music of The Destitute still captured everything in its power.

"So, if you had no problems, and if you basically changed nothing, then that has to lower the chances of there being a safety risk."

"I suppose," he said, wavering under Charlie's cool logic. "But how can we be sure?"

"OK, well, I can check that for you. It will take a bit of time, but I can tell you now, it's time I'm prepared to invest if it stops all the things you and I have worked for from being torn down by some jumped up bastard of a bureaucrat making huge flawed leaps of thinking from the fact Layla got a little squashed tonight."

A little squashed. As her head cleared, the now insistent protests of her aching shoulders and hips suggested it was more than a little. She wanted to rip off her jeans right there and show Charlie the bruises that surely must be there. But she understood her argument. This could have been one small freak incident. Not enough to ruin everything for two people she cared about.

"Take me up to the castle," she said, opening her eyes. Their heads swivelled towards her in unison. "Yeah, I heard," she said. "And I agree with Charlie."

"But how can you be sure, Charlie?" Finn protested. "Sure enough?"

"I have all the footage from last time. And I have tonight's, up until the point I saw what was happening to Layla. I'll go back through it, and see what's different, if anything. I'll tell Tess and Brayden it's all on them tonight. They won't mind, they're both hungry for a chance to shine. And I'll work on reviewing film all night if I have to. "

"I'll do it with you," he said.

"Don't you trust me?"

"Of course I trust you," he said. "But I know how it was set up a lot better than you do. So it makes sense. And, to be honest, after this, I don't think I'll sleep tonight, anyway. I'm wired."

"OK, you take Layla back now. You're OK, hun?" Charlie's concerned face appeared in front of hers. "Not going to topple out of there, are you?"

Layla summoned a smile, and words more confident than she felt. "Promise I'll be good, no more drama."

"I'll buckle her in to be safe." Finn reached across for the belt and she winced as his hand scrabbled against her hip, searching for the connection.

"Right, I'll just let Tess and Brayden know they're on; tell Safiyah she's sleeping without me tonight and then join you up there." Charlie marched off back to where she'd stationed her two assistants.

The golf cart jerked forward with a soft hum, and Layla closed her eyes as they made their way towards the castle.

Layla could hear quiet breathing beside the bed, interspersed with the faint rustle of a page turning. When she opened her eyes, she stared into the gloom of an unfamiliar ceiling, dark wood high above her. She turned her head to the left, toward the faint ripple of another page turn. By the light of a small glowing lamp, Patti McGill sat with a large leather-bound book in her lap. Aware of Layla's movement, she closed the book with a soft slap and reached out a hand to smooth back the unruly tangle of Layla's hair.

"There you are," she said, her smile kind. "How are you, sweetie?" She stroked Layla's cheek with a warm, gentle hand.

"Ah..." Layla hesitated while her mind took its first tentative steps, probing her body, and strangely, to her surprise, found no real pain pushing back in answer. "Ah... you know, I think I'm OK."

"Well, you've had a few hours' sleep. The best healer of all."

She was right. That's why they put people into an induced coma, forcing the body to take the rest it needed. Her body had needed no such coaxing, grabbing it willingly. Sleep had slipped across her with ease, in what seemed like mere moments after Finn had helped her into the enormous bed.

"I'll send for Isabel. Get you some tea perhaps."

Patti reached over to the wall beside the bed, pressing a small button in the centre of a discreet brass surround. In the quiet house, the faint tingle of a bell sounded, summoning the loyal Isabel. It was only a matter of minutes before the thin housekeeper appeared, bearing a tray with a steaming mug of tea and a bowl that smelled a lot like macaroni cheese.

Isabel smiled at Layla as she placed the tray on a side table. "It cheers my heart to see some colour in your cheeks, my dear. It gave us quite a scare when Finn brought you in."

"Yes, good news isn't it?" said Patti, beaming proudly as if she herself had conjured an awake talking Layla. Perhaps she had. There was an ethereal, almost magical aura around Patti McGill that spoke of hidden depths. However, the smile evaporated from Patti's face as Isabel passed the tea. With narrowed eyes and a sudden deepening of her wrinkled brow, she intercepted the mug before it reached Layla's outstretched hand. Passing it beneath her nose, the frown deepened.

"No, Isabel, not the yarrow. Not in this case."

"But I thought she'd most likely have some bruising, with what he said—about her being squashed against that fence?"

"Yes, normally I'd agree, Isabel. But as I said, not in this case. And not the comfrey, either." Layla caught a knowing glance between the two women.

"Perhaps the chamomile?" Isabel suggested. "That won't harm—"

"Perfect." Patti cut her off, the abrupt tone surprising.

Another odd glance passed between them, and Isabel bustled off, removing the offending tea. Despite not being fully awake, and the surreal quality of finding herself here, in an enormous bedroom in the castle, Layla's curiosity was momentarily piqued. With a scant knowledge of herbal remedies, her medical mind pounced on the moment as a possible new source of useful information. But before she could shape that thought into a question, Patti was on her feet, pulling back covers.

"How about we have a wee look, shall we?" she said, her gentle hands tugging at the neck of Layla's t-shirt so she could peer at her shoulders for damage. Enjoying the soothing attentiveness, she relaxed with eyes closed and drifted peacefully on the edge of sleep. But something about the exchange between the two women continued to nag at her.

"Why not the comfrey? Or yarrow?" Layla said, opening her eyes and meeting Patti's gaze.

Patti's lips pursed, and she paused. This uncertainty how to proceed was a stark contrast to her previous kind efficiency.

"I'm sorry, I presumed as a doctor… but of course maybe in New Zealand you don't have to deal with so much of this sort of thing." She waved a casual hand in the air, as if to make light of the conversation. Her apologetic tone suggested her words were an attempt to be tactful, and not cause Layla's medical knowledge to appear lacking. "They're wonderful herbs. But not for pregnant women."

Layla's fogged brain processed the words slowly, rolling that one most important word around and around in her head, tossing it back and forth to view it from all sides. Pregnant. True, she hadn't had a period for months. Not since… but she'd written that off to the trauma, her body's response to the punishing grief. In the same way as she'd assumed the bouts of nausea, that had now thankfully passed, were part of the painful adjustment to a world without Will. She'd noted their cessation as a small positive sign she was starting to heal.

Her hand instinctively fell to her stomach, tracing the slight curvature, in awe at the realisation that a part of him lived on there, inside of her. But the immediate thought that he'd never get to see this child triggered a brutal stab of pain to her heart. Seeing her stricken face, Patti moved to sit on the bed, hugging Layla to her chest as the tears fell.

"Oh my poor darling," she said, the instinctive response of a mother in her soft embrace, the hand stroking her hair, the murmured wordless sounds of comfort falling naturally, interspersed between Layla's sobs. "I didn't realise. You had no idea."

"But how did *you* know?" Layla snuffled against the scratchy wool of Patti's shawl. She could feel Patti's small smile against her hair.

"There's a look women have about them. It's like that little life inside of them glows. I knew the moment I met you. Despite the sadness in your eyes, there was this beautiful aura around you. But

I imagined how hard it must be, that you'd be having this baby on your own, and expected you wouldn't be sharing that with strangers, not until it became obvious."

"Do you think anyone else knows? Other people might have seen it too?"

She felt a twinge of guilt. She was having a baby. Yet she'd come here with a promise to serve this community for a year. Would they judge her harshly, thinking she'd signed that contract, knowing she couldn't fulfil it, and that she would let them down?

A gentle shake of Patti's head calmed those thoughts. "No, I doubt that. Just me, and now Isabel. Other people are so caught up in their own worlds. These things aren't so obvious as they are to people like us. And don't worry, I'm sure when it becomes unavoidable, people will be happy for your news."

It was as if this woman could read her mind, and not only hear her thoughts, but decipher the tangled jumble that floundered inside. As if her life wasn't already complicated, with all she'd endured in these past months.

Isabel returned a few minutes later, and taking in the scene, made the astute decision to take up her own position on Layla's other side, coaxing her gently away from Patti's shoulder, and with small encouraging noises, ensuring that she took some first tentative sips at the tea.

"Oh love, you didn't know," she said, with a gentle squeeze of Layla's shoulder. "You needn't worry. You've done such a grand job of caring for the people around here these last few months, and now we are all going to take care of you, if you'll let us. And the wee one too."

And she let the two women do just that, finishing her tea, accepting mouthfuls of the sticky but delicious macaroni cheese, and then allowing herself to be tucked back under the heavy covers, where their weight and the effects of the chamomile lulled her back into sleep.

A while later, she stirred with a terrible thirst. Flicking on a bed-side light, she found the cooled remains of the chamomile sitting beside it. She tested a small sip, and the sweet delicate taste brought the memories of earlier surging back. Again, her hand automatically fell to her stomach.

Of course, she'd have to tell Charlie soon. She deserved to share in the bittersweet knowledge that Will wasn't completely gone. And she needed to tell Charlie for her own selfish reasons—how else was she to survive the months ahead? And survive them she must, for the sake of this precious spark of life inside of her. She would need her friend.

But she'd let Charlie sort out the worries of last night first. Maybe she should even wait till the festival was over, not distract them from this priority. A few days wouldn't make any difference. Once it was done, she would forge ahead with the conversation that must come.

And as for Finn, the already complex dynamic between them was disturbing. In amongst the welcome and comforting gestures of friendship, she saw increasing signs he was already far beyond that in his thoughts about her. He tried hard to suppress them, but lost the battle on an almost daily basis in small ways that others might never notice, but advertised it loud and clear to her: a look behind his eyes, an undercurrent to his words, a sudden adjustment of his body. And perhaps she noticed them, because she too felt things for him beyond gratitude for the refuge of his company, as he extended kindness to a lonely woman in a strange place.

But a cautious voice in her head warned her away from them. Anyone who had been there would agree that the emotional land-scape of the newly-bereaved was an unpredictable and dangerous territory, and expeditions to its deepest, darkest places inadvisable without careful preparation. There had been too little time since Will's death to explore its closest regions, let alone map its full extent, or consider venturing further to discover what lay beyond.

Finn lay in that beyond, and this pregnancy like an unexpected river sprung up between them. She needed time to navigate that before she could even contemplate meeting him on the other side. The possibility that when she did, he might not still be there waiting for her brushed her with sadness, but it was a risk she must take for the sake of herself and this baby.

Maybe In Another Life

Dallblane Castle, Scotland - July 2022

WHEN LAYLA WOKE, THE first thing in her line of sight was the neat pattern of Charlie's iridescent braids that had replaced Patti's tumble of loose dark hair. Arrows of light from the centre of last night's hastily pulled curtains suggested a sunny morning awaited behind them. It lit up Charlie's pale skin; her face immovable as if sculpted from marble, and her mouth fixed in a single tense line. Layla felt a rush of dread. They must have found something bad, if this was how Charlie waited for her.

"Charlie?" she said, and her friend turned towards her, a mask of normalcy pulled down over the previous look of concern.

"Hey," she said, "I didn't want to wake you."

"You didn't. And even if you had, it's fine. I slept well thanks to Isabel's chamomile tea."

"I bring good news to start the day," Charlie said. "Especially good since Finn and I stayed up all bloody night to find it. But yeah, we found the problem."

"That's great."

"And the best thing is, it's an easy fix."

"So what happened? What was different?

"They moved one entrance from the hospitality area a little further down this time. Funnelled people in too close to the lighting tower on the left. And so it compressed things in that area more than the last festival. And of course it was worse when it was one of the big acts and the area was pretty much at capacity. It was freaky when I played it sped up. You can see exactly how it happened—streams of people moving, flowing into the main crowd, and one small backwater suddenly overwhelmed. Finn's had them move the gate back already. Just a bloody shame it took you getting caught up in it for us to find that out."

"I'm so relieved, for both of you. When I saw your face so serious, I thought there was something really wrong. You would tell me if there was, wouldn't you?"

The question ripped off Charlie's mask once more. And anxiety about what lay behind it unsettled her. Layla had known this woman more than half her life, but she'd never observed the expression that swept over her face at that moment. Charlie was bold, brash, confident, and unwavering. She didn't always think her words through; sometimes she was downright tactless, and certainly never too paralysed to offer them. So it was unnerving to see her frozen like a deer in the headlights, as if fearful to provide the answer to Layla's simple question.

"There is something," she said. "But I can't tell you. I need to show you."

Entering the downstairs room, Layla's eyes immediately focused on Finn, slumped forward, elbows on his knees, his head cupped in his hands. He sat in a winged chair beside the vast oak desk that dominated what Charlie called her mission control. Housed in the old Earl's study, the bank of video monitors and computers did resemble

NASA headquarters. The modern technology looked out of place against the backdrop of wood panelling and towering bookcases of leather-bound volumes. His mother sat alongside him, a wistful look on her face, as if she'd known something they didn't all along.

At the sound of their footsteps, Finn sat up, and she saw Charlie's exhaustion mirrored in his eyes. Lack of sleep, scrutinising screens for hours, and a cloud of worry hanging over him had taken their toll on Finn. He summoned a small, tired smile and reached out one hand to pull her onto his lap.

She was still unused to these gestures, torn between enjoyment of the little ways he let her know that when the time was right, he wanted to be more than friends, and the guilt that by accepting them she might in some small way already be edging towards a life after Will. And now, the new knowledge of her pregnancy dictated she push that away. But she mustn't think of that.

"So, what's up?" she asked him. "It has to be something out of the ordinary to have Charlie so rattled."

"Yeah," he said, with a resigned sigh, "it's something—something quite extraordinary. Let her talk you through it."

Charlie settled at a keyboard and immediately a monitor lit up.

""OK," she said, "so what you're about to see is from 2019. It's the final night, and, the same as this time, The Destitute are book-ending the festival. I chose this because I knew the crowd size would be fairly similar." Layla could see the towering stage, the metal barriers, the crowd huddled in close. "So this clip is near the end of Phoenix Alferez's set. The Destitute played next."

"Yeah, I remember," Layla said. "Will and I were standing next to you. It would be over there, just out of frame." She pointed to where the media area had been off the top left of the screen, and Charlie nodded.

"So Will was there too?" Finn asked, brows raised in surprise.

"Oh yeah," Charlie said. "Layla wasn't expecting him to arrive in the UK for a week or so. He and I organised a little surprise for her on the first night, so he was there pretty much the whole time."

"That's even more freaky," Finn said. "So all of us are there on that night, at least in the version we remember."

"And I'm absolutely sure we were there because I wasn't going to risk missing The Destitute a second time," she told him. "The first night, just before they came on, there was a call for a doctor backstage. In the end, it wasn't that serious—one of the security team had an asthma attack. Looks pretty scary if you've never seen it before. But she had her puffer, and we got it under control fairly quickly. Not quickly enough for me to avoid missing half of The Destitute's first set."

"So, knowing all of that, now I'm going to let it roll and I'll zoom in on the centre." Charlie paused, hand poised above the key. "That's where you need to look."

As the first frames came to life, Charlie zeroed in on a small section of the crowd, perhaps three deep in from the front. Behind her, she heard a sharp intake of breath and felt Finn's body tense beneath her. He already knew what was on that film, and whatever it was, it was something so shocking that it still had this effect on him.

The image that now filled the screen was of a man and a woman; the man tallish and dark, the woman perched on his shoulders, tiny and blonde. His arms looped over her thighs, steadying her above him. She raised her hands high, clapping to the music, stretching skyward and swaying to the rhythm. As the powerful stage lights splayed backwards and forwards, bathing her in their glow, they picked out a trail of tattoos on her arms. A unique and recognisable pattern of flowers and ribbons flowed from her wrists to where the thin straps of a white singlet crossed her shoulders.

As the music ended to a clash of guitar and drums, and Phoenix Alferez belted out her final powerful note, the man spun around and despite the slight pixilation, there was no doubt that she stared into her own pleasure-glazed eyes with Finn's exultant gaze turned upwards towards her.

A rolling wave of nausea hit her, and the world spun. Only Finn's arm tucked around her waist prevented her from spilling onto the floor at his feet, her body unable to hold its own weight. Charlie sprang to her feet and leaned in to offer support. Layla grasped at the air, but her lungs lacked the power to take it in.

"Layla, Layla, you gotta breathe, honey," Charlie urged. Layla clutched at her throat, constricted so tight she struggled with the simple rhythm of inhaling and exhaling.

"Let's get her on the couch." She felt Finn's arms underneath her as he swept her into the air. He took the weight of her limp body as if it was nothing.

"Damn." Through the fog, she heard Charlie spit out the words. "I can't believe we were so bloody stupid. She's already been through enough, and then we drop this on her."

"Calm down Charlie. That's not helping." Finn's voice was steady, and she clung to it. "None of us are thinking straight at the moment. She had to find out sometime."

For the third time that day, she opened her eyes to the dark wood ceiling above, the comfortable hug of the mattress below, and the shadow of a sentinel at her side. This one held her hand in his, rubbing her fingers absentmindedly. It felt good, safe, soothing, and she squeezed in gentle acknowledgment of his comfort.

"Hey there," he said, offering a reassuring smile.

"Hey," she said, finding her voice returned and an unexpected sense of calm. It might have been easier if the last twenty-four hours had simply been a strange dream. But her rational mind told her it wasn't. Now she wanted to place this day in a neat box where she might consider it from a safer viewpoint, objectively, without the earlier crippling emotions. And objectively but not singly, because this man—who'd become her friend and who had tactfully let her know that if the time was right, she need only say the word, and he would be her lover—was enmeshed in this too.

"How you doing? You've got a bit of colour there now." He traced her jaw with one finger, his eyes assessing her for himself. His touch sent a little shiver through her, half bliss at the intimacy, half fear, as she remembered the things she needed to tell him. She ripped her mind back to focus on his question.

"You know, I think I'm doing OK." She made her own tentative assessment of her body, reaching out to limbs, and fingers and toes, before a quick check that the churning nausea in her centre was gone, finding nothing but a gnawing hunger.

"Well, you can't imagine how relieved I am to hear it. Charlie was right—we should have better prepared you for that revelation."

"And how could you have done that? I don't think there's any easy way to lead into something like that. I doubt I'd have believed you without seeing it for myself."

"Yeah, well, to be honest, I'm not sure what to believe anymore. That two versions of us might have been in the same place at the same time, it defies any explanation I know. I'm starting to think I should have paid more attention in my physics classes and I might have a better idea of where to at least begin to understand it."

"Maybe we're not meant to understand it."

He gave a brittle laugh. "That's exactly what mum said. Of course, she totally believes in the possibility of some parallel universe, one she thinks has given us a gift. We shouldn't ask why or how, just accept it, make use of it."

"In what way? How?"

He sat in silence, swallowed hard, and dragged his eyes away. Standing awkwardly, he moved to the window, where he stood silhouetted against a surprising Scottish noonday sun that beat down on the festival outside. Strands of music drifted from the main stage, a cheerful, upbeat pop melody. He kept his back to her, as if meeting her gaze in this moment was too difficult.

"She thinks that this is a sign. I told her about the incredible pull I felt towards you—it was there even from the moment Charlie sent through your photograph so I'd know who to look out for at the airport—and she says this is the reason for it. She says it's telling us this attraction is not only reasonable, but inevitable because in some other life we were together. However, I'm struggling with that."

"Well, that makes two of us. When you put it into words, it sounds like fantasy. But when you see that video..." It was strange seeing the two of them captured like that, and that last look exchanged between them—even the memory of it triggered goosebumps.

"Exactly." He sighed. "Until a few hours ago, I believed that on that night in 2019, at that moment, I was backstage arguing with Mick Harrison about whether the supply of cocaine was an unwritten but implied condition of his contract."

"For real?" She'd thought meeting these modern-day gods might be fun, but obviously not.

"Oh yeah, Mick is the real deal rock star, drug habit and all. So it was a memorable conversation, to say the least. And I bet if I called Eric Walters up, he'd remember it too. Even though he's more used to rock stars behaving like divas than I am, I'm sure anything to do with a big personality like Mick is more unforgettable than most."

"So, you're sure, and you have a witness. Just like I'm sure of where I was that night, and Charlie is, too."

The freakish but unassailable truth was there in the video: that somewhere, on the other side of time, there was a Finn, and a Layla, living a life that was frightening in both its similarity and difference to this one.

And where was Will in all of this? She couldn't believe that any other version of herself would be so different as to cheat on a man she loved. Among her many faults, disloyalty was not one of them. So if in this other time and other life she was with Finn, then she wasn't with Will. She wasn't sure she wanted anything of a life where

Will hadn't been part of it. Would to never have loved him be worse than having loved him and lost him?

"So we're not losing our minds," he said. "We can accept what we saw. It happened."

"But Finn, it happened there. Not here. So, does it really change anything?"

"Maybe." He hesitated before turning back to her. "Layla, you know how I feel about you. But it's never sat comfortably. The timing was all wrong. It seemed way out of line for me to even admit that I felt something for you when you've got so much going on. You didn't need me to complicate things. So maybe, this video, if it shows some connection between us, well I suppose it's a 'get out of jail card', a reason, an excuse. It allows me to feel like less of an arsehole for hitting on you."

"I never saw it that way, Finn. I mean, yes, of course I've noticed—that you're attracted to me—but I've always felt you acted so carefully around me. You've always been respectful of my... situation."

She'd watched him fight his feelings as he tiptoed around her fragile state. And sometimes she'd wished he hadn't. Layla realised that had things been different, she wouldn't have hesitated to encourage this man. Kind, funny, talented, unselfish, loyal, all the qualities that made him a wonderful friend. And she knew firsthand how a strong friendship could pave a path to passion and love. Maybe the universe would deliver her another opportunity for that, maybe even with Finn. But not right now.

"I've tried, believe me," he said, "but there's been times I overstepped the mark."

"Perhaps a little," she said, a smile tugging at her mouth when she thought of the night in his studio, "but I've never felt pressured into doing something I didn't want to do. I always knew if I'd asked you *not* to do something, you would have. So it's OK. You don't need to worry."

"Thank you," he said. "So, Layla, I might have got this all wrong, but—" He hesitated, as if weighing his words, and then pressed on. "I felt that the attraction wasn't just in one direction. That maybe you felt something too. Looking at that film, it wouldn't be totally unexpected."

It would have been easier to lie to him. Say she felt nothing beyond the friendship they'd forged. But he'd been straight up with her. She needed to return it.

"You're not wrong Finn. I do feel something for you. Same as you. From the moment I saw your picture, there it was. I didn't want to face it, but I guess now I have to."

She saw the flicker of hope at her admission and hated herself for what she was about to do. She slid from the bed and cupped his hands in her own, already glazed with a sheen of sweat. Dread sat heavy upon her shoulders, a dull weight bearing down on her. She let her head fall forward, her hair a tangle shielding her face. The deep breaths gave her power but caused her pain. The coward inside of her slyly suggested avoidance. It wasn't too late to shy away from her decision. But her heart, bruised as it was in accepting what must be done, still whispered encouragement. If she cared for him at all, she owed him honesty. She met his gaze, hoping he might read in her eyes how desperately she didn't want to hurt him.

"Finn, what you said—about the timing being wrong—it's even more so than you think." His mouth collapsed in a thin line, his jaw tensed, and she could see him swallow, preparing himself as a dawning understanding of what was to come edged forward. "I'm pregnant. And that makes things extremely complicated. Just when I'm starting to relearn who I am, as an individual, not one of a couple, now I have to learn to be a mother, to a child without a father. All alongside keeping the promise I made to the people of this village to care for them."

He swayed in front of her, as if he was a slender tree slammed by an unexpected blast of wind. But surely he knew this might come? After all, she'd only reiterated what he'd admitted minutes ago, that this was not the time. And now damn it, she could see him regather himself, stand tall again, the careful processing of his thoughts flowing across his face. He was about to try to talk her around. And part of her weakened at the tantalising thought of not having to do this alone, but with someone like him by her side. She leaned into it, willing him to convince her she was wrong.

"Layla, that's even more reason for us to be together. You need someone to be there for you. You don't have to do this on your own. Move in here. Let us look after you. Let me look after you. I swear, I'll never ask more of you than you're prepared to give. All on your terms. Always. I promise."

All she had to do was say yes. The word sat there, teetering on her lips. She stood at a fork in the path, hesitant about which way to go. One direction offered companionship along the way. The thought of not having this baby on her own was so tempting. But that path was also crisscrossed with complicated emotions that she wasn't yet ready to grapple with. The other path was a lonely one, but time spent alone on the route would buy her space to consider her future. She knew which she had to choose.

"Finn, I'm not saying never. But I am saying no. I have to put myself first and doing that means having time by myself. To sort things out."

A brief flash of pain flickered across his face, as if she'd slapped him. But it was gone in an instant.

"You're right," he said with a regretful smile, freeing his hands and taking a small step back. "You absolutely need to prioritise yourself and the baby. When you're given a precious opportunity like this, no one in their right mind would expect otherwise, certainly not me. I know what this must mean to you, and there's no way I'd make it more difficult in order to satisfy my own selfishness. But know that anything you need, you only have to ask. For you—I'll do whatever you need with no hesitation—and no expectation."

He slipped out of the room and she traced the sound of his going, the steady beat of footsteps along the hallway, more muted on the carpeted stairs, before fading into nothing behind the dull thud of the steel door as he headed for his studio. She had done the right thing, but that knowledge didn't ease the aching gap inside her when she thought of the days to come.

35

Big Sisters

Dallblane Castle, Scotland - September 2022

FINN SAT AT HIS desk, furiously typing a reply to the fuckwit at a Glasgow hire company who failed to realise that in order to be paid for a service, that service must be delivered—the reason Finn was disputing his invoice. Fortunately, six weeks out from when the last helicopter had lifted off with the members of The Destitute safely on board, and the rows of dusty and hungover festival goers had trailed out the gates vowing to return next year, he'd dealt with most of the small residue of minor annoyances. Now he spent his days immersed with Eric, working on the exhilarating task of signing acts for Rock The Castle 2023.

As he hit 'Send' with an emphatic click of his mouse, he noticed the top corner of his screen: 5:50 pm. It was as if his internal clock registered the time, and every evening still triggered a silent alarm to remind him it was time to head to the clinic to meet Layla. And every evening, a small hopeful part of him watched for a text to come, summoning him to join her and resume their old routine. It didn't, but he was confident that one day it would. Give her time. First time round it was the wrong time. One day it would be the right time. He wasn't a patient person—except when it concerned Layla. In those three short months of seeing her daily, he'd learned there were a lot of things he could do if the stakes were high enough.

Walking away from Layla was the hardest thing Finn had ever done, but it was also his proudest moment, and the one that gave him the most hope. By doing so, he'd proved to himself beyond a doubt that this wasn't a simple infatuation; he loved this woman. For the first time in his life, he'd put another person's happiness so firmly ahead of his own. And it was incredibly freeing. He believed this time he'd really escaped the insidious tentacles of anxiety that had dogged him all his life. It had made him a selfish person, always on high alert for the next thing coming to attack him and send him into a frantic spin.

Being with Layla had taught him that by putting the emotional wellbeing of another first, it was possible to put aside the overwhelming emotions that had always swirled around him, propelling him in directions he didn't want to go. He'd let himself be swept along by them, like a leaf on the river, sometimes whipped along with the current, other times waylaid in dangerous eddies.

Losing Layla had forced him to grow up, and think about what he really wanted out of life, beyond simply stepping up to the unwanted responsibilities that had arrived on his doorstep. His father had produced the expected 'heir and a spare'. And as the 'spare', Finn had naively thought that the title and all that accompanied it would never come to rest on him. It had, but with the second festival making a tidy profit and cemented as a regular event on the summer music calendar, he'd met that challenge.

However, he now knew that the really important things in life had nothing to do with money, and bills and taxes. The real challenge lay ahead of him—to show Layla it was possible to find happiness more than once in your life, that you could have more than one true love. And she deserved that.

"Finn?" His mother's frowning face appeared in the doorway. "Shouldn't you be leaving soon?"

"Ahh, shit," he said, yanking open a drawer and rummaging for the keys to the BMW.

At seven pm, a small plane from Stornoway would land at Glasgow and he'd better be there to meet it. His brother-in-law, Gary, was an amiable giant, a bearded Viking lookalike with arms like hams grown huge from hauling on fishing nets in the waters of The Minch. Finn didn't like to think of what those large sausage-like fingers might do to his scrawny neck if he incurred Gary's wrath. And given how besotted Gary was with his sister, leaving her languishing at the airport, when eight months pregnant, might be the thing to ignite it.

As he sped towards Glasgow Airport, he thought about the last time he'd driven this road, belting along in the Daimler, hopelessly late and fearful that Layla, this woman who spoke to him even from her photograph, would meet him and, at best, think he was a dick. He didn't fear that anymore. She'd willingly spent too much time in his company for that.

He missed the intimacy of spending time alone with her. Their daily debrief had allowed them to offload the troubles of the day, followed by conversations that ranged from their favourite movies (his: the latest iteration of Dune; hers: Bohemian Rhapsody) to why New Zealand was simultaneously home to the worst ice cream flavour in the world (Goody Gumdrops, tasting of bubblegum with chewy wine gum lollies scattered throughout) and the best ever (the strangely named Hokey Pokey).

It was the closest he'd felt to another human being, the most he'd ever let down his guard with anyone. Having known that blissful freedom, each cell in his body now craved it with a deep, all-encompassing ache. But he was prepared to live with the withdrawal symptoms, steeling himself with the belief that in time the demands of his addiction would be satisfied and this time without her would one day be a brief moment buried in the past.

He still worried that without seeing her, except in polite exchanges when he'd encountered her in the village, without that nightly connection, she wouldn't understand the commitment he was prepared to make to her. He might lack Gary's physical prowess, but he was just as determined to fight for Layla's happiness in any way he could. Finn slammed those thoughts away, writing them off as a sly last-ditch attempt by his anxiety to invade his mind. He was done with that, determined it wouldn't allow him to second guess himself ever again.

When he saw Star appear through the doorway in arrivals, he was relieved he'd risked a speeding ticket to arrive in plenty of time. The most enormous baby bump embellished her tall slender frame, and the effort of carrying it was etched on her face. A slow waddle replaced Star's usual determined stride. He looked across to where a row of wheelchairs stood and wondered if he should offer one. Only the thought she might bash him over the head with the particularly enormous example of her ever present tote bags she wielded today caused him to swallow the suggestion.

Star didn't smile often, but when she did, it lit up her face like the sun. Despite her obvious tiredness, on catching sight of him she still summoned the energy to flash one his way, before picking up waddling speed to engulf him in as close as was possible to a hug with the beach ball shaped container that held his niece pressed between them.

She didn't object when he wrestled her gigantic suitcase off the carousel and hefted it into the back of the car. It was a sign of how much things had changed. His athletic and fiercely independent sister, currently held hostage by her body's tiny tenant, was happy to have him fetch and carry.

"So, tell me about this doctor," she said as they swung out of the airport onto the M8. Typical of Star, to not mess around with small talk.

"Layla?" he said, mustering a nonchalant tone. "Oh, she's a great doctor. Fully qualified in obstetrics. Delivering babies is a specialty. You and wee Freya will be in excellent hands there. And cool in a crisis. You heard about the night old Rabbie Williams rolled the digger..."

She cut him off, shooting him one of her sharp looks. "I don't need a list of her credentials or her heroics, Finn. I'm sure you checked her out properly before you let her loose on the village. After Dr Jean, nothing less would be acceptable. No, you know exactly what I mean. What's up between the two of you?"

Trapped in a car with your interrogator in the passenger's seat was the worst place to be. You couldn't exactly fling the door open and leap to safety, hitting the ground in a spectacular roll like an action hero. For a moment, he considered pretending he needed to stop for gas. Maybe he could go to the loo and leap out a window, leaving Star to drive herself. That's if she could even fit behind the wheel. But where was a bloody gas station when you needed one, anyway? He hadn't realised how sparse they were in this patch of motorway. And knowing Star, she'd already have thought of that, checked the gauge and would call him out on the lie.

"So, Mum's been talking," he said, buying himself time to gather his thoughts. He wondered how much his mother had said.

"Yes, well, she let a couple of things slip. But it's you who needs to do the talking." Her exasperated tone left him no option. He sighed, and wearily set to doing as he always did in the face of the immovable force that was his sister.

"Layla and I are just friends." He saw the line of her lips tighten. "OK, so in the first few months she was here, we became close friends. Too close really, considering she'd not long lost her husband. Anyway, then she discovered she was pregnant. No, it's *not mine*," he said, seeing her startle. "Do you really think that little of me?"

"No, of course not," she said, her grumpy tone suggesting that for an instant she may have jumped to that conclusion. "But it's a surprising extra complication."

"That's one way to describe it. Anyway, I'm giving her some space."

"You don't sound overly happy about that."

"Not really. But I don't have much choice in the matter. I'm playing the long game here, Star. And she's worth it. You'll see when you meet her."

"How long is this long game likely to take, do you think?"

"I don't bloody know. Jesus, Star, this is a woman who's lost the love of her life, who's grappling with pregnancy on her own. And who, to her surprise and mine, found we had a compelling mutual attraction. There's a bond between us we can't explain. It's complicated."

"Look, don't get all pissy with me. I'm worried about you, Finn. You forget, Mum and I were at the frontline when things collapsed with Niamh."

"And so you, if anyone, should be able to see how far I've come since then. And how different this situation with Layla is. Six weeks ago we agreed to back off, take some time, create some space. Six whole weeks and do you see me locking myself in the house, a non-functioning, non-communicative pathetic excuse for a human being?"

That stopped her onslaught. She stared out the window, watching the golden grain filled fields flit by, kissed by the summer sun that still lingered here in this part of the world. It was so different from her remote windswept home, where even the summers were cool and the winters long and harsh. But Star possessed a mental and physical toughness that made her well-suited for island life, and he knew that even now, if she could, she would be there.

No wonder she was extra feisty today. Coming here now, leaving Gary to join her closer to her due date, might be the sensible decision, but wasn't one she'd taken lightly. He felt a little bad sparring with her so fiercely when she was obviously struggling. But damned if she didn't bring that fighting spirit out in everyone. She turned to him, and he saw that she'd used the silence to form a different approach.

"Finn, honey, you're right, you're doing amazing. I *can* see that." The softening of her voice was more disconcerting than when she berated him. She reached across her hand, large for a woman, larger than his, and squeezed tight. "I just couldn't bear to see your big, beautiful heart get so badly broken again. And no matter how wonderful she is, there's this other guy lurking in the background, and he's always going to be there."

Her conciliatory tone worked its magic, and he responded in the same way. He didn't want to fight with his sister. The abrasive questioning was Star's love language and while it was difficult to be on the receiving end of it, it came from a place of genuine concern for him. And today with an ability to out the elephant in the room. William Leroux.

"You're right, he is always going to be there. I get that. And not only in the background, but every day through his child, too. But, you know, I'm good with that. Remember Star, all my life I've been the guy that comes after. I've never been anyone's number one." He couldn't help the trace of bitterness that crept in and saw the immediate concern that flared in her eyes.

"Don't you think you should look for someone who will make you their number one, not just a replacement?"

"No one can ever replace her first husband. Not me, not anybody. But I do think she and I have a future together. I'm not setting out to compete with the guy or to replicate the life she had with him. That's a road to disaster. Layla and I need the chance to make our own new life. And I'm prepared to wait until she's ready to take that chance."

"Wow, you've really thought this through, haven't you?" He caught the touch of admiration in her voice. Star never gave her approval willingly, so that was a good sign he might win this one.

"I've had six weeks to think. Like I said, this is the long game. I'm holding onto the belief that if she can love like that once, she can love like that again. She can love *me* like that. It just needs time."

She gave his hand one last squeeze, then closed her eyes, tipped her head back, and hummed along to an annoying pop song on the radio. What Star didn't know, and he might never tell her, given her sceptical nature, was that he had a trump card up his sleeve. He and Layla had a bond that defied logic, defied time, defied the normal rules of love. And he was certain they were destined to be together in this life, as they were in that other life. All they needed was time.

Ten o'clock phone calls from Charlie weren't unusual. Her creative muse had no respect for polite business hours. She didn't hesitate to phone him any time of the day or night when she wanted to run an idea past him, or was overwhelmed by a burst of enthusiasm or hit with a flash of inspiration. While the advance for the documentary met her immediate financial needs, Charlie was too smart to pin everything on one project, so juggled it around a string of other jobs. He wondered if she slept some weeks, but it was if she had some little internal dynamo supplying limitless energy. She never sounded tired or weary of the life she'd made for herself.

But tonight, work wasn't on the agenda. It was as if she and Star had some freaky mind meld going on, with him and Layla as the focus. Charlie's interrogation was less brutal but equally effective as his sister's. God, befriending Charlie was like gaining a second big sister who took way too much interest in his life. Star's direct questioning had opened up the Layla situation and forced him to defend his actions. Now here was Charlie, a few hours later, compelling him to confront the wisdom of his approach.

"Have you seen her at all?" It sounded like an accusation. But one he probably deserved.

"Ah, Mum and I took over a couple of chairs for the sunroom last week," he said. "And I saw her a few days ago when she dropped in to collect one of the soy candles Isabel's been making. God, you'll notice when you next get up here—the entire house smells like..."

She cut him off swiftly and without mercy. "No bloody diversionary tactics, Finn. You won't shake me off with talk of candles. I've already heard enough to know why she sounds so damn sad."

"She seemed fine to me."

"Because you only talk to her with the buffer of someone else there. Of course she'll make sure it looks like she's doing fine when your mum or Isabel are around. But she's not. Far from it. If you'd found a few moments to talk to her one on one, you'd know that."

That was exactly what he'd been avoiding, always making sure she didn't have to face him on her own. Now Charlie insisted he'd got it wrong.

"Oh, God," he said, with a sharp exhale of breath. Her words had ripped away all the confidence he'd built, shattering his belief that his handling of the situation was as Layla wanted.

"Look," Charlie said, sensing his distress from afar. "It's pretty fucked up, but it's not all your fault. I know she thought it was for the best, so you've supported her in that. But it's not working, Finn. You both went cold turkey. One day you're in her life, the next you're out. You've left her all alone. She's been through that once this year, and she won't make it through a second time."

He hadn't thought of it like that, not daring to compare his absence from her life to the gaping hole of Will's death. It was nothing like that. Surely it wasn't at all the same.

"She seems OK whenever I've seen her. And no one else has mentioned it."

"She tries to put on a bright face. She's good at that. And people in the village are really kind to her. So, of course, they think she's doing fine when she's smiling at them, saying thanks for whatever damn thing they've brought for her this week."

Finn had seen the steady parade of women up the hill. He hoped Layla was already eating for two—she'd need to with the amount of food going into that house. And it was fortunate the baby would be born in winter. Given the flying fingers of Dallblane's knitters working overtime, this baby would have a wardrobe on a scale previously unseen. It was as if they'd taken that old saying 'It takes a village to raise a child' and put it into practice. There was no doubt Layla endeared herself to them all. But of course it was the care and concern of neighbours, and people who she mattered to as the village doctor. She deserved more than that.

"OK," he said, "so if she needs more of me in her life, what do I do?"

"I think you have to weave your way back into it. Quietly. Not go leaping in there," she warned. "But go gently."

He'd come a long way since meeting Layla. He could do gently now. He could do gently for her.

36

Small Miracles

Dallblane, Scotland - September 2022

LAYLA USHERED MOIRA DUNCAN back into the reception area with a satisfied smile. She and the elderly woman had initially crossed swords over Moira's struggle to balance her Type 2 diabetes against a love for sweet things. Although Dr Jean's notes revealed no such thing, Moira had insisted that the previous doctor had discussed her diet in great detail and was perfectly happy with her daily intake of a nice piece of Battenburg cake with her morning cup of Earl Grey at the village tea shop, a few of her favourite lemon curd shortbread with her afternoon cuppa, and after dinner, a generous serving of whichever pudding she'd created for her unmarried forty-year-old son, Terrence, who still lived at home. Layla had firmly argued otherwise. Today, on this third visit, she'd won the battle.

However, Layla was also forced to admit that this increased receptiveness to her advice by the older women of Dallblane may well be as much to do with Jocelyn Wallace's influence as her own capable manner. Since Rabbie's accident, Jocelyn's dramatic retelling of the incident, particularly Layla's role in it—"If it wasn't for Dr Leroux I'd be visiting him in the churchyard"—was not only a village gossip favourite, but had definitely upped her credentials amongst the group she'd found hardest to build a relationship with.

As she steered Moira to Raylene's desk, she glimpsed her last patient of the day. A tall blonde woman, maybe fortyish, sat with hands clasped over her protruding stomach, the pop of her navel pushing up against the fabric of a stretchy dress. She smiled at the woman's pose. It was an intuitive thing she'd found herself doing, even from that first moment of knowing she was pregnant, that need to protect the life growing inside you with an unconscious movement of your hands.

She slipped back into her examination room to take a quick scan of the woman's details. Mrs Cameron was visiting from Stornoway. Where was that? She was still hazy on Scottish geography. The appointment was for a pregnancy check-up. She had to be at least thirty-six weeks, possibly thirty-seven, judging by her size. The efficient Raylene had already attached notes from Mrs Cameron's own GP and Layla clicked on them to brief herself before calling the woman in.

The name leapt out at her from the screen. Mrs Star Cameron. It had to be. How many people named Star would show up in Dallblane? Seeing her full address confirmed it. Stornoway, Isle of Lewis. Finn had told her his sister lived on the Isle of Lewis and now she was sure his sister sat in her waiting room. She felt an unnatural twinge of nervousness, as if somehow treating this woman brought him once more back into her world, as if he were some satellite caught in his sister's gravitational pull, and now she was dragged into orbit with him.

Layla pushed thoughts of Finn away, put on her smiling doctor's face, stepped into the waiting area and extended a hand to Star, who used it not simply in greeting but as an aid to heaving herself from the chair. The examination proceeded smoothly, with both mother and baby appearing perfectly fine four weeks out from her due date, apart from the fact that the baby girl's size was at the upper end of normal. That explained Star's hugely distended stomach. But she was a tall woman, and she'd laughed it off, saying if Layla was to meet her husband she'd know why she was about to give birth to an Amazon.

"Anything else you need to share with me?" Layla asked. "Any unusual sensations?"

"Nothing unusual. Had a bout of Braxton Hicks this morning. My mother panicked, thinking it was all about to happen in her kitchen. But I've had them now and again right through, so I knew I just had to breathe it out. Probably brought on by the travel."

Layla frowned. "So you didn't notice any difference this morning from the previous times?"

"No," Star shook her head, patting the huge curve of her stomach. "Not particularly, except this little one's anxious grandmother hovering over me, worried that she's about to deliver her own grandchild."

"And you haven't had any more since this morning?"

"No, just a few well-placed kicks from Freya to let me know she's awake and ready."

"Well," Layla huffed in concentration, weighing all the information in her head. "If it was the early onset of labour, I'd have expected them to have re-occurred across the day at shorter intervals. And I should have seen some changes to the cervix. With neither of those things happening, it sounds like Freya might have to be patient and tough it out in there a little longer. So I think you can pop your clothes back on and we'll get you to make another appointment for a week from now on your way out."

"How about you?" Star asked from behind the curtain as she dressed.

"Me?"

"How long till your baby's due?" Star waded out of the cubicle with a smile, flopped into a chair and tried to slip on her shoes while struggling to see her feet. Layla stepped over to help her.

"I'm five and a half months. Sorry, I didn't think it was that noticeable yet." Her as yet tiny bump was easily concealed under the shift dresses of her comfortable work wardrobe.

"It's not," said Star. "My brother told me you were having a baby."

Layla froze at the words. One mention of him and her heart leapt into a wild beat, as if the echo of Finn's drums lay in wait in her head, springing forward at the slightest reminder. Bent over Star's feet, she kept her head down, fearing her disorientation might be obvious in her eyes.

"Oh, of course, you're Finn's sister." She tried to keep her voice neutral, but it wavered over his name. "He told me you'd be coming here to stay." She stood and headed for the refuge of her chair on unsteady legs.

"Look, Layla." Star met her gaze directly, pausing a couple of beats before pressing on. Her eyes lacked the warmth of Finn's, being a more determined shade of brown. "I know this might seem a little out of line, but as we sort of know each other, or at least know about each other, do you mind if I ask you a personal question?"

"Ahh, no," Layla said, wishing she could say otherwise, but feeling trapped and with her paralysed brain unable to retrieve one of her standard well-practised doctor's answers for tricky questions.

"It's not really any of my business, but I care about him an awful lot. So, do you see any future between the two of you? Maybe not now, but at some time?"

Layla closed her eyes, her breath coming in a shallow staccato. She took it in hand, forcing it into a slower beat. When she opened her eyes to face the moment, Star's expectant stare had softened. And as she spoke, it melted even further. It seemed Star appreciated her responding in the same direct manner.

"Star, your brother is one of the most beautiful human beings I've ever met. He took such good care of me from the moment I arrived. And not only did he look after me, and show me friendship, he taught me I could laugh again, gave me moments of happiness that made me forget this whole shitty year for just a little bit. I never expected that would happen so soon. In the early days after my husband died, I was convinced it would never happen again. Apart from the appalling timing, I don't regret anything about meeting your brother. He did so much for me."

"And he loved you," she said. "He *loves* you."

"And that," Layla said gently, "is why we need this space from each other. Star, it would be selfish of me not to give him that. I know he'd have taken me on without hesitation, with all my baggage, my screwed up emotions, my messy life. But now it's more than me he'd be taking on. There will be a child. Not his child. If he wants to be with me, he has to accept a lifetime not only with me, but with this child—that's not his." Her hand once again found its natural place, resting on her belly, seeking that first faint flutter of her baby's movement.

"That's true," she said. "Being a good father to someone else's child isn't something any man could do. But Finn knows what that looks like. He understands the commitment."

"I don't get it. How could he know?" Even from someone he was close to, it seemed a confusing assumption to make. But Layla was wrong.

"Our father, Peter, was not my biological father. He met and married my mother when I was five years old."

Layla had seen their family photos decorating a sideboard in the formal dining room: Euan and Finn, dark like their mother, and tall blonde Star, always towering over her brothers, facing the camera with a confident smile, in some pictures her father's hand resting on her shoulder. Here was the reason.

"But from that moment, I never doubted he loved me, and even when Euan and Finn came along, nothing changed. Do you know that if it had been legally possible, I would have been his heir? In Scotland, women can inherit a title. But not adopted children, male or female. I know that upset him. He was so desperate for us to be one family, always careful to treat us exactly the same. So although I couldn't inherit, he made provision for me. On my twenty-first birthday, he called me into his office to hear the family lawyer explain that he'd invested a sum of fifty thousand pounds in my name. My father might not have created me in the biological sense, but he created who I am, he and mum. Finn had an incredible man as his role model. If you let him, Layla, he would love you, and he would love your child."

Star stood and quietly gathered up the huge tote bag that lay in a puddle of soft leather beside her and slipped out the door.

Fifteen minutes passed, and Layla didn't move. Notifications popped up on her screen, but she ignored them. Nothing was more important than those four words. *If you let him.* It was as simple as that. And as difficult. If she let him.

Raylene's bright ponytail bobbed in the doorway. "I'm off now, unless..." Her freckled face creased in a frown. "Layla? Are you OK? Is there something else I can do for you?"

Layla blinked herself back into the moment. "No, all good Raylene. Thank you."

"Well, enjoy your evening." And she was gone, leaving Layla to contemplate another lonely night in the cottage, dinner for one and the mindless clatter of the television, while a few hundred yards away was a man who would love her. If only she'd let him.

A day later, once again, Layla sat in the dark, feet up on the coffee table, sprawled in front of the television. This was her regular week-night viewing, *The Chase*. Her favourite chaser, Jenny The Vixen, battled with an exceptionally dim group of competitors tonight, dispatching them with calm efficiency. Layla cringed as yet another of Bradley Walsh's team, Bernard from Taunton, left the stage, a trail of incorrect answers in his wake. Given she herself had answered all the questions correctly, she pondered on an alternative career as a professional quizzer, but rejected the idea immediately. She loved her job, loved this place and gave thanks every single day for Charlie, who had seen what she needed when she herself couldn't.

The knock on the door at this time of the evening caught her by surprise. Usually, the trail of well-wishers from the village popped by in the mornings. With the days drawing in a little now, the oldies avoided venturing out after dark.

When she opened the door to find Finn standing there for the second time in one day, although it was unexpected, it wasn't unwelcome. In fact, answering a knock on her cottage door this morning, to find him alone on her doorstep, had coloured the rest of the day in a warm glow. The slightly perturbing thoughts of him, planted by Star the previous afternoon and that had lingered into the night, had dissolved in the early morning sunshine. This morning she'd faced the reality of Finn with nothing but pleasure at the opportunity of an abbreviated form of their precious nightly debriefs.

Sent to deliver a few of the last of the season's tomatoes from Patti's greenhouse, she'd enjoyed the ease with which they'd slipped into their old conversation. He'd talked of Charlie and the whirlwind of activity surrounding their joint project. She'd shared a picture of Jimmy's new baby girl, pictured with the doting father, and they'd laughed at how her brother's extreme mullet had strangely come back into fashion. It was as if little had changed between them and she supposed that was a good thing. Maybe time was working its soothing magic over another trauma in her life.

Tonight though, Finn's face wore a worried frown, and she guessed straight away that it wasn't Layla, but Dr Leroux that he came for.

"It's Star," he said. "She says the baby's on its way and Mum and Isabel agree. Don't think there's time to even get her to Cluanie, let alone Glasgow."

"No. Trying to get to a hospital would be a bad idea," she said, already tying on her trainers. "I'm sure you'd prefer your niece born here than in a car on the side of the road."

He laughed at that. "I'm sure Star prefers it to be here too, but she's starting to panic."

"I only saw her yesterday," Layla said, shaking her head, puzzled that there had been no sign. She grabbed her bag, and they set off up the driveway. The castle loomed ahead of them, its normally bland face dotted with extra lights. That alone suggested something was up.

"This has come on quickly."

"Ah. No. It hasn't," he said as she struggled to match his long, anxious strides. "She's been having pains all day. But any time someone suggested this might be it, she shouted them down, saying it was just Brighton... Brixton..."

"Braxton Hicks."

"Yeah, that's the one."

"OK, well, she knows what that feels like. Poor thing, she's put up with that for months. I imagine if she says this pain tonight is different, then she's probably right. We are about to deliver a little girl into the world. How amazing is that?" She couldn't help grabbing his hand in excitement at the thought.

"We? I don't think I'll be of much bloody use."

"You're on moral support duties, you, and Patti and Isabel. That's likely to be as important as anything I do. No chance of her husband getting here?"

"No, he's out on a boat somewhere. Even if he was ashore, there aren't any more flights tonight. We've sent a message to him."

"It's sad he's going to miss the birth."

"Oh, I don't know about that," Finn said with a grin. "Knowing Star, it might be safer for Gary if he's not too close when things get rough. After all, he's jointly responsible for this."

"Bloody men," she said, giving him a playful punch on the arm, "leaving us women to do all the hard stuff."

As they raced through the front door, a wail from above suggested that things might already be getting rough. Upstairs, a distressed Star walked the length of one of the large bedrooms, supported by Patti and Isabel. Her blonde hair hung in lank tendrils around her face, sweat beaded across her forehead, and her mouth tensed in pain as another contraction rolled across her. She stood hunched as Patti ran a soothing hand across her daughter's back.

"I think I'll try Gary again," Finn said, heading for the door.

Layla didn't blame him for opting out. This was a confronting sight for anyone who'd not experienced it before, even though to her eye, things appeared to be proceeding normally, although rather rapidly.

Star summoned a grateful smile. "Please," she called after Finn, in between a gasp as she straightened a little. He hurried out the door, leaving Layla to assess the situation.

"How long between contractions?" Layla asked.

"About five minutes," Isabel replied.

Layla maintained her mask of calm as they steered Star to the bed. This baby was definitely in a hurry. She was relieved they'd made the call to stay here rather than attempt to drive to a hospital. She could handle this, despite slight niggles about this being a first pregnancy, so she had no history to draw on, and the size of this baby, so well-developed even not at full term. Star might not be in for an easy time, but it seemed likely that it would be over with quickly.

After a long hour of alternating between Star walking back and forth, her two steady supporters at her side, and perching her overflowing bloated form on the small loveseat while they took turns at massaging her back, Layla knew that the now ferocious contractions called for a different approach. Once again they settled Star on the bed, and a quick examination confirmed that everything was falling into place for Freya to make her entrance into the world.

The door flew open, and Finn rushed to his sister's side, perching on the bed with his phone in hand.

"It's Gary," he said, holding it up in front of Star's face. A large round face with a thick forest of beard filled the screen. Still on a fishing boat somewhere in the dark waters off the coast of Lewis, they'd come into range. Gary, making a last check of his phone before turning in for the night, had seen the flurry of messages.

"I'm here for you, love," he said.

There was a tremor in his voice, but all Star seemed to hear was the comfort of her husband's words. She fixed her gaze on him and he stayed with her right through until the moment the high-pitched squawk of a newborn bounced off the walls of the bedroom and beyond. Gary's smile was as wide as the sea, and mirrored on the faces of the family who welcomed its newest member, already surrounding Freya with love. It was beautiful to observe, but also provided a sad reminder that when her own baby came, there would be no father to hold it close, no family to embrace it, only her.

Layla sat in the comfortable hug of a large wingback chair. The twin forces who ruled this household, Patti and Isabel, had insisted she stay the night. She was in the same expansive room as they'd put her to bed on the last night of the festival. She couldn't prevent it transporting her back to the bizarre events of that twenty-four hours, and the twisting maze of emotions.

Although perhaps on some subconscious level she'd known she was pregnant, Patti's recognition had forced her to confront it. The initial shock and the pain of Will's absence from what should be a moment of shared joy had at the time caused her to think the universe was unkind to send this baby. But she had quickly accepted it as the greatest gift, a chance for their love to live on in the world.

And then on top of that, the revelation that life as she knew it was not in fact her only life was one thing too many to cope with. However, in the last few weeks, she'd had so much time on her own to think about that, too.

While the existence of that other life had raised so many unanswerable questions, it had also provided answers. She understood why she'd been drawn to this place when the old Layla might have baulked at Charlie's suggestion, choosing to stay with the known and familiar despite the pain that would bring. She knew why feelings of déjà vu had stalked her wherever she ventured in Dallblane: the pub, the village streets, the rambling shops, and, of course, here in the castle. And she had a reason for the magnitude of those feelings when she stepped inside it, amplified in the wood-panelled rooms, the wide staircase, the homely kitchen, and of course, in Finn's studio.

Finally, it allowed her to forgive herself for what had seemed an unnatural attraction to a man she thought she'd only met in a photograph, to give permission for her to explore those feelings. The way he'd now catapulted back into her life after six lonely weeks of separation seemed to suggest perhaps it was time for her to follow Star's words, and let him back in, maybe let him love her.

With a small tap, the door nudged open, accompanied by the subtle wafting aroma of chamomile. "Mum's orders," Finn said with a smile, setting one steaming mug on a side table before sitting on the bedside, sipping at his own. "Even I wasn't prepared to argue with the Dowager Countess tonight. For all her protests otherwise, I swear she slips on the title and all that goes with it when she decides it's time to order everyone around."

"She was great tonight. It might not have been a planned home birth, but it all went like clockwork thanks to you lot."

"No, thanks to you," he said. "I'm in awe of how you do this stuff. Just like the night with Rabbie. People relax knowing you've got everything in hand."

"Well, thank you. But don't underestimate what the rest of you did. Star really needed a team around her tonight to give her confidence. Having your baby at home when you're not expecting it could have been really frightening."

"I admit to finding it very bloody frightening. I swear I felt every contraction myself." He screwed up his face at the memory. "And my god, the noise of it, hearing her scream like that... shit it was so bloody awful. It's hard to believe every single one of us is here because someone endured that."

He shook his head in wonderment at what he'd observed in his front-row seat, sitting with his arms wrapped around his sister the whole time, the phone held in front of her while her husband shouted encouragement. Each time Layla had glimpsed Finn's tense white face, she knew he'd have preferred not to have been there. But he'd done it for Star, and for Gary.

"Making it possible for them to share the experience was a wonderful gift, Finn. Without you, they'd not have had that moment together. Though you still look a little traumatised by the experience."

"Even watching it from that distance, I think it scared the shit out of Gary, too. Even so, he wouldn't have missed it. And he'll be here by lunchtime tomorrow. Little Freya gets to meet her daddy properly." He leaned back in the chair, eyes closed, his dark hair a tangle and weariness laying heavily on his face. "God, I'm tired," he murmured, "and all I did was hold a bloody phone."

It was after midnight and they were all exhausted. Patti and Isabel had ordered Finn and Layla to bed, insisting they would maintain a shared vigil, each in turn sitting in the room where Star and her baby slept peacefully.

Again she thought about that baby coming into the world surrounded by family. How amazing that so soon after her birth, the first hands to stroke her tiny head and marvel at her delicate fingers and toes were those of people who would treasure her. Remembering the gentleness with which Finn cradled the small bundle in his arms, already enchanted by his niece, tugged at something deep inside. She closed her eyes too, turning the sensation over, trying to put a name to the emotion but thwarted by her tired brain.

She heard Finn slurp the last of his tea, and rise from the bed. She opened her eyes to see him standing over her. He cupped one hand softly under her jaw and placed a tender kiss on her forehead, his lips lingering there for a moment. With her head buried against that warm stomach, his smell was intoxicating. Even the nearness of him triggered a pulse of something—want, or need? She drank in the feeling of pleasure at his touch, the gentle hiss of his breath against her hair as he spoke, igniting that tiny spark of potential that had lain dormant these past weeks.

"I'm so glad you're here, Layla. It's been too long."

Underneath all the bustle of the household tonight, something had quietly shifted between them. No longer did she feel like she broke some rule by letting him into her space. Maybe this was the first step to letting him love her.

Even tucked in under crisp sheets and the comfortable weight of covers, sleep danced around the periphery, pirouetting away on elusive feet each time she thought it in her grasp. The adrenaline rush of earlier events hadn't yet fully subsided, and it fought back against the soothing properties of the chamomile.

Frustrated, Layla decided to attempt some of the relaxation techniques she'd taught to patients. Maybe they would deliver the rest her body craved. She began with some deep breaths, occupying her churning mind by counting the rhythm, pushing other thoughts away with the steady beat. Next she quietly reached out to her exhausted body, sending slow tentacles of thought towards each of her weary limbs in turn and then down through her torso, shoulders, neck, chest, abdomen... and it was there that her silent query received an unexpected reply. It wasn't her imagination. A second small flutter, like the beat of butterfly wings, confirmed it.

Well, hello there, little one. She sent the words out with a loving caress of her stomach. Until now, its gentle curve was the only evidence of her baby's growing presence. *Mummy can't wait to meet you. But we must be patient, my sweet. Only halfway there.* Another subtle pulse flickered as if her body's tiny inhabitant tapped out its own coded message in reply.

Although months away, thoughts of the birth triggered other troubling thoughts to take hold. How different her own little one's welcome to the world would be to that of baby Freya. How different her own experience of birth would be compared to Star's. Her mind scrolled through the images—Patti and Isabel pacing the room, offering reassuring words as the pain became more frequent; Finn an arm wrapped across Star's shoulders, pushing back his fear so she might be less fearful; Gary's deep voice across the phone line sending loving encouragement; a dreaming newborn, eyes squinted shut against the world, clasped to Finn's chest as he looked down at her in wonder.

The reality of her situation struck with brutal force. Without the luxury of a support network, the home birth she'd always hoped for was impossible. Instead, she would be in some stark Glasgow hospital room surrounded with kind and well-meaning people who would ensure the physical safety of her and her child, but not that of her heart. If things went to plan, at least she'd have Charlie. Despite Charlie's claim that she could well prove totally useless, she was so grateful that her friend had blocked out two weeks either side of her due date.

But what if the baby came early or late? She'd have no one. And the most cruel thought of all forced its way forward, bringing hot tears and wracking sobs: for her child there would be no father to hold it and quietly marvel at the miracle of its existence.

37

Coexistence

Dallblane Castle, Scotland - September 2022

FINN FLOPPED ONTO THE bed and stripped off his t-shirt, tossing it on the floor while debating whether it was worth even trying to sleep. He rested his head in one hand, briefly massaging the dull ache in his temples until the worse ache in his arm made him think better of it. Fuck, it hurt.

The torture of holding his phone at arm's length, with Star leaning against his chest while she veered between determined panting and feral screams, had left him with a searing pain from wrist to shoulder. Not to mention his legs that even now harboured an uncomfortable residual tension. Crammed in against the headboard behind her, his legs folded beneath him, fierce cramps had forced him to grit his teeth and remind himself the pain was nothing compared to what his sister was going through.

He considered venturing down to the studio where, on sleepless nights, picking up an acoustic guitar and losing himself in a lazy strum usually did the trick. However, it seemed unlikely his stricken left hand would cooperate enough to press string against fret. Anyway, he'd realised the other day how rarely he hid down there to escape life these days. Instead, lately it was a productive diversion from the craziness of work.

This new habit of taking a break mid-afternoon to mess around with a few songs had begun to deliver results. He'd decided this week they were shaping up well, almost to the point he might take a punt and send them to Dervla McBride. It was her voice he imagined as he wrote. And it was her of all the musicians he'd connected with this past couple of years that he trusted to hold his hand when he took that leap and opened up his intimate world to the scrutiny of others.

Since he'd started writing, he'd discovered there was a weird ever-present tension in the creative process. He and Charlie had talked about it one day, how even she, so outwardly confident and desperate to share her creations with the world, also feared what the world might have to say about it. And so it was a given that he, the stereotypical introverted artist, felt both that same driving need to take his intensely private music and his words and release them to the world while pushing down the anxiety of how that world might receive them.

Still, it was the only real source of anxiety for him these days. Even Star, for all her initial misgivings about how he had handled the Layla situation, admitted she could see he'd finally learned how to manage those wild emotions that had leapt out of nowhere and dragged him down since he was a kid. So now when he settled himself behind his drums and dove into the music, it was for the pure enjoyment of layering rhythm over rhythm, his mind, his body and the beat of his heart all consumed in the momentum. No, he wouldn't go downstairs tonight.

Sleep should have come easily in a silent house. In the west wing, he'd left his mother sitting in quiet vigil, forsaking her own bed next door to watch over her daughter and her grandchild. She'd insisted on taking the first stint, positioning herself in a comfortable chair with knitting in hand. The familiar gentle click of her needles was the soothing backdrop for the exhausted mother and her baby. Next door to them, Isabel grabbed a few hours of sleep before taking her turn.

But here in the east wing bedrooms, neither of the two occupants slept. Although the sturdy stone outer walls of the castle buffered the noise of the outdoors, these wood-panelled interiors did little to stop sounds from within. Even the small sound of a woman crying.

His first cowardly thought was to head downstairs to the studio, the one place he could be sure not to hear it, because to hear it meant he needed to do something about it. *Don't you fucking dare.* His mind was quick to stomp on that bullshit notion. Without any further hesitation, not even stopping to grab a shirt, he went to her.

Although he opened the door with care and brushed it closed behind him with barely a whisper, she stilled as he approached. Curled into a tight foetal position, she looked so tiny, so vulnerable lying there in the vast bed. He was unsure of what to do, what to say, only knowing that he needed to offer some comfort. God, he loved her, and it gutted him to hear her in pain like that. So, although still wary, he gave way to the surge of protectiveness, moving to lie beside her, his body bracketing hers.

She smelled so fresh, her newly-washed hair still damp from rinsing off the heat and blood of the evening's work. He inhaled it with the lightest of breaths, so as not to spook her. As he looped one arm across her waist, her own came up to meet it, trapping it there close to her. He could feel the slight swell below his hand, not visible under the loose shirts she'd taken to wearing, but so very present, pressing against the stretchy t-shirt fabric of her top. Such a neat, dainty curve, in stark contrast to the confronting expanse of Star's bare ballooning belly when he'd come into that bedroom tonight.

As if sensing his awareness, Layla drew his hand down lower, and he splayed his fingers over her stomach, thinking in awe of the beating heart, the growing life inside of her. *So fucking amazing.* It wasn't something he'd thought about much before tonight—how absolutely incredible it was.

But as he lay there, her baby resting beneath his hand, the heightened knowledge that in a few short months, she too would face the same ordeal as Star, brought a twinge of fear. She was a tough little thing, and he knew she'd face it with the same staunch attitude that had already got her through so much. Even so, things could go wrong and the thought of losing her was unbearable.

"I felt it move tonight." There was a faint glimmer of a smile in her words.

"Wow. What was it like?" He couldn't begin to imagine what she was experiencing.

"You know, when someone lays a light kiss on your neck? That's what it's like. Just a brush of sensation, so gentle, but also so powerful. Except it's coming from inside you."

"That's amazing."

"Yeah, guess I won't be feeling so kindly towards it when it decides kicking me is more fun."

"Oh, I bet you will."

"Yeah," she sighed. "I will."

"So what's it telling you? Is it a girl or a boy?"

"You know, for a little while there, I felt it was a girl. But something happened tonight when I felt it move…" Her voice wavered. "I dunno. It just made me think it's a boy. Will didn't say as much, but I know he wanted a boy." At that, she fell quiet, the slight tremble beneath his hands signalling the return of her tears.

"Layla," he breathed, after a few minutes, each controlled sob shuddering through her, tiny sad waves lapping against him. She didn't answer, but gripped his arm even more tightly around her. "You know, you can talk to me about him, if you want. If that helps."

If he was ever to have a future with her, he must do this. He must make her realise he'd never expect to claim that part of her she'd given to William Leroux. He'd never expect her to surrender her memories, or her love for this man. It was possible for him and William to coexist, if not companionably, at least tolerably, for her sake. She sat up slowly and in the faint light, he could see the sheen of tears still fresh on her face as she gazed down at him, her eyes still uncertain.

"I mean it," he said. It might not be easy to do this, but it was necessary. And it would get easier with time. He swallowed hard. "Layla, anything you want to talk about, you can talk to me. Anything. Anytime."

She reached across him. "Thank you," she said, brushing the lightest of kisses on his forehead before picking up her phone from the bedside table.

"Let me show you," she said, beginning to scroll through photographs. "This was William."

38

Home

Dallblane Castle, Scotland - September 2022

LAYLA STIRRED A LITTLE, and then sank back into a grateful doze, appreciating the warm, comfortable body curled around hers, and the strong, reassuring arm draped across her. She relaxed to the regular rhythm of his breathing and let its steady beat lure her into sleep once more.

When she woke properly, as a slash of sun angled the light of a new day across her face, she saw he was gone. For a moment she questioned her memory, but she traced the rumpled sheets beside her, hinting at the shape of him. And on the dented pillow next to hers, the lingering woody smell she recognised as his aftershave confirmed it: Finn had stayed with her through the night. Not only stayed with her—he'd allowed her to talk, to laugh, to cry, and as they'd edged back into sleep, she knew he'd also allowed her to let go of Will just a little, and maybe enough to face this next part of her journey without him.

She swung her feet over the bed, scanning for her jeans and the shirt Patti had loaned her last night. She needed to put her own needs aside for now and go check on her patient.

Over in her west wing bedroom, Star sat propped up on a mountain of pillows in the enormous bed that seemed to be a feature of every bedroom in the castle. Her mother sat beside her watching the newborn feed.

"Oh great. She's still feeding well then?" Layla asked. The hungry little one sucked with determination, while Star looked down in blissful approval.

"Yeah, looks like she's got her father's appetite," Star said with a grin.

"Well, that's one less worry. It can be frustrating to get them feeding sometimes, but looks like you two have got it sorted. No discomfort?"

"No, all good, for now. Not sure I'll feel the same way when she gets teeth."

Patti laughed. "I remember thinking bottle feeding might be a good alternative at that point. You were brutal, my darling," she said, stroking her daughter's hair affectionately.

"You haven't been here all night?" Layla asked her.

"No, no," she reassured. "Isabel took over about five, but I couldn't manage more than a couple of hours sleep. Too excited. So I'm here and she's downstairs making us all breakfast. We dispatched Finn to help, although it wasn't easy to convince him to leave this wee darling. I think she's got a doting uncle wrapped around her little finger from day one."

"And that's how we do it, my sweet," Star said proudly, her hand gliding over Freya's downy head. "Wait till Daddy gets here and you can charm him, too."

"Perhaps, since it looks like she's finished," Layla said, noting Freya slackening her grip on the nipple with a small satisfied hiccup, "I should give you both a quick check over?"

"That's a great idea. I'll go and lend a hand in the kitchen and bring up some breakfast soon," Patti offered.

Star pulled her mother towards her with a grateful hug. "Thanks Mum. That would be great. I'm bloody starving."

Once her work was done, and satisfied that mother and baby were doing well, Layla made her way to the kitchen, her own stomach gnawing with a vicious hunger that was exacerbated by the smells drifting across the hallway. Baby weight aside, she was sure she'd gained extra kilos through the regular deliveries from this kitchen. Isabel and Patti seemed to be simultaneously running their own versions of *Master Chef* and *The Great British Bake-off* from within the castle.

Apart from the food, sitting to eat breakfast with other people was a treat. It was amazing how much she'd missed such small ordinary activities as sharing a meal. There was a blissful sense of normality, to sit with Finn and Isabel around the huge country style oak table, eating homemade crumpets dripping with bright yellow butter and golden syrup, washed down with a generous hit of caffeine.

"I guess you have to thank Freya for deciding to arrive on a Friday night," Isabel said. "No clinic patients waiting for you this morning."

"Yeah, that's a relief," she replied. "Although this is nothing compared to when I worked in the ED. You got so used to running on no sleep that having a full eight hours before starting a shift felt strange. Sleep deprived is your normal state."

A tiny voice in her head repeated it. Normal. That word again. Normal. It was what she craved, a life that wasn't turned upside down, a life where you could take pleasure in the everyday things. *This* could be her normal. Waking up to Finn. Sitting around the breakfast table together. Being part of this family.

How odd that she should feel more at home here on the other side of the world in the house of an Earl and a Countess than in her own family. They loved her in their own rough way, but they'd never understood her. That drive for learning and a career had marked her as a cuckoo in the nest. And the family she'd married into had always considered her an aberration, one that, given time, their son might tire of. She was sure that for them, the only good thing to come out of Will's death was never having to see her again. The feeling was mutual.

But this family had scooped her up like one of their own and made her feel like she had a part to play in it. She was sure this wasn't merely an idea conjured by the lack of sleep. Yesterday, once more, the world had shifted ever so slightly and the life she lived irrevocably altered. Today she lived another life, and with the way he looked at her, and his subtle but relentless attentiveness to her, Finn had made it very clear: this could be her life, if she was willing to choose it.

"Thank God for coffee," he said, pouring a second cup and emptying the plunger. Isabel, reading that as a sign more caffeine was required, automatically whisked it away and headed for the scullery. Finn heaped sugar into the cup and took another gulp. "Gary's flight gets in around noon, so I need to head down to Glasgow to pick him up. Fancy coming along for the ride? Play loud music and talk nonstop to keep me awake?"

"I thought you'd want to take the Daimler? A bit of fresh air to blow out the cobwebs."

"That's right, I forgot you've only seen Gary's great big hairy face. There's no way his even bigger hairy body would fit in the Daimler." It seemed none of them had been exaggerating about Gary's legendary size.

While her sleep-fogged brain might have welcomed the opportunity to go back to her own bed, the thought of doing another so completely ordinary thing with Finn won out. Maybe this was how you created that new life, taking one small step after another, each little action building on the last. And while none of them might be hugely significant on its own, you would one day look at them woven together and celebrate what you'd made.

"OK," she said. "I will, if only to keep you from falling asleep. Can't have you running off the road. Star wouldn't forgive any more delay in getting this family of hers together. But I'll need to go home first. I think another shower and some of my own clothes."

"Before you do, there's something I need you to see."

He sculled the coffee and rose, stretching down a hand to her. He led her across the broad hallway and into the vast room that was Charlie's workspace whenever she came up to Dallblane. It largely sat empty while she was in London. Finn preferred his own smaller sunny space on the opposite side. Today, the dark room exuded a steady calm far different from the wild energy that filled its walls when Charlie was in residence. At those times, the frenetic pace of her work seemed to sweep through the entire castle, pulling everyone else along with her. The faint smell of one of her favourite Jo Malone orange blossom diffusers still marked this as Charlie's space.

From a desk came the low hum of a computer. In the centre of the room crouched an oversized leather couch as big as a bed, used by Charlie to catch a nap when pulling an all-nighter. Finn sat on it, patting the space beside him. In front of them, one of the huge video monitors waited on standby, lazily blinking its single red eye.

She sat tucked in close to him, unsure of what was going on. But when he took one of her hands and clasped it tightly in his, while the other reached for a remote, she knew. With one click, the monitor sprang to life and there on the gigantic screen, footage of the final hours of Rock The Castle 2019 rolled across in front of them; the images zoomed in to almost life size. Sound poured from speakers dotted around the room, enveloping them as if they were really there in the thick of the throbbing crowd.

That first time, Layla had viewed it like a horrified onlooker watching a car wreck playing out in front of her. Seeing it again, knowing what was to come, it held not fear, but fascination. Here was evidence of something that defied the accepted rules of time and space and challenged her to cast off any preconceived ideas of how her life would play out.

She couldn't help but smile at the girl on the screen, thrusting her arms upwards in time to the music, the same music pulsing through her body now. And the joy radiating from that Layla seemed to drift through the air, swirling towards this one, little threads of sheer happiness spiralling around her, before settling in her chest with a warm glow as if they'd found their home.

At the moment where the camera swung around, capturing both of them in its lens, Finn hit pause. There they were, suspended in time, his upturned face meeting her gaze, their identical expressions of delight in that moment.

He pulled her close, resting his head on her shoulder.

"Look at us," he said, his voice low against her ear, thick with emotion. "Look at you. Your face…"

He was right. If you'd been searching for one image to sum up the word 'happy', this could be it. When was the last time she'd looked like that? Or felt like that?

"In all the time you've been here, I've never seen you look like that. And I've never, ever felt like that guy up there. And I want to."

"You deserve to, Finn. You're always looking out for everyone else, never for you. You deserve to be happy."

"And so do you. And right there in front of us is the answer. There we are in 2019, together and happy. And we could be again. That could be us."

Six weeks ago, she'd thought it was all so complicated. But she'd been wrong. It was, in fact, quite simple. As simple as accepting that six months on from the worst thing to ever happen in her life, she had a choice.

She chose happiness.

"I think that could be us too," she said quietly.

He looked at her with surprise. "For real? My god, I thought you'd have a long way to go before…"

She took the remote from his hand and pressed play. Watched the girl on the screen slide off his shoulders, watched him spin around to take her in his arms, watched her stumble into them, laughter spilling over, watched him kiss her deeply, saw the look that passed between them. And she hit pause. She longed to replicate that look. She and Will had looked at each other like that. It was captured forever in Charlie's pictures of them in Tahiti in 2014. And there it was again—her and Finn, also unwittingly captured by Charlie, in some parallel version of Dallblane in 2019.

"That's all the reason I need right there, that and what you did for me last night."

He pulled her onto his lap. And she relaxed back against the safe space of his chest. "I know that wasn't easy for you. Hard to talk about what you've lost."

"Yeah. It was. But you let me talk. It *was* hard, and it will be for a long time. You see when I look up there, while I see us happy...in love..." That's what it was, that look on their faces—love, pure and simple. "I also see a life where Will and I weren't together. He's not there with me. And he's not here either. In this one I've lost him, and in that, he was never mine."

"Maybe there are others, other lives. In fact, the rational part of me says there has to be. Others where you and he lived a long life together, maybe had this baby together." His hand brushed her belly in gentle reassurance.

The words triggered a brief burst of hopeful optimism. She accepted the idea. It made sense, if there was any sense to be found in this bizarre situation. However, a strange unexpected twinge of melancholy accompanied that acceptance.

"Yeah, maybe. But you know that makes me a little sad too." Her voice came out in a whisper, her hand gravitating to his cheek. "Because there are other lives where I might never meet you. And I think my life would be poorer for that."

"That's OK," he said, tucking one straggling curl behind her ear, the brush of his fingertips along her jaw soothing. "You're with me in this one, and to me, that's all that matters."

His lips met hers, the kiss tentative at first, but her mouth responded instinctively, offering permission. As her lips melted into his, he let his hunger for her show, letting free the deep longing he'd held back so carefully.

When he pulled away, his face was serious. "And when you're talking to Will, because I know that you always will now and then, tell him he needn't worry. Tell him I promise to look after you. And his baby."

Layla sat snuggled against Finn, who had minutes earlier slapped one book closed and picked up another. The room was quiet and still, a stark contrast to the joyful bustle of the McGill family earlier in the evening. The only sound was the odd spit of sap from what remained of the huge logs Gary had hefted into the hearth. Small flames danced, a safer tamer version of the inferno he'd taken such pride in creating. It left the enormous lounge room still warm an hour after the rest of the family had made for their beds.

Upstairs, little Freya slept alongside the new parents. It was fortunate the McGill household sported huge beds, large enough for her giant of a father and long-limbed mother to share.

Patti and Isabel, no longer buoyed by the excitement of the new arrival, had by dinnertime both looked every bit of their seventy-plus years. Even so, Finn had to practically order them to go to bed, pointing out that Star had promised to stay on for a couple of weeks so they would have plenty more time to get acquainted with the newest member of the family.

"What are you reading?" she asked, pulling herself away from the hypnotic flames.

He turned the cover towards her. *The Storyteller*. Dave Grohl.

"Why doesn't that surprise me?" she said, shaking her head in amusement. This man seemed to live and breathe music.

"How about this?" he said, picking up the recently finished paperback from the side table. *A Beautiful Mind.*

"Ah," she said. "More things that define Finn McGill. Not only is he a music man, but also possibly a mathematics nerd."

"Unfortunately, it's all true," he said. "But being a numbers man, right now I'm calculating the odds of you saying yes to something. I'm hoping we've got a lot of nights for you to learn about me," he said, "and for me to learn about you." His dark eyes shone with intensity. "Starting with tonight. Stay?"

So much hung on that one word between them. But the answer was simple. There was a new surety about what she wanted. What she needed.

"Yeah," she said, unwavering in the face of that overt desire in his eyes. "I'll stay."

"God," he said with a huff of relief. "You're going easy on me, aren't you? Each time I ask you something thinking 'I'm really pushing the boundaries here', you quietly say yes. I'm not sure what's…"

She trailed a finger down those sensuous lips, silencing him.

"After you fell asleep last night? Well, I couldn't. My mind wouldn't rest. It was as if I had almost all the pieces of a puzzle; I was so close to seeing the whole picture. But there was something missing. Something small but important. And then, today when you played the video. I knew. It was the final piece I needed to understand what the picture looks like. And the picture is us."

"Have I told you I love you?" he said.

"You don't need to. I've known for ages, even though I refused to put that word against it. I tried to push it away. Star reminded me of that."

His dark brows knitted together in a frown. "Star? When?"

"I don't want you to be mad at her. She was trying to help. And she did. It was when she came for her appointment. On Thursday. Well, let's just say the appointment wasn't all about her and the baby."

"My bloody sister. She's like a ballistic missile. Once she gets fixated on something, there's no deviating from the course. God, I'm sorry."

"I'm not. If you stop to look past her direct manner, she's really rather wise."

He snorted at that, but took her hand and gave it a squeeze. "Perhaps."

"Star said I needed to let you love me. She's right. And when I think about that, it's not at all difficult. In fact, that's the easy bit. What she didn't say, but is more important—I needed to let *me* love you."

"Wow," he said, eyes wide in shock. "We sure are covering some ground kind of fast here." He linked his fingers through hers, one thumb rubbing back and forth, sensing her need for a soothing touch.

"Yeah," she said, "but I learned the hard way that if you shut out that possibility, if you fail to recognise that it's love, or if you do, but you're too scared to tell that person in case they don't feel the same way, or you keep telling yourself the time isn't right..." This was so hard, revisiting the mistake she and Will made. It sat there inside her, a jagged lump of rock in her throat, the rough edges scraping painfully as she tried to push the words past it. "Well, you will live to regret it."

He lifted her hand to his lips, placing a delicate kiss. "You don't have to fear this person not feeling the same way. If you were to feel about me even a fraction of the way I feel about you..."

"But that's it," she said. "I do. I loved you there wherever there is. And I love you now. You are such an easy man to love. And it's not only because there's some connection between us, across time, or across space. It's not simply some residual memory of you. It's *you*. Here, now. I love you."

He kissed her deeply. Then, without another word, rose to smooth down the fire, pulling across a screen to protect against stray sparks. Stretching a hand towards her, his dark eyes held a promise of something, a promise she would ask him to keep.

"Come to bed. To sleep," he added. "I want to wake up with you in the morning."

She took his hand and followed him. She wouldn't go home to the cottage tonight. He was her home now.

Epilogue

Dallblane Castle, Scotland - December 2023

LAYLA WATCHED WITH PRIDE as her one-year-old levered himself to standing position, his chubby little fingers surprisingly strong in their grip on her jeans, his face a study in determination. He'd be walking soon and then what would they do? A castle full of antiques and a curious toddler were not a good mix. She must ask her mother-in-law. After all, it seemed Patti had raised two boys here without them destroying the family heirlooms.

Meanwhile, Lachlan William McGill used his newfound ability to balance on two legs and held his arms wide in supplication. Layla, on a laugh, whisked him into the air and held him at arm's length, studying the cherubic face as all the bittersweet emotions that surrounded this child washed over her.

His green eyes were her own, but the playful glimmer in them, the developing pert nose and the lazy knowing smile were his father's. Lachie's pale hair hadn't made up its mind yet whether it would mirror her platinum curls or fade to Will's darker blonde. But no matter what direction it chose, no one who had known William Leroux, would ever doubt that this child was his son. She inhaled his sweet baby smell, as if in it she might catch a fleeting reminder of Will, the essence of his father imprinted in his genes.

It was Will's birthday today, her second without him. At first, as the date had crept closer, nagging worries as to how she might face it had also nudged their way forward, unbalancing her world. Last year, with a newborn, she'd been so overwhelmed with love for this child she and Will created together, it had seemed like he was still there and, with Finn's steadying presence, somehow the day had passed unmarked. This year, she felt like she owed Will more. Perhaps simply holding his boy close while she silently told him how much she still loved him, would always love him, would be enough.

The kitchen door swung open and the other man she loved, and would always love, walked towards her, his arms outstretched demanding his own cuddle with the squirming child.

"Lachie!" The little boy's head swung towards him, his lips curling in a smile of joy

"Da," he cried and Finn's face crinkled in delight. This was a new thing. His babyish babble had in the last few weeks morphed into distinguishable words. "Ma", had been swiftly followed by "Da" and only yesterday "Ga", Lachie's attempt to say "Grandma". That's what she'd chosen to be known as, although the word didn't exactly cause images of Patti spring to mind. With her long waves of hair and ethereal dresses, she more resembled some beneficent dark angel that drifted around the castle hallways, leaving a faint spicy smell in her wake.

Finn snatched the child up, then flung him high in the air, to the accompaniment of happy squeals. Next, seeing the exposed skin of a pale tummy, he caught him in his arms and blew a raspberry on the tiny navel. The squeals became an infectious giggle that spread to Layla.

God, she was so lucky to have found this man who loved her so unconditionally and loved her child as his own. She whispered a silent thanks for Charlie, who had pushed her towards him, perhaps even in those dark days holding some subconscious knowledge, buried deep down, that Finn could be the one to heal her grieving heart.

"Right, I'd better deliver this rascal to Mum," he said. "And let you get to work."

Work. It didn't really feel like work, doctoring to this small community. It was more an act of gratitude, giving back to the place and the people who'd provided a refuge when she'd needed to escape from the reality of losing Will. Burying herself in their problems, meeting their needs, had allowed her to focus on more than herself.

"And you're still up for lunch with Adam? He's bringing his wife, Gemma, as well. Company for him on the drive, I suppose. I bet she'd love to meet you—she's a Kiwi too."

A friend of Finn's, another son who'd inherited a crumbling castle and saved it by partnering with the National Trust, had passed on Adam Platt's details. Although income from the festival had pushed Dallblane back from the edge of ruin, and the spin-off businesses were doing well, Finn was open to the idea of trading off a little autonomy in return for government assistance. After weeks of email conversation, Adam had suggested he come up from Edinburgh in person.

"Sure, that would be great," said Layla, rising to gather her bag. "I don't mind." She might also welcome company, something to keep the melancholy thoughts from drifting in today.

"OK, me and my main man here..." he said, bundling the squealing bundle of child under one arm, "will pick you up from the clinic at one."

While she'd won half the battle, insisting the morning walk down to the village was good for her as she made the daily transition from mother to doctor, Finn had maintained their old daily ritual, meeting her at the clinic each afternoon. Sometimes they'd take up their favourite seats at the pub, other days wander back up the hill hand in hand, sharing the little details of their day. Now Lachie was older, Finn might bring him, either in a backpack or, if the weather wasn't so friendly, in the child seat that was a permanent fixture in the rocket red sports car.

"Yeah, I should be well finished. Only four appointments in the diary today." The winter days worked in her favour. With the locals reluctant to venture out in the cold unless it was really necessary, she could limit the clinic to mornings through these months. And when the sun barely rose before nine, sleeping late to open at ten am didn't seem at all lazy.

With a heavy wool coat, fleece-lined gloves, and the loops of her scarf pulled tight, she had almost everything required to face the crisp morning. The soft brush of her lips against Lachie's smooth forehead and Finn's parting kiss, as always, deep and lingering, heavy with the promise of his love, triggered a warm glow inside—and provided the final thing she needed to sustain her through the hours away from them.

She stepped out into the pure Highland air, and despite its cold sharp edge, breathed deep in thanks for choosing the fork in the road of her life that had brought her here.

Closing her laptop, the final patient's notes carefully filed, Layla turned to place the weighty pharmaceutical manual in its slot on the bookcase. Her eyes met the line of photographs on the top shelf. Some workplaces discouraged such displays of personal items, expecting their doctors to be faceless, neutral, bland. But here they were welcome, a reassurance for her villagers that sitting across from them was not only a doctor capable of meeting their medical needs, but a wife, a mother, and a friend; she was someone they could relate to, trusting her empathy for their own lives as genuine, grounded in experience of life with all its highs and lows.

She hadn't deliberately placed them that way, but those of her past life, before Dallblane, formed the backdrop. There on the left, Will and her in Tahiti, not a wedding photo but an impromptu moment; the laughter that they'd really done it, got married, lighting up their faces, their love captured by Charlie's practised eye. She couldn't help but reach for him, tracing the cheek, the jaw, resting her fingertip lightly on his lips, the remembered feeling of them pressed against hers still a jolt of memory. She clung to it still, not wanting to conceive of a time when she might be unable to retrieve it.

Next to it stood the tight five, one of the few photos of all of them, snapped by a kind lady at the next table at the resort. Charlie, her cool ethereal beauty, contrasting with Tristan's irascible grin, and dear Leo, his warmth shining in those dark eyes; not family by blood, but her true family, flanking the two of them on their wedding day. She remembered how good it felt, to stand with Will's arm across her shoulders, safe and secure, knowing he'd always be there for her, as would these friends. And he was. She often felt him near, his whispered encouragement, his quiet approval, and the sense he looked out for her still, a calm presence in the background.

"Happy birthday, my love," she said, reaching out a hand to touch the final photo. Surfboard under one arm, still dripping, with the wetsuit pulled down to his waist, barefoot in the black Piha sand, the pure effervescent joy of doing what he loved beamed from him. She remembered snapping it as he tossed a cheeky comment at her to cover his slight embarrassment that his half-naked body should be the subject of her camera lens. That total lack of awareness as to how beautiful he was had hooked her from the very first moment. But what was inside of that boy, and the man he'd grown into, had exploded her initial attraction into a deep, all-encompassing love that would always endure. "Happy birthday." The pain of her loss still jabbed at her with fierce thrusts, often without warning, triggered by a word, a smell, a song. Today she'd known they'd come. Today she'd known they'd hurt.

She heard them before she saw them, a bubbling child's half-formed words and a man's low indulgent tones in reply. Finn appeared at the door, with Lachie propped on his hip, the small blonde head tucked in against his shoulder, smiling up at him from under pale lashes. But Finn's own gaze locked onto her welling eyes and he immediately sprang forward to capture her in the curve of his free arm.

That was the beautiful thing—as Finn took in the sight of her he knew without any need for explanation—but even more than that, there was no awkwardness at him finding her there, tear-stained and heartbroken. He was secure in her love, unafraid that he shared it with a man from her past. He pressed a kiss on her forehead, sweet and reassuring.

Turning to the photos, he stretched Lachie's hand towards the two that took centre stage. The first was on their wedding day. In this one she cradled Lachie in her arms, a smiling five-month old, oblivious to the reason for all the fuss, merely curious at why Auntie Charlie kept pointing her camera at them. If anyone doubted this thing that arced between Finn and her was love, those doubts would be swept away by this one photograph. Charlie had made it visible.

The second image was newer, the three of them on a late autumn family picnic at the loch. Patti had been more than willing to capture her son's happiness, and the reason for it on film.

Finn proceeded to guide Lachie in their new ritual. Taking one tiny finger in his hand, he pointed it at the pictures of Layla and then tapped it against her chest. "Ma." Lachie repeated the word, wide-eyed at this still novel discovery that his mother could exist in two places at once.

They went through the process again, locating Finn. Her heart fluttered as the little mouth solemnly said the word. "Da." When it came to the pictures of himself, Lachie made no attempt at his name. Perhaps he struggled with the concept that the child in the picture bore his name. Or maybe the softer 'L' sound eluded him. It would come.

Finally, Finn stretched the child's fingers towards the photo of Will. "Daddy." He'd said it every day for weeks, but today she heard the slight catch in Finn's voice. Lachie paused with small brows knotted in concentration at the challenge of two syllables. "Dee."

"Good boy," Finn said. "Daddy."

"Da." "Dee."

"Yes," Layla said, stroking his head. "Daddy."

Layla recognised the small shock on Gemma Platt's face when she entered the library. In her past life, patients in the ED had worn that same expression, realising that the young tattooed woman with Marilyn Monroe hair was a fully-fledged doctor. Today, Gemma was struggling to understand that Layla, clad in jeans and a sweater with a restless baby in her lap, was in fact Lady McGill, the Countess Dallblane.

"Gemma, grab a seat," she said, flailing one hand at the nearest chair while depositing Lachie onto the rug at her feet. "Can I offer you a coffee? Or tea? Something to warm you up, since it's freezing outside and those bloody men of ours didn't think to bring you in straight away. Lunch won't be too far off."

Snow threatened, early in the season for sure, but not unheard of.

Gemma smiled with grateful eyes, "God, yes, I'd kill for a hot drink. Thank you. Coffee would be great."

Layla stretched out her hand to ring the small bell on a side table. It still didn't sit well with her, ringing for servants. And when it was only the three of them, she'd stroll out and make drinks for herself. But with the increasingly mobile Lachie on the rampage, crawling at top speed for Gemma's booted feet, it might be safer to let Isabel take charge of the refreshments.

Also, as Finn had patiently explained to her, Isabel might be basically family, but she took pride in doing her job. They paid her well, and she took it as a personal slight if Layla sidestepped her too often. Particularly when there were guests, it was easier to go with the long-established rhythms of a noble household.

"He's beautiful," Gemma said, laying a hand on the tiny blonde head bowed over one of her boots, playing with the ends of the velvet ribbon laces. "How old?"

"Just turned one," she said. "I'm steeling myself for the trouble he's about to unleash when he starts walking. And it's not far off."

"But worth every ounce of it," said Gemma. "You're very lucky."

And she was lucky. Life hadn't always been kind. Robbed her of Will. Robbed Will of this, the chance to watch their child grow from baby to man. But life had given her Lachie. And Finn.

"So, how long have you been in Scotland?" Layla said, steering the conversation away from herself and the day's small underlying sadness that again edged its way forward.

"Since late 2019."

"Oh, so you rode out the pandemic up here?"

"Yes. You too?"

"No," Layla said with a grimace. "I was working as a GP in South Auckland. That community bore the brunt of it in New Zealand, so it wasn't an easy or pleasant time." Gemma appeared as startled by the revelation that Layla was a doctor as she'd been on finding she was the Countess. "I came over here in 2022, as the GP down in the village. That's how I met Finn."

"And became a Countess," Gemma said through a laugh.

"Yes," Layla said, breaking into a grin. "Although his title was probably the least attractive thing about him."

"Will he be allowed to keep it if he gifts the castle to the National Trust?"

"Oh yes, I think that it's attached to the family, not the buildings."

"Then it will pass to the little one some day." Gemma smiled indulgently at the small boy who was now crushing the hem of her skirt in his hands.

"Ahh," Layla paused. Now this was getting awkward. Oh well, it was common knowledge around here that Lachie wasn't Finn's child. It would save the visitors having uncharitable thoughts when they saw the two of them together later on, noting father and son bore no resemblance whatsoever. And it seemed that somehow, on this day, the universe was challenging her to face her loss, to speak of it, to make it real.

"No, you see, when I met Finn I had just lost my husband." She took a slow, deep breath and pushed back a small sigh. "He died in an accident. And I didn't know it, but I was already pregnant with Lachlan. Finn's his adopted father. And while they are progressive with the peerage here in Scotland, with daughters allowed to inherit, they don't recognise adopted children. So no, Lachie will forever be 'The Honourable Lachlan McGill'. Although if he grows to be anything like Finn, I doubt he'll bother using a title if he can avoid it. We are pretty ordinary people once you get to know us."

As if to emphasise this point, Finn burst through the door in faded jeans and a well-worn sweater, looking less like a lord and more like the gardener. He and Adam were still in the middle of an animated conversation. It appeared their menfolk had hit it off.

Lunch in the kitchen, at the huge oak table that was its centre, further cemented the air of normality that Layla and Finn liked to surround their family with. Patti swooped Adam and Gemma into her orbit like they were long-lost cousins and they appeared in her thrall, captivated by her lyrical retellings of stories from the castle's past.

Gemma insisted on cradling Lachie on her knee until he became tired and fractious. Layla knew the only answer for this was bed, and Gemma seemed reluctant to let the child go, offering to come along and tuck him in. The two women sat beside the cot, Layla humming softly and stroking the curls till he succumbed to sleep.

"It must be hard," Gemma said softly. "All you've been through."

"It's been the hardest two years of my life. But you get through it, in the end."

"A loving husband and this little boy must help."

"It does," said Layla. The conversation was taking a deeply personal turn for one between two people who'd just met, but something about this woman made her feel it wasn't intrusive. "And I know a lot of people must wonder how I could jump into this with Finn so quickly... after." Gemma simply stared at her with those amber eyes, as if she understood, but Layla still felt a need to explain further. "You see, Finn and I knew each other... before." How else could she describe it? "So, we had history. I suppose that got us here a little quicker."

"Sometimes life pulls you to the right people at the right time."

"It does," said Layla, with a small laugh. If only she knew. "Speaking of which," she said, her voice still hushed, "probably time we got back down there to see what those two men are cooking up behind our backs. Bloody Scots, you can't trust them not to be up to something."

"Can I ask you one thing before we do?" Her question was cautious. "It's just... I'm curious."

"Go for it," Layla said. Life in a small village had taught her there was no point attempting to be secretive.

"It's just, from the moment I saw it, I've wanted to ask. About your ring. The design looks familiar. It's a Nik Francovic, isn't it? Since you're from Auckland, I thought it might be."

"Yeah, it is, in fact."

She rubbed one finger across the winged heart. It was as impractical for wrangling a baby as it had been for seeing patients in the clinic. So most of the time it lived in its midnight blue box in her bedside drawer. But she'd put it on this morning, as a reminder of the love it represented and the man who'd given it to her. Finn had signalled his approval, taking her hand to place a soft kiss on it. How lucky she was that he understood and had never made her choose; allowing her love for Will to sit lightly alongside her love for him. "That and the wedding band below. See." She tilted her hand so Gemma could see the golden v-shaped ring cradling the heart. "From my first husband. I still have the band Nik made for him, too."

"Beautiful. He's so talented."

"Do you have some of his jewellery too?"

"Just a pendant. A tuatara," she said. "Reminds me of home. Speaking of which, we need to head for ours soon. Adam will want to get on the road. One drawback of Scotland in December—dark at four o'clock."

"Yeah, takes some getting used to." Layla took one last glance at Lachie, checking he was still asleep before following her downstairs. A day she'd dreaded, expecting to spend it wallowing in sadness, had passed pleasantly. And it felt like they'd made new friends.

Layla stood in front of the full-length mirror surveying the curves of her body, tracing the string of pearl-shaped marks on her abdomen, like a necklace, the imprint of her child upon her. She smiled at the thought of his little arms reaching towards her as she pressed a goodnight kiss on skin so soft. And his cartoon character voice shaping his word for her brought the sweetest delight.

Ma. The shortest but most precious name of many she bore, now nested comfortably amongst the others. They sat upon her in layers, none ever discarded, each a reminder of who she was.

Layla Angell, the name of a young girl forced to be a fighter, who'd overcome the drawbacks of that name and the family who claimed her by its existence.

Layla Leroux, the name of a woman who'd learned what love could be and would always treasure the faint remembered touch of the man who had taught her.

Layla McGill, The Countess Dallblane, the most ironic. She'd surprised herself, finding that she who'd looked at such lofty titles with scepticism should not only wear the title but feel a genuine warmth from the way the villagers used it. Perhaps that was because the respect they offered her was earned, a tribute to her work tending to their needs, knowing her first as simply Layla, a doctor they trusted.

But tonight, it was the mother gazing back at her, a little triumphant smile tugging at her mouth. She didn't need Patti snatching yarrow and comfrey away as Isabel lingered in the pantry, deciding which tea to make. She didn't need the plastic test kit with its two pink lines. The only reason she'd bothered taking it was that little doctor's voice niggling in the back of her head, insisting she be sure before she told him. It was going to blow his mind.

She slipped into the familiar antique bed, the width so great you almost needed a map to find each other within it. His brows arched in surprise as her hand traced a path from his chest, following the dark line of hairs to the neat v between his legs. Sweet Finn, he'd not have expected this from her tonight, not this night when the past pressed in against the present a little more boldly than usual. She hadn't expected to want this herself. But she did. Wanted him. Wanted the man who was her present and her future.

Their lovemaking was slow and tender at first, each silently enjoying the familiar rhythms of each other's bodies, with no need for words. But as the heat rose between them, so their voices rose too, that need to vocalise the exquisite joy of their coming together overtaking any rational thought.

"And that, my love," he said with a grin, as she lay panting across his chest, "is why we will *never* have a bedroom in the west wing. Not that I think Mum and Isabel are under any illusion what goes on in this room. I don't think they need to hear it to confirm it."

"Well," she said, unable to prevent a sly smile from drifting across her face, "soon they'll have something else to confirm it."

She sat up, still astride him, staring down at his tangled hair, plastered against his forehead all lank and sweaty. He was so damn beautiful, even all dishevelled like this. Especially all dishevelled like this. She imagined a child with those dark curls, those lips, that curious expression.

"What?" he said, with a puzzled shake of his head against the pillow.

"God Finn, for such a clever guy, you can be really dense some-times."

"Cruel," he said, adjusting his lips into a hurt pout, which only made him look even sexier. If he was up for a second round tonight, with him looking at her like that, she was in.

"OK," she said. "Let me help you out here. Do you remember the first night we ever made love?"

"Twenty-third of October 2022," he said. "We came home after having the Sunday night roast special at the pub. I'd drunk way too many beers, came home a bit merry, and this sexy wee thing took advantage of me. Still one of the best days of my life."

"Yeah, yeah," she said. "As if you had no say in the matter. I seem to recall us both making very sure we consented to what happened when we got home."

"Yeah," he said. "But I could never say no to you. You only have to look at me and I get hard. God, you don't even have to be present. I only have to *think* of you looking at me and I'm gone."

She cuffed him playfully. "As if it's any different for me. I saw you making those puppy dog eyes at me across the dinner table while I tried to keep my mind on the conversation with the Platts. You don't exactly make it easy."

"I never said being with me would be easy. But I sure like it when *you* are." He raised a brow.

She ignored that little invitation. "Anyway, back to that night. Do you remember me sitting here, just like this, and you sat up?"

He sat up now. "And I wrapped my arms around you and kissed you like this," he said, plunging his tongue into her mouth before she could speak. She took her time to enjoy the kiss before gently fending him off.

"And," she said, looking downwards, "do you remember what else happened while you were kissing me?"

"I do," he said with a snort. "A certain little guy decided his mother had been ignoring him and chose that moment to give you a swift kick to let you know he wasn't happy about it."

"Right," she said. "A baby in his little earth ship docked in between us." She paused and ran her hand over her stomach, now bearing only the slight curve that hinted of her first pregnancy. "Like now."

His eyes flickered up from her stomach to meet hers. Recognition dawned. She'd seen so many emotions ripple across his face in the time she'd known Finn. He wore them close to the surface, felt them with an intensity she didn't always understand. But she understood the pure joy that lit him up so completely now. She knew he wanted more children, but, as with everything, his respect for her past made him patient. And now his patience was rewarded.

He almost crushed her within his arms, and his kiss was rough.

"Still room for a family of four in the Daimler—just," he said, pulling away with a laugh.

To hear those words, her heart leap so hard, surely he must feel it against his chest. A year ago she'd hoped they might forge a family out of the wreckage of her life, that Finn could live up to his ambition to be the man his father was, to love her child as his own. There was no doubt—he'd said it—a family of four: Layla and Finn, Lachie and this new baby. She could picture them now, two dark heads and two blonde, zipping along the road to the loch, smiles on their faces mirroring the little convertible's smiling grill, while the wind whipped their identical curls into a frenzy.

A wail sounded from the adjoining bedroom, and the image evaporated.

"I'll go," Finn offered, snatching his discarded boxers from the floor and pulling them on.

She reached for a robe. The sweat drying on her skin had produced a prickle of goosebumps, despite the warmth from the vents that pumped a steady stream of air, usually countering the chill of the old uninsulated walls.

Finn reappeared, a now giggling Lachie in his arms, the source of his distress forgotten by his father's soothing presence. "Think he slept too long this arvo. Now he's up and ready to party. Aren't you buddy?" He tickled the sliver of exposed tummy, causing the giggles to erupt into raucous squeals.

She reached for the child, pulling him down to sit in her lap. Finn tucked in behind them, his chin resting on her shoulder.

"How good is this?" he said, pressing a kiss against her cheek. She could feel the upturn of his mouth, the words a breath on her hair. "To hold my entire family in my arms."

Layla sat in the centre of a circle. Her husband's solid arms formed one arc, safe and warm. Her child's arms clasped around her neck formed the other, his little head resting against her breast, lolling back into sleep in the safety of her embrace. And deep inside her, the tiny seed, not yet moving, its rapid heartbeat still undetectable, but through its quiet presence anchoring her here, in this family, in this love, in this life.

If you loved this book, I'd appreciate it if you have time to leave a review on your favourite retailer, review site, or social media. Use the QR code to visit my website www.carolinecorvin.com.

Receive your free bonus *Tangled Hearts* short story *Five,* as well as updates on new releases.

Sometimes you find family where you least expect them. Layla's about to step onto the bus that will take her to her new high school...and a future she never imagined.

Acknowledgments

Every book is special. But this one feels more special because it came into being during a tough time in my life. Escape into Layla's world allowed me to put my own troubles aside for a while, and seeing her get her happily ever after helped me hang on to belief in my own. Once again, David, my best friend and partner in the highs and lows of life, has offered his quiet, steady support. My editor Jacquelin Cangro is always a joy to work with. Having someone else who can offer wise guidance while laughing and crying with you over a story is a rare gift. As is the friendship forged through a chance encounter with a writer on the other side of the world. Thank you, Lauren, for your unfailing encouragement and the understanding that only another person on this crazy but thrilling journey can provide.

Caroline

Read More

Take a look at the first chapter of the next book
in the *Tangled In Time* series

TANGLED PAST

Betrayal

University of Edinburgh, Scotland - November 2017

THE WORDS FLOWED LIKE an enchantment, the man's voice casting its spell. It captured Cassie in velvet handcuffs. She made no attempt to resist.

"Full house," he said, staring out at the crowd with wide eyes, as a woman fumbled at his lapel, adjusting a tiny microphone. "They must be in the wrong room."

The self-deprecating comment; the flush that crept up his neck as he realised the microphone had thrown his words out to the entire lecture theatre; the embarrassed smile; all these small gestures immediately endeared him to her and others in the audience.

Yes, his observation was correct: there *were* a lot of people in the lecture room, and they *were* all here to see him. At least a hundred had voted against making a run for home before the threatened early-season snow coated Edinburgh so they could listen to his words. With a rustle of papers and a click of a pointer, he began.

"So, good evening ladies and...." He hesitated for a moment. There wasn't a single man in the group. "...ladies." The melodic rise and fall of his accent caressed the ears of every woman in the room, and their collective silent sigh washed across the space.

The title slide 'Outlander With The Castle Hunter' featured a larger-than-life portrait shot that only confirmed he was a good-looking man, although in real life less severe than the image on screen. Her eyes followed the sensuous curve of his lips that relieved an otherwise angular face. The straight nose, slash of cheekbones, and pale skin were unlined apart from a crinkle at the eyes that held a suppressed smile. That smile seemed to lie in wait, ready to spring forth in delight at the effect of his next utterance on the assembled women.

"First of all, I'll apologise in advance for disappointing you—I'm not a Fraser or a Mackenzie. Not even a Fitzgibbon." Laughter rippled across the room, warm waves radiating towards him. "For this final session of the day, you'll have to make do with me—Simon Buchanan. And as you can probably tell from just looking at me, I'm no brawny Highlander."

Another small titter of amusement bubbled in his direction. Not a sturdy red-haired Jacobite warrior as described in the books or brought to life in the TV series, but a mid-thirty-something university lecturer. His athletic build and sleek wave of hair as black as the heart of an English garrison commander completed Cassie's assessment: Doctor Simon Buchanan was strikingly attractive. She wondered if he knew it. Surely a man of his age would have heard it, seen it reflected in the admiring eyes of women. But even if he was aware of the effect of his appearance, his humble manner of speech and a slight awkwardness projected back at the audience suggested a refreshing lack of arrogance.

"However, I do know a thing or two about castles," he smiled. "So, come with me on a journey."

In that moment, Cassie decided she'd be perfectly happy to go anywhere this stranger led. She envisaged him a Pied Piper, a long line of women following, mesmerised—but with her elbowing past, determined to be first.

Another click and the screen behind him sprang to life, video images taking them soaring high above castles and lochs before diving low to circle ancient battlements.

"Nothing is more romantic than a castle. When writers, and indeed filmmakers, take us to a castle, they're tapping into our fantasies of times past, of bold heroes and despicable villains, of sworn enemies and passionate lovers."

His eyes met hers, and Cassie gulped in air. Did she imagine it, or was his direct gaze deliberate? Did it linger a moment longer than it should? She forced herself to study the cover of her notebook. *My Secret Thoughts Lie Within These Pages*. The playful gold letters stared back. Even the 'Duly Noted' stationery chain had conspired against her. Maybe it was a small sign from the universe legitimising this sudden instant attraction she felt for a stranger, despite eight years of marriage to the one man who had ever made her heart lurch at the sight of him—until now. She risked a surreptitious glance and let out her breath in relief that his gaze fell elsewhere.

But it was only a temporary reprieve. Simon Buchanan's sweep of the room turned back in her direction and again they made eye contact, and this time she was sure of it—a hint of that unexpected chemistry projected back at her.

She could just get up and leave. No. This close to the end of the day, she must complete her mother's assigned mission: attend every session of this one day exploration of the history behind a much-loved series of books. Blair had read the first when it came out, back in 1991. Now battling cancer, revisiting the fictional world of her favourite author and repeatedly watching the spin-off TV series, gave her mother respite from thoughts of an uncertain future.

There was no way Cassie could bail on this session. Besides, seated in the middle of a row, leaving the lecture theatre without creating a disruption was virtually impossible. The last thing she needed was to draw attention to herself. So she vowed to tough it out, no matter how uncomfortable.

An hour of exquisite torture followed. The startling sensation of having Simon all to herself took hold, making her feel like the other hundred women in the room didn't exist. A flush of embarrassment surged across her neck and face each time he made eye contact. Surely it must be obvious for all to see?

The pleasure of basking in his presence mingled with thoughts of future pain when confronting the empty notebook pages, reminders of her failure to completely fulfil the task. Discomfort niggled her, as she anticipated the awkward scene to come. What reason might she offer her mother for her paralysis? Detailed notes of every other session filled the book. The pages allocated for this one lay bare, the blank lines an accusation of negligence. And oh, how her mother loved those castle scenes. With three weeks left before she'd have to offer up the notebook, she might find time to read and research—bury herself in the library, scour Google for obscure facts that might replicate the musings of a Scottish castle hunter.

Stabs of guilt assaulted her at the thought of Nik, her husband. She could still hand on heart, say she loved him. She didn't doubt he loved her. Although, it was no longer the wild tumultuous love of teenagers. Facing the inevitable changes as they'd grown into adults wasn't easy; they were such different people from the two naïve kids who'd pledged a lifelong commitment. Even now, they were determined to honour that commitment, but both would admit they had struggled lately. It wasn't only the emotional challenges of their evolving selves. Weathering the shitstorms that had come their way, rather than drive them closer in solidarity, had caused them to pull apart.

Physically, they had barely spent a day apart in eight whole years. Not healthy probably; and it made this separation hard. But she'd had no choice but to remain in Scotland on her own. Nik had already abandoned his work for two months to be here with her.

She couldn't object when he'd asked to return early, making his own family pilgrimage along the way.

Meanwhile, she sat here focused on this academic eye candy. Unbidden, but certainly not unpleasant impulses circulated deep down in her centre. Nik was the only guy who triggered this lustful longing in her loyal body. Now a stranger had provoked the same. Nik was the only person who understood her, with an instinctive deep knowledge that seemed to touch her soul. Now another man had brushed against it.

Was this cheating? If Nik should pick up the damn notebook and flick through it, would he see those pages and know that in her mind, in her heart, in her soul, she'd cheated on him? Were these blank pages evidence of betrayal?

As the lecture ended, she rose from her seat. Her eyes met Simon's again in a brief glance—of what? Attraction? Knowledge? Recognition? Whatever it was, she knew she had to leave, abandoning that sweet carrot of possibility dangling in front of her. She forced herself to go, moving in mechanical steps towards the door. His smile just for her now turned to the throng of women who'd poured from their seats. Some thrust copies of a book at him for signing.

Walking through the vaulted ceilings of the cloisters, she reached for the swirl of emotions that circled the corners of her mind, separating the strands to examine each more closely. Shame that she'd even allowed herself to give in to this crazy instant infatuation. Fear that it was a symptom of some hidden flaw within herself. Dread that it was a warning one of the numerous tiny fissures in her marriage was about to rupture, unleashing devastation. Regret for something that might have been. And a sweet melancholy that she must leave Simon Buchanan behind.

And leave him she must, relegating him to a surreal temporary insanity best forgotten; the product of an overactive imagination, as she clutched at what was real.

Stepping out into the chill night, she shook her head free of the disturbing thoughts. She recognised the fresh sniff of snow in the air, familiar from childhood winters in New Zealand's deep south. She rummaged in her tote bag for a hat, pulling it on to contain the strands of her hair whipped by the icy wind off the cobbles. Cursing the absence of her gloves, left behind in her hurry this morning, she plunged her hands deep into the pockets of her coat. With her phone still on silent, a vibration against her fingers signalled an incoming call. She pulled it free to peer at the screen. Blair Tremayne.

"Mum?" she asked. "You're up early. It's only six a.m."

"Oh darling, I couldn't sleep with the excitement. How was it?"

"It was fabulous, Mum."

"And you took lots of notes, I hope? And maybe a few photographs? I want it all."

"Yes Mum, of course I did," she lied.

"Thank you, my darling. It will be almost as good as being there." Cassie caught the faint hitch in her voice. An unexpected thread of worry surfaced.

"Mum? Are you OK?"

"Of course, yes. I'm just a bit tired." She unleashed a girlish giggle. "You know me, never been a fan of early rising. But today I had a reason." There it was again—the faint tremor in her mother's voice hidden under a cheerfulness so bright it didn't ring true.

"I can't wait to see you, Mum. It's been amazing here. I'm proud of myself for doing this. But I'm ready for home."

"I think Nik's ready for you to both be home, too." She could hear her mother's smile across the miles at the mention of him. Her so-called 'second son', they talked often. "He's not happy about having to leave you there on your own."

Guilt at her crazy preoccupation with that man in the lecture theatre slapped hard at her again at the mention of Nik. What the hell was wrong with her? The pressure of this last couple of months weighed heavily. But with the retrospective exhibition of her mother's art coming to an end, the worst was over. All that remained was to oversee the packaging of those precious pieces that would never be for sale, ready for their journey home. Perhaps she wasn't coping with that final responsibility as well as she'd thought. Whatever the reason, she needed to bury the whole shameful hour deep down in the past. It was time to focus on more important things: the safe return of the paintings, and getting back to her life.

"Yeah, I know Mum. I hate it too. But it's not for much longer." Her voice echoed off the stone buildings flanking her.

"Are you outside?" Her mother's concern for her child sprang forth, even though thousands of miles separated them.

"It's OK, Mum, they're predicting snow, but it's not here yet."

"I'll not keep you talking then. Get yourself back to the apartment before you freeze. Talk to you tomorrow."

"OK, love you Mum."

Her mother's call had pulled her part way back into normal life, but to secure herself there, she must talk to Nik. She flicked her phone to the World Clock. What would he be doing at eight o'clock on a Saturday night in Dubrovnik?

Most guys of his age would be tourists checking out the bars and the pretty girls, hoping to hook up for the night. But he would more than likely be sitting in a little house in the old town, making stilted conversation with his grandparents. Yes, while Nik unselfishly spent his time doing something for his family, his wife walked the streets of Edinburgh fighting off treacherous thoughts of a Scottish stranger who, for some inexplicable reason, had forced his way into her mind.

With one last firm shove, she pushed Simon Buchanan away. She turned her focus to the most important contact in her phone and dialled her husband's number.

More From Caroline

Tangled In Time

A free-spirited artist, a wandering astronomer, and an instant connection. Is their future painted in the stars?

Landscape painter Blair Silvestri hasn't time for stargazing —or love. It's her immediate, more precarious situation that she needs to focus on for now. Daniel Tremayne spends his life looking skyward. Maybe that's why he's made such a mess of all his relationships so far. A trick of time throws them together, but also threatens to tear them apart.

Tangled Threads

What if her future lies
in a time tangled past?

Now the last of those who loved her are gone, there's nothing left for young teacher Kate Moreton in New Zealand. It's time for her to forge a new life. Pinning her hopes of finding friends, family—and maybe even love—elsewhere, she heads for the bright lights of London. What Kate doesn't know is this journey will lead her to two men, two loves, and two lives. And offer a future lifeline when her world falls apart.

Tangled Paths

"In a world full of limitless lives,
of endless possibilities, I will always find you."

Sarah Mitchell always put family first. Now, freed from self-imposed exile in her hometown, she's ready to jump back on the academic path she sacrificed for others three years ago. It's her time to choose a path. Or is time going to choose for her? When Sarah's future seems destined to be defined by loss, will time's tangled paths deliver her a second chance at happiness?

Tangled Past

**When the past holds you in its power,
is love enough to set you free?**

Cassiopeia Tremayne isn't looking back at her sleepy hometown. Facing the future, all she can see is her dream of being a writer, just there on the other side of her final high school year. But Cassie's future also includes navigating the turbulent waters of two parallel but intertwined lives, forcing her to confront truths about herself, her family and the men she loves in two separate worlds. And when those worlds collide, will love give her strength enough to rewrite the past and become the hero of her own story?

About the Author

WHEN NOT WRITING, YOU can usually find Caroline with her nose in a book from any one of an eclectic mix of favourite genres. While officially a resident of Auckland, New Zealand's stunning City of Sails, she has become adept at juggling her love of writing alongside her other magnificent obsession of travelling the world. Caroline didn't set out to write romance, but her characters took control the moment she let them loose on the page, reminding her that finding happily ever afters are the reason she's one of those people who sometimes reads the last page first, just to be safe.

Follow Caroline Corvin on all your favourite
social media or review sites!
Visit her website: www.carolinecorvin.com

www.ingramcontent.com/pod-product-compliance
Lightning Source LLC
Chambersburg PA
CBHW050850210726

48290CB00004B/1161